BOOK I

Table of Contents

Main Characters

Amara Johnson: Born prematurely and facing numerous challenges throughout her life.

Jenny Alonso: Amara's biological mother struggles with addiction.

Nathan Okechukwu: Amara's biological father, struggles with addiction.

Mr. Tony Adamu: Amara's first foster father.

Mrs. Tony Adamu: Amara's first foster mother.

Mrs. Jamaila Peterson: One of Amara's foster mothers.

Tailor Marcus: Foster mother who cares for Amara, discovers family secrets.

Anene Marcus: Foster father who cares for Amara, supports his partner Tailor in uncovering family secrets.

Mr. Chimezie Johnson: Amara's final foster father.

Mrs. Chimezie Johnson: Amara's final foster mother.

Mrs. Amal Johnson: Amara's foster grandmother provides wisdom and support.

Dr. Paul Antoinne: A local doctor who inspires Amara to pursue medicine, becomes her mentor.

Dr. Paul's son - Xavier: Studying medicine, following in his father's footsteps.

Lilly Adebayo: Amara's close friend provides support and encouragement.

Emily Carter: Another friend of Amara's from his childhood school.

Ramos Czeches: Amara's childhood friend from her former neighborhood.

Ayala Poulet: A school bully who tries to undermine Amara's achievements.

Vivian Puslovic: A classmate of Amara's struggling with self-doubt.

Mrs. Njideka Musa: The respected coordinator of the student support office at Amara's school.

Rev. Okafor Christian Solomon: A clergyman who encourages Tailor to uncover her family's secrets.

Ms. Thompson Ivy: A seasoned social worker who helps place Amara in foster care.

Chapman Mesut: A member of the ambulance crew who provides a health check on Amara when she is taken into government care.

Serjeant Kazley Green: A police officer who helps ensure Amara's safety during her removal from her parents' home.

Mrs. Chinenye Okon: Amara's neighbor who reports concerns about her well-being to the authorities.
Jude Okon: Chinenye's boyfriend who supports her during the process.
Mr. Nohra Sharma - Jenny and Nathan's Former School Teacher
Anelia Pawson: Chinenye's friend who provides comfort and support.
David Schmid: A young man admitted to the hospital with symptoms like the mysterious illness from the past.

Key Locations

Igili Village: Amara's birthplace and childhood town, where much of the story takes place.

Igili River Niger part (Oshimilli Edei): A secluded spot where Jenny, Nathan, and their friends gather.

Igili Sports High School: The school where Jenny and Nathan meet and fall in love.

Igili Community Centre: Location of the child protection and services department office.

Neonatal Intensive Care Unit of Igili: Where Amara spends her early days after being born prematurely.

Igbuzor Village: A neighboring town where Amara lives with the Johnson foster family.

Amara's childhood neighborhood: An unspecified area where Amara grows up with her parents.

Tailor and Anene's home: One of the foster homes where Amara lives.

Tailor's family farmhouse: An abandoned property that holds secrets about Tailor's family history.

Amara's school in Igili: The school Amara attends before moving to Igbuzor.

Johnson residence: Amara's final foster home with Mr. and Mrs. Chimezie Johnson.

Igbuzor Metropolitan Area: The bustling city where Amara and her friends celebrate their graduation.

Academy of Human Sciences, Zaria: The prestigious school where Amara is accepted to study medicine.

Dr. Paul's clinic: The local clinic where Dr. Paul practices medicine and offers Amara an opportunity to gain experience.

School library in Zaria: Where Amara is studying when she receives the unexpected phone call.

Private hospital (New Age) in Igbuzor: The hospital that contacts Amara about the mysterious illness.

Prologue

An amazing, thrilling, and puzzling journey is about to begin under the golden light of the setting sun in the middle of the lovely town of Igili. This is the story of Amara, a child whose severe future hunger persisted even in her mother's pregnancy.

Her longing and wonder-filled eyes reflected sunlit golden rays. They were entrances to a restless spirit seeking a world distinct from her present. Her relentless, overwhelming craving for grandeur set off an almost ravenous need for thrilling events well beyond her reach.

Like a famished child tending to her mother, her hunger transformed into restlessness and a need for more. But that same hunger will dictate her future in the next few days. Every room's curtain fluttered as she prepared to enter Igili, as if extending a warm welcome. Under this warm welcome, however, lay a world filled with challenges. The road ahead would be challenging, filled with twists and turns that would test her resolve to the limit. Still, Amara wasn't alone. In this small village, the spirit of adventure thrived, welcoming each new day with optimism and determination.

Our ancestral ground, Amara, will welcome you at first arrival. As the road opens out more, the farther you go on this trip. The whole planet waits for your arrival with subdued breath. For in your narrative, people see mirror images of their own hopes and goals. They discover echoes of their own bravery and inner strength along your beautiful journey.

This goes beyond Amara's account. This is the story of every individual who calls Igbuzor and Igili home. This is a story of achievements and hardships, as well as perseverance and optimism. And it all starts here—in the cozy embrace of the dying sun's illumination.

The air thickens with expectation as darkness falls and shadows start to dance on the walls of every Igili house. Something is approaching. Something substantial. It also raises questions about the experiences Amara is ready to face in this world. What obstacles will she encounter? Above all, will she possess the drive to get beyond them? Once again, welcome to your home, Amara; this is Igili.

Your lifelong journey is just beginning…

PART 1

YOUTHFUL EXPERIMENTS

Chapter 1

Turbulent Start

Today, in the charming town of Igili, two remarkable young people from Ogbaru's own nation, Jennifer (Jenny) Alonso and Nathaniel (Nathan) Okechukwu, reached a pivotal moment. Their hearts pounded together, caught in the fog of young love and discovery. As they went through their days exploring every corner and cranny of Igili villages, their laughter echoed throughout the streets. From tree climbing in the rich forest to chasing fireflies in moonlit meadows, their friendship blossoms like wildflowers over their beloved town.

On this fateful day, the golden rays of the sun gently welcomed Nathan and Jenny as they sat in the crowded corridors of Igili Sports High School. The young people set upon a road that would irrevocably swing their course in life.
Jenny, a lovely and refined ballet dancer, walked elegantly across the corridors. Her every action exuded her passion for the creative art and affection. On the other hand, Nathan was a friendly and athletic young man who attracted everyone around him in curiosity. His confident gait and mischievous grin caught the sporting mood of the school. Benevolent in his look, he was a fiery, curious individual longing to experience the world beyond his chosen field of expertise.

Their paths first collided in a sad ballet-dance pair production. Jenny, with a flowing white tutu, stood stiffly near the dance floor. Her pulse hammering with eagerness, she waited for her beloved dance partner. She was unaware that fate had other plans in the meantime. Nathan came bringing his own wardrobe. Their routes curved from that moment on like the branches of an ancient oak tree.

Jenny is a young woman whose heart seemed as clean as morning dew. Her unearthliness charmed everyone who saw her. Her laughter sounded like the most exquisite symphony, and her perfect grin could make even the darkest of evenings dazzling.
Nathan, a beautiful and fascinating young guy who drew people in just by virtue. His mischievous grin and clear blue eyes radiated a

beauty that would have warmed even the roughest of hearts. Every gathering included him due to his keen wit and audacious attitude. Nathan maneuverers his way through the crowded hallways of Igili Sports High School; his eyes glistened with wicked intent. He spoke easily and cleverly weaved his words into an array of tension and comedy. His mesmerizing style clearly revealed his inherent ability to make everyone around him feel special.
"Ah, there he goes," a junior student murmured from the corner of the room. Nathan's infectious smile illuminated the room, drawing people to him like moths to a flame. Jenny seemed attached to Nathan's confidence and charm; she felt drawn toward him without control.

Like their other high school friends, Jenny and Nathan soon found themselves in a romantic relationship, enjoying the freedom and excitement of being young lovers. Their playground was weekends; they relished the opportunity to rebel. Driven to feel the forbidden pleasures of adulthood, they gave in to the seductive vices of smoking cigarettes and tasting alcohol.

Chapter 2

Fateful Night

Every day looked to be pleasant when the young lovers enjoyed one another's company—in the neighbourhood or at the school ground. However, these days, they are no longer mere high school students, but rather recent graduates deeply in love with each other.

Jenny and Nathan met with friends in a remote area besides the well-known Igili River Niger section known as Oshimilli Edei on this Saturday night as the sun sank below the horizon, bathing the earth in a golden glow.

Their pulses pounding with the thrill of the future, they laughed and spoke with pals Kene, Jake, Morata, Ade, Lou, and Nnadi.

"Hey, Lou, pass me that cigarette," Nathan said, his voice tinged with inquiry and assurance. Jenny saw him drag, the brightness of the fire lighting his face. She had a flutter of exhilaration in her breast, a need for the same forbidden pleasure.

Jenny stretched out with quivering hands and grabbed the cigarette from Nathan. She felt an adrenaline surge go through her veins as she lifted it to her lips.

Smoke choked her lungs, leaving her tongue tasting both sweet and sour. She felt released in that instant, as if she had passed a boundary into a world free from regulations.

The group of young pals descended further into the seductive realm of experimenting as the evening went on.

Before they all went home for the evening, they handed bottles of wine around, their contents disappearing with every instant.

Chapter 3

Reckless Paths

Like every other weekend, a stunning sun rises in the village of Igili, marking an exciting day for the young people living here. Nathan and Jenny stumbled into Jake, one of his friends from yesterday's river trip, just outside their home. Looking forward to a great night out, Jake was eager to have his friends join him on the evening adventure at a local pub.

"Nathaniel, my friend, I beg you to come tonight on an amazing adventure!" Jake shouted out, his eyes burning with fervour.
"What manner of party do you speak of, Jake, you are the funniest son of the soil?" With a mixture of curiosity and anxiety, Jenny, Nathan's friend, gazed at him. "Is it really important to go?"
Jake grinned slightly, his voice exuded eagerness. "Oh, sweet Jenny, this is not your typical gathering. It's for the best of all and cool kids!

Nathan's inherent curiosity caught him. Under her gentle approach, little Jenny, with great will, extended out and firmly gripped Nathan's arm. Her touch made Nathan shudder down his spine, as if it might change their paths of life.
Nathan, a dubious buddy, looked upon Jenny for solace.

Nathan burst out laughing. His strong laughter echoed across the street, exuding festivity and friendliness. "Very well, very well," he said, his voice somewhat amused. "We will go to this wonderful party." His comments showed some promise. They got ready and then proceeded to the gathering.

Jenny and Nathan walked hand in hand over the busy throng as the sun started to drop and the wonderful celebration took on a golden tint. Electric energy electrified the air, as though the very heart of expectancy were hanging there.

The gathering was eagerly embraced by many familiar faces from their days as Igili High School students and village members.

"Nathan, look! Mr. Nohra, Jenny shouted and pointed, her eyes widening with delight at the sight of their old math teacher waving at them from across the courtyard. Oh, I do remember him. I haven't seen him in years.

Jenny laughed, her heart bursting with yearning. His demystification of mathematics seemed to come naturally to her. "Let us go say hello," she urged.
Moving amid the crowd, they greeted old friends and caught up as they went. Laughing and intense debates permeated the air as they went back over treasured memories of shared occasions.
Mr. Nohra smiled politely as they arrived. Jennie! Nathan! His eyes shining with excitement, he said, "It's so wonderful to see you two getting into adult life now!" "You two were consistently among my top students." In what state have things been?

As the evening progressed, Jenny and Nathan descended into a sea of memories, their hearts ablaze with belonging. Not just a celebration of remarkable individuals, the memorable event was a memorial to the ongoing bonds of their community—a reunion of hearts and spirits.

Chapter 4

Fate Twists

Standing side by side with hands entwined, Jenny and Nathan revealed a deep look that was beyond words. Jenny replied softly, "I never imagined I could feel such intense emotions." She showed fragility and shock.

Holding her hand firmly, Nathan added, "Jenny, I promise you that I will always stand by your side, unwavering in my commitment to you."

The noise of friends' rumours tested their friendship to the very last degree and may have caused division between them. They persevered together, overcoming various challenges right from high school. Every morning's bright beam caressed their worn-out faces, consoling one another in their hug. Their love guided them over the darkest of gloom like a lighthouse.

They came to see they could surmount any obstacle together. Still, the storm intensified with daily adult life experience. The immense power of its blasts shook their fundamental basis of love. Their hearts started to store doubts, whispers of mistrust, and dread.

Attached to memories of their gentle touch, they fought a swirl of whispers and gossip from intimate friends and strengthened their affection. The flame flared brightly even amid adversity.

They continued then; their hearts connected like the limbs of a robust oak tree. They knew that love was not always straightforward and involved sacrifice and compromise. They were ready to give their all, however.

Weeks turned into months, and Jenny noticed changes in her body. She first related it to the strain of their stormy relationship. But as the days passed, she began to recognize the truth. She is pregnant. Jenny's heart soared with a combination of joy and fear as she gave Nathan the news. The directions these young people choose to follow are still unknown. But in that moment, as they held one another near, they understood they would create this new chapter together.

PART 2

THE GIFT OF NATURE

Chapter 5

Miracles Amidst

Like an unexpected miracle, both excitement and fear greeted Amara's birth into the world. Born only twenty-eight weeks into her mother's pregnancy, she weighed just 925 grammes. Her weight could be likened to that of a delicate water bottle. Her little and delicate look belies her fragility; her soul had a secret power.

Amara started her fight for life within the newborn intensive care neonatal unit's walls. Her early days were filled with the sound of beeping monitors and subdued medical staff murmurs as she negotiated the unknown road ahead. She kept proving her relentless will despite the difficult obstacles ahead of her with every hour that went by.

Amara's parents, Jenny and Nathan, observed their daughter with mixed feelings of awe and concern. As Jenny held Amara in her arms, she experienced a tremendous sensitivity in her heart. Her beautiful and subdued voice created a pleasant lullaby in the room, softly lit, created a loving environment around the mother and her priceless child as she offered her skin-to-skin hugs.

Jenny was in awe of Amara's exquisite beauty, particularly her little fingers, which appeared to be masterpieces created by fate itself. Jenny was in wonder at the miracle of life as she felt the outlines of those little fingers with her own. Time appeared to stop, so she could savour each second of this amazing trip.

Amara's mother experienced a unique blend of emotions, as the burden of duty blended with an inexplicable joy. Jenny sensed an unbreakable tie developing between her and Amara as she cradled her softly.

As Nathan leant in and gave Jenny a soft kiss on her forehead, his voice permeated the room, indicating his great respect. The sensitive moment seemed to stop time, as if everyone else in the universe had vanished. Their obvious relationship reflected the immense affection they had.

Jenny's eyes opened, and she looked into Nathan's eye with a combination of love and vulnerability. In that brief instant, a rainbow of feelings travelled quietly between them—unspoken words only they could grasp.

As the sun sank beyond the horizon, bathing them in a warm golden glory, the mere existence of her captivated him. As if nature herself were celebrating her beauty, the soft wind rustled through the leaves bearing the pleasant aroma of budding flowers. Overwhelmed with love, he couldn't resist speaking; his words carried a great tenderness that reflected in the darkness of the evening. "She is absolutely perfect," he said, his voice barely audible, as if he was worried about upsetting the delicate equilibrium around them.

Amidst the immaculate medical room, filled with the strong scent of antiseptics, a group of machines emitted beeping sounds. The room hummed with the steady reminder of the precarious life that hung on the verge. She lay on the immaculate white sheets, her body seeming ethereal, like a little flower trapped in the uncertainty. Her face had lines of concern, highlighted by the gentle halo cast by the faint fluorescent lights. Time seemed to stop within those walls, as if the whole cosmos had stopped waiting for the conclusion to develop. Beside her stood the world's greatest nurse, a steadfast anchor amidst the chaos.

Amara boldly confronted the difficulties ahead from the minute she was born. She entered a world of uncertainty, having been born before her time. Still, her spirit was strong and determined, unaffected by the enormous challenges ahead. The world seemed to pause in anticipation as she inhaled deeply, seemingly aware of the incredible journey this petite yet resilient spirit was embarking on. Fear and excitement permeated the air as her presence upset the natural equilibrium and put her in a world where she would require enormous bravery and will to flourish.

Weary but determined, Dr. Monique Fernandez, a neonatologist, walked towards the incubator with a steely sense of drive refined by years of relentless professional commitment. Though she felt the clean walls of the neonatal critical care unit closing in on her, she stayed concentrated, staring at the frail life before her.

A tiny life teetered on the brink inside the incubator. She spoke gently, "Hold on, my dear child," her voice full of a combination of hope and anxiety, and the gentle glow of the lights overhead produced almost magical ambience. The words hung in the air like a soft song, dancing softly on the edge of their awareness.

The chamber was softly golden, as if the sun itself had taken cover behind its walls. Dr. Monique, standing beside the bedside, had silver-streaked hair and kind eyes. Her thin fingers intertwined with Amara's tiny, delicate ones. Amara remained motionless, pale and feeble, her breathing faint and laboured. Jenny fought her battle with love, softly speaking into her tiny one's ear, infusing the air with a desperate calm

Chapter 6

Addictive Shadows

Amara's life story was horrific, one that evolved with a mix of pain and hope as Nathan had battled illicit drug addiction and aimed at recovery. Nathan and Jenny's hearts were full of hope and concern; they had spent countless hours by her side since birth.

Finally, the time they had been anticipating had arrived. Little and satisfied, Amara had surmounted her medical obstacles and now got permission to leave the hospital. Her young parents, filled with both relief and excitement, were preparing to welcome their beautiful daughter home.

As Amara's parents meandered throughout the hospital corridors, they thought back on the path that had brought them to this moment. Her radiant smile and kind demeanour reassured Jenny and Nathan, acting as a beacon of hope on their journey to healing.
Jenny, a young lady who had spent a lot of time depending on alcohol for comfort, found herself caught in a swirl of foggy nights and sad mornings. But Amara sensed a fresh sense of direction that energized her worn-out spirit when she entered her life. Jenny had been craving Amara's regular emotional support, which became her driving force in life.

Nathan, on the other hand, had always been a free spirit who jumped from one dangerous adventure to the next. His drug addiction totally consumed him, and he felt lost and cut off from the surroundings whilst under the influence.

Ready to embark on an amazing journey, Nathan and Jenny entered the lovely world of parenthood, full of love and excitement. As their beloved daughter Amara embraced her new responsibilities, she seemed to radiate enormous strength and fortitude. Every day was full of incredible happenings as they saw their child's great determination and strength.
Amara had an inexhaustible enthusiasm that never ceased stunning

her parents with her brilliant eyes and cherubic traits. She had conquered all obstacles right from the start, relentless in her pursuit beyond all expectations. Rising boldly and deliberately, Amara remained a symbol of hope during hardship.

Jenny would frequently murmur gently, pointing Nathan's attention to their darling little baby, Amara, who slept soundly in her crib. The moonlight's warm brilliance slowly seeped through the curtains, producing beautiful shadows on the room's walls.
Jenny and Nathan adored these quiet moments when the world appeared to be on hold as they observed their precious daughter. Amara slept peacefully and looked like an angel with her lovely face and cherubic head. Her small body lifted and dropped in a gentle rhythm, a sign of the peace all around her.

Jenny felt a great surge of love and protection as she marvelled at the beauties they had created. Nathan would only nod in agreement, his eyes fixated on his beloved daughter, unbroken, few words but a heart full of love. His eyes spoke a mix of pride, sympathy, and unwavering devotion, like windows to his soul.

One could almost feel the invisible bond between father and kid as he stood there silently verifying the relationship at that instant. This was a connection existing only in the domain of raw emotions and transcending words.

Chapter 7

Early Years

Amara's early years purportedly weaved with strands of affection and unflinching support, like a lovely fabric. Lucky for her, her parents had overcome drug addiction. Their extreme will to provide her a better life was a lighthouse of hope. From the moment she opened her eyes to the world, love enveloped Amara. Having experienced their own individual struggles, her parents found strength in one another and were now prepared to boldly meet the demands of parenthood.

Every word and deed clearly revealed their love for their daughter. Jenny, Amara's mother, is a lady of amazing fortitude; she has battled addiction nonstop since she became pregnant. She had fought her inner demons for her family as much as for herself. Having started a road of self-discovery, she had arrived at a level of unquestionable will. She wanted to have a lasting influence on the great canvas of the earth.
She embraced her actual potential with wide arms, shedding the doubts and fears that had earlier dogged her with every day that passed. She boldly started her road into the future, radiating from inside a fresh confidence that brilliantly highlighted her direction.

Over time, Nathan and Jenny find themselves increasingly entangled in the unpredictable twists and turns of life's journey as young partners. Once merely a possibility, the road has now transformed into a beautiful tapestry of memories woven with threads of pride and gratitude. Looking back in time, people marvelled at the unanticipated events and changes that had brought them to this point.

Their initial meeting, two forlorn souls in an uncertain world, seemed like just yesterday. They were unaware at the time that their paths would intertwine, destined to embark on a journey together that would profoundly transform their lives.

The unrelenting grip of youthful experimentation, which led to addiction, has consumed their lives, casting a dark cloud over their once vibrant existence. Little did they realize, however, that a sliver of hope was just waiting to shine on their road to atonement, out of the shadows.

Amidst the turmoil and hopelessness, they received a great gift: Amara, their daughter. Her arrival ignited a blaze of resilience and determination within their hearts.

Chapter 8

Fragile Balance

Sadly, the monsters that had tormented Nathan and Jenny came again, their hold tightening over Nathan's wounded spirit. A terrible turn of events, Nathan's relapse served as a sobering reminder of the unrelenting nature of addiction.

Jenny quickly realized that her former demons had ensnared her. She finally gave in to the attraction of drugs and alcohol once again, despite her best attempts to stay on the road to sobriety. It was a leisurely dance with temptation—a steady decline. It was originally simply a passing idea—a murmur in the rear of her brain. But as the weight of her previous misdeeds weighed on her and the demands of life piled up, that murmur grew louder and louder until it drowned out all reason.

The news came as a shock to their friends and relatives in their neighbourhood. It echoed down the hallways of their lives, leaving a trail of incredulity in its wake. The unexpected turn of events this naive couple had to deal with took friends, relatives, and even their reliable therapists by surprise.

In the field of human relationships, where ties are created and memories are spun, this disclosure created shock waves that reverberated broadly. Those who had laughed, cried, and spent many hours of understanding with others suddenly found themselves bereaved and trying to make sense of the incomprehensible depths of this unanticipated turn of events.

Whispers of incredulity mingled with subdued chats within the circle of companions, akin to trying to fit a jigsaw puzzle with missing pieces. Every individual hung to their memories, frantically looking for any clue that would have predicted this unanticipated turn of events in their common story. How could they have overlooked the minute subtleties—the hidden flaws in the façade that now appeared so clearly obvious?

Nathan's heart sank as he absorbed the weight of this unexpected event, realizing the news was no longer a secret reserved for Jenny and himself. He never expected his community to learn about their usage so quickly, and the news hit him like a tidal wave, threatening to drown him in a sea of hopelessness. Still, he held onto a glimmer of hope despite such destruction.

His thoughts flew, frantically looking for a sliver of a solution—a means of getting above the seeming surmount challenge presently before him. Despite the weight of disappointment trying to break his spirit, he resisted its stifling hold.

He stood firmly by the side of his loving partner and adored daughter, their unbreakable link acting as an anchor in the turbulent sea of life, driven with relentless will. Together, they discovered they were once again on the brink of a difficult road to recovery, one full of unknown challenges.

Adversity did not break their spirits; rather, the love that entwined their souls strengthened them. They had seen storms before, rising each time stronger and more robust. This would be the same.

Their hearts full of optimism and their minds clear of doubt, they set upon this difficult journey together. Days stretched into weeks, and weeks into months as they negotiated the maze-like healing hallways once again. Countless doctor's visits, therapy sessions, and the relentless search for some kind of normality defined the difficult journey. Still, they pushed on.

The path ahead was filled with perilous turns that could have easily diverted their entire existence. It was a road that tested their resolve and nearly plunged them into despair.

At times, it seemed as though all hope had vanished, leaving only darkness. But two spirits entwined by the same fight, Jenny and Nathan, resisted the grip of their addiction. Their stubbornness glowed brightly in their hearts, a flame unquenchable.

They battled fiercely against the demons, threatening to overwhelm them with every ounce of power they could summon. And at their lowest points, when the weight of the world felt intolerable, they took comfort in the constant support of those by their side.

Friends and relatives banded around them to provide a lifeline of love and support.

Their shared conviction that Jenny and Nathan could transcend their situation once again became a lighthouse of hope, leading them over the turbulent seas of healing. This fight called for a profound reflection and a deep dig into their souls, not just physical might. They had to face their demons head-on with unflinching resolve, tackling their anxieties.

Although it was a challenging journey that necessitated confronting the root causes of their addiction, it was an essential step towards their recovery.
Day by day, they made small progress, gradually approaching the light at the end of their journey.

Chapter 9

Hope Beacons

The events of the preceding several weeks had permanently changed Jenny's spirit, a sobering reminder that the fight against addiction was an unrelenting road requiring constant will and the unflinching support of loved ones.

Having seen personally the terrible force of addiction as a teenager, Jenny had always known of its risks. She didn't really appreciate the scope of the fight, however, until her late father, Emeka Danjuma Alonso, fell prey to its grasp. Her father had always been the centre of the party; his contagious laughter and unbounded vitality illuminated every room he entered. But behind that brilliant grin was a darkness that may have consumed him.
It began innocuously enough, with some drug experiments at parties. Jenny's late mother, Mrs. Aisha Alonso, originally discounted it as a phase, a rite of passage many young fathers experience. Emeka's experimenting, however, developed into a full-fledged addiction as the months passed—a relentless beast that would not let go of his delicate soul—and finally brought about the breakup of her family.

Jenny watched helplessly as her father's life collapsed when she was a little kid. The formerly energetic and ambitious young man turned into only a shell of his former self. A life of homelessness took centre stage in lieu of his hopes and aspirations.

However, Jenny possessed an immense heart. Her mild demeanour exuded sympathy and tenderness; she hugged her loved ones softly. She was the glue keeping their family together; her flowing auburn curls and eyes glistened with a trace of mischief.
Her unwavering love and unwavering faith in the strength of unity guided them through the most challenging times.

Amara, their beloved daughter, was particularly brilliant, serving as a symbol of strength and optimism. Her contagious laughter and limitless curiosity brought life to their lives. Her energy, as vivid as a kaleidoscope of hues, painted their lives in delight and astonishment.

She was a continual source of inspiration throughout all the ups and downs, reminding them of the beauty present in the most everyday events. They negotiated the storms life presented together. Still, the trip had been long and challenging, with periods of uncertainty.

With their false promises of brief comfort, drugs had captured Nathan in a vicious cycle of self-destruction. Though he tried so hard to escape this stifling habit, he discovered he was always giving in to its enticing grip.
Nine long months had gone by, full of both achievements and disappointments. He had sadly relapsed three times rather than one, despite their best efforts. Each relapse appeared to be a blow to their hopes, casting doubt on their future.

Always the rock, Jenny had been clinging closely to her determination. But the weight of it all appeared to sap her as the days stretched into weeks and the weeks into months. Her resistance started to be undermined by the weight of his relapses and the difficulties of their shared path.
Nathan also felt the weight of their situation. As he watched the lady, whom he loved fight to keep herself afloat, the guilt accompanying each relapse tormented his conscience. He wanted to be the stability she needed—the mate she was due. But like a persistent beast, addiction has a way of separating even the strongest ties.
Deeply in their hopelessness, a deadly idea started to take cause. Desperate for respite from the suffering and tiredness, Jenny was thinking unfathomable thoughts.

Every day seemed to intensify the allure of the drug that had captivated Nathan. It whispered promises of a fleeting escape from their common world, a brief break.
Jenny turned to face Nathan, her eyes desperate, and her voice shook. She knew she could not stand it alone anymore; the weight of the world appeared to lie on her skinny shoulders. Her problems had become too weighty and threatened to break her spirit.
Always the dependable buddy, Nathan turned to face Jenny. The bedside lamp warmly illuminated the worn-out wooden furniture in the barely lit room. Jenny stood on the edge of the bed, her voice filled with a mixture of hope and despair.
Her eyes glistening with unshed tears, she said, "I need you to be

strong for us, for Amara." Her voice wavered, indicating the anxiety
that had seized hers. With his emotions weighted with his words,
Nathan looked into Jenny's eyes. "I know, Jenny," he said, his voice
a blend of sympathy and guilt.

Jenny gazed outward; her gaze driven. Though the weight of the
world appeared to sit on her shoulders, she resisted letting it break
her spirit. She turned to her partner; her voice was resolutely
constant.

She began with urgency, saying, "I know it's hard, but we cannot
afford to give up now. No matter the challenges ahead, we must keep
fighting. For you, Amara, and for us."
Her words lingered in the air—a rallying cry. Jenny's thoughts
recurred, her eyes filled with worry as she gazed at her boyfriend,
Nathan. She realized something had to change—the weight of the
welfare of her family lay mostly on her shoulders.

The addiction that had gripped Nathan threatened to split their once-
happy house apart. For a moment, Nathan pondered, his eyes fixed
on the distant horizon. Jenny's remarks weigh heavily on the
atmosphere. The words resonated deeply in his mind, bearing
immense significance. For you, Amara, and for us.

It had become his mantra, his compass, during challenging times.
Though he felt a great weight of obligation on his shoulders, he
would not waver. Nathan stared determinedly into his partner's eyes;
his words full of relentless will.
"I promise you, Jenny, I will do whatever it means to overcome this
addiction and become the partner and father you and our daughter,
Amara, truly deserve."
As Jenny listened to Nathan's moving comments, her heart was full
of both hope and anxiety. She had witnessed the suffering addiction
had inflicted on their once peaceful house and the damage it had
caused to their family. But here, at this instant, she saw the guy she
had fallen in love with all those years before.

Nathan's path to rehabilitation has been turbulent, with both times of
hope and hopelessness. Addiction's grasp had tightened over him,
poised to split his family apart.

Chapter 10

Hope Glimmers

In the months that followed, demons haunted Nathan and Jenny's lives, entangling them in a complex web of destiny. The universe seems to have worked to cross their paths and link their lives in an amazing dance of connectivity.

As time passed, Nathan and Jenny grew closer, their hearts thumping in unison.

One of the bases of their current relationship is their love for Amara, which helps their connection develop daily. Among many diaper changes and restless nights, Nathan and Jenny found a wonderful feeling of direction. They remained together because they both wanted the greatest life they could for their beloved daughter. Unknown to them, the next events would be shocking and historic, permanently changing their feelings and perspective. Their lives started to entwine in ways they never would have imagined as the day went on.

In the immense distance of life's uncertain road, we often come across unanticipated bends. It may be as basic as choosing the incorrect road, work stress or missing a train. The captivating narrative of a roaring sea now engulfs them. The tides of destiny smash on the coast, echoing unexpected and strong love, of course.

Destiny carried them to a peaceful riverbank as they travelled through this gripping tale. Amara was a little miracle for Nathan and Jenny, who were formerly content and worry-free; they now had to deal with the difficult challenges of parenting without enough preparation. The river and the ocean symbolize the fluctuating emotions that shape their intertwined lives, as drug abuse intensifies the burden of parenthood. With unimaginable depths, their love is as vast and unbounded as the ocean.

Jenny sometimes feels totally buried in the tangle of obligations in life. She had not chosen this road deliberately; it felt heavy to tend another life when she could hardly take care of her own. Jenny had always been kind, attracted to the delicate craft of tending to others. She had followed a calling that had diverted her path, and now the weight of her choices rested on her worn shoulders.

With every stride reminding her of the sacrifices she had made, the road ahead seemed to go on forever, into the future. Her thoughts drifted over the memories guiding her to this place as she strolled. Amara heard the laughter of her loved ones resonate in her head. She had once felt like a lovely symphony of joy.

Every month was filled with unique occurrences that combined to create a unique arras of memories over time. Amara discovered she was controlling the unanticipated swings in her parents' lives. Like a fragile flower breaking through the cracks of a concrete sidewalk, her resiliency developed over time, determined to blossom despite the harshness of her surroundings.

Amara's road mirrors the turbulent environment that seemed to surround her. Her life had been emotional, turbulent, and full of challenges and issues. But in the chaos, she found a startling ability inside herself that she had not seen before.
It appears the universe was conspiring to challenge her to her limits and test her ability to withstand the pressure.

Chapter 11

Painful Decisions

Often faced with the difficult decision of separating children from their families and homes where they are supposed to feel safe and loved, devoted social and human services personnels—who carry the weight of many challenges in their loving hearts—may find tranquillity and safety within the scope of their honourable obligations.

Ms. Thompson, a seasoned social worker, sat opposite a couple with a reputation in the respite and foster care sectors in her modest and neat office, located in the child protection and services department building of the Igili Community Centre. The couple appeared distressed and emotional in the tense room. Saying farewell to a child they had grown to love was a terrible reality they were negotiating. Kind and compassionate, Ms. Thompson has devoted her life to helping families negotiate the challenging terrain of foster care. She'd seen many reunions, each distinctive. Conversely, the agony in these foster parents' emotions had a significant impact on her.

The child had benefited much from the parents under question, Mr. and Mrs. Tony Adamu. They created a caring and encouraging environment where the little spirit can grow. Loving this child as their own, they had poured their hearts and souls into her; the prospect of saying goodbye hurt.
Ms. Thompson couldn't help but respect the Adamu's as she listened closely to their passionate pleas and connected with their suffering. Their tears demonstrated their deep love for the child and their unwavering dedication to her welfare.

She understood that bringing a child back to their birth family was a challenging and emotional occasion full of both happiness and grief, but family restoration is a great outcome they hope to achieve daily. The situation underlined the force and possibilities of the human soul's ability to grow and heal. But it also meant bidding farewell to a chapter in their life that had grown to be indispensable.

Ms. Thompson, calm and kind, reassured the Adamu's that their love and care have had a long impact on the child's life.

Ms. Thompson said she was sorry; her voice laced with regret and reminded them that their responsibilities as foster parents were not quite clear-cut. Her apologies had weight; hence, her words lingered in the air, heavy and residual. The room became quiet, and everyone felt the tension clearly.
All of them were waiting, hardly breathing, to find out what she would do going forward. Her usually confident and purposeful gaze now reflected the soft golden light of the lowering sun over the lovely town. The residents of the town were living in this wonderful site, each story closely entwined with the others like a gorgeous masterpiece.

Two souls bound by destiny, Jenny and Nathan, discovered they were at the heart of a gripping story within a rich needlepoint of life. Hidden in a quiet part of town, Jenny and Nathan's little house offered a refuge of love and companionship. Their lives were full of laughter, hopes, and a close awareness of one another.
But on this evening, as the outside world became even darker, an unexpected turn of events shook their usually peaceful lives. Jenny's next-door neighbours, who have grown fond of young Amara, are an inquisitive couple who enjoy chatting and are fascinated by what lies beyond Jenny's curtains. As they peered through the tiny layer of fabric, they couldn't help but be afraid and very worried about their close little friend, Amara.

Jenny's neighbours observed the dancing, flickering shadows on her house's walls; their hearts were beating in sync with hers. Mrs. Chinenye Okon dreamed of becoming a mother herself—a dream that nature refused to allow her to realize; a strange sense of terror was rising within her. Chinenye sensed a strange presence in the house next door today, akin to a cunning beast lurking in the shadows. In weeks she had not seen any evidence of life emerging from beyond the walls. She didn't even hear the usual whisper of conversation, nor did she see any laughter or flashing lights.
A disturbing silence seemed to envelop the house, leaving Chinenye restless and nervous. Her heart drove her interest as it rushed against her chest like a wild animal imprisoned in a dimly lit place. Her

hands trembled with fear and desperation, and beads of sweat glistened on her forehead as she reached for the phone.

Like a flickering flame amid a storm, her expectation of a rapid rescue became stronger with every second that passed. Like a lifeline at this moment of severe need, she gripped on to the emergency hotline number she had etched into her brain. Her fingers glided across the keyboard, each stroke resonating in the quiet room as she dialled the emergency numbers. She could hear the silent scream—a wonderful mix of yearning and urgency.

The diligent social worker, Ms. Thompson, was totally absorbed in the stack of paperwork on her desk. Working with numerous families, her thoughts were constantly racing. Driven to finish her tasks before the day concluded, the consistent ticking of the clock on the wall reminded her of the passing of time.

Her phone broke the peace at her job as she was about to start reading another case file. Startled, she hurried for the phone, her pulse thrashing with both panic and excitement. She felt the weight of obligation settle on her shoulders and a flash of will be coursed through her veins.

She acknowledged the gravity of the situation, realizing that the safety of a helpless baby was at risk. Resolved, she started a path that would test her will and bravery.

The sun was lowering, and its low point in the sky created long shadows over the still region. Usually, Ms. Thompson's thoughts, as she hurried over the typical areas heavily affected by drug users, were filled with concerns for the welfare of each child. She was unable to see their fragile faces, filled with uncertainty and anxiety, out of her mind. She dedicated herself to confronting the horrific reminder of the world's depravity that the image brought.

She grabbed her coat quickly and felt the cool fabric on her fingers. She grabbed her keys off the table, their metallic jingle blending with the din of her racing ideas. She encountered an unusual puzzle that beckoned her to uncover its secrets.

Her head was whirling with possibilities as she ran for the door. What might she be expecting at the scene? Will it be a terrible catastrophe or an incomprehensible riddle she must answer? Her curiosity in the ambiguity only motivated her to discover the truth.

Outside, there was fresh air full of expectation. Her pulse pounding, the streetlights danced in time, creating long shadows that moved in time. Every action she took revealed her unquestioning dedication to her obligations.

She entered her car, shattering the silence that had enveloped the neighbourhood with the piercing wails of police sirens resonating down the calm residential street. The unexpected disturbance aroused the interest of bystanders who stared out their windows in a mixture of wonder and anxiety.

Among those present was Mrs. Chinenye Okon, a middle-aged woman well-known for her curious nature and relentless enquiry. From the comfort of her lovely living room, Mrs. Chinenye watched the dramatic incident unfold, widening her eyes. The police trucks' flashing lights cast a terrible glare over the serene surroundings, therefore generating a tense and negative atmosphere.

Her heart throbbed with eagerness as she thought about the reason for the authorities' sudden and quick response. The siren noise assaulted the serene surroundings as Mrs. Thompson listened tensely. Clean blue uniformed police hurried up to the large front entryway of the tall mansion. Their words were urgent, mirroring the weight of the recently experienced event.

As the welfare officers approached the opulent home, their hearts thumped in their chests, and adrenaline coursed through them. Knowing the stakes were great, they felt the weight of their obligation bearing down on their shoulders.

Mrs. Chinenye, tried to hear portions of the conversation next door. Her senses sharpened, and her ears pitched up as she listened carefully. Her hearing suffered from the whispers that passed through the little walls of her lovely abode. Something about the fascinating meeting caught her attention and aroused her curiosity.

Under the lace curtains, Chinenye could only hear fragments of the conversation. Little Amara, whose body was delicate, found herself curled in a tiny corner where she could hear subdued but clear voices dancing on the brink. She fretted; her body shook and shuddered wildly.

With only a sliver of moonlight peeking through the frayed curtains, the room was dark. Whirling shadows draped the walls, forming amazing figures that seemed to parody her imperfections. Outside, the wind howled ceaselessly, it's sad cries echoing across the empty streets. The storm unleashed its wrath on the street, with rain pouring at the windows like a beggar begs to enter.
Suddenly the rain started to pour in floods. A soft breeze whispered around the trees, fluffing the leaves and releasing the wonderful aroma of newly blooming flowers. The stillness of the evening suggested something remarkable was about to happen.

Amara lost herself in her thoughts and felt her heart skip a beat before hearing the soft sound of approaching feet. The repeated rhythm in her ears caused her pulse to speed. Only the distant chirping of crickets broke the terrible silence in the air. Her anxiety, which had gone deep into her bones, was intolerable.

Strong and determined, Ms. Thompson had always shown an amazing ability to see issues before they developed. Tonight was no different; she would carefully assess the family circumstances before making any decisions. Standing there, her mind was racing with many questions. Sitting in the poorly lit room, a lone person slumped on the edge of a worn-out chair. Under the light of a candle, Amara tear-stained face shimmered to produce a dark shadow across the room.

She gripped her most valuable possession, a beloved stuffed animal that had been her constant companion over many nights of solace, with shaky palms. The entire crowd appeared to be in a state of gentle understanding and sharing her loss. Her emotions weighed down her weak shoulders, threatening to throw off the delicate equilibrium she had laboured so hard to achieve.

She took comfort from her favourite stuffed animal, even in the darkest of her sorrows. Once vibrant and active, its fur now revealed the marks of many events.
Chinenye, the neighbour, blushed as she stood near the fence separating their backyards. Her voice quivered with annoyance, clearly revealing her deeply felt emotions. "I couldn't bear this any

longer," she yelled, her words hanging in the air with immense contempt.

Chinenye leans on the fence, looking for comfort and encouragement in her neighbour's suffering. Their shared problems would help her relax. "The continuous noise from outside felt like it was filling every part of me while I was sitting in my modest home," she said.

"The loud, persistent sounds of shouting at each other outside my window, resonating through the walls, nearly made me pass out then sudden silences." Since this young couple came into this home, the peaceful neighbourhood I had grown to adore has suddenly become noisy and chaotic, and I could not find even one minute of serenity. The sounds of car horns seemed to permeate the air before the neighbour's house became quiet, like a tomb. To show how much he loved her, Jude Okon, Chinenye's lover, could not help but stare at her with a sad expression. The wrinkles on his brow conveyed a deep sense of tension and concern.

He could not bear the thought of Chinenye experiencing any form of suffering, as if the entire weight of the world rested on his shoulders. Their eyes locked briefly, and they exchanged a subdued knowing. Together, they have surmounted numerous challenges, side by side addressing different aspects of their married life.
Their bond, forged through numerous challenges, remained unbreakable. Jude understood Chinenye deeper than anybody else. Jude could sense when Chinenye, a woman tormented by persistent restlessness, felt limited within the confines of her living room.

Her heart pounded, and waves of feeling swept over her entire life as she could feel the weight of her emotions descending on her. Her mind was filled with a flurry of ideas and emotions, making it challenging for her to relax, as she remained uncertain about the well-being of her small companion residing in the adjacent house. As she paced back and forth with each step, her inner wrath intensified. With these two, one mind convinces the small baby she is secure. Once a haven of safety and protection, her home now seemed stifling, as if its walls were relentlessly pushing on her. Chinenye's spirit was restless, yearning to break free from the confines of her own thoughts. She yearned greatly to be free from the bonds that held her back, to travel to uncharted territory, and to find a world beyond her cozy house.

But where was her illness originating from? Deep under her tormented psyche lie certain secrets. The question dogged her, one she was eager to solve.
As she walked back and forth, her thoughts drifted to a far-off past, recalling a love she once cherished but eventually ended in grief when she suffered her third miscarriage.

PART 3

DARING
SEPARATIONS

Chapter 12

Heartbreaking Separation

The days before Amara's return from the hospital saw a sequence of horrific incidents, including a bustle of guests arriving and leaving, loud sounds, and echoes of Jenny and Nathan's strong voices cutting deep into Chinenye's consciousness like glass fragments. These memories left scars that did not heal. The swift sequence of events rendered Chinenye completely defenceless and plunged her into terror. The air was heavy with unspoken evil, and the walls appeared to be murmuring secrets. She couldn't describe the sense she felt—that an invisible power had contaminated the very essence of her dwelling.

The last several days had been a whirlwind of activity and doubt. Mrs. Chinenye stumbled into a sequence of confusing events, each more confusing than the next. Strange sounds in the middle of the night started it all, resonating over her mental hallways like a melancholic song.

Her sleep became more difficult to find because restless nights full of vivid nightmares seemed to linger even when she was awake. However, the ethereal disturbances were not the only things troubling Chinenye. Other clear indicators of things going wrong were there.

Some unseen force seemed to guide objects away from their intended places in strange directions. She felt the weight of the circumstances bearing down on her; dark shadows danced in the corners of her eye, followed by a sudden silence akin to that of a mortuary. She immediately felt a sense of relief. Her heart heavy, she reluctantly embraced the reality that her only choice was to call the emergency numbers.

She had made numerous calls, consistently reaching out to those necessary to defend and serve society, as well as the children. However, she was dismayed that no one had shown up to help her for such a long time. The officials were evasive even after weeks passed.

Her wrath and despair became stronger with every missed call. She had reasoned that by requesting help, someone would pay attention to her distress signal. But the immense emptiness of indifference seemed to swallow her cries.

Alone, she began to question the fundamental basis of civilization. How could a mechanism meant to protect its occupants fail so horribly? Where were the law's defenders when she most needed them? Her mind was spinning with thoughts, which only served to intensify her search for help.
She continued to call out despite the lack of answer; her voice became more resolute with every attempt. She dialled number after number, clearly determined that someone would ultimately answer her phone. Still, the silence persisted, disparaging her efforts and isolating her.

There was a sliver of hope along with the wrath and grief. But today the light breeze rustled through the leaves, creating a soothing melody that appeared to match Chinenye's hammering pulse speed. She gently grabbed her phone and felt a little tremor go through her quivering fingers this time.

Desperate, the air seemed heavy, as if the heavens themselves were sobbing with her. While seeking comfort with her dear friend Anelia, who happened to be visiting at the time, Chinenye's shaking fingers had dialled the emergency number. Every ring of the phone seemed to reverberate throughout the room, raising the suspense that hung there.
As Chinenye softly talked to Anelia, her voice trembled with both hope and anguish. Their bond turned into a lifeline, a lighthouse of hope amid the storm that tore within as much as outside. Anelia gave Chinenye a comforting presence, a strong tower of support, and her own eyes full of empathy.
Together, their lungs seized in expectancy as the call connected on the other side, and both watched as the services arrived and saw her efforts at last pay off.

Two welfare officers stood side by side, fixated on Amara, as the rain started to flood in. Seeking protection from the harsh realities of her existence, she huddled in a corner, her tiny body draped in torn clothing.

Once a place of warmth and delight, the room itself now serves as a depressing reminder of time passing. Abandonment and neglect have left scars on its once vibrant paintings and walls. The air smelled strongly of decay, mixing with the faint whispers of buried parent dreams.

The darkness of the event concealed the identities of the two onlookers, who watched Amara with both curiosity and anxiety. The mystery she presented captivated them, drawing them to her like moths to a flame.

On the opposite side, Chinenye, Anelia, and Jude gathered close to the yard fence, their ears listening for any whispers of knowledge that could escape Nathan and Jenny's home. As they waited for any clue of what was going on behind closed doors, the air was thick with expectancy.
With their hearts pounding in their chests, the house sank into an odd calm. The walls themselves seemed to be anticipating the next step in this enigmatic story: breathing.

The once-busy sounds of everyday living had given way to an unsettling quiet that made their spines shiver. Other emergency services arrived at the location, intensifying the sense of urgency and anxiety that dominated the surroundings. A strong reminder that something significant was happening within the four walls came from the blazing lights and sirens.

Anxious glances passed among Chinenye, Anelia, and Jude as their minds whirled with questions. Why would such a sudden voice stop occur? Are we certain that everyone inside was safe? Their desire to understand the situation intensified as the uncertainty consumed them.

Expecting to hear even the tiniest murmur of conversation or rustle of movement, they listened carefully. However, all they encountered was an eerie silence that seemed to persist perpetually. Time had stopped, and they were in an anticipatory state. Their senses sharpened, and their thoughts went wild as they stood there; every moment seemed to last forever.

The weight of the unknown sank down on them, and logical thought became impossible. They needed solutions—any hint as to what was happening behind those closed doors.

Their minds created a multitude of scenarios, each more horrible than the next as they listened attentively. Combining curiosity with fear produced a potent mix of emotions that may have overwhelmed them. Still, they kept looking for a fix.

The surroundings seemed to have become unbearably weighty, suppressing any trace of sound that dared to challenge the quiet. The space itself seemed to be breathing, its walls vibrating with energy. Faced in the low light, the two individuals locked their eyes in an unsaid conflict of will. There was clearly tension, sparking with an electric power that appeared to charge the air they breathed. They counted each breath to avoid upsetting the fragile balance on the brink of collapse.

The first person was firm, their shoulders aligned, and their posture constant. Amid an ethereal quiet, when time seemed to stop, one disturbance broke through the peace. Beautiful yet extremely sad, the sound of Amara's soft sobbing echoed throughout the room.

Every tear that fell down her cheek was a mournful symphony that spoke to her soul—a symphony of anguish and yearning. Amara, a beautiful newborn, discovered that darkness surrounded her. Her heart yearned for serenity, weighted with unfulfilled expectations and unspoken words.

Surrounded by remnants of the past, she found herself alone in a desolate landscape. The wind's ghostly whisper piercing through the lifeless limbs enhanced the terrible mood. Her heart ached as Chinenye turned to face her assumed buddy, Amara. Once vibrant and full of life, Amara now lay in front of her, her delicate form hardly seen beneath the torn coverlet covering her weak body. Thoughts of happier days at Jenny and Nathan's home, when laughter and joy permeated every inch, swamped Chinenye. But suddenly, the soft sound of Amara's feeble breaths broke the silence. Chinenye's gaze stayed on Amara's face; her once-glow complexion now was pale and strained.

The creases in her brow revealed the numerous battles she had engaged in, both internally and externally. Ms. Thompson, the kind social worker who evaluated the matter and is now ready to receive Amara, glanced at Chapman, who had assessed Amara with pity in her eyes and a soothing tone in her voice. Her temperature was above limits.

The scene in front of them was chaotic, with ambulance drivers frantically rushing around to tend to the emotionally damaged youngster. Their voices were hardly audible in the centre of the tumult; they talked in low whispers. "I understand your concern, Chapman," Ms. Thompson remarked, her words flavoured with empathy that only someone with her history could have.
She understood the importance of maintaining calmness and composure in life-threatening situations. As a member of the ambulance team, Chapman Mesut had been especially struck by what he saw in front of him; he is the first witness of a health check on a child ready for government custody. His face reflected the weight of the circumstances, and his eyes revealed a mix of exhaustion and anxiety.

Though he had devoted his life to serving others, sometimes the weight of that responsibility felt almost intolerable. Among the hustle and rush, Ms. Thompson reached out a soothing hand, gently resting it on Chapman's shoulder. Despite its small size, this gesture demonstrated a deep understanding of the emotional toll their line of work may cause.

With years of expertise, beauty, and grace, Ms. Thompson descended softly to the level of a nervous child. Her kind and calming voice exuded comfort and certainty. Amid her anxiety, she reached out a calming hand to Amara, a kind smile on her lips, expressing protection and assurance.

Wide-eyed and trembling, Amara sought comfort in Ms. Thompson's company; her kind and empathetic approach provided much-needed reprieve from the strong feelings that had consumed her now. At that moment, a relationship developed between the two that cut beyond age and situation.
Finding loving homes for those who had been abandoned in the vast sea of uncertainty had been Ms. Thompson's lifetime dedication to a deserving cause. "We shall whisk you away to a haven of security,"

she said, her voice filled with a physical sense of urgency.
Arriving on the scene, experienced and alert police officer Serjeant Kazley Green had heightened senses and tuned instincts. Before Mrs. Thompson emerged from the shadows with Amara, he took a quick and practiced look over his shoulder to make sure his surroundings were secure.
Kazley's eyes probed every nook and cranny, seeking any potential predator lurking in the darkness; the dimly lit alleyway appeared to hide secrets beneath its murky depths. Standing there, a defender of the night, he carried enormous responsibility on his shoulders, prepared to meet whatever challenges lie ahead.

Jenny and Nathan, unaware of the events unfolding around them, had supposedly fallen asleep in their living room.
A massive downpour washed over the little village as the heavens opened once again, drowning everything in its path. The constant rain seemed to reflect the growing discomfort of the residents. The heavens themselves seemed to be sobbing tears of anguish and loss.

The streets were empty, their usual liveliness replaced with a disturbing quiet. The repetitive pitter-patter of rain on the street cobblestones and rooftops played a melancholic tune throughout the evening.
From one fresh face to another, Amara's wide eyes ran with a mix of fear and wonder. She was confused and ignorant of what was happening, as if a storm of upheaval had swept over her innocent head.

Holding a worn-out dummy, Amara struggled to understand the world around her; its rubber teat brought solace. The din of voices, jostling bodies, and the bustle of movement overwhelmed her senses. She yearned for a familiar face—a peace in the thick of the chaos, maybe from her parents.
But all she found were strangers, their features a tangle of anxiety and enquiry. Their eyes, ablaze with sympathy and curiosity, gazed down at her. They appeared to be attempting to unravel the mystery that this young child, engulfed in a sea of ignorance, also presented. She clung to her dummy, the one constant in her often-shifting surroundings. Its presence in her mouth brought calm, a brief break from the emotional tsunami threatening to overwhelm her. Every

sucking gave her a little escape from the confusing world she had
been living in.

Amara kept staring at the unidentified faces as her mind flew with
enquiries. Where are her parents? Why weren't her parents there to
comfort her? Her universe was changing—to what? Her little
shoulders carried enormous weight from the uncertainty, which
threatened to break her delicate soul.

But amid the disarray and uncertainty, optimism started to show. Ms.
Thompson's soft touch and consoling words were a lifeline, a
lighthouse in the shadow. Amara hung on that warmth, her heart
longing for the familiarity and protection of home.

As the evening deepened and the rain continued, it carried Amara
away to a place she knew nothing about. Her surroundings became a
kaleidoscope of colours and noises—a tornado of dizziness that left
her bewildered and afraid.
However, she clung to the idea that her parents were out there,
searching for her and longing to welcome her back into the warmth
and protection of their arms. Even during the storm, she persevered.
She was unaware that her journey was just beginning—a complex
path that would test her resilience and determination in ways beyond
her imagination.

Chapter 13

Turbulent Transition

Let's explore Amara's stormy journey into the unanticipated realm of foster care at the age of eleven months. Every family she encounters shapes her stubborn nature through a whirlwind of emotions and challenges.

Amara finds herself perched on the edge of yet another peculiar mansion, her heart pounding.

The door creaks open, revealing Mrs. Jamaila Peterson, an austere woman. With a frigid voice, she says, "Welcome to your new home." Amara's eyes stray over the room in search of any sign of consolation, but all she discovers are empty walls and a depressed mood.

Days stretch into weeks, months into years, as Amara's pure spirit works to fit the austere rules and cold surroundings of the Peterson's mansion. Her inner spirit, nevertheless, yearns for something more—a feeling of belonging. She longs for a family that will love her totally.

One evening, Amara is sitting alone in her room, shedding tears, when she hears a gentle knock on her door. She quickly wipes away her tears and opens the door to find Mrs. Jamaila standing there, her expression softened. "I know this hasn't been easy for you, Amara," she says. "But, even if it doesn't always feel like it, we are here for you."

Amara was moved to another carer looking for a child under the age of seven to look after only a few months with Mrs. Jamaila's family. Amara's heart raced as she walked down the unusual hall of her new foster home. She was apprehensive as much as delighted. Would this be the place she could finally feel at home?

Amara walked into the living room, staring at Tailor and Anene, her new foster parents. Their kind smiles gave her hope and helped her quickly relax. She had no idea; however, this was just the start of an incredible journey full of challenges, love, and unanticipated twists.

Amara had a horrific first day at her new school. The children mumbled and stared at her, making her uncomfortable. She, among the sea of fresh faces, identified Lilly, a girl who seemed to radiate kindness. Their bond became strong, giving Amara solace amid trying circumstances.

Tailor and Anene were handling their own difficulties as foster parents in the meantime. Attending meetings, making medical appointments, and navigating the complex foster care system, they worked assiduously to fulfill Amara's needs. Their relentless dedication to Amara's welfare revealed the strength of love and encouragement.

But just as Amara was adjusting to her new existence, a fresh twist of recollections began to disturb her midnight sleeps; nightmares of flashbacks and wonderlands of dreams in an imagined universe were waking her every night. Dreaming, Amara saw herself in a universe where she lived at home with her biological father and mother (Nathan and Jenny) and moved houses with them from Igili town to different places.

Amara moaned in one of her Wonderland Daydreams, staring at her father as her eyes became frustrated.

Amara said, "Thank you so much, Lilly," after her observation of Lilly emerging from the bathroom and showing her small cool places in the school. "Being a member of this group makes me very happy; she added."

"You're not exactly joining any typical company, Amara," Another friend Emily said. "We are the selected ones, doomed to fight the forces of darkness and save the world."

"Could you save the earth?" Amara inquired. "That sounds like an intense scene from a horror movie." Where do we even start?

"This is like some homework, we will be challenging all the bullies together," Lilly said. "We will face many challenges, fierce opponents, even betrayal from within our own ranks."

"Betrayal?!" Amara questioned, widening eyes.

At the end of the school day, the three girls appeared to have formed friendships and headed back to their own homes. Lilly, on the other hand, sees it more as a collection of well-chosen women than as a straightforward friendship. Although both women had succeeded in their respective classes, one of their friends, Amara, still suffers from the shadows of previous adversity.

On her way back, Amara is still getting her bearings at Anene and Tailor's home; she went in gently and carefully but had Tailor, who was having afternoon tea in the front, to lift her spirits.
"You are a part of our family, sweetheart," Tailor remarked, her voice honest and kind. She gently grasped Anene's hand, a gesture that told volumes about the strong bond they had developed in the months after Amara's placement in their care.

Amara couldn't help but smile, feeling a strong sense of belonging that had until now slipped her. Amara relaxed coolly after walking inside her room.

Chapter 14

Uncovering Secrets

Just as they are relishing the cool air rustling through the thick grass around Amara's new house, a stranger strolls through their front yard. Meanwhile, her foster parents are enjoying their last coffee of the day in the evening while they listen to the distant chatter of birds returning to their nests.

"Hi there, lovely evening weather, isn't it?" a passing stranger said.
"Absolutely," Tailor said fervently.
"Be cautious Mrs tailor, and don't do it like they did; they know why they kept it all in your old family building," the stranger advised.

Tailor laughed it aside but then remembered she had never met this guy who had just passed by and how he knew her name. What had just happened confused Tailor.
Tailor asked Anene, seated beside her, "Who was that man?"

"I have no idea," Anene responded, shrugging. "He does look like the new clergyman who had just moved into the new church building, Rev. Okafor, or a similar name, but I am not sure due to the unfamiliar disguise and nightlight, I have heard the Reverend has connections with the ancient histories of all the neighbouring towns and events of the past through his family," Anene responded, shrugging.
Her surroundings seemed to melt away as she kept the stranger's remarks in her brain. "Be careful; don't do it like your father's generation, Tailor," he had warned, his voice full of anxiety and hurry.
Tailor went to bed that night, having a succession of dreams she couldn't remember, but she did remember a man looking like the same man warning her in one of her dreams: "Your family's farmhouse has communal secrets that must be kept secret. There are forces at work here that you cannot comprehend."

Tailor couldn't understand why the stranger had picked her over Anene or Amara or what secrets her family's house may have. For years, it has been in their family, a comfort and familiarity passed down from generation to generation.

Tailor kept expecting to see the same guy, whom she had bucket lists of questions ready to ask him in a minute, but the stranger was nowhere to be seen another evening while she was having her regular evening coffee in the front yard with Anene.

"Anene," Tailor said cautiously. "Do you think what the stranger said about our family's farmhouse's harbouring secrets could be true?"
"Do you think what the stranger said about our family's farmhouse's harbouring secrets could be true?"
Anene cast a focused look at her. "I don't know," he responded warily. However, there is only one way to find out.

Mrs. Tailor had a terrible feeling of dread as the dusk sky became a deep shade of orange. She had always found immense fascination in the rituals and tales from long ago around the house of her ancestors. She had barely begun to develop an emotional bond with the newly adopted kid under their care, and suddenly this stranger had arrived to obliterate her innocent soul using cryptic words.

Before her, the years had passed down stories of lost love, hidden riches, and strange happenings. Conversely, Tailor had always dismissed them as common folkloric tales intended to entertain and captivate. She now began to doubt, however, if those tales were accurate. The stranger's remarks had piqued her interest, connecting with her on a level she had never acknowledged before.

"What secrets might our family's farmhouse possibly hold?" Tailor asked Anene.
"I'm not sure, honey," Anene answered. "But I'm willing to help you find out."
Why did she receive advice to remain cautious and not act? Tailor decided as the last of the light disappeared over the horizon. After her regular morning coffee the following day, she would discover the truth at whatever cost.

She rose from the veranda and made her way to their family's abandoned farmhouse, located just a few kilometres away from their magnificent mansion, which her grandparents had left empty for years.

Anene said as they approached the main door, "Are you sure about this?"
Tailor nodded strongly. She said, "I have to know."

The morning light sprang in as Tailor opened the ancient farmhouse door, casting long shadows on the floor. A crowd, their expressions full of enthusiasm, had gathered outside at Anene's invitation, in case anything within the structure required additional assistance. Among them, Tailor saw familiar faces, including neighbours and clients. The entry door groaned open to expose a poorly lit hall. Tailor stopped momentarily, her heart thumping in her chest. She couldn't withdraw now, however. She inhaled deeply and walked inside the vacant house, her feet resonating.

Tailor looked at room after room for any clues that would help explain the riddles her family's house kept. Neglected objects, fading pictures, and dusty furniture told the tale of earlier generations. But behind the surface, there was much more.

Her heart sped as Tailor made her way to the attic. The stranger had hinted that the secrets resided in this very location. She opened it with shaking hands, exposing in an ancient, encrypted wood book the many atrocities her family had committed in the past—including stealing and exchanging people's children during delivery.

The ancient, scribed documents hidden in their farmhouse captivated tailor, persuading her that her ancestors had committed more terrible crimes over decades of slave trade. As she left the house, her pulse was pounding like a grinding machine.

Mrs Tailor dives into the complex network of modern human emotions. This web links hope and despair, joy and suffering, and love and hate. From the perspective of Tailor's foster child Amara, we witness the complexities of controlling these emotions in a world that can appear overwhelming; however, Tailor's feelings quickly change.

Tailor, who had secretly promised to reveal her family's secrets hidden in the abandoned farmhouse, finds herself further entangled in her own complex web of emotions and disappointments.

Tailor said, "Anene," shaking her head. "I'm not sure I can handle this; what I've found... it's too much."

Anene reached around with her arm. "We'll get through this together," he said laughing. "We'll uncover the truth, regardless of how painful it may be."

Thank you, Anene; Tailor nodded. Together, they kept searching for the truth in hopes of uncovering more of the atrocities hidden on their family property.

Deeper historical research revealed that reality was much more complex and horrible than they could have imagined. Despite this, they remained steadfast in their pursuit of the truth.

Tailor and Anene continued their research, discovering more about the horrible facts hidden in their family past. They found evidence of betrayal, dishonesty, and even murder. Despite the horrific and uncomfortable journey, they remained determined to uncover the truth.

As they descended farther into the past, they began to assemble a complex web of lies and deceit born over millennia. They discovered that their family had belonged to a covert club with considerable authority and influence in the area, allegedly responsible for so many of those horrific murders.

What she had found stunned Tailor. Her family's culpability for such horrible atrocities astounded her. But she discovered as she kept searching for solutions that reality was even more convoluted than she had first thought.

She discovered that her family had been involved in a power struggle that pitted them against their own relatives and neighbours. They had been compelled to make difficult choices that finally brought them down a sinister path of killing hundreds of their own family members in a lethal assault.

Tailor was questioning what she had ever known about her family and her place in the world as she battled to come to terms with what she had learned. Not sure who she could depend on, she felt lost and alone.

Anene was there by her side all through it. He listened as she opened her heart, offering consolation and encouragement where it was most needed. Together they faced reality and began to heal from old wounds.

Tailor finally realized that she could not alter the past. Her background would always include the mysteries of the farmhouse her family owned. However, she also realized that she had the power to shape her own destiny. She might choose to follow a different path from dishonesty and betrayal and leave a fresh legacy for her family and herself.
The tailor eagerly awaited with renewed determination and longing. Though she was ready to meet whatever challenges lay ahead, she knew the road would be tough. And she knew anything was possible when Anene was by her side.

Knowing the background of her family, Tailor felt compelled to right the past mistakes. She decided to use the family farm as a site of healing and reconciliation. She invited the relatives of her forebears who had suffered to come share their stories.

This was a challenging journey filled with suffering and anger, but also with understanding and forgiveness. Tailor's daring and tenacity inspired Anene in the meantime. Anene resolved to use his journalistic skills to uncover the truth about his neighbourhood's past.

His series of pieces on the covert society and its activities set up a communitywide discussion and introspection. News of Tailor's efforts attracted support from unlikely sources. People from different walks of life volunteered to help restore the farmhouse and turn it into a community hub for residents and visitors.

From what they learned, they planned events and workshops meant to foster understanding and reconciliation. The revelations about the history of her foster family had a profound influence on Amara, Tailor's foster child. Upon learning of the revelations, Amara experienced a conflict between feelings of wrath and betrayal and a desire for understanding and forgiveness.

With Tailor's guidance, she began to sort through her emotions and find solace in her foster family's history. One day, while sifting through old records at the farmhouse, Tailor came across a letter from one of her cousins.

It was a sincere apology for bringing about loss and a call to pardon from future generations. Tailor felt relief reading the letter. She could learn from the past and aim for a better future, even if she could not change it.
Tailor's journey finally taught her own strength and endurance, as well as the mysteries of her family. She came to see that while the past shapes us, it need not define who we are. Love, compassion, and forgiveness aid in the healing of even the most severe wounds.

Still a mystery was the stranger who had set things in motion. Tailor, on the other hand, stopped being afraid. She felt she could overcome whatever challenge lay ahead. At the farmhouse, Tailor watched the fields as the sun set, filled with peace and hope.

Tailor's farmhouse became a lighthouse of hope and healing for the village as the days stretched into weeks and then into months. Laughing, crying, and deep conversations suddenly animated the once-deserted construction. People from all walks of life came to exchange their stories, become closer, listen to the stories of discovery, and heal past hurts.

Anene's writings about their path to farmhouse discovery created a wave of change in the neighbourhood. People started to reconsider their beliefs and practices, which promoted more respect and knowledge of one another. The disclosed ancient secret society's authority began to fade.

Amara felt inspired to emulate Tailor's bravery and aspirations. As one of the young individuals responsible for running the children's story room, Amara began assisting the village's little souls in navigating their emotions and overcoming their past.

One day, a familiar person visited the farmhouse. Although they couldn't confirm it based on his brief glance, it appeared to be the same stranger who had initially sent the message to Tailor and

Anene. Now they saw him; all had begun thanks to Rev. Okafor who
appeared as a stranger to them. His father had abandoned its
practices after learning of its terrible continuing activities, but he
revealed himself to be one of the descendants of the evil organization
that had helped execute the group plans; he left Igili village long ago
as a child to go to Igbuzor, then to Wirad village, and only returned
to notice the farmhouse was now a bushland from historical tales and
abandoned. Rev. Okafor, who was only temporarily appointed to the
Igili village, will be returning to his main church branch at Igbuzor
Town where he will mastermind a sinister plan to unseat their local
mayor.

He thought Tailor might influence the required adjustment, so he had
notified her. He informed Tailor, "I knew you were strong." I was
confident in your ability to handle the truth and use it to effect
change.
Tailor said she appreciated his trust in her. Though the past had been
full of suffering and sorrow, it had also brought her to this point: one
in which she may change things.

Tailor's goal was eventually more than just learning the mysteries of
her family. It was about learning to forgive, finding her own inner
fortitude, and using her past to create a better future. She also
questioned if she had made the correct choice as she looked out over
the fields that had hitherto held so many mysteries.
Tailor and Anene stood at the farmhouse door as the sun fell, gazing
out at the fields glowing warmly in the evening.

Tailor turned to face Anene, the last of the sun's light flashing back.
"Anene," she said, hardly audible above a whisper. "Do you feel we
acted morally?"
Anene looked at her with knowing eyes. "Tailor," he said, "we did
what we needed to do. We discovered and disclosed the truth. That
was all we could do."
But what if those changes everything? Tailor said, her voice shaking
slightly. "What if people look at us differently now?"
Anene reached out and squeezed her hand, trying to calm her down.
Then let them," he said angrily. "We can only live our truth; we
cannot control how others see us."

Tailor nodded, finding confidence in his statements. She turned back to face the fields, her heart a strange mix of desire and fear.

Anene said, "Tomorrow is a new day," softly. "And we'll face it together, whatever it brings." Rising from the past, they returned to the farmhouse prepared to face an uncertain but hopeful future.

PART 4

BUILDING OF THE VEINS

Chapter 15

World Weights

Amara's heart continually sinks as she contemplates the continuous upheaval that seems to define her life, stays with foster parents who are juggling their own family issues, and changing her carers. Just as Amara was beginning to find consolation and a sense of belonging, an improbable destiny intervened, ripping her from her newly discovered comfort and thrusting her into a foreign land.

At least she wouldn't be completely separated from the familiar people and places that had been her lifeline; therefore, this time, Amara and her dear friends found mixed comfort in the fact that the move was still within the confines of her Favorite town.

One constant protective factor in Amara's often shifting environment—school—offers a ray of optimism among the tumult. She could still catch flashes of the companions she had grown to treasure here; their presence gave some consistency in an otherwise turbulent life.

Despite the unfavourable circumstances, Amara found solace in the brief break that maintained a certain level of routine. Amara wondered how long this break would continue as she negotiated the hallways of her new house. Will she find herself displaced once more, forced to adapt to unfamiliar surroundings?
Her youthful shoulders bore a heavy burden from the uncertainty, yet she resolved to fully embrace the present and cherish the fleeting moments of stability that came her way. Among the swirl of transformation, Amara's fortitude came through. Particularly with a scientific fair just over the horizon, she refused to let the events of her past define her destiny.
She was determined to pursue her studies, thrive, and ultimately overcome the challenges. Amara's spirit intact, she clung to hope despite the unknown. She was evidence of the human spirit's resiliency and a lighthouse of hope among hardship.

Her narrative reminded me that there is always space for development and learning, even within turmoil and uncertainty. She therefore continued her path, her heart full of optimism and her mind open to the many opportunities that lied ahead.

When Tailor and Anene decided to continue caring for only their respite foster child Ethan, Amara learned she would receive a new foster parent.

Amara sat with her pals Emily and Lilly today in the classroom, sharing with them her recent moves away from Igili village.

Emily's voice was full of empathy as she gently said, "I know this is very upsetting." Her eyes, bursting with compassion, fixed on Amara, thereby expressing a profound feeling of sympathy. She seemed to have reached inside Amara's heart at that instant, knowing the conflict swirling there.

Emily's comments were a lifeline, a lighthouse of hope amid the turbulent sea of Amara's life, not simply a passing comment of understanding. Her compassion was like a consoling salve, calming Amara's tormented heart and providing her with a sliver of hope among the turmoil.

Emily's empathy demonstrated the connection they formed, forged in the crucible of mutual understanding and shared experiences. Amara realized she was not alone in her battle. She had Emily at her side—her constant support pillar of strength in her life.

Amara believed she could overcome anything with Emily's help, even if the road ahead presented obstacles. Emily was more than just a companion on Amara's journey through life.

Lilly also became quite sympathetic to her friend Amara as the sun caressed the horizon and sent a pleasant glow over the undulating hills. Sitting on an old wooden bench, they were staring at the busy city plaza in front of them.

"It must be so challenging for her," Lily said, her voice soft and somewhat grieved, "always having to adapt to new environments and unfamiliar faces."

With her eyes reflecting the fading light, Emily nodded softly in accord. Lily shook her head gently, trying to fathom the immensity of what was ahead of them. Her voice trembled with incredulity as she said, "I can't even begin to comprehend."

"But I guess it's better to find oneself in a situation that, while not perfect, offers some stability and safety than an unsafe environment," she said deliberately.

Emily nodded once more; her eyes stayed on Lily. As they sat in silence, each lost in their thoughts on Amara's situation, the room was motionless.

Conversely, Amara maintained consistency in her normal thinking; her spirit was intact; she was a monument to human perseverance, a lighthouse of hope amid adversity. Lily and Emily found immense appreciation for their friend's tenacity and brilliance while they sat there.

Mrs. Njideka, the respected coordinator of the student assistance office, entered the room, commanding attention with her presence and radiating warmth and power. She smiled broadly enough to light even the darkest evenings as she approached a group of young girls who had met earlier that morning to talk about the forthcoming science fair.

Mrs. Njideka was more than just a coordinator; she was a mentor and a source of inspiration for the children; her comments filled the room with passion and determination as she discussed the need for curiosity and learning. Her address reminded them that the scientific fair presented a chance for learning and development rather than just a contest.

Mrs. Njideka's words resonated throughout the room, lighting a spark within every child and turning them from science fair attendees into explorers setting upon a journey of enquiry.

Warmly and with real concern for the girls' friend predicament, Mrs. Njideka asked them, "Is everyone okay?"

Emily responded, "We're fine," with a kind smile and a thank-you tone in her voice. Though they flowed naturally from her mouth, the words had deeper resonance within her.

Their combined ideas drifted toward the suffering of those innocent souls stuck in the turbulent whirlpool of continually changing foster homes as the debate progressed. Their situation loomed large in the air, a dark shadow over their conversation.

Mrs. Njideka emphasized that everyone should pay close attention to this issue because we understand the great difficulties these youngsters faced, including the heartbreaking reality of leaving one temporary refuge and entering another.
The concept of their journey, rife with uncertainty and instability, captivated us and heightened our sensitivity. Mrs. Njideka, a wise and elegant lady, gently tilted her head to indicate she understood the entire scenario.

Her sympathetic and understanding eyes silently sent a thank-you note. "Yes, I absolutely get it," she said gently, her eyes sympathetic. "For them, it can be rather difficult."
Her speech had a trace of empathy, as if she had gone through the difficulties they encountered directly. She felt a twinge of pity for their situation as the weight of their obligations seemed to fall on her shoulders.
So, driven relentlessly, she sets out to find the ideal support structure for every kid caught in the web of such a fragile situation.
She searches for the illusive answer nonstop every day; her heart is full of kindness, and her intellect is bursting with creativity. Mrs. Njideka understands the responsibility of guardians, who bear the sacred duty of guiding these young minds towards the path of knowledge.
She meticulously explores every avenue and uncovers every detail in her extensive quest.

She closely reviews every facet of the educational system in search of creative ideas to enable these pupils to overcome their difficulties. Mrs. Njideka's goal is more than just academic support; it's about establishing a loving environment where every student feels valued and understood, about realizing each student's unique needs, giving them the tools and resources they need to flourish, and about building a community where every student feels seen, heard, and valued.

Mrs. Njideka is a lighthouse of hope in this enormous search for knowledge and insight, guiding the road for others who come after her. As she travels, she carries with her the hopes and dreams of every student she serves, fuelling her will to build a better future for all. Her relentless dedication and tireless efforts are evidence of her commitment to her students and her passion for education.

"I can't even begin to fathom the depths of emotion that Amara must have experienced," Emily murmured gently, her eyes full of a combination of wonder and enquiry. Her eyes, a combination of desire and sorrow, stared out the window. The wind carried the sounds of a life she had never known as it murmured through the woods.

Emily's heart ached for Amara, unable to comprehend the experience of living without a permanent home and experiencing constant displacement and relocation. She saw Amara's loneliness, her need for stability, and a feeling of belonging, but Emily also saw Amara's fortitude and will.

Emily found tremendous inspiration in Amara's fortitude against hardship. Though she knew Amara's path would be challenging, she also knew she was not alone; she had teachers who encouraged her, friends who loved her, and an entire community cheering her success.

Graceful and kind Mrs. Njideka had a soft grin on her face. There was a great awareness of the need for stability and security in the huge system where many lives crossed and entwined.

Among the many souls seeking comfort in its embrace were children, innocent entities thrown into a world of doubt and anarchy. With its complex network of support and care, the system saw the extreme need to provide these young people some kind of stability—though transitory that may be.

During their tumultuous journey, they realized that a brief respite from the chaos could be crucial. For these kids, who knew only the challenging facts of life, the system turned into a refuge. It gave them a refuge, somewhere they may find comfort and a sliver of hope.

Their loving embrace sheltered them from the harsh reality of the

world and gave them the opportunity to recover and flourish. Amid confusion and uncertainty, they found a sense of belonging—a sense of love and care.
Despite its best intentions, the system often failed to provide the stability and security these children so desperately needed. Their young brains suffered from the incessant turmoil and never-ending cycle of house-to-house relocation; they ached for a place they could really call home.

The challenges these children faced did not crush their spirits; instead, they demonstrated incredible tenacity in the face of adversity, bravely and determinedly overcoming each one. They were an homage to the force of the human spirit, a lighthouse of hope amid difficulty.

Looking at these young people, Mrs. Njideka felt pleased because she knew that, with the correct assistance and direction, they could overcome any challenge that came their way and thus reflect the potential they had. They were fighters, eager to face life, not just survival.

Deeply lost in contemplation, Lily gazed into the emptiness as Mrs. Njideka reiterated in the calm haven, "Our primary goal is to surround all students in foster care with a sense of safety and love." Lily contemplated her ideas, her eyebrows drawn together. Tension charged the air as everyone considered how to ensure these pupils had a clear road ahead.

Every attention turned to Lilly, a young student with a focused attitude. Mrs. Njideka, a lady of grace and poise, was there to provide responses. She nodded elegantly in accord, her eyes glittering with knowledge and compassion.
The pupils' choices started to affect the decisions made by the system from a young age; the guardians, constantly conscious of their needs and wants, took extreme care to consider them when inviting children into their custody.

It was a delicate dance, a balancing act between leading and caring, making sure their little charges were heard and cherished. This habit only became more noticeable as the relevant youngsters established

their own distinct personalities and goals throughout the years.
Ever alert, the guardians knew how important it was to respect these
choices, as they would help each fledgeling soul realize its actual
potential. Of course, everyone wanted the other person to find solace
and pleasure in their new home.

It was a global need—a basic one that cut across countries and
civilizations. Whether one was a tired traveller seeking comfort in a
distant country or a family displaced from their old surroundings
because of displacement, the goal was the same: to establish a
sanctuary where one could really belong.
Finding a place to call home is a very basic need in this wonderful
fabric of human life. Emily sighed with relief, her eyes briefly
shutting as she absorbed the consoling words; it was a natural
impulse that drove people to flee and start roots.

Mrs. Njideka said, "That's good to know," her voice tinged with
thanks and a trace of fresh calm. Emily responded, her eyes
glistening with gratitude, "It must make the transition a little easier
for them."
"It definitely will help," Mrs. Njideka responded, her voice
somewhat grateful.

One truth stands out above all others in the wide tapestry of life: the
need to build a loving and supportive environment for those we love.
We make numerous choices and decisions.
Souls can only grow and realise their own potential in the embrace of
love and encouragement. When it comes to parenting children, this
reality holds even greater significance. Every parent, guardian, and
caretaker longs to see the children in their charge not just survive but
really flourish. The human heart harbors a common craving that
transcends time and civilization.

Intricacy conceals a process within the realm of minute details,
where emotions intertwine, and choices carry significant weight.
However, its objectives remain clear and consistent: ensuring the
welfare of a precious child. This ultimate objective is like a
lighthouse of hope gently lighting the road ahead, guiding stars
illuminating the route.
Emily and Lilly nodded gravely; their features marked with gravity.

Emily's voice rang out with passion and force. "We should all do our part to support the children and their carers," Emily said, her words bearing the weight of obligation.

Her unflinching determination permeated the air, as if she had drawn from a reservoir of power running through her own body. Emily obviously believed totally in the cause; her enthusiasm kindled a fire inside her that would not go out.

Those who listened found her words resonating in their hearts, inspiring a feeling of direction. Lilly nodded in accord, her eyes shining with conviction. Her words poured knowledge and insight into the room as she spoke. For those who heard it, the phrase—so basic yet powerful—hovered in the air and connected with their hearts.

"After all," she said, her voice softly cadenced, "raising a child requires a whole village effort."
Those words became weighty in that instant, each assembled soul considering the truth buried inside. Mrs. Njideka listened to her beautiful student's comments and wore a kind grin.
"I'm delighted to hear those words, my dear girls," she said with a charming grin. Looking at your little face, a sliver of hope sparked in my worn spirit. The sight of such compassion and understanding touched the depths of my heart; they are so uncommon on our turbulent planet.

It was evidence of the human spirit's resilience and a lighthouse among the uncertainty's shadows. Your presence is evidence of the need for compassion during a period when apathy and indifference appeared to rule.

Your very attentive listening to the hardships and tragedies of others was a healing agent for their damaged spirits. Your ability to relate to and comprehend the events of others is truly remarkable.

Your empathy and understanding act as a lighthouse of hope, reminding us of all the power of empathy and the need to help one another. Your comments today not only warmed my heart but also kindled hope for a better future. We envision a world where every child, regardless of their circumstances, receives the necessary love, care, and encouragement to thrive.

Keep in mind that your words can affect your surroundings while traveling. You are change agents prepared to transform the world, not simply pupils.

Amara chose to pause at the same time and found herself on a park seat staring at the busy school playground. Though the weight of the world seemed to be falling on her, she clung to a sliver of optimism for the forthcoming scientific fair.

She wondered about the difficulties everyone could be experiencing as she watched the rush of activity around her. A small boy, who had just dropped his ice cream cone, interrupted her thoughts as she watched his ice cream cone break across the pavement.

Seeing this, a known family friend of the boy smiled gently, stooped down to meet the boy's eye level, and said, "Don't worry, little man. Accidents happen. "Here, get yourself another ice cream," he said, taking some money from his pocket.

The lad's look shifted from regret to excitement as he ran towards the ice cream vendor; his mistake lost memory. As Amara saw this conversation take shape, she grinned. Even though it was a small gesture of kindness, it brightened someone's day, served as a reminder that goodness persists despite life's challenges, alleviated her burden, and instilled renewed hope and motivation for her science fair participation.

"If the boy family friend can make the child's day better with such a simple act," she said, "then I, too, can make a difference with my science fair participation."

Rising from the bench, Amara headed out, prepared to meet whatever obstacles lay ahead.

Emily and Lilly felt a flood of will when they elegantly left the room after their meeting with Mrs. Njideka. A fresh sense of direction imbued their emotions, as if the weight of the earth had lifted off their backs. Their spirits appeared to flare from the electricity in the air surrounding them.

Relentless determination stoked their emotions, igniting a dormant fire. Their hearts beat in perfect time, reflecting the rhythm of their common will with every instant that passes. Deep within their hearts, they held a profound understanding that the world was not merely a blank canvas for their imaginations, but a vast canvas poised for instant transformation.

Still, driven by the immensity of the work, they held to an unflinching determination to help these students—such as Amara—by means of the major cause of progress. Armed with a relentless will to plant seeds of change, one little deed at a time, they set off a road with every day that passed.

Their goals were neither extravagant nor ones for the limelight of attention. Rather, they took comfort in the simplicity of their work, as they knew that even the tiniest actions might have a lasting impact on the fabric of life.

They found the actual force of their aspirations in the quiet times, far from the din of the outside world. In a society too often marked by indifference and apathy, they decided to be the agents of compassion. They knew that the road they had decided upon was not a simple one, as it required constant dedication and relentless endurance.

Despite the difficulties, they welcomed them with open arms, understanding that the path to change often paved with obstacles. With every stride they made, they were prepared to meet the difficulties, learn from their past, and keep becoming stronger. Emily and Lilly knew their road would not be simple; they knew transformation was a gradual process often full of obstacles and disappointments. They also understood, however, that every effort—no matter how tiny—may change someone's life. They resolved to contribute to the improvement of their surroundings through their own actions.

As they entered the world with optimism and resolve, Emily and Lilly knew they had each other and their community to help them overcome any challenges in the coming science fair and help their friend Amara wherever possible. With this in mind, they proceeded, one step at a time, prepared to make a difference.

Their narrative reminds us all that we have the power to effect change in our own ways, that every act of kindness matters, that every word of encouragement can make a difference, that we can be compassionate, sympathetic, and supportive of those around us, and, most importantly, that we have the strength inside us to persevere and overcome adversity.

Chapter 16

Adverse Triumph

Amara sat at her desk working on her new college textbooks, obviously committed to her studies. Amara's journey into a new family led her to the nearby town of Igili. Fortunately, her new home is just a short drive away from her previous college, which is why she had maintained her continued enrolment at her school. Her brow wrinkled as she descended into the depths of knowledge, resolved to blossom intellectually. Amara's new foster parents, Mr. and Mrs. Chimezie Johnson, who had been instrumental in realizing her potential, did not overlook her remarkable dedication.

Amara's academic ability had soared under the Johnsons' loving guidance. At her school, her diligence had made her a brilliant star among her peers. Her love of information deepened with every day, guiding her towards an almost limitless future.

Amara was studying in her bedroom one evening when she heard Mrs. Johnson's familiar voice startle her. "Amara, supper is almost ready! For a while, the appeal to nutrition diverted her from her academic endeavours and reminded her of the need for balance in life. Sighing, she closed her textbooks, knowing that her road to academic achievement will go on after a well-earned meal.

Satisfied with the sustenance that awaited her, Amara sat at the dinner table with her foster parents. She had a deep respect for the Johnsons as they traded stories and laughed. Their ongoing encouragement had not only created loving environments but also inspired her to want to excel academically.

After lunch, Amara returned to work, reenergized and prepared to tackle the challenges that lay ahead. Knowing her foster parents thought she was capable; she went back to study with fresh energy. Her will remained strong throughout the night, guiding her towards a time when her dreams would come true.

Amara kept growing intellectually, and her constant search for knowledge paid off. Her foster parents' unwavering encouragement and her own perseverance transformed her into a true student. She knew her journey was just beginning; hence, with every milestone, she became closer to her objectives.

Amara's academic achievements proved her determination and the love she got in her new foster family. She felt her future held opportunities as she sat at her desk reading over her textbooks. She was sure she could surmount any obstacle and create a path to success with the Johnsons at her side.

""Amara!" From the kitchen, Mrs. Johnson screamed, her voice filling the house. The little Amara lifted her gaze from her schoolbooks, a charming smile flickering at the rims of her mouth. Closing her books, she headed towards the dining room, where Mrs. Johnson's culinary wonders permeated the air and awakened her senses.

Mr. Johnson couldn't stop giving Amara compliments as they gathered around the table, a symphony of flavours just waiting for them. "Amara, my darling, your academic performance is really remarkable."

Amara blushed; a delicate pink hue crept over her cheeks as a rush of warmth surged across her chest. She couldn't help but experience a surge of success.

Her voice full of thankfulness, she added, "Thank you so much, Mr. Johnson." "I will be forever grateful for your steadfast support as well as Mrs. Johnson's invaluable guidance. Without your combined support, I could not have done what I have."

Chapter 17

Adventure Calls

The golden orb of the sun softly warmed the busy rooftop of her new house as it sank into the painted canvas of the horizon. From this new day, an unwavering decision mirrored the fiery flames of determination within Amara's soul; her eyes glitter among all the bustling Igbuzor urban roads.

She held her torn notebook, its old pages filled with quickly scrawled notes and beautiful images depicting aspects of her visions. The beautiful symphony of laughter and lively conversation awakened her senses as she glided naturally through the crowded streets. She moved expertly amid the wave of people, like a professional dancer gliding over a hypnotic sea of humanity.

On the far side of the room, she immediately recognized a familiar voice. "Amara, please wait for me!" pleaded Ramos, a childhood friend from her previous placement. The intense pursuit caused his breath to become somewhat laboured as he approached her.

"Have you in fact heard of my admission into the prestigious Academy of Human Sciences?" Amara exclaimed, her face ablaze with both exhilaration and terror. "Can you check if this is accurate?"

"Ramos, yeah! Are you crazy?" A wonderful quiet fell over the crowded city as Ramos checked the news. Acceptance into the esteemed Academy of Human Sciences, Zaria, was a significant achievement for Amara—one that not long ago had looked like a far-off fantasy.

"Amara," Ramos said, his voice full of love. "For every one of us, you have always been a wonderful inspiration. I always appreciated your energy and perseverance.

Amara grinned at Ramos; gratitude abounds in her heart. "Thanks, Ramos," she said softly. But I couldn't have done it without people like you and the Johnsons.

Just as they were about to begin their conversation, a commotion erupted from a nearby alley. Under the leadership of the notorious bully, Ayala, some of their former classmates emerged from the shadows.

"Ayala," Amara said coolly under the extra pressure.
"Amara," hissed Ayala. "I heard about your tiny achievement of getting into the prestigious Zaria university. Having everything on a silver platter simply because you are in care must be fantastic".

Two other former classmates of Amara's gathered around her as she listened to Ayala's speech. She was aware he was trying to annoy her, but she wouldn't let him ruin the occasion.
She said softly, "Ayala." "I have put much effort into my successes. I had to work hard for them; they didn't just come to me.

Ayala mocked her remarks but said nothing more. He understood he could not dispute fact.
Amara switched back her focus to Ramos as Ayala and his friends disappeared into the night. With a firm and resolute whisper, she said, "Let's go home."
Driven to celebrate Amara's achievement and get ready for the challenges ahead, they left the crowded street behind and headed to the Johnson house.
Amara and Ramos considered the events of the day as they returned to the Johnson house, the city lights shimmering like far-off stars. Though Ayala's nasty remarks had cast a shadow over their pleasure, the news of Amara's admission to the Academy of Human Sciences had delighted them.

"Amara," Ramos disturbed the silence. "Don't allow Ayala's comments to colour you out. You have put a lot of effort into accomplishing your objectives. You are deserving of it, everyone knows it.
Amara nodded, a determined look on her face. "I know, Ramos," she said. "I won't let him ruin this for me."

Mr. and Mrs. Johnson prepared a surprise party for her back at the Johnson house. There were balloons in the dining room and a placard saying, "Congratulations, Amara!" The sight made Amara smile, effectively removing the sour flavour from Ayala's comments.

Amara was delighted for the love and encouragement she had discovered in her new family as she sat down to celebrate. Despite all the challenges she had faced, she believed she was heading in the right direction to achieve her objectives.

Her story reminds all of us of the transformative potential of loving and encouraging environments, as well as the fortitude and relentless strength. Amara is now looking forward to their high school graduation party tomorrow.

Chapter 18

Deserving Reunion

The joyful celebration filled the air with a sea of emotional messages, each expressing words of congruence and best wishes for Amara and others. Her graduation and subsequent admission to the prestigious Zaria Academy of Human Sciences ignited a flurry of excitement and admiration among her friends, relatives, and acquaintances.

The messages inundated her with a tidal wave of love and encouragement, each message serving as a testament to the impact she had on those around her. Glancing over the many messages of congratulations, she felt pride and thanks bubbling up within her, warping her heart with delight. It had been long overdue, the culmination of years of effort and sacrifice.

Amara was marvelling at her human abilities as she savoured the warmth of her victory. The scene hummed with excitement as the children celebrated their high school graduation and admission to tertiary institutions. It was a major event—a gathering of loved ones celebrating the accomplishments of their precious children.

Parents beaming with happiness and guests clinking glasses in celebration made the room alive with love and pride. Warmth and friendship abound in this scenario, which is evidence of the constant love and encouragement these remarkable people received.

As the sun sank below the horizon, a warm golden light covered the little hamlet, welcoming Amara and her closest companions. Among them was Lilly, a lovely, energetic child with a kind heart.

Lilly found herself complimenting her friend Amara as the evening wind swept across her hair. "Lilly," Amara said, startled, "you're too kind."
Lilly growled, "I'm just telling the truth. You have worked so hard, and you deserve all the credit."

The two friends savoured a peaceful period of insight; their relationship became stronger through their common struggles. She grinned brilliantly and sent her beau her sincere congratulations. She had always had perfect trust in her own talents, thinking she had a mind fit to get him into any school she wanted.
Amara answered Lilly's praise, and her eyes sparkled with thanks. Amara's genuine gratitude was evident in her radiant smile. Her voice was kind and genuine as she said, "I am truly grateful for your kind words, Lilly."

A compelling drama plays out on the enigmatic arena of life's great stage, where dreams take flight and fortunes entwine. There are many personalities created by this intricate fabric of life, each with its own traits and goals.

One person stands out from the throng: their ideas sparkle like a lighthouse in the night. Still, Amara started remembering her travels to this point as the evening became darker. She thought back on the many hours she had spent studying, the costs she had paid, and the obstacles she had overcome. Though it was a journey with challenges and difficulties, it also offered development and self-discovery.

A poignant moment emerged between Mrs. Johnson's mother, Amal, a wise and seasoned soul, and Amara, the young girl who had found peace in her loving embrace, as the vibrant celebration continued to sweep the room in an aura of delight and festivity.

The old lady leant in closer to Amara, her voice resonating with the echoes of unmet ambitions and goals and her words flowing with the knowledge only age could provide. "You, my darling," she uttered, her voice a gentle melody amidst the sounds of laughter and music, "have the ability to achieve anything your heart longs for."

A universe of possibilities opened before Amara, as if she had properly borne the weight of a lifetime's worth of aspirations and regrets. Mrs. Amal Johnson, Amara's foster grandmother, had persevered through life's challenges and emerged resilient and knowledgeable.

Amara had a flash of optimism and resolve at that instant, as if the cosmos itself had worked to get this wonderful message straight into her spirit. Indifferent to the two spirits' strong interaction, the party continued around them. On the other hand, Amara saw something in that intimate moment.

Amid the joyful throng stood Vivian, a little child with relentless clarity in her gaze. She was a formidable presence, captivating everyone around her with a fierce determination. She lifted her gaze to meet Amara's wise grandmother with a sense of anticipation. Her pulse was pounding with a mixture of exhilaration and anxiety as she bore the weight of a recent letdown.

Her less-than-perfect marks had kept her from accessing the sought-after doors of her intended college. In the little living area, Vivian fixed her gaze on Amara's grandma. The streaming flames of the fireplace softly illuminated the ancient furniture and formal graduation images on the walls, whirling across the room.

Vivian enjoyed a quiet period of reflection as her ideas battled a dilemma that had been weighing heavily on her heart. "But Grandma Amal," she hesitated, her voice barely audible. "What if Amara didn't make it into the Human Sciences College?"

Vivian's voice trailed off, her worry lingering in the air, and the room fell silent for a while, the delight of the celebration fading into the background. With her eyes full of knowledge and compassion, Mrs. Amal Johnson moved to Vivian, gently grasping her hands in hers.

Her voice was calm and reassuring. "Success is defined by your determination, resilience, and willingness to learn and grow, not your college or grades." She spoke.

She added, "You are a bright and determined young woman," stopping momentarily to let her comments sink in. "And I have no doubt that, whatever college you attend, you will do fantastic things."

Tears welled up Mrs. Johnson's eyes, and Vivian nodded, a little smile flickering on her lips. Vivian's talents weighed heavily on her worn-out mind, and a residual concern seeped into the shadows of

her consciousness: "What if, I wondered, what if I'm not good enough?"
The glittering stars of the vast night sky seemed to tease her self-doubt. She seemed very vulnerable, as if the cosmos itself were working to discredit her value.

Like many of her friends, Vivian had always felt optimistic about her capacity to face the persistent uncertainty that had crept into her life. Realizing she had to face her uncertainties head-on; Vivian felt a surge of resolve. Her heart thumping in her chest, she inhaled deeply and mumbled to herself, "I am good enough," her voice almost audible. "I am capable; I am strong; I will succeed."

A long sigh accompanied her as the words came out, bearing the weight of dashed hopes and despair. Like a merciless shadow, the question had covered her dreams and veiled the road she had so fervently aspired to follow. Her truth abruptly appeared before her, presenting a bitter reality to confront.

The wise and caring grandmother of Amara glanced at her with warm and sympathetic eyes. The concepts of these young minds had caught her attention and set off a response that would stay with their hearts.

Amara's grandmother started speaking in a voice as faint as a whispering breeze. Her comments have the weight of compassion and lifetime experience. "Life is full of ups and downs, and how we handle those situations defines us. Even if your desired institution doesn't accept you, it doesn't mean you can't pursue your goals. Where you study is less important than what you do with opportunities."

She stopped to consider what she had said. "You are all here because you are capable and talented people who excelled inside the walls of high school. Don't let one setback define your future. Use it as a steppingstone to reach greater heights. Have faith in yourself, strive diligently, and never surrender your aspirations.
As she concluded her speech, the young students listening stopped; her words had touched everyone present, understanding that their path was just beginning, and they could choose their own destiny.

Vivian turned to look at Mrs. Johnson with fresh intent. She said, "Thank you," her voice full of gratitude. "I will keep your words close at hand as my compass."

While the party went on, Vivian was optimistic about the future. Looking around at the faces of her loved ones, she realized she would always have their love and support guide her down the road. She knew she had the courage and will to conquer any challenge that came her way.

With a quiet smile on her lips, the grandmother's quiet voice filled the room, focusing all her attention on her beloved granddaughter, Amara, thereby fostering love and compassion.

Lilly, a childhood friend of Amara, engaged in a heartfelt conversation with her grandmother and a friend today. Since their infancy, the two had been inseparable, their hopes and desires seeming to blend effortlessly. But tonight, their discussion took a more sombre turn as Amara discussed her intense ambition to be a doctor, just as their neighbourhood general practitioner, Dr. Paul, had said.

"Dr. Paul has been a lighthouse of hope and healing in our community," Amara's grandmother said respectfully. "He has devoted his life to helping others; his dedication to his patients is really inspirational."
"I want to be just like him," Amara said, her voice confident. "Like Dr. Paul, I wish to change people's lives."

Lilly expressed with great emotional resonance, "Amara, I have no doubt that you will become an amazing doctor." You always helped others, and I know you will likewise in your career."

Mrs. Amal began, her voice full of concern and questions, "Have you been made aware of the mysterious ailment that has befallen our modest Igbuzor town since the late 1980s?"

Amara nodded slowly, curious eyes wide. She had surely heard whispers of a strange disease that had engulfed their community and spread like wildfire through the close-knit neighbourhoods that year; it almost reached other towns, including Igili. An unsettling silence has replaced their previously vibrant surroundings, seemingly draining the town's entire energy.

"Yes, Grandma," Amara answered—hardly audible above a whisper. "I have known about it."

Mrs. Amal nodded, resolution and anguish shining in her eyes. "It was a difficult period for our community," she said, her voice rich with feeling. "Many people became sick, and we had no idea what was causing it. Dr. Paul was there for us. He laboured around the clock, day and night, to discover a cure."

Amara listened attentively, respect for Dr. Paul pumping in her heart. She understood she wanted to be like him—a healer in times of disease, a ray of hope among hopelessness.

"Dr. Paul's son is following in his footsteps," Mrs. Amal said with a proud undertone. "He is also learning medicine, much as you, Amara."

The rapid and unrelenting spread of the illness had sparked a frenzy of fear and anxiety throughout the town. Whispers about the mystery illness had permeated the streets, creating a path of concern in their wake.

One man stood strong in the thick of this ambiguity, his relentless search for answers driving him on. That is Dr. Paul, now in old age but always a source of inspiration for the next generation. Dr. Paul, an eminent physician renowned for his relentless dedication, was captivated by the hunt for the secrets of this perplexing illness that year.

Day and night, he laboured hard in his lab, reading many research papers and medical publications in search of any clue that would bring him near a solution. His once-perfect workplace had transformed into a chaotic conflict, filled with half-empty coffee cups, bottles of various medications, document stacks, and evidence of drug abuse. Handwritten notes covering the walls created a scene of connected ideas and speculations.

Driven to heal the illness that threatened to wipe out his beloved neighbourhood. Dr. Paul gave up sleep and personal comfort in service to this goal. The dedication of Dr. Paul to his community really inspired me. His relentless search for a solution and his relentless efforts demonstrated his integrity and love for his community.

Originally a shining example of precision and order, his workplace has turned into a chaotic battlefield in the struggle against the mysterious illness. Notwithstanding the chaos, there was a distinct will and goal.
Dr. Paul's dedication and enthusiasm encouraged his son to decide to carry on his father's legacy. He decided on medicine because he wanted to change people's lives and serve his community. Amara also expressed a similar wish. She saw Dr. Paul and his child as a mirror reflecting her own aspirations and goals.

Dr. Paul was very dedicated to his profession. Whether he was spending late evenings reviewing research papers or spending many hours with his patients, his unwavering determination never wavered. It captured his lifetime passion for medicine and his real will to change the course of events for everyone he came across.

His profound knowledge left everyone in awe, and it wasn't just his enthusiasm that captivated me. Dr. Paul was a scholar, researcher, and teacher as well as a doctor. His extraordinary attention to detail and a comprehensive awareness of the human body in handling every situation revealed his obvious medical competence. His knowledge went beyond textbooks; years of practical experience and continuous study had an augmenting effect.

Rising straight and declaring her lofty objective, Amara, a young woman driven to help others, had eyes glistening with resolution, mirroring the fire burning within her. Her profound trust in the ability of compassion and the possibility to change the lives of those around her drove her down the path of selflessness and service.

She stood among the best students in the town, as if the entire essence of the academic environment pushed her to go on a path of change, to make her mark on the world in a manner that would never fade. She felt a rush of purpose.

The centrepiece of this frenzied conversation was Amara, a young, aspirational woman whose voice rang over the nighttime air. "But I believe that with the latest inventions, if such a disease resurfaced, we would defeat it straight forward," she said, her eyes flashing with unshakeable conviction, "that with knowledge and dedication, there is a solution."

Amal looked at her grandchild and smiled kindly. The little girl's words filled the air, encircling Amal's heart and igniting it with an amazing sense of pride.

Amara's voice was full of thanks as she greeted Dr. Paul; her eyes gleamed with respect for the man who had been her continual inspiration.

Dr. Paul went over to the stately man with grey hair and a calm demeanour, Amal. His voice was full of anxiety, but his piercing blue eyes appeared to gleam with delight as he talked. "Mrs. Johnson Amal," he continued, sounding rather regretful. "I couldn't help but find myself softly pulled into the orbit of your conversation, Amara. Stay true to your dream, and you are most welcome to practice at my clinic during your field education placements."

Mrs. Amal approached the elderly man, Dr. Paul, whose grey hair framed her beautiful face. Amara's heart accelerated, and she wore a startled look as she listened to Dr. Paul speak.

The well-known doctor, renowned for his knowledge and compassion, had just presented an unexpected offer. This opportunity, rich in experience and development, had the potential to transform her life in ways she could never have imagined.

Amara's mentor along her medical career has been Dr. Paul, with his greying hair and kind smile. His advice and consistent support have been very important during her journey. He was now providing her with the opportunity to enhance her knowledge and refine her talents. Once her class starts, Amara's practicum year—a turning point in her medical school career—will be upon her. Amara, a feisty young child, was shocked by the sudden proposal she had just received. The words hung in the air for a while, leaving her paralysed in wonder.

On the other hand, her determination took control immediately, and she quickly composed herself, resolving not to let her emotions dictate her actions. Usually inquisitive, her hazel eyes now convey amazement and concentration. She couldn't turn down the unexpected offer, even if it seemed only half promising.
"I would be truly honoured, Dr. Paul," she said, her voice full of authenticity and a great smile on her lips. Her words came easily and carried with them respect and adoration. Her eager and eager gaze met his.

She immediately recognized that this was not a typical opportunity. Along with providing an opportunity for her to grow and learn, Dr. Paul's offer acknowledged her diligence and commitment.

Dr. Paul grinned at Amara and had beaming twinkling eyes. "I have no doubt that you will maximize this possibility, Amara," he said boldly. "You have the intelligence, drive, and dedication needed to excel in the medical field; I'm thrilled to see you grow and flourish."

Little Amara started a life-changing path toward her ambition of becoming a doctor. She had a caring heart and a strong will to influence her community.

She embarked on a journey that would test her resolve, challenge her intellect, and challenge her boundaries, all the while fuelling her unwavering commitment to serving others. Amara felt her dreams weight on her shoulders with every stride. Despite her deep-seated knowledge that this was her destiny, it proved to be a challenging journey.

The countless hours she spent reading textbooks, the restless nights she spent preparing to get into medical school, and the sacrifices she made were all part of her happy payoff for pursuing her ambition. Amara's goal went beyond mere education and skill development to include an investigation of the intricacy of the human body, the secrets of medicine, and the healing techniques.
She wanted to be a brilliant doctor, one that changed people's lives in addition to healing illnesses. She wanted to encourage the weak,

comfort the hurt, and give hope to the hopeless.

She knew the road ahead would be filled with challenges as she embarked on her journey. She was ready nevertheless to face them. She held convictions about tenacity, education, and personal development.

The celebration had ended for the day, but for Amara, who is now a medical student at the prestigious medical institution in Zaria, far from home, it was a step ahead in her path. To deepen her knowledge of the human body, it is time to visit classes and libraries. It helped her to remember her goals and purpose. She reaffirmed her dedication to her goals, yet the path to achieving them appeared paved with obstacles only the most resilient could withstand. Could Amara negotiate that difficult road?

Epilogue

Two years have passed already at the university, yet today Amara was deep in her studies in the school library in far-off Zaria when she received an unplanned call. It had originated in Igbuzor City from one of the nearby private hospitals. On the other side of the line, the desperation in the voice made her spine shudder. "Amara," the speaker said, "we need you here right away," but the connection broke off before she could respond.

Amara clutched the phone, her heart pounding. Though she had no idea what lay ahead at the hospital, she was sure her journey would take an unanticipated turn.

As Amara disconnected the phone, the urgent appeal from the hospital continued to play in her ears, causing her heart to race. Though doubt clouds her head, she realizes she must act quickly. What could possibly be so urgent that we require her immediate attention?

Her footsteps resonated in the empty corridors as she hurried out of the library, gathering her belongings to head home. She felt as if her life was about to undergo a permanent transformation as she stepped out into the cool evening air.
Amara's mind flew between worst-case scenarios and tried to remain calm as she travelled to the private hospital at Igbuzor. Upon her arrival, the emergency room was evidently bustling with frenetic activity. Doctors and nurses hurried around; their features marked with concern.

During the chaos, Amara spotted Dr. Paul and quickly approached him, who had also received a summons. "Dr. Paul, what is happening? I had a call."
Dr. Paul looked at her, his face serious. "Amara, thanks for being here. We have a problem that calls for your particular viewpoint and expertise."
He took her to a patient's room, where a young guy lay still on the bed, his skin pallid and clammy. Dr. Paul said, "This is David."" He arrived a few hours ago with symptoms consistent with the enigmatic

disease from years past. It's the same disease your grandmother mentioned which is why they called me.

Shock widened Amara's eyes. Despite having heard tales of that terrible period, she never imagined she would face it directly. "But how can it be possible? I believed the disease was gone."

Dr. Paul gave his head a shake. "We thought likewise. However, it appears to have resurfaced, and we need to act quickly to control it and provide a remedy. I believe in you, Amara. Your medical skills, mixed with your unique viewpoint—growing up in this neighbourhood and hearing the stories—may be the secret to cracking this riddle.

Amara felt the weight of duty falling on her shoulders. She understood she had to rise to the challenge for her whole community as much as for David. She took into consideration her grandmother's words about the strength of knowledge and commitment in the face of hardship.

Amara nodded deeply and inhaled. Dr. Paul, I'm ready. Let's cooperate to solve this and rescue our town.

Amara felt her fate as she descended into the medical riddle. From her early birth to her admission into medical school, all her challenges and victories had brought her to this point. Just where she should have been, she was fighting for the health and future of her beloved community.

However, Amara discovered through further research and patient interviews that the illness was only the beginning. Igbuzor's past held hidden secrets—someone was willing to commit murder to maintain silence.

Amara understood she had to be cautious, balancing her medical obligation with exposing the truth. She could sense the darkness encroaching, ready to destroy everything she had diligently worked for. She would not allow fear to stop her. Amara, with the support of her family, friends, and Dr. Paul, was determined to transform her town and illuminate the darkness, irrespective of the costs involved.

Amara knew her road was far from over as the sun sank over Igbuzor, casting eerie hues of crimson and orange across the sky. The sickness was just the beginning; it was a sign of a much more serious disease afflicting her community.

Amara prepared herself for the battles, personal as well as medical ones. She was unaware of the secrets, foes, and costs she would face. Despite everything, she refused to rest.

After a last glimpse at the fading light, Amara returned to her task, prepared to face whatever obstacles the night—and the future— might present.

BOOK II

Main Characters

Amara Johnson: A young medical student and doctor facing personal and professional challenges as she navigates her medical career and a new chronic illness diagnosis.

Jiu Adekunle: Amara's supportive partner who stands by her side through her health struggles and helps her find strength in love.

Dr. Patel Sharma: Amara's mentor at medical school who provides guidance and support throughout her journey.

Lilly Adebayo (Amara's childhood close friend): Offers emotional support and encouragement to Amara during her studies and health challenges.

Dr. Lilly Ibrahima (Amara's medical school roommate and colleague): Works with Amara at the Togo community health center and expresses concern for her well-being.

Constable Yen Chan with the Wirad Police Department who delivered news to Amara.

Dr. Rodriguez Mendez: Amara's supervisor during her clinical rotations at the Togo community health center who recognizes her passion for serving underserved communities.

Mrs. Thompson Ivy: Amara's former social worker who visits her at the Hope for Tomorrow Foundation, expressing pride in Amara's achievements and the impact she's making.

Destiny Yar'adua: A teenager on routine medical checkup.

Liam Adams: A teenage patient Amara befriends during her rehabilitation who is learning to navigate life in a wheelchair and serves as an inspiration to Amara.

Dr. Singh Bilal: The specialist who diagnoses Amara with myositis and helps her understand the challenges and treatment options for her condition.

Jasmine Kante: A young patient at the Togo community health center who Amara connects with and helps to open about her traumatic experiences.

Darius Tamova: A foster child mentioned as one of the many youths Amara has encountered and advocated for through her work at the community health center.

Maria Santos: A young mother and fellow patient at the rehabilitation hospital who is recovering from a stroke.

Ms Santos Ebenezer: Nurse at Togo community health center

Emily Carter: Another friend of Amara's from his childhood school.

John Mambo: An elderly patient at the rehabilitation hospital who is recovering from a broken hip and is determined to dance at his granddaughter's wedding.

Sarah Melaye: Amara's physical therapist at the rehabilitation hospital who guides her through her recovery and provides emotional support.

Rajendra Kumar: Amara's lab partner during her medical school anatomy class who commends her natural ability.

Key Locations

Academy of Human Sciences: Where Amara attends medical school in Zaria.

Abuo Ekanem campus: One of the campuses of the Academy of Human Sciences in Zaria.

Togoo Community Health Center: Where Amara completes her clinical rotations and later establishes the Hope for Tomorrow Foundation Clinic.

Wirad Private Hospital, Togo Road, Wirad: The location of the private hospital where Dr. Lilly Ibrahima works.

The Enugu Specialist Rehabilitation Hospital: Where Amara undergoes physical treatment and therapy for her myositis diagnosis.

Amara's School Hostel apartments: Where she lives during her medical school years at Zaria and her health struggles.

Dr. Patel's office: Where Amara seeks guidance and support from her mentor.

The lang park: Where Jiu finds Amara sitting on a bench, reflecting on her health challenges.

Amara's childhood bedroom at the Johnson family home: Where she sorts through her parents' belongings after their passing.

The Johnson family home: Amara's foster family's house, where she spends time with Nuss and Zarah after their parents' death.

The Igbuzor community center: Home to where Amara established the Hope for Tomorrow Foundation, Clinic and hosts the annual gala.

Igbuzor town: The town where Amara grew up.

Wirad: The neighboring town to Igili and Igbuzor.

Amara's dorm room: Where she lived with Lilly during one of her medical rotations school years.

The hospital cafeteria: Where Amara and her colleagues gather during their shifts.

The examination room at the Enugu specialist Rehabilitation Hospital: Where Amara receives her myositis diagnosis from Dr. Singh Bilal.

The physical therapy gym: Where Amara undergoes rehabilitation at the Hospital with the help of her therapist, Sarah Melaye.

Prologue

The sun dropped over Igbuzor, throwing brilliant orange and light pink tones over the sky that would have been ideal for another beautiful day. Perched on the balcony of her family residence, Amara watched the last of the day fade into darkness. She took a long breath, enjoying the fresh evening air and the sensation of possibilities that seemed to hover about.

Six months had passed since she received that fatal call from the private hospital in Igbuzor—six months since she had returned to her hamlet to confront an undiagnosed illness that threatened to wipe out her people. Faced challenges never seen in that era, Amara had pushed herself to the limits of her medical expertise and personal fortitude.

She remembered the hectic days and nights she had spent reading medical articles, conversing with colleagues, community leaders and striving to uncover the truth behind the pandemic.

They overcome all the difficulties, too. Through sheer will, outstanding collaboration, and a sequence of lucky occurrences, Amara and her colleagues found the source of the disease and developed a treatment strategy. In addition to healing a community and saving lives, Amara emerged from the ordeal with renewed confidence in her medical abilities.

As the first stars began to spark in the darkening skies, Amara felt a familiar thrill of excitement. Tomorrow she was going back to Zaria to continue her studies at the renowned Academy of Human Sciences. This was the next stage of her road, a chance to grow in knowledge and ability in ways she had only dreamed of previously.

Amara felt a twinge of apprehension even as she anticipated this new chapter. The events of the preceding six months had shown her the volatility of life and the speed of change. She considered the patients she had assisted as well as the relationships she had created with her peers and the community. She considered Jiu, who had been by her side through it all, his unflinching support a balm for her worn soul. She also thought about her foster parents and her real parents who had lost their lives to drugs.

Her chest ached as their memories reminded her of everything she had lost and gained. But it was also a source of strength, a motivating factor guiding her to be the greatest version of herself and to use her skills and compassion to change the world.

As the last light faded from the skies, Amara turned back towards her bedroom, where a half-packed suitcase was resting open on her bed. She knew that the road ahead would be challenging and that sometimes doubt, worry, and exhaustion would hit.

She was prepared to face the challenges ahead with unwavering clarity. She wants to be a doctor who loves her town, fashioned in the furnace of adversity and cooled by the power of her own unbroken spirit. Her journey had yet to begin.

PART 1

MEDICAL CRUCIBLES

Chapter 1

Orientation Recurrences

Her journey began just two years and six months ago, but the grand halls of the esteemed Academy of Human Sciences seemed to tower over Amara as she stepped onto the vast Abuo Ekanem campus in Zaria today, embarking on a new journey as a medical specialist trainee, her heart pounding with a mix of excitement and trepidation. Her hard-earned white coat sat heavy on her shoulders, a physical reminder of the amazing path she had followed to reach this point.

Amara considered the meandering route that had led her to the threshold of her aspirations as she negotiated the sea of expectant faces. Her parents battled drugs; thus, she experienced a turbulent upbringing marked by instability and neglect. But destiny had intervened in the form of the Johnson family, the foster parents who had adopted her and showed her the transforming power of pure love.

With the unwavering support and encouragement of her beloved childhood friends, Emily and Lilly, Amara surmounted the challenges faced as a child of the system. She had given her studies her all, fought over murmurs of uncertainty and discrimination, and found her position at this stronghold of medical school. Now Amara was filled with thanks for the family of choice who had raised her and believed in her ability as she passed the threshold into the sacred halls of study. She quietly promised to make them proud and to respect their confidence in her by giving her training all she could.

A touch on her shoulder shocked Amara from her thoughts. She turned to see a small young lady with a dazzling smile and a halo of curly hair.

"Hello! Brightly extending a hand, the girl remarked, "I'm Lilly, your new roommate." It appears that both of us are new to this hectic medical   environment.

Amara grinned back, drawn right away by Lilly's friendliness. "My name is Amara; I had a childhood friend with a similar name, but it seems like I've recently met another Lily who follows a different academic path." Really? Oh's really, it's lovely to meet you," Lilly said, shaking Amara's hand. "I suppose we will be negotiating this journey   together."

As the two new colleagues headed towards the Abuo Ekanem campus medical student's introduction hall, Amara felt a flutter in her chest. She was aware that the path ahead would be demanding, with many hours of study and clinical training. She was driven by a deep-seated desire to become a doctor who could truly transform people's lives, and she was determined to face every obstacle head-on.

Amara and Lilly entered the auditorium, which hummed with the enthusiastic conversations of their fellow future doctors. Amara sat up straight in her seat, her eyes gleaming with expectation as the lights darkened and the dean stepped on to do his welcoming speech.

"Welcome, future healers," the dean said, his voice booming out with authority. "You are starting a great road that will try your mettle, challenge your presumptions, and finally help you to become the compassionate, competent doctors our planet so sorely needs."

Amara felt a surge of intention as the words swept over her. This was it, the start of everything she had laboriously gone for. Though she knew the road ahead would be difficult, she was willing to give her heart   and   soul   to   be   privileged   to   serve   others. Amara's thoughts turned to her loving foster parents, seeing them pleased, tear-streaked faces from their parting embrace. She quietly promised to be the type of doctor who would touch lives with the same compassion   they   had   always   shown   her,   making   them   proud.

Amara   inhaled   deeply,   straightening   her   shoulders   and   turning forward to confront her fate. She knew she would meet the challenges with the unquestionable power and will that had taken her this far. Amara let herself see a future where everything was conceivable for the first time in her life, and she was ready to pursue it with all she had.

Amara looked to Lilly with a grin as the orientation ended and the room once again buzzed with excitement. She felt the flame of a fresh friendship flickering. Ready to enter the rigors, thrilling world of medicine, they poured out into the brilliant sunlight together.

Chapter 2

Fire Trials

Her five-am alarm broke the silence before dawn, startling Amara into instant consciousness. She turned over and let a quick touch silence the constant beeping. She smiled quietly. Lilly moved beside her, letting out a subdued groan of protest.

"Is it morning already?" She whispered, her voice heavy with the weight of sleep. "I felt as though I just closed my eyes." Amara sat up, wiping the residual bleariness from her eyes. "I know, it's horrible," she said. "But at 7 a.m. sharp, we have an anatomy lab. If we are late, Dr. Singh will have our heads." Lilly sighed dramatically and pulled herself straight, her locks shooting out at odd angles. She stumbled towards their communal coffee maker and said, "Remind me again why we signed up for this torture."

Amara laughed as she slipped from bed and started gathering her daily belongings. "Because we're addicted to punishment, who wants to make a difference in the world?"

Actually, the first few months of medical school had been much more demanding than Amara had expected. Classes ranging from sunup to sunset covered everything from biochemistry to physiology to patient evaluation techniques over the course of the full day. She and her friends laboured over textbooks and case studies in the few hours between classes, trying to keep up with the relentless flow of fresh material.

Still, Amara discovered she thrived on the challenge even with the long days and late evenings. She delighted in the intellectual rigidity of her studies and the way each new idea built on the previous to create a complex world of medical knowledge. Her fellow students, a varied collection of gifted, determined people who shared her love of healing, also inspired her frequently. Of course, in the swirl of learning, there were times of uncertainty and frustration. Amara occasionally struggled to balance her rigorous academic schedule with her desire to participate in extracurricular activities and maintain a social life. As one of the few students from a low-income household, Amara occasionally encountered subtle prejudice and reduced expectations from certain lecturers and classmates.

But Amara would not let those challenges stop her. Often burning the nighttime hours in the library long after her friends had left, she immersed herself in her studies with single-minded concentration. She also made a point of looking for mentors like Dr. Patel, a gifted surgeon noted for his dedication to diversity and equality in medicine.

Under Dr. Patel's guidance, Amara began exploring methods to give back to her community, despite her busy schedule as a medical student. Starting at nearby high schools, she shared her tale and inspired children from underprivileged backgrounds to choose professions in science and medicine. She also urged the government to launch a mentoring programme that pairs first-generation medical students with supportive upper-class men and faculty advisers.

Amara felt a flutter of satisfaction at how far she had come as she hurried across campus to her anatomy lab, holding a thermos of coffee and mentally going over the convoluted network of nerves and blood vessels she needed to memorize. Despite the long road ahead, she was determined to seize every opportunity for learning, development, and service.

Amara inhaled deeply, then opened the door of the anatomy lab, prepared to meet whatever obstacles the day presented. Despite her understanding that becoming a doctor would be the most challenging thing she had ever done; she was deeply aware that she was exactly where she was meant to be.

Chapter 3

Forging Ahead

As Amara crouched over the prone body on the stainless-steel table, her gloved fingertips gently probing the exposed muscles, the fluorescent lights buzzed above. With her eyebrows furrowed, she mentally matched every building to the meticulously memorized schematics. "The flexor digitorum superficialis," she said, gently raising a long, thin muscle. The median nerve innervates it, and the ulnar artery provides its blood supply.

Her lab mate Rajendra Kumar nodded kindly across the table. "Well done, Amara," he replied, giving her a brief grin. "You're naturally at this."
Feeling a flush of delight at the compliments, Amara returned the grin. She and Rajendra bonded easily on their first day of anatomy lab. He had a keen intellect and a ridiculous sense of humour that could cut through even the most stressful times of their dissections; he was a conscientious worker. Amara was astounded at the complexity of the human body on display as they methodically explored the forearm. Every muscle, neuron, and artery fit together like the gears of an extraordinarily complicated machine, all cooperating to allow the marvel of movement and sensation. These kinds of events helped Amara remember why she had chosen this path, despite the long hours and constant sacrifices. The beauty of the human body and the opportunity to understand and repair it inspired her ambition to succeed.

And shining she was, often scoring highest in her class on tests and getting compliments from her teachers for her sharp analytical mind and relentless work ethic. Amara, however, yearned for more than simply intellectual achievement. She craved to use her developing knowledge and abilities to really improve the quality of life for those most in need. Amara therefore gave her all to her fledgling mentoring program for minority pre-med students while she was not in class or studying. She set up seminars and panels to link wide-eyed undergraduates with prominent doctors and researchers who might illuminate the roads ahead.

From the Cultural Diversity and Inclusion Office to the Office of Community Engagement, she began building a network of friends across the university. Her efforts did not go unreported. Many student groups soon sought Amara for leadership positions due to her reputation as a fervent supporter. When her mentors and colleagues nominated her for a prestigious national fellowship honouring emerging leaders in medicine, she was astounded by the outpouring of support. Of course, the Honors and successes came with some demands. Sometimes Amara felt the weight of tremendous expectations pressing down on her little shoulders as her fame kept rising. As a lady of colour blazing paths in a typically homogeneous profession, she understood that every action she took was under scrutiny.

The persistent anxiety that she lacked the intelligence, ability, or resilience to merit her place at the table sometimes crept in under the imposter syndrome. But Amara found courage in the unwavering support her foster family and friends had always exhibited in her potential throughout those self-doubting years. She considered Lilly, her study companion and present confidante, who always seemed to know when Amara may want a late-night pep to talk or unplanned dance party in their dorm room. She also leant on the wise counsel of Dr. Patel, who reminded her that the people she affected along the road defined actual achievement rather than titles or medals.

Driven to live up to the trust people had put in her, Amara pushed herself to new heights with their support and her own grit powering her. She recognized that her path involved much more than just personal success. It was about opening doors, removing obstacles, and clearing the path for the next generation of healers.

Amara experienced a renewed sense of purpose as she removed her gloves and confidently nodded at Rajendra Kumar. She was confidently moving forward, one anatomy lab and leadership position at a time, towards the promising future she knew lay just beyond her work. She was also very eager to welcome it.

Chapter 4

First Cut

Amara held the knife over the pale, waxy skin of the dead, her fingers shaking just slightly. Breathing deeply and steadily, she felt the weight of her classmates' eager looks on her. On their first day of full-body dissection, they worked on isolated body parts for weeks, learning the language of anatomy one muscle and nerve at a time. However, now they would uncover the entire enigma of a once-living, breathing human being.

Amara paused, a surge of feeling almost drowning her. She knew cognitively that this time would arrive. But standing here, knife in hand, the truth of what she was about to do struck her with visceral power.
She considered the person this body had previously been—someone with aspirations, loves, and sorrows. She questioned their life narrative and the pleasures and tragedies they had experienced on Earth. She also owed a great deal of thanks for the amazing gift they had given— their earthly vessel for the honourable cause of training future doctors.

Dr. Patel interrupted Amara's dream by gently clearing his throat. She looked up to see him nodding encouragingly, his eyes kind and sympathetic. "It's a profound moment," he whispered softly, his voice low enough for only Amara to hear. "Sit back slowly.

Honor the weight of what we are about to do. Amara nodded and bit hard against the knot in her throat. She then brought the blade to flesh with a last, centering breath and made the first, intentional cut. Amara found herself sliding into a kind of meditative concentration as she worked, her hands moving with increasing confidence as she revealed layer after layer of the latent architecture under the skin. She was astounded by the precise arrangement of every organ, the exquisite blood vessel lacework, and the muscular sinewy power. It was like seeing, in breathtaking detail, a symphony of form and function performed with the labour of a skilled artisan. Amara couldn't fully get rid of the anxiety she had experienced at first, but she lost herself in the nuances of the dissection. With each unveiling of a new building, she felt an increasing burden of duty. One day, she would assume responsibility for diagnosing, treating, and defending these tissues and systems. The margin for mistake was minuscule, and a fall may have disastrous results.

A few days later, Amara found herself struggling to keep up with the rapid-fire questions during Dr. Singh's infamous "hot seat" sessions. The weight of that knowledge struck her squarely. Renowned for his rigors with a Socratic approach, the stern-faced anatomy teacher would drill pupils on minute minutiae until they either emerged victorious or collapsed under duress. This was not the case with Dr. Patel.

Amara felt like she was floundering, her head blank, as Dr. Singh asked her more vague questions regarding the blood circulation to the duodenum. As the stillness persisted, she could feel her cheeks heating and hear her classmates shifting uncomfortably. Just as she was about to sink into a sea of shame, she felt a small kick to her foot. She looked down to find Lilly sat beside her, giving her a subdued thumb beneath the table. Amara was sufficiently snapped back to herself by that little act of support. She inhaled deeply, closed her eyes, and sharply visualized the relevant anatomy. Her eyes widened as she recognized the distinct response in her mind. She spoke with a quiet confidence, observing as Dr. Singh's eyebrows rose in surprise and then curtly nodded.

The moment was a revelation for Amara. She knew she did have the information, buried far down in the caverns of her brain; she simply needed to trust herself enough to reach it under duress. She also recognized the remarkable power of a supportive network to rely on during challenging times. Amara addressed her studies from that day on from a different angle. Driven by a terrible feeling of obligation to her future victims, she pushed herself into learning every minute detail. She also made a point of tending to the friendships and mentoring relationships that would help her get through the difficulties ahead.

Late into the evening, she studied anatomical schematics and sometimes found herself returning to that initial, formative cut. She would also silently pray for the great honour of learning from the most personal secrets of the body, as well as for the strength and encouragement of those who travelled beside her on this lifetime trip.

Chapter 5

Emerging Purpose

As Amara walked over the sliding doors, the busy hallways of the Zaria community clinic hummed with a tangible vitality. Her clean white coat was a lighthouse of peace among the controlled anarchy. Her first day of clinical rotations, she could hardly contain her enthusiasm at the idea of at last using her acquired abilities in service to actual patients. As she checked in with the harried-looking receptionist and went over the patient list she would be seeing, one name caught her attention: 14-year-old Destiny Yar'adua is here for a regular checkup.

Something about the girl's age and the general reason for her visit niggled at the rear of Amara's consciousness. Foster children often fell through the gaps of the healthcare system, their needs forgotten in the mix of overloaded guardians and overworked case workers. From her own youth, Amara understood all too well bouncing between placements.

Amara headed to the exam room, where Destiny awaited, her pace quickening in the direction of a goal. She knocked gently and then came in, staring at the adolescent girl seated nervously on the exam table's crinkly paper. Destiny gazed warily, her shoulders hunched defensively, even as she gave Amara a cautious smile. She donned a too-big sweatshirt that swamped her skinny frame and tied her hair up in a sloppy ponytail.

"Hi Destiny, I'm Student Doctor Johnson," Amara replied kindly and held her hand. "If it's agreeable with you, I will exam you today with few questions." Destiny shrugged; her eyes flicked momentarily to Amara's before flying away. "Sure, whatever," she said, murmuring.

Amara nodded, not bothered by the teen's reluctance. She understood too well that years of instability and unfulfilled promises might destroy the trust that defensive and mistrustful foster children build.

As she began the standard assessment, Amara casually discussed school and her interests while keeping a close watch for any signs of neglect or abuse. She pointed out a fading mark on Destiny's forearm and observed how she shivered just a little at unplanned touches.

Amara gently asked about Destiny's home life and support system, probing a little more. The evasive and imprecise responses suggested that Destiny bounced between too many places, never truly settling before uprooting again.

Empathy and irritation tightened Amara's heart. She was aware of the statistics, which showed that foster children were more likely to experience poor school performance, mental health issues, and chronic illness. How does the system often allow the very children it claims to protect to fail?

An idea started to develop in the back of Amara's mind, nebulous at first but becoming more concrete with every query and silent disclosure. How would it be possible to provide children like Destiny with more constant, thorough treatment? A one-stop shop that combines case management, physical and mental health treatments, and educational help would be ideal.

Amara had seen first how easily underprivileged children may slip through the gaps. However, she also recognized the immense resilience and potential awaiting development beneath the surface. Amara's brain was whirling with options at the end of the visit. She handed Destiny her card and urged her to reach out anywhere, for any reason at all. As she watched the guarded girl sneak out into the waiting area, Amara quietly swore to do everything in her power to create something better.

Over the next two weeks, Amara immersed herself in research with a fervour that matched her most focused study sessions. She read public health publications and policy papers, contacted community leaders and mentors, and developed budgets and program designs.

Amara became increasingly sure she knew this was her actual calling. It wouldn't be easy; nothing worthwhile has ever been simple. She was aware that she would face resistance from a deeply ingrained system that was opposed to change, as well as doubters who questioned the viability of her ideas.

Amara, however, has never been one to run from a difficulty. She also firmly believed that this was a battle worth enduring. Every child deserves a chance to flourish and reach their infinite capacity. And Amara would be held accountable if she hadn't dedicated her life to giving them that chance.

Amara's pulse raced with anxiety and expectation as she at last sat down with Dr. Patel to present her concept for a thorough foster care facility. However, her mentor's eyes sparkled with excitement, and his head nodded before she had even finished her spiel, which astounded and delighted her.

"This is exactly the kind of creative, systems-level thinking we need more of in medicine," Dr. Patel continued, his grin broad and pleased. "Amara, you will undoubtedly make significant progress." And I will be by your side at every stage.

Tears sprung to Amara's eyes at the confirmation, the sensation of her several identities—foster child, activist, future physician—slotting into place like tumblers in a lock. She was aware that there would be a thousand more challenges and failures. But Amara felt superhuman at that instant, driven by her own fierce conviction and the confidence of her master. She was a lady driven by a goal; a brilliant arrow aimed towards the heart of injustice. She was just beginning as well.

PART 2

SHATTERED LIVES

Chapter 6

The Loss

Amara woke up from a long, dreamless sleep with great agitation, reaching for her phone. She slid over and moaned, reaching for the gadget among her messy nightstands. The brilliant screen displayed an unidentified number, and Amara momentarily thought about ignoring it. But something pushed her to respond—a whisper of discomfort, a gut pull. She sighed, then swiped to answer the phone.

"Hello?" Her voice sounded irritable and foggy. "Please let me talk with Amara Johnson." On the other line, the voice sounded clear, authoritative.
Amara scowled, then became totally alert. "Speaking. Who's phoning?"
"Ms. Johnson, this is Officer Yen Chan from the Wirad Police Department. I have some unsettling news to share.

The words that followed rushed through Amara's ears as if they were coming from a distant place. An accident has happened. They said he was a drunk motorist. The Johnsons, who had taken her in and loved her as their own, and her parents, the only ones who had ever truly cared, were gone. That's precisely what happened on a dim rural road, amidst a tangle of metal and the screech of tires.

A wide pit of anguish threatened to consume Amara from within. She barely noticed the officer's subdued sympathies as she acted. She found herself free falling amidst the debris, feeling as though her entire life had suddenly vanished from her grasp.

The next days were a haze of numb incredulity broken by burning stabbings of pain. Amara felt strangely disconnected from her own body as she worked through the procedures of organizing a funeral and received the emotional hugs of family friends. She seemed to be unable to halt the ceaseless unspooling as someone else's life disintegrated in slow motion. Nuss and Zarah held her up while her siblings leant on one another for support. Even their constant presence, however, couldn't stop the flow of loss, threatening to drag Amara down. Now resonating with the ghost of their laughter and love, every inch of the Johnsons' once-vibrant house appeared haunted by their absence.

Amara sought to bury herself in her studies as a diversion, a lifeline to hang on to amid the storm back at the university. But the words floated before her, their meaning lost in the mist of sadness and tiredness. She discovered she was zoning out in lectures, her head far from the fluorescent-lit academic halls.

Lilly and Emily from her hometown of Igbuzor and her childhood friends made every effort to help her; they brought casseroles and sat with her in solidarity while she blankly looked at the wall. Amara, however, was withdrawing into the dull cocoon of her loss. She began missing social gatherings and study groups and stopped sending SMS. A wall had grown around her heart, keeping everyone and everything at a distance.

In the face of her spiralling gloom, even Jiu, her constant rock, a friend turned partner, appeared powerless. He held her as she wept, caressing her hair as she lay asleep for many hours. But no kind of compassion could pierce the frozen shell of bereavement covering her.

As the weeks dragged into months, Amara began to feel like a ghost in her own life. She followed the guidelines of courses and clinical rotations, but the spark that had previously propelled her vanished under the weight of her grief.

Her grades started to drop; formerly excellent test results fell into the category of almost passing. Professors who were worried about her drew her aside for polite pep speeches, but their comments seemed to her like white noise. Nothing seemed to matter anymore, not her studies, her struggling organization, or the future she had once been so intensely motivated to build.

Late one night, Amara sat on the floor of her childhood bedroom, surrounded by boxes of her parents' possessions, and felt something change. The numbness that cocooned her for so long started to break, then a seething rage at the injustice of it all took front stage.

She reflected on all the challenges she had overcome in her early life, the courage and resiliency that had carried her far, and the loss of the one family she truly cared about. She considered her parents' unflinching faith in her ability and their constant encouragement of her to pursue her goals in front of any challenges.

Amara realized that she could not allow their loss to shatter her. She owed it to their memories as much as to herself—to keep striving for the bright future they had always seen for her. With all the relentless dedication of the whole family, they have made sure she is ready for her profession.

She shook hands and pulled out her laptop, searching for the office location of a highly qualified therapist Dr. Patel had mentioned, who had experience working with patients such as Amara, his name is Steve Martinez, a neurologist and clinical psychologist. She scheduled herself for a session; it was time, she realized, to begin gathering the fragments. Learning to survive in a world without her parents appeared highly unlikely.

Since it is what they would have wanted for her. The child within her, who had already experienced numerous storms, was more resilient than she realized. She was more resilient than anything life could throw at her.

Amara began to move slowly and laboriously, one foot in front of the other. She knew that the path ahead would be long and meandering, and that there would be days when the loss would seem as if it could break her.

But she also knew now, with a calm, unwavering belief, that she would survive it. She would emerge from the crucible of this loss, transformed by grief, strengthened by resilience, and even more fervently committed to a life of meaning and service. Her road map would be the love and legacy of the Johnsons. Amara vowed to honour them.

Chapter 7

Picking Pieces

The morning light slanted over the kitchen table, casting golden trays on the dust motes swirling there. Amara held her coffee cup and peered out the window to see a couple of squirrels playing in the backyard oak tree of her family's house in Igbuzor. After her father's death four weeks ago, she returned home and found the house strangely still, devoid of the cozy buzz of their presence. Amara noticed remnants of their love gestures wherever she looked: the hand-stitched throw pillows on the sofa, pencil marks measuring her and her sibling's heights on the doorframe.

Their absence seemed like a tangible pain, a hollow place pulsating with every breath behind her breastbone. Amara, however, was learning day by day to live with the suffering. She allowed the pain to wash over her in waves, but she refrained from letting it submerge her entirely.

Her weekly therapy appointments with Dr. Martinez had evolved into a lifeline—a secure harbor to help her navigate the storm of emotions still whirling around her. At first, Amara was reluctant to talk to Martinez, as she thought there was nothing that could help reduce the intensity of her emotions. However, she found that expressing her anguish, her fury, and her terror somehow diminished their intensity. It felt as though by calling them out, she might begin to control them.

Dr. Martinez had urged Amara to rely on her support network and allow her loved ones to share the weight of her loss. And in those first few weeks, she had begun to gently, hesitantly, lower the barriers she had set up. She allowed her friend Lilly to take her out for coffee and commiseration in Igbuzor, and she sat silently as Emily delighted her with stories of their childhood adventures in the area. Sholina, the Mayor of Igbuzor, has also expressed her respect for Amara and her family with many flowers on their doorstep and several visits. Her long-time friend, Jiu was also available for leaning shoulder. Her pillars of support had been Nuss and Zarah, the only other individuals on the planet who truly understood the depth and shape of her grief. Laughing and sobbing over lost memories and fading pictures, they combed through the wreckage of their parents' lives.

Zarah was the one who discovered the stack of letters and cards their parents had carefully chosen throughout the years, each one a picture of a priceless event in time. Amara had crafted a crayon artwork for Mother's Day featuring six-year-old stick figures surrounded by mismatched hearts. After a particularly violent argument in his teens, Nuss had penned a tearstained epistle pleading for pardon. On the eve of her college graduation, Zarah sent a sincere note thanking them for their constant support.

Reading those words and feeling the echo of her parents' unbounded love set something free in Amara. She allowed herself to really feel the whole weight of her loss for the first time since that horrible phone call. Great, sheaving sobs rocked her frame as Nuss and Zarah hugged her close, their own tears mixing with hers.

It was a turning moment—the first fracture in the cold numbness covering her. Amara started the process of thawing gradually, painfully, letting herself feel the whole range of her emotions free from control or anxiety.

As she unravelled the intricate web of her loss, she resumed the practice of journaling her heartfelt thoughts. She also started to find comfort in little, quiet moments of delight: the gentle weight of Jiu's hand in hers, the first hesitant crocus blooms peeking through the snow.

Amara knew that the pain of loss would always accompany her existence, and she would never cease mourning her parents. But she was beginning to realize that even in the midst of grief, there might be beauty and significance. That loss might strengthen her capacity for empathy, for valuing the priceless relationships that still existed, but not define her.

A little piece of paper flew out between the covers one day while Amara was sorting through an old family album box. She grabbed it, and shaking fingers helped her to straighten the wrinkles. Her mother sent a message in her customary looping script.

"Amara, my lovely daughter," started it. "I understand that sometimes in your life, the path ahead appears rather dark and steep." You may feel overwhelmed by the weight of the world. "You are stronger than you realize; however, no matter how strong the storms are raging around you, you have a light within you that never goes out."

Tears distorted the words as Amara read, her mother's voice ringing in her head as clear as if she were standing next to her. "Keep in mind that every challenge and suffering serve to shape you into the woman you were born to be. And know that your father and I will always be besides you, supporting you at every turn, wherever your road may go. Our amazing, courageous, gorgeous daughter loves you to the moon and back.

Grasping the message to her bosom, Amara felt a surge of mixed pain and thanks erupt in her throat. Her parents knew even then the challenges and successes she would face. They had placed their unwavering trust in her and provided her with the resilience to overcome any challenge.

And Amara pledged, at the same instant, to honour her confidence in her. She aimed to collect the pieces of her fractured life and reassemble them into something new, powerful, and purposeful. She would keep constantly with her the love of her parents—a talisman against the gloom. She would also use every bit of her genius and perseverance to create a legacy and life worthy of pride.

Amara took a deep breath, slid the letter into her pocket, and reached for the next album. She still has numerous lessons to learn and numerous memories to cherish.

But Amara felt a flutter of hope rekindling in her breast, the first since that terrible day. She didn't break, but she endured beatings and abuse. She also understood now, with bone-deep clarity, that she would emerge from the ashes of her tragedy stronger than ever.

Chapter 8

Lurking Shadows

Overhead, the fluorescent lights buzzed, creating strong shadows on the Academy of Human Sciences teaching hospital linoleum floor. Leaning against the wall, Amara battled the flood of tiredness that may have pulled her under.

She had returned to her medical school three months ago, re-entering the chaos of academics and clinical rotations. At first, the diversion had been a pleasant respite, a means of easing her ongoing anguish from loss. But Amara discovered she was having trouble keeping up with the unrelenting speed as the weeks went on.
She was still coming up for labs and lectures, following the rules of a decent student. But the fire that had driven her—the blazing need to succeed—had fizzled away. Some essential flame within her seemed to have extinguished along with her parents' life, leaving only ashes and nothingness.

Amara was sliding. She knew it. She could see it in the way her professor's brows wrinkled when she stuttered over a question and in the worried looks Lilly sent her when she slept off in the midst of a study session. However, she struggled to summon the determination to care, to break through the barrier of apathy surrounding her.

Instead, she found herself seeking escape through alternative routes. After a long shift, she started with a drink or two to numb the acute edges of her suffering. However, Amara soon found herself yearning for the temporary distraction that alcohol offered.

She understood she was on a perilous road, and she was jeopardizing what she had laboured for. But when the bottle called, the consequences seemed distant and insignificant compared to the joyous numbing it provided.

Amara's friends reached out to express their concern and offer encouragement. However, she pushed them away, retreating deeper within herself each day. She could not stand the sympathy in their eyes or the unquestioned questions hovering between them.

Jiu, who had been one of her rocks during those initial horrible weeks, too appeared lost. He had given up his plumbing job, kept his clients waiting, and drove back and forth from Igbuzor to Zaria to assist Amara. He comforted her during her grief and caressed her hair as she lay curled in a ball on her bed. However, Amara lacked the means to bridge the chasm of pain and self-destruction that separated them.

She reminded herself she was adjusting and that she just needed time to deal with her loss. Deep down, however, Amara knew she was disintegrating—the finely spun fabric of her existence ripping at the margins.

One rainy night, Amara staggered out of a nearby bar well after midnight, and the situation escalated. She had lost track of the beverages she had consumed, the faces of worried students blending in a mist of whisky and hopelessness.

The world slanted dangerously about her as she flowed unsteadily along the wet pavement, and she felt a sudden surge of nausea like a freight train. As tears tore her body, Amara slumped over and started to cough into the gutter.

Her knees ached on the cold pavement, and as hot tears mixed with the rain on her face, she wondered how long she would remain kneeling there. When she did glance up at last, however, she discovered she was gazing into a set of known eyes.

Dr. Patel saw her across the road, his face etched with sympathy and anxiety. With a firm and consistent grasp, he extended a hand to assist her in getting upright.

"Amara," he whispered gently, his voice piercing her mental fog. Let's get you home.

With her self-destruction on her chest, shame blazed through Amara as she let him lead her to his vehicle. She couldn't meet his stare as he guided her into the passenger seat; she couldn't find the words to explain how she'd let herself descend so low.

The trip to her hostel apartment was silent, with the only sound being the consistent pattern of rain across the windscreen. Dr. Patel turned to face her when they at last arrived at her building, his countenance grave.

"Amara, I know you're hurting," he murmured softly. "I find it impossible to even picture the suffering you are enduring. However, this approach—drinking and seclusion—is not the solution".

Amara felt her throat tighten as hot tears pounced at the edges of her eyes. She wanted to protest—to protect herself. Deeply, however, she knew he was correct.

Her voice breaking, she said, "I don't know how to do this." "I don't know how to keep going without them."

Reaching out, Dr. Patel rested a consoling hand on her shoulder. "You're not alone, Amara," he added with much conviction. "You have so many people wanting to support you through this—loving you. But you must allow them in."

He stopped to fix her eyes. "Your parents had faith in you. They were aware of your impending greatness. Let their death not be the thing that veers you off that road".

His comments knocked the air from Amara's lungs like a kick to the belly. She felt something break apart within her—a dam of need, sorrow, and agony.

She also realized that he was correct at that instant. She couldn't continue to run away from her pain or carry on in this manner. She owed it to her parents and to herself to fight for the future they had always seen for her.

Amara shivered and nodded, tears streaming down her cheeks. She said, "I know," in whispers. "I know I should seek for help or support. Simply put, I have no idea where to start".

Dr. Patel smiled sadly and squeezed her shoulder. "Let those who love you support you," he says quietly. "Start by believing that one day at a time you are strong enough to get through this."

Closing her eyes, Amara felt the reality of his words sink into her bones. She knew it would not be simple. There would be numerous setbacks and mistakes, moments when the darkness seemed to consume her entire existence.
She knew now, with a quiet, certain conviction, that she was not alone. Her hands were prepared to grasp her when she faltered.

And Amara emerged from the automobile into the rain-soaked night, breathing deeply and steadily. She had a long road ahead of her, a path of healing and self-discovery that would try her in ways she did not yet see.

But she felt a flutter of optimism sparking in her breast, the first in months. A little, tenacious spark suggests better days ahead.
She was Amara Johnson, the dreamer and daughter of fighters. She was determined not to let this break her.

Chapter 9

Bind Ties

Amara walked out onto the porch of her childhood house today as the sun was just starting to rise and the skies were softly pink and gold. She watched the world open around her while cradling a hot mug of coffee in her hands and savouring the warmth.

Three weeks had passed since that soggy evening in Dr. Patel's automobile, and it was during these three weeks that Amara decided to begin her healing. The journey had not been straightforward; there were days when the allure of the bottle was almost overwhelming, and moments of vulnerabilities and times of weakness.

But Amara had persisted, grasping the lifelines the people she loved had thrown her. Both Lilly's are like relentless friends, at least she has someone who took her out for early morning runs and late-night study sessions, both at her hometown and at her university. Their laughter and Amara always mixed with tears as they leant on one another for support. They discussed everything and nothing.

Emily had been a quiet, consistent presence, always available with a listening ear and a shoulder to weep on. Reminding her that it was alright to take a break from the weight of her loss, she had arrived at Amara's door with handmade food and ridiculous movies.

Finally, Jiu appeared, providing her with comfort and stability. As she opened her heart, he would have held her and whispered love's words of encouragement into her hair. Never pushing or evaluating, he had been patient and sympathetic while Amara fought to unwind the knots of her suffering, always present in all the many ways she needed him to be.

Day by day, Amara had started to sense her depression's cloud lifting slowly. She began eating regular meals, sleeping better, and even sometimes smiling. Small slivers of light were peeking through the blackness as if the coldness that had encased her for so long was at last beginning to melt.

She understood she still had a long way to go, and that healing was a trip rather than a destination. For the first time in months, Amara experienced a surge of hope for the future, with the possibility that she could emerge from this crucible stronger and more resilient than ever before.

Amara's thoughts turned to her parents—to the legacy of love and fortitude they had left behind—as she drank her coffee and watched the neighbourhood come alive around her. She knew they would be pleased with her for battling her way back and for refusing to let their deaths crush her.

She also understood, however, that they would want her to rely on the family of choice that had gathered around her in her darkest hour, the network of support she had developed. That was the essence of real love—about the bonds that link; it did not die but lived on in the hearts of those left behind.

The sound of a vehicle approaching their family home's driveway shocked Amara from her dream. She glanced up to find Nuss and Zarah clambering out, their arms loaded with shopping bags and brilliant grins.

"Morning, sis! Nuss cried out and sprang up the porch stairs to give her a bear hug. "We arrive bearing supplies for breakfast!!"

Close behind, Zarah kissed Amara on the cheek with passionate compassion in her eyes. "And by supplies, he means enough food to

feed a small army," she said. "You know how Nuss gets in chef mode."
Amara laughed, filled with a surge of love and gratitude for her crazy, amazing siblings. "Well, I'm hungry; thus, I hope you brought appetites."

The three of them headed into the kitchen, the air smelling warmly of freshly prepared coffee and bacon sizzling. Amara felt calm come over her as they worked side by side, cutting vegetables and mixing eggs.

Family, she understood, was all about this. She cherished the tears and laughter, the intimate jokes, and the shared memories. No matter how long it had been or how far they had wandered, their ability to take up just where they left off was remarkable.

It was more than just blood, genes, or legal records. It was a conscious decision to stand by each other every day, through both the good and the bad times.

The table creaking beneath their feast, Nuss lifted his glass in a salute as they sat down to eat. "To the Johnsons," he added gravely, unshed tears shining in his eyes. "To the Johnsons, the people who raised us and the ones we have chosen along the way." May their love always guide us now.

"To the Johnsons," Zarah and Amara said, their voices charged with feeling.
And Amara felt a tsunami of love and belonging sweep over her as they clinked their glasses together. She was aware that the road ahead would be lengthy and meandering and that uncertainty and gloom would periodically surface.

She knew now, with a deep conviction, that she would never have to walk it alone. She had an army of love behind her, a tapestry of souls permanently woven into the fabric of her existence.

And that knowledge, that unwavering trust in the connections that bind, would serve as her beacon amidst the challenges that lay ahead. She was Amara Johnson, the daughter of dreamers and fighters, a sister and friend to the toughest hearts she knew.

And taken collectively, they might withstand any tempest, conquer any anxiety, and clear any barrier. Anything was conceivable as long as they had each other.

Chapter 10

Painful Purpose

With Amara standing at the front of the packed lecture classroom, her heart thumping in her chest, the place hummed with a tangible vitality. Her stomach fluttered with both dread and excitement as she gazed out at the sea of expectant faces before her.

Six months had passed since that terrible night in the rain, six months before Amara decided to start climbing out of the depths of her sadness. She had worked hard in that period to reconstruct her life and find meaning and direction after her terrible loss.

Determined to make up for lost time and demonstrate to herself and everyone else that she remained the intelligent, motivated student she had always been, she had resolutely returned to her studies. She had also started to cautiously and laboriously reawaken the emotions and aspirations that had previously driven her.

But through her work with the foster care community, Amara had truly found her path once more. Working together with Dr. Patel and a group of committed volunteers, she put her heart and energy into creating an outreach program, thereby making her vision a reality.

And now Amara felt a surge of pride and purpose swelling in her chest as she stood before a room full of her fellow medical students. Here she was presenting her program and sharing the work that had evolved into her lifeblood after her death.

She inhaled deeply to ground herself and then started her presentation. She talked passionately about the difficulties foster children experience and the differences in health results and educational success that afflict this vulnerable group.

Through her work, she told tales of the young people she had encountered—young people who had surmounted enormous challenges to pursue their aspirations and create meaningful lives. She then described her idea for a whole clinic combining mentoring and educational assistance with physical and mental health treatments.

Amara could hear the mood in the room changing as she talked, the first mistrust giving way to a mounting sense of exhilaration and opportunity. Her students slanted forward in their chairs, their eyes ablaze with wonder and respect.

The cheers were deafening as she finished, a tsunami of affirmation and support sweeping over her. Overwhelmed by the outpouring of passion for her art, Amara felt tears pricking at the margins of her eyes.

A crowd of her colleagues immediately surrounded her as she emerged from the stage, eager to congratulate her and delve into her program. With elegance and passion, Amara answered their questions; her heart grew with every indication of interest and support.

Then, glancing out of the corner of her eye, she saw a familiar person headed towards her. Jiu had a pleased smile; his cheeks split wide. Pulling her into a firm embrace, he said, "Amara, that was incredible!" "I am really, quite proud of you."

Amara responded, feeling a surge of love and thanks for this guy who had been her support during the worst of times. She melted into his hug, realizing that you hadn't told me you were coming in today. "I couldn't have done it without you," she said into his chest. "Without all of you."

Jiu withdrew, his eyes ablaze with emotion. "You're wrong about that," he remarked gently. "This was all you, Amara; my presence was just a surprise given your meeting behaviour today. You embraced your suffering and converted it into something exquisite that will impact people's lives. Your parents would be very proud of you.

Amara felt a familiar feeling of loss at the mention of her parents—a lingering aching she knew would never completely go away. She also experienced tranquilly, a gentle acceptance that they were still with her, directing her actions and motivating her from some other dimension. "I hope so," she said, fighting back tears. "I hope I'm bringing them pride."

Jiu clasped her face in his hands, his eyes sharp with belief. "I know you are," he insisted. "Every day, by leading a life of compassion and meaning, you are respecting their legacy. They could not have demanded a finer daughter."

Amara nodded. Let his comments seep into her soul. She understood he was correct—that continuing the love and devotion of her parents would be the best way to honour them.

And Amara felt a fresh will rising in her chest as she turned around in her heart at the faces of her friends, at her students, and at the network of support she had created. She had a long path ahead of her—a lifetime of effort to serve the most vulnerable among them.

However, she now realized with profound clarity that she was exactly in her right place. Every suffering and agony—every setback and grief—had been guiding her to this calling.

Amara Johnson, the desired daughter of warriors and dreamers, was a lady forged in the crucible of loss and rebuilt in the flames of purpose. She was just beginning as well.

PART 3

SERVICE CALLS

Chapter 11

The Apprentice

As Amara walked through the sliding doors, the whole town of Togoo Community Health Centre buzzed with a barely controlled anarchy. Her neat white coat was a lighthouse of calm among the bustles. She quickly nodded to the harried-looking receptionist before heading back to the staff lounge to gather her belongings.

Amara couldn't contain her excitement at the prospect of finally applying her acquired skills to assist real patients. It was her first day of yet another clinical rotation at the Centre. She was more than ready to enter the tough, hands-on task of healing after over three demanding years of classroom education and simulated practice.

Amara felt a flutter in her gut as she slid into her scrubs and attached her ID card to her lapel. She was aware that the path ahead would be demanding and that she would have to deal with unpleasant diagnoses and complicated issues. She also understood, however, that this was what she had been preparing for, what she had given her heart and soul for as long as she could remember.

Amara inhaled deeply and straightened her shoulders as she headed to the clinic floor, prepared to see her first patient of the day. She encountered a tall, slender man with a charming smile and auburn hair.

Warmly waving a hand, he replied, "You must be the new medical student." "I am Dr. Rodriguez, one of the centre's visiting doctors." Over the next few weeks, I will be your supervisor.

Amara shook his hand firmly, giddy at the idea of learning from such a seasoned and esteemed doctor. "It's a pleasure to meet you, Dr.

Rodriguez," she added with a lively voice. "I'm Amara Johnson, and it makes me great to be here."
With his eyes wrinkling around corners, Dr. Rodriguez nodded favourably. "I have fantastic things to say about you, Amara," he continued. "Your reputation as a fervent supporter of underprivileged areas comes before you. You would suit really well here."

At his remarks, Amara had a flash of pride—a confirmation of all the effort and commitment she had put into her fledgeling outreach program. "Thank you, sir," she responded, bowing her head slightly. "I'm eager to learn from you and the rest of the staff here." Clapping her on the shoulder, Dr. Rodriguez was showing friendship and welcome. "Well then, perhaps we should start? Our whole day is ahead of us." Then he took her onto the clinic floor, a swarm of activity humming with healing and hope.

As the day progressed, Amara found herself completely engrossed in the demanding yet incredibly fulfilling job of patient care. With his soft bedside approach and careful explanations, she followed Dr. Rodriguez from exam room to exam room and marvelled at how he appeared to relax even the most nervous patients.

Always taking the time to listen to his patients' worries and patiently and sympathetically answer their enquiries, she observed as he negotiated difficult medical histories and perplexing symptoms using a sharp diagnostic eye. She also began to personally observe the numerous challenges faced by the low-income immigrant populations the centre served.

There were language hurdles to overcome; some of them spoke only their native tongues; cultural difficulties to negotiate; and the constant spectre of poverty and marginalisation hovering over every interaction. Amara observed patients suffering from chronic diseases, compounded by a lack of access to nutritious food and secure shelter. Parents were forced to choose between filling a prescription and putting food on the table.

She also saw, however, the amazing resilience and fortitude of the human spirit—that even the most damaged and shattered bodies could recover with the correct mix of medical treatment and caring care. She also began to deeply observe the vulnerability and optimism that accompanied each visit, and the unwavering trust patients placed in their therapists.

Amara lingered in the staff room as the day came to an end, her head whirling with fresh ideas and new information. Dr. Rodriguez poked his head in, sporting a knowing grin.
Settling onto a chair across from her, he murmured, "Quite a day, huh?" "How is your mood?"
Amara drew a deep breath, attempting to articulate the whirl of feelings running through her. "Overwhelmed," she said, admitting it still in a positive sense. Today seems to have taught me more than my first year of medical school did. Dr. Rodriguez laughed and nodded knowingly. "That's the beauty of hands-on learning," he remarked. "Only so far can textbooks and lectures get you. The real education takes place on the floor, among actual people and actual issues."
He leant forward, his face becoming grave. However, it's important to acknowledge that your emotions are quite normal. This task is not simple. It exhausts you both physically and emotionally. It's normal to feel overwhelmed and question your suitability for it. Amara nodded, her throat swelling with lumps. She was all too aware of the weight of self-doubt and the anxiety of not being enough. Dr. Rodriguez placed a comforting hand on her arm. "But Amara, from what I have seen today, you possess what it takes. You

possess the compassion, knowledge, and tenacity to really improve the lives of your patients. This is a rare and valuable quality.

Tears were pinging at the edges of Amara's eyes, a surge of thanks and will building within her chest. She understood that the path ahead would be long and meandering and that doubt and hopelessness would periodically surface. However, she knew with a calm, unwavering confidence that she was exactly where she should be. "Thank you, Dr. Rodriguez," she replied gently, her voice rich with feeling. "I cannot explain how much that means to me."

He grinned kindly, gently squeezing her arm, then stood to go. "Get some sleep, Amara," he said. "Tomorrow is a fresh day with fresh opportunities to change things and fresh challenges. And I have a sense you will achieve fantastic things."

After his departure, Amara found herself alone with her thoughts and the weight of her calling.
She was aware of the lengthy road she would be travelling—a lifetime of learning and development and helping. With a strong, unquestionable faith, she also understood, however, that she was prepared to welcome it with all she had.

She had been striving for this, pulling herself up from the depths to achieve it. This was her chance to carry on the compassion and sacrifice of her parents.
And so Amara grabbed her belongings and left for the waiting world, breathing deeply and with a heart full of direction. Born of love and fashioned in the furnace of grief, she was Amara Johnson, healer and activist. She was just beginning as well.

Chapter 12

Empathic Powers

Amara walked fast and deliberately into the Togoo community health centre for another normal day of work; the light was just beginning to shine over the horizon. Inheriting from her mother, who thought the calm hours of the morning were the most valuable time of the day, she had always been an early riser.

Amara felt a surge of excitement at the idea of yet another day serving her patients as she swiped her badge and pushed through the staff door. < She had thrown herself into the job with a passion and determination that had won her the respect and admiration of her colleagues in the weeks since she had begun her clinical rotations.

She had remained late to reassure nervous parents, read over medical publications to identify the most recent therapies for difficult diseases, and furiously fought for her patients against insurance rejections and administrative red tape. With each small victory, every grateful smile or relief, Amara experienced a clearer sense of direction and an increased dedication to her profession.

A harried-looking nurse stopped Amara as she headed to the staff lounge to take a quick sip of coffee before morning rounds. "Dr. Johnson, thank goodness you're here," Ms. Santos Ebenezer, the nurse, exclaimed, her voice tense with fear. "A teenage girl who is new to us is not interacting with anybody. We are concerned about her; she is in exam room three."
Amara felt a hint of discomfort as the nurse's words revealed more to this situation than initially appeared. She nodded fast and placed

her coffee on a table close by. "I'll take care of it," she replied, mentally mulling over the various ways a reluctant adolescent might have arrived at the clinic.

Amara inhaled deeply, centring herself, then gently knocked on the door as she walked towards exam room three. After hearing a subdued "come in" from inside, Amara pulled the door open, absorbing the image before her.

A little girl, no more than fifteen or sixteen years old, huddled on the exam table, her tiny figure overwhelmed by an enormous sweatshirt. Her face turned away from the door, but Amara could feel the strain in her shoulders as her fists clenched and unclenched in her lap. "Hi there," Amara remarked gently and with a non-threatening tone. "Amara, feel free to refer to me as Dr. Johnson. I can assist you right now."

The girl remained riveted on the wall across from her without responding. Amara moved forward cautiously not to crowd her personal space. "I know coming to the doctor can be scary, especially when you're not feeling well," she said, her voice calm. "But you should know that you are safe here; we will keep all we discuss private."

At that moment, the girl's head sprang up, her eyes locking with Amara. Their vivid green colour matched unshed tears and a sort of apprehensive defiance, which made Amara's heart hurt. The girl continued, her voice thick with feeling, "You don't know anything about me." "You don't know what I have gone through or what I have had to do to survive."

Amara fixed her sight firmly, unbroken in the face of her suffering. She responded gently, "You're right." "I have no idea what your narrative is. I know how it feels to feel alone and like the world is against you."

She paused to thoughtfully consider her next words. You know, I've lived in foster care before. My journey began when I was a newborn and continued until I transitioned out of the system. I understand, at least partially, how difficult it might be to imagine that anyone could truly care about you.

Amara's comments caused the girl's eyes to widen, a flutter of astonishment and identification spreading across her face. "You were a foster kid?" she asked in a voice that was almost a whisper.

Amara nodded, a depressed grin dragging at the edges of her lips. I was. Nor was it simple. Sometimes I felt like giving up, as nobody would always understand what I was going through. However, I also had individuals who believed in me and stood up for me when I was unable to fight for myself.

She hesitantly stretched out and lightly rested a hand on the girl's arm. "If you would allow me, I want to be that person for you. Without judgement or criticism, I aim to assist you in acquiring the necessary treatment and assistance.

The girl remained quiet for a long time, her eyes searching for any trace of dishonesty or sympathy. But what she discovered was a great reservoir of empathy and compassion—an acknowledgement of the wars she had fought and the wounds she bore. She nodded finally, a single tear running down her face. She said, "Okay," her voice breaking. Alright, I'll try.

And with those basic words, a link was created, one that would prove to be the first step on a long and challenging path to recovery.

Amara listened over the next hour as the girl—Jasmine Kante—pushed her narrative out. She described a childhood of neglect and abuse, of hopping from one family member's house to another without quite finding a place to belong. She spoke of the tragedies she had gone through and the frantic steps she had taken to dull the suffering. Amara also kept room for her through it all, providing words of comfort and affirmation to reassure her that she was not alone and that there was still hope for a better future.

By the time Jasmine emerged from the medical room, tears had covered her face, yet there was a glimmer of cautious faith and potential. Amara understood that Jasmine would want continuous help and resources to mend the scars of her past and that the path ahead was lengthy.

However, she was deeply aware that this was her intended role. She had the power to significantly impact her patients' lives by sharing her personal story and demonstrating empathy and understanding towards those marginalized by society.

Her head raised a bit higher and her feet a little lighter as she watched Jasmine leave the clinic. Amara felt a rush of pride and purpose swelling in her breast. This was what it meant to be a healer—to use one's own suffering as a link to reach others, to provide hope against hopelessness.

She also knew, with a strong and unquestionable belief, that she would spend her whole life doing precisely that. She was Amara Johnson, shaped in the furnace of her own hardships and committed to lightening the load of others who came after her. She was also just beginning that process.

Chapter 13

Tomorrows Hope

Amara walked over the double doors, her arms laden with a stack of papers and a set to her jaw, while the Igbuzor community centre hummed with tangible energy. She nodded quickly to the receptionist, then turned back to the little office she had seized as her temporary headquarters. It was a beautiful time at her clinical rotation at Togoo.

Nine months had passed since Amara first proposed a comprehensive foster care clinic to Dr. Patel and the hospital board in distant Zaria, a period marked by numerous meetings and late-night grant application reviews. But now, at last, all her effort was beginning to pay off, and her concept had arrived in her hometown of Igbuzor.

Having partnered with a nearby organization, she had obtained a pilot grant that was sufficient to operate the clinic for a year. She had also put together a crack team of volunteers ranging from seasoned doctors wishing to give back to the community to medical students keen to get practical experience and other human services providers. The Hope for Tomorrow foundation starts here, it is officially lunched and registered now by Amara.

However, Amara recognized that the work was just beginning. She envisioned the clinic as a form of treatment that would holistically meet the requirements of foster youngsters. The clinic would integrate mental and physical health services, along with mentoring and educational assistance, offering a comprehensive solution for children who have fallen through systemic gaps.

Amara felt a rush of enthusiasm at the idea of realizing her ambition as she relaxed in her chair and started organizing the stack of papers on her desk. She had witnessed personally the terrible effects of trauma and instability on foster children's lives, as well as the ways in which it may ruin even the brightest prospects.

She had also seen, however, the amazing resiliency and promise hidden under the surface—the way a little amount of aid and encouragement may transform a struggling child into a confident, competent adult. She also committed to fostering an environment that fosters the development and honouring of such potential.

Amara's thoughts strayed to the numerous young kids she had met during her rotations at the community health centres while she worked. Children like Jasmine, despite witnessing terrible atrocities, maintained a strong hope for a better life. Children such as Darius, a bright and science-loving adolescent, had transitioned between a dozen different schools without truly settling down. She considered the many hours she had spent pushing for these children to get the tools and money they needed to flourish. And she felt her chest bursting with fresh drive and purpose.

Amara awakened from her dream, frightened by a knock at the door. As she raised her head, she saw Lilly staring in with a broad smile on her face. Lilly mocked, "Hey there, boss lady," and sat down in the chair across from Amara's desk. "How's world-changing going now?" Laughing, Amara felt a surge of love for her confidante and friend for years. Lilly first had volunteered to assist with everything from grant writing to community engagement. Amara pointed to the stack of documents in front of her. "I'm sifting through paperwork, attempting to manage everything effectively. A nonprofit founder lives a glamorous life."

Lilly nodded compassionately and reached to grasp Amara's hand. "I know it's a lot," she continued, her voice softening. "But Amara, what you are doing here is amazing. These children get an opportunity at a future they would never have otherwise had."

Overwhelmed by Lilly's degree of trust in her, Amara felt tears pricking at the corners of her eyes. Her voice heavy with feeling, she added, "I couldn't do it without you." "Without all of you. We are a team, and I am fortunate to have such exceptional people around me". Lilly laughed, wickedness glistening in her eyes. "Well, we're pretty amazing; it's true," Lilly said, flinging her hair over her shoulder in an overly arrogant gesture. "But Amara, never sell yourself short. You are the spirit and heart of the project. We simply follow your lead".

Amara shook her head, a rueful grin pulling at her lips. "I don't know about that," she responded gently. "Some days I feel like I'm just stumbling about in the dark, hoping I'm doing the right thing." Lilly leant forward, her face becoming grave. "Listen to me, Amara Johnson," she insisted. "You are exactly where you should be, doing exactly what you should be doing." Since we were only a pair of wide-eyed medical students, I have known you, and I have seen you develop into this amazing force for good in the world.
She stopped, staring at Amara with a ferocity that made her shudder. "Your parents would be quite proud of you," she said, her voice softening. Even then, they understood that you were destined for greatness. Look at you today, doing something that will change the lives of future generations.

Amara felt a knot forming in her throat, a surge of emotions almost certain to explode. She nodded politely at Lilly and fought tears back. "Thank you," she said, her voice almost heard above the abrupt surge of emotion. "Thank you for always being there, for believing in me even while I didn't believe in myself." Lilly grinned, a kind, sympathetic smile that spoke more than words could express. "That's what family does," she answered, rather succinctly. "We back each other and raise each other. And you, Amara Johnson, are the sister I never had but always wanted."

They sat silently for a long time, allowing Lilly's words to lay over them like cozy blankets. Amara felt serenity and direction seep into her bones, a peaceful assurance that she was exactly where she should be.
At last Lilly got up and brushed phantom lint off her scrubs. "Well, I'd better get back to the grind," she remarked, teasing Amara. "You know, these people are not going to heal themselves," she said. Amara laughed and shook her head kindly. "Go on, then," she urged Lilly toward the door. "Go help save some lives. I will simply be here, hidden under mountains of documentation. Lilly stopped at the entrance and turned back to stare at Amara gravely. "Remember what I said, Amara," she advised gently. "Here you are doing incredible things. Never question that.

Then, she vanished, leaving Amara alone with her thoughts and the burden of her calling on her shoulders. As she turned back to her workstation, she noticed a framed picture of her parents, a constant reminder of the love and heritage that had shaped her. They had their arms around a much younger Amara, their features ablaze with pride and delight, and they were smiling in the photo. Whispering, Amara said, "I hope I'm making you proud," running a finger over their radiant faces. "I want to respect all you taught me about service and compassion."

Deep in her bones, she felt they would be proud of her, watching over her even now and supporting her from some other dimension. She could handle even the worst days with that unwavering faith in the love that had shaped her.

Amara went back to her work, her mind already spinning with ideas and possibilities, inhaled deeply, and felt a fresh sense of purpose.

She had a clinic to create, lives to transform, and a future to influence.

She was also ready to dedicate her entire being to achieve her goal. She was Amara Johnson, a lady shaped in the furnace of love and loss—daughter of warriors and dreamers.

Chapter 14

Harsh Realities

Amara is back again to complete her clinical placement. It has not been an easy task juggling her medical residency placements with her newfound NGO at a different location, but she is keen in getting it all done. The fluorescent lights buzzing overhead cast a severe glare on the linoleum flooring of the busy Togoo's emergency room. Leaning against the nurses' station, Amara battled the flood of tiredness that may have pulled her under.

It had been a terrible change, a continuous assault of sorrow and tragedy, leaving her raw and wrung out. Two patients had died after a protracted struggle with cervical cancer and a college student who had overdosed on fentanyl.

Despite her best efforts—many hours spent reviewing their records and speaking with experts—Amara had not been able to rescue them. And she carried hard on her breast the weight of that failure—the crushing sensation of impotence against such senseless loss.

She closed her eyes and inhaled steadily. She understood, intellectually, that death was a part of the work; that no matter how hard she tried, she would always have patients she could not rescue. That awareness, however, did not help her to lessen the pain in her heart or the persistent thought that she ought to have battled harder. "Dr Johnson?" A timid voice interrupted her reverie, and Amara opened her eyes to see a young nurse standing before her, clutching a chart to her breast. "We have a new patient in exam room four," the nurse said, her voice tense and filled with barely suppressed emotion. The nurse identified a six-year-old boy who had multiple bruises and a seemingly fractured arm. CPS has been contacted."

Amara's stomach dropped, a cold terror covering her like a blanket.
She always suffers most from cases of child abuse; the echoes of her
own turbulent upbringing still ring true in her ears.
She nodded fast and grabbed the chart from the nurse's extended
hand. "Thank you," she murmured, her voice sounding empty even
to her own ears. "I will take it from here."

Amara sharpened herself for what lay ahead as she headed into the
test room. She understood all too well the indicators of neglect and
abuse—the haunted expression in a child's eyes when they had
seen and survived the unimaginable.

She opened the door to see what was ahead of her. The little, dark-
haired youngster huddled on the test table had tears on his cheeks
and his arm tucked defensively against his breast.

"Hello," Amara murmured, taking slow, deliberate steps that led her
to the table. "Although you could call me Amara, my name is Dr.
Johnson. I'm here to make you feel better.

With wide, terrified eyes and a quivering bottom lip, the lad looked
up at her. His voice was almost audible over the monitors as he said,
"I want my mum."

At the raw vulnerability in his voice—the desperate cry for comfort
and protection—Amara felt her heart seize. She understood, with a
terrible certainty, that his mother was probably the one who caused
his injuries; the one person meant to be watching after him had
instead turned into his tormentor. "I know you do," she answered
softly, maintaining a calm voice. "But just now, we have to
concentrate on ensuring your wellbeing. Tell me what happened to

your arm."

The lad stopped, his eyes darting over the room as if he were looking for a getaway. "I fell," he replied at last, the words rushing out. "I fell while using the monkey bars."

Amara nodded, her look precisely neutral. She had heard that explanation a hundred times before: the well-worn falsehood youngsters uttered to hide the truth, gradually destroying them to protect their abusers.
"I see," she remarked, reaching out to carefully inspect his arm. That must have been rather terrifying. Coming here to obtain aid was rather bold.

Amara kept up a consistent stream of soft reassurances while she worked, gently guiding the lad to unwind and talk. She inquired about his preferred TV programmes and toys, as well as about his soulmates.

And gradually, cautiously, he started to reveal more—about the shouting and the punching, about the evenings he went to bed hungry as the home ran without food. He expressed his feelings of guilt and terror, expressing a deep desire for someone, anyone, to bear witness to his agony and put an end to it.

By the time the hospital social workers arrived to handle the issue, Amara was emotionally exhausted, and her heart weighed down by the boy's narrative. She left the exam room, gave herself some time to gather herself, then started her shift.

Even as she moved on to the next patient and problem, Amara couldn't shake the image of the boy's haunted eyes and the way he had clung to her hand like a lifeline.

With a profound understanding, she realized that this was the driving force behind her decision to become a doctor and her unwavering dedication to the foster care facility. She had experienced personally the terrible effects of trauma and neglect, so she understood how it may destroy a child's feeling of safety and self-worth. She also resolved to do everything in her power to speak for those children and fight for their right to a future free from suffering and anxiety. She was prepared to bear the weight of their experiences on her own heart, even if it meant bearing witness to the most brutal facts of human brutality.

Her own childhood hardships shaped her into Dr. Amara Johnson. She would not stop until every child had the opportunity to develop, heal, and flourish. Regardless of the expense, a tree they claim does not create a forest.

Chapter 15

Change Ripples

As Amara moved through the packed hallways, the Igbuzor community centre in Block B was a swarm of activity, her white coat a lighthouse of peace among the turmoil. Feeling a flush of pleasure at the activity and excitement filling the area, she nodded and smiled at the patients and families she passed.

Nine months had passed since the Hope for Tomorrow Foundation's founding. The past nine months were filled with challenging days, sleepless nights, triumphs, setbacks, and everything in between. However, Amara experienced a profound sense of fulfillment and direction as she observed the tangible manifestation of her vision by now becoming a qualified Doctor and NGO founder. Attending the medical facility as her main work and administering her foundation as two jobs for one Amara present a problem. Still, Amara would always add, with a pat on the back, "When life knocks you down, you have two choices: stay down or fight back. "I am not the kind of person to remain so depressed".

She had given this initiative her all, assembling a group of committed volunteers and community partners to establish a one-stop shop for foster children, their carers, and their families. Under one roof and everything totally free of charge, the clinic provided everything from regular check-ups to mental health counselling to educational help.

It had not been simple; from money constraints to bureaucratic red tape, there had been many obstacles along the route. But Amara had confronted every obstacle with the same tenacity and will that had guided her through her own chaotic upbringing—the same strong conviction in the need for compassion and community. Her efforts had also begun to pay off, gradually but definitely. Weeks of waiting lists plagued the clinic, always packed solidly. From children who were flourishing in school and in life owing to the tools and direction they had received; Amara had gotten sincere thank-you cards from parents who at last felt supported on their path.

However, the clinic's impact on the broader community was perhaps its most significant contribution. Speaking at conferences and seminars, testifying before local authorities, and organizing support from companies and organizations throughout the city, Amara had developed into a passionate advocate for foster children.

Her relentless work had drawn media attention—stories in the local newspaper and even an evening news slot. Suddenly, the suffering of foster children—so long unnoticed and disregarded—was front and foremost in public awareness, driving a larger discussion on the need for institutional reform.
Amara understood that many more lives to touch and futures to change still needed effort, and she could, however, not help but dream of what lay ahead as she headed towards her little office at the rear of the clinic.

She had just relaxed into her chair, ready to delve into the never-ending stack of papers on her desk, when a gentle tap on the door shocked her from her concentration. She yelled, "Come in," hoping to see one of her volunteers or an inquisitive reporter looking for a quotation.
But as the door opened, Amara saw a face from her past that flooded with mixed emotions, one she had never expected to see again. "Mrs. Thompson," Amara said, breathing softly and rising gently to stand. The elder lady entered the room. Mrs. Thompson had been Amara's initial case manager and social worker, the one

who had placed her with the Johnson family years ago. She had been in Amara's life nonstop in those early, turbulent years, offering direction and encouragement as she negotiated the ups and downs of the foster care system.

Years had passed since Amara last saw her mother after her retirement; the Johnson's had taken Amara under their wing, and the weight of everything that had transpired in the interim loomed large between the two.

"Amara," Mrs. Thompson whispered gently, unshed tears glistening in her eyes. "I wanted you to not mind my dropping in like this. I simply had to see you."

Amara shook her head, a lump rising in her throat. She said, "Of course not," pointing Mrs. Thompson in the direction of a seat. "It's quite wonderful to see you." They just stared at one another for a long minute, absorbing the changes time had produced. Mrs. Thompson's hair was greyer, her face more wrinkled, but her eyes still radiated the same kindness and compassion Amara recalled. Mrs. Thompson broke the silence at last, "I've been following your work and growth." "What you've created here, Amara, is rather remarkable. You are truly making a significant difference in the lives of these children.

At the compliments, Amara had a flash of pride—a validation of all the blood, sweat, and tears she had put into the clinic. "Thank you," she replied gently. "It has been unquestionably a labour of love. But without the basis you helped build all those years ago, I could not have done it. Mrs. Thompson waved her hand dismissively. "Oh, I was simply working at my job," she answered. "It was you who grabbed the ball and started running. You are the one who refused to let your past define you and transformed your own suffering into direction."

Overwhelmed by Mrs. Thompson's depth of trust in her, Amara felt tears pricking at the edges of her eyelids. "I had good role models," she remarked thinly. "The Johnsons...they demonstrated to me what unqualified love looked like. And you never gave up on me, even when I gave you every justification." Mrs. Thompson reached out and lightly squeezed Amara's hand. "I knew from the moment I met you that you were special," she replied gently. "You possess an inner brilliance that nothing could diminish." Now, observe yourself; your brilliance is so immense that you are guiding others.

They sat silently for a long time, allowing Mrs. Thompson's words to rest over them like a benediction. Amara felt a calm assurance that she was precisely where she was intended to be, seeping into her bones.

Finally, Mrs. Thompson stood up and gently straightened her skirt, her hands quivering slightly. "I should be going; it's a bit of a distance to Igili Land for me," she responded, sounding somewhat reluctant. "But Amara, you simply wanted to know how pleased I am of you. How appreciative I am of having even a little role in your path.

Amara also got up and gave the elder lady a strong embrace. She said, "Thank you, in a whisper with immense emotional weight. You trusted me and encouraged my presence with the Johnson family. I would not be here without you.' Mrs. Thompson gave her a hug back, her own emotions mixed with Amara's. She said, "You always possessed brilliance, sweet girl." "I just guided you toward seeing it in yourself." Then she vanished, leaving Amara alone with her thoughts and the burden of her heritage.

She went back to her desk and looked at a framed picture of her younger self—a thin, guarded youngster with watchful eyes and a powerful will. In that instant, she felt a surge of love and gratitude for that little child, remembering all the struggles and scars that had shaped her into the woman she was today. "We made it, kid," she said, running a finger over the fading picture. "We made it out the other side from the fire."

And Amara felt a fresh sense of direction and resolve fill her chest as she relaxed back into her chair, eager to return to the task that had become her life's calling. She had a clinic to manage, lives to transform, and a future to Mold.

She was also prepared to continue shining her light into the darkest corners of the foster care system to continue fighting. She was Dr. Amara Johnson, a woman shaped in the furnace of love and sorrow, a lighthouse of hope for everyone who came after her.

PART 4

MINDFULLNESS MATTERS

Chapter 16

Invisible Enemy

The alarm clock tore through her lovely slumber, waking Amara to see gentle morning light streaming through her window and pushing her to wade through waves of tiredness. She groaned silently and stretched a worn hand to muffle the sharp sound, feeling the weight of many restless nights squarely upon her awareness.

Amara lay in bed looking at the ceiling, unable to ignore the pulsating pain that seemed to infiltrate every thread of her existence. Slowly, sneaky tiredness crept up on her like a robber at night, gradually sapping her vigour and strength.
She originally attributed it to the unrelenting demands of her profession—the long hours at the hospital and her foundation offices—and the emotional toll of seeing so much misery and suffering. She had always been the kind to challenge herself to the absolute limit, to give her all towards her passion and goal.

But Amara felt something was very wrong as the weeks stretched into months. The tiredness had given place to a constellation of other symptoms: muscular weakness, joint discomfort, and a deep, painful stiffness that made even the most basic motions seem like a tremendous effort.

She had attempted to grit her teeth and go on as usual, power-through it. But the unseen adversary that had settled into her body appeared to become more powerful every day, sapping her vitality and fogging her once-clear head.

Wincing at the protest of her tight, painful muscles, Amara pulled herself from bed. She stood before the mirror, marvelling at the image that met her: the black bags under her eyes, the pallor of her complexion, the slouch of her shoulders beneath the weight of her invisible load. She understood she had to get treatment before whatever was destroying her body did permanent harm; she could not continue like this. However, a strong, visceral fear gripped her as she considered allowing anyone to see the flaws she had carefully hidden behind her strength and resiliency.

Throughout years of crises and need, Amara consistently stood as the unwavering source of support. Her identity had been based on her capacity to bear the weight of the world and provide the unquestionable basis on which others may rely.

But Amara started to experience a growing sense of powerlessness and hopelessness as she faced an adversary she couldn't see or fight. When she could not muster the energy to get through the day, how could she be the healer, the champion, or the force for change she had always aimed to be?

Amara sighed heavily and pushed herself to get ready, wincing at the agony shooting across her hands as she buttoned her top. She glanced at the clock and knew she was already running late for her clinic shift. She got her keys and luggage ready for the day. She knew she would have to put on a brave front, to fight through the pain and tiredness and be the strong, unflappable Dr. Johnson everyone knew and depended on.

But Amara couldn't escape the sensation of gloom hovering over her like a black cloud as she emerged into the brilliant morning sunshine. She sensed a profound unease in her bones, certain that the journey ahead would challenge her in ways she had never encountered before.

By the time Amara arrived, the clinic was humming with activity; the waiting room was full of people from all walks of life. She nodded quickly to the receptionist and turned back to the staff room, where she slumped into a chair with a subdued sigh.

"Rough night?" a voice inquired, prompting Amara to turn and see Dr. Lilly, her former college classmate from Zaria, standing in the doorway with a worried expression. Amara questioned Lilly, "Hey Lilly, happy to see you but am confused, what are you doing here? I assumed you were now permanently with the newly opened private hospital along Togoo Road." Lilly nodded. "Yes, I assumed you too Amara is now permanently employed at the newly opened private hospital along Togoo Road." Amara laughs. Aside from the ward rounds, Lilly asked, "What are we supposed to accomplish today?"

Amara feigned a smile, even though it seemed odd for Lilly to suddenly appear in her thoughts. She dismissed her friend's worry with a disdainful gesture. "It's just the usual, darling," she replied, trying to soften her tone. Lilly grins adding, "too much labour, not enough sleep." Amara responded, you understand the challenges of working in two different locations. After my shift here, I will head straight to a couple of meetings at my foundation".

But Dr. Lilly was not buying it. She moved across the room and sat down next to Amara, her eyes searching her face for the truth beneath the fake bravery.
She whispered gently, "Amara," her voice tinged with anxiety. "I knew you. Something seems off to me. You have been pushing yourself to the limit for months now, and it is taking a toll on you".

Amara felt a knot in her throat, a sudden, strong need to release herself, to allow someone else to take the weight of her anxiety and suffering for just a little while. But the words would not come; the habit of self-reliance, of never letting someone see her weak, was too strongly rooted. Instead, she replied, "I'm fine," with a hint of dishonesty in her voice. "I'm just a bit worn out; that's all." A strong cup of coffee can solve everything.

Though the sound of a code blue over the intercom cut her short, Dr. Lilly seemed like she wanted to protest. Adrenaline pumping through her restless veins, Amara sprang to her feet and ran for the medical department.
Amara and her colleagues worked feverishly to stabilize a patient who had gone into cardiac arrest; the next several hours passed in a haze of confusion and desperation. Ignoring the black spots dancing at the margins of her vision and the screaming protest of her muscles, she pushed herself to the brink.

Amara couldn't get rid of the feeling, however, that she was waging a losing struggle against her own body even as she battled to rescue the life before her. Every movement and every choice seemed to be saps of what little power she still had.

Amara was trembling with fatigue, her scrubs drenched in sweat; by the time the patient stabilized, she was transferred to the ICU. She staggered back to the lounge and fell on the sofa with a stifled moan.

She must have fallen asleep because Jiu was softly waking her, her face marked with concern. Citing that she believes Amara needs a break, Dr. Lilly had called Jiu to see if he was free.

Lilly began by describing how the hospital's medical director had reached out to her as a professional support person, hoping to have an honest conversation with Amara face-to-face, given their friendship. However, despite Amara's typical bluster, she refused to admit her exhaustion and instead pushed herself back to the boundaries. Lilly highlighted that some healers tend to neglect their own needs, while others occasionally exhibit excessive concern for their patients or others. Jiu acknowledged that Amara had travelled a long road and that a respite would not be terrible, but it is entirely up to her to welcome the summons to rest her body and spirit.

"Amara?" Jiu replied gently, his voice tinged with anxiety. "Are you okay?" Lilly mentioned you weren't feeling well. Amara blinked up at him, feeling a sudden, intense surge of emotions. The tears she had been suppressing for so long started to run down her cheeks as the dam of her well-crafted serenity finally broke.

She said, "No," her voice breaking. "No, I'm not feeling well. Jiu, something is wrong with me. There's a serious issue with me, but why are you here? When did you arrive?"

Those remarks unleashed a cascade of emotions. Amara told the full story: the tiredness, the suffering, and the growing anxiety she had been steadily ingesting for months.

Jiu paid careful attention, his face a mask of affection and concern. When she finally stopped, he reached out, gently squeezed her hand, and then asked her to gather her luggage so they could continue.

"We'll figure this out," he declared resolutely, his eyes ablaze with will. "Whatever it is, we'll deal with it together. Amara, you are not alone in yourself. You never were."

Amara nodded, a flutter of optimism starting in her chest. She realized she would have to face the unseen adversary that had settled in her body, and her journey forward would be long and challenging.

But she felt she could face whatever lay ahead—with Jiu by her side and the love and encouragement of her friends and family. Driven by her own unyielding spirit, she was Dr. Amara Johnson, shaped in the furnace of hardship. She would not allow tiredness to break through either.

Chapter 17

Hard Road

The antiseptic white walls of the examining room suffered a severe glare from the humming fluorescent lights above. Her heart thumping in her chest, Amara sat on the edge of the paper-covered table, waiting for the pathologists to come back with test findings.

Jiu appreciated Amara's attendance for the exam; she noted that the tiredness Amara may experience sleeping off on a lounge chair is not typical.

Three weeks had passed since that fatal day in the lounge, when Amara had at last come clean to Jiu and herself that something was very wrong. The past three weeks were filled with constant visits, injections, and scan operations—the objective, cold touch of medical equipment. Jiu said that, regardless of one's own knowledge, seeking assistance when one believes they need it is a wonderful strength. Amara had always taken immense satisfaction in her strength and in her will to meet any obstacle. She felt a growing feeling of powerlessness and despair, but as she sat there, her body hurt, and her thoughts whirled with a thousand terrible possibilities.

What would happen if the results of the testing turned out to be extremely negative? What would happen if she faced an opponent she couldn't outrun, outfight, or even win? She was deeply, deeply afraid of losing her freedom and burdening the people she loved. Startled from her whirl of ideas, Amara heard the door opening. She glanced up to see the expert she had visited, Dr. Singh Bilal, walking solemnly into the room. "Dr. Johnson," he replied, his voice artfully neutral. "Thank you for waiting. Having your test results, I am worried I have some tough news to share.

Amara's stomach dropped, a cold perspiration starting on her forehead. Quietly nodding, she prepared herself for the worst.

"The tests have verified that you have a rare autoimmune disease, myositis," Dr. Singh said, his words like physical blows. "This disorder causes inflammation and muscular weakness, which results in the symptoms you have been experiencing fatigue, pain, and stiffness."

Amara felt as if she were underwater, and Dr. Singh's words seemed to be reaching her from a considerable distance. Myositis it is. On her tongue, the word seemed alien, a weird and terrible intruder in the terrain of her body.

She was able to articulate, "What...what does that mean?" Her voice sounded tiny and delicate, even to her own ears. Is treatability possible? Will I be, okay?" asked. Dr. Singh's expression softened as a flicker of sympathy passed over his features. Dr. Singh softly replied, "Myositis is a chronic condition as you know, but as a doctor yourself, we cannot rule out anything depending on an individual's body." "Although there is no known cure, therapies exist to help control symptoms and slow down the disease development. It will require continuous care and control; occasionally, you may experience flare-ups or periods of increased weakness and discomfort.

Amara felt a blow to her abdomen, her breath exploding out in a painful gasp. Continuous. No treatment exists for it. Her mind kept repeating the words, a death signal for the life she had always envisioned for herself. Amara is aware of these medical diagnoses, yet she currently uses a wheelchair and has the courage to not push herself down the stairs.

"I know this is a lot to take in," Dr. Singh said, his voice kind but forceful. "But you should know you are not fighting this alone. On our team, we have outstanding experts who will help you create a treatment plan and provide continuous assistance. Many people with myositis may also have full and active lives with appropriate treatment and care.

Amara nodded, numbly trying to process the magnitude of the information she had just received. She had always been the one who healed and raised others; she was the caregiver. The idea of being on the other side of that equation—requiring care and assistance herself—was almost intolerable.

Her voice was just above a whisper as she whispered, "What...what happens now?"

Dr. Singh leant forward, his eyes fixed steadily on hers. "We start fighting now," he replied simply. "We start with a course of high-dose steroids to help lower the inflammation in your muscles, and we'll track your development very carefully. You must adjust your lifestyle: pace yourself, get enough sleep, and pay attention to your body's demands. Although it won't be easy, I am confident that you possess the will and fortitude to confront this challenge head-on.

Amara drew a long, quivering breath and felt a flutter of will in her chest. She had overcome obstacles before the death of her parents, the difficulties of her early years, the unrelenting pressure of her career. She had always found a means to transcend the suffering and emerge on the other side stronger.

She was also prepared to repeat the process. She was Dr. Amara Johnson, a woman forged in the crucible of hardship. She was determined not to let this illness define or diminish her. "Okay," she responded, her voice becoming louder with every syllable. "Alright, let's start this. Allow us to fight."

And with those words, Amara set out on the arduous path ahead—one marked with uncertainty and hardship but also with optimism and the unquestionable assurance she would not travel alone.

Chapter 18

Love leans

The wind blew over the long park walk, sending a flutter of fall leaves skittering across. Bundled in a warm sweater and scarf, Amara sat on a bench and watched the world pass with a sad heart.

Four months ago, she received her diagnosis, which led to a continuous cycle of doctor visits and treatment, marked by both positive and negative days. Although the high-dose steroids had lessened her muscular inflammation, they had also harmed her body and psyche.

Amara felt like a stranger in her own flesh, her once-strong limbs now weak and wobbly, her once-sharp intellect suddenly cloudy and forgetful. She had always taken great satisfaction in her independence and in her ability to grit and fiercely manage whatever life presented.

But now, as she battled a chronic ailment that seemed to be gradually sapping her health and vigour, Amara felt a growing sense of helplessness and despair. She had felt compelled to miss work at the clinic to distance herself from the lobbying and campaigning that had always been such a basic component of who she was.

Amara was aware of her suffering, despite her efforts to put on a brave front and convince her loved ones that she was doing well. She felt like a weight, a sapping of the time and effort of everybody around her.

Amara shivered along her spine from a sudden blast of wind, thereby tightening her coat about herself. Closing her eyes, she could feel tears burning behind her lids. "Amara!" a gentle voice cried out, and she turned up to see Jiu staring at her, his face marked with worry.

He took her hand in his as he settled next to her on the bench. "Hey," he whispered softly, his thumb gently tracing peaceful circles on her hand. "I reasoned I might find you here."
Amara felt a knot developing in her throat—an instantaneous, intense emotional surge. She had been working so hard to be strong and to present a brave front for Jiu and everyone else living with her. But at that instant, with his loving hand in hers and his eyes glistening with compassion, she felt her carefully built barriers start to fall apart.

Her voice faltering, "I'm so tired, Jiu," she said. "Feeling like this, or like a shell of myself, makes me so exhausted," she said. I'm not sure how to accomplish this." Jiu grabbed her close and tightly embraced her with his arms. "I know, my love," he said, his voice vibrantly emotional. "I understand it's difficult. But you're not alone in this. I am here, and nowhere is where I'm headed.

Amara felt the dam within her crack, and the tears she had been stifling for so long started to run down her cheeks. Her body quivered with the weight of her tears, and she clung to Jiu like a lifeline.
She coughed out. "I'm scared," she said, her words muffled against his chest. "What this implies for my future, for our future, scares me. I neither wish to burden you nor myself".

Jiu drew back, hands rising to cup her face. With his eyes fixed on hers, he continued, "Amara, listen to me," sharply. "You would never be a burden to me." The toughest, bravest, most amazing woman I have ever known is you, the love of my life. And I shall be by your side no matter what at each stage of this trip."

Amara experienced a flood of love and thanks, a warmth that seemed to drive away the cold of her uncertainty and anxiety. She slanted forward, her forehead pressing on Jiu's.
She murmured, her voice heavy with emotion, "I don't know what I did to deserve you." "But I am so glad you are in my life."

Jiu grinned and planted a gentle kiss on her lips. "You deserve the world, Amara Johnson," he added quietly. "And I want to spend my life giving it to you."
Nestled in one another's arms, they sat there for a protracted while, allowing the love that flowed between them to be the salver for their tired souls. Amara understood that there would be many more times of uncertainty, anxiety, and sadness, as well as a long and challenging journey ahead.

She knew with a deep conviction that she wouldn't have to walk it alone. She knew that Jiu, her family, and friends were all ready and prepared to assist her in carrying the burden, to steady her when she faltered.

Amara leant into the love all around her, letting it be the anchor tying her to hope and opportunity, breathing deeply and steadily. She was Dr. Amara Johnson, a lady shaped in the furnace of hardship and anchored by the strong ties of love.

Chapter 19

Odds Defied

Amara walked slowly but deliberately toward the physical therapy gym, the corridors of the rehabilitation centre humming with a hushed intensity. Ten months had passed since her diagnosis—ten months filled with demanding treatments, disappointments, and small difficult victories.

But at last, she was beginning to feel like herself once again. While Amara still had a long road ahead, the drugs and treatments were helping her gradually regain strength and vigour.

Amara heard a symphony of noises as she pushed open the gym doors: the whirr of the exercise equipment, the thump of the treadmill, the soft encouragement of therapists leading their clients over their paces.

She made her way to the mat, where her own therapist, Sarah, a kind-eyed lady, was waiting for her. Sarah smiled warmly to meet her, her eyes creasing at the corners. She reached out to give Amara a soft embrace and murmured, "Amara, it's so good to see you." "How are you feeling nowadays?"

Amara inhaled deeply and checked her physical condition. "I feel better," she said with a hint of surprise in her voice. "Although my muscles hurt and I'm still fatigued, it's not the same type of bone-deep tiredness I used to experience. It feels as though I can now discern a brighter future ahead."

Sarah nodded, her face one of comprehension and support. "That's fantastic to hear," she said. "You've been working really hard, and it pays off. Though I know it hasn't been simple, you're progressing remarkably.

Amara had a surge of thanks and will. She recognized that the relentless support of her medical team, along with the hours of hard labour and endurance she had invested in her recovery, were mostly responsible for her development.

Amara allowed her thoughts to stray toward the other patients Sarah had seen during her stay at the rehab centre as she led her through a sequence of stretches and exercises. Maria was a young mother learning to walk after she had a stroke. John was an old guy who had fractured his hip and resolved to dance at his granddaughter's wedding.

Liam, a young lad paralysed in an automobile accident, was navigating the world in a wheelchair. Due to Liam's sardonic humour and unwavering attitude, Amara developed a connection with him during their mutual physical therapy visits.

Amara felt a flood of respect and affinity as she watched him, wheeling herself over to the parallel bars with a look of great resolve on his face. She was all too familiar with his difficulties—the times of anxiety, irritation, and hopelessness.

She also sensed in him, however, the same resiliency that had seen her through her own worst days, the will to refuse to let his circumstances define or confine him.

Amara considered her own path—the many hours she had spent in this very gym, pushing herself to the edge of her capacity. She recalled the times she had wanted to quit when the suffering and tiredness had felt intolerable. Driven by the love and encouragement of her family and friends, as well as by the awareness that she had so much to offer the world, she continued throughout. And now Amara felt a fresh sense of purpose and resolve as she gazed around at the other patients labouring to take back their lives.

She understood that her road was far from over and that many more obstacles were ahead. She was also deeply aware that she possessed the strength and determination to face these challenges head-on.

Amara made her way over to where Liam was resting as her session with Sarah ended, a sheen of perspiration on his forehead and a pleased smile on his face. "Look good out there, kid," she remarked, tapping his fist with her own. "You will be whirling around the rest of us soon."

Liam chuckled, wickedness gleaming in his eyes. "I'm uncertain about that," he responded. However, I refuse to let this chair define me. I have too much left to accomplish in my life.

Amara felt a knot form in her throat, a surge of emotions almost ready to explode. She reached out to grasp Liam's shoulder, expressing unity and understanding. "You have that right," she remarked gently. "We still have a lot of living to do. And we will accomplish it on our own terms, regardless of what life presents."

And with those words, Amara saw fresh hope and possibilities flooding her chest. She had gone so far and battled so hard to recover her life and her sense of self. She also understood, with a strong and unwavering belief, that she would keep fighting, keep challenging the odds, for as long as she had breath in her body.

She was Dr. Amara Johnson, shaped by the love and encouragement of those who believed in her, born in the furnace of hardship. She would also not allow anything, even her illness, to stand in the way of the brilliant and wonderful future that awaited.

Chapter 20

Healers Heart

Today, Amara left the rehabilitation centre for the last time, when the sun was just beginning to rise, and the heavens were delicately pink and gold. She took long breaths, enjoying the chilly morning air and the feeling of the warm rays on her face.

The journey had been filled with numerous hours of medical treatments and physical therapy, marked by both victories and setbacks, along with everything in between. At last, after months of struggle and determination, Amara was returning home to continue her journey.

She remembered those early days after her diagnosis, when fear and uncertainty had almost overcome her. She recalled the periods of despondency when the anguish and exhaustion had seemed terrible and when she had wondered if she would ever feel like herself once again.

Despite being a fighter, a survivor, and a woman with an intact spirit even in her darkest moments, Amara never lost sight of her true self. She had found strength in the unwavering belief of her medical team, the resilience that had always burned brilliantly inside her, and the love and encouragement of her family and friends.

And now Amara stood on the threshold of a new chapter in her life, pride and accomplishment pouring over her. She had boldly faced the toughest challenge of her life and emerged wiser, more determined than she had ever been.

As Amara headed to the car, where Jiu was waiting, she couldn't help but think back on the lessons she had picked up during her stint at the recovery centre. She had a big grin. She had discovered a quiet resilience inside herself that got her through even the darkest of days. This was a fresh kind of power.

She had learned to depend on others, appreciate help and support when she needed it, and find enjoyment and significance even in trying circumstances. She had also become close to her fellow patients, a community of warriors who had struggled alongside her for their lives.

When Jiu gently hugged Amara, she experienced a tsunami of emotions. She grasped him tightly and let the tears she had been holding back run down her cheeks at last.

"I'm so proud of you, my love," Jiu remarked, his voice full of affection. "You have shown such incredible courage and fortitude during this whole process. You inspire every one of us."
Amara pulled back, a misty smile on her face. Her subtle addition was, "I couldn't have done it without you." "Without all of you. Having you in my life makes me extremely happy."
Jiu held her face in his hands, love and respect flashing in his gaze. "You are the strongest, most beautiful woman I have ever known," he shot out viciously. "And I'll be with you throughout our lives."

And with those words, Amara felt serenity and fulfilment sweep over her. She knew the road ahead would not be easy, and she would have to face many obstacles. She knew, nevertheless, that she had the will and fortitude to meet these obstacles squarely. Driving out of the treatment centre, Amara felt waves of excitement and potential running through her veins. They had given her a second opportunity at life, a means to change the world, and a means to really welcome every day.

She also knew, with great and unquestionable clarity, that she would not waste one minute of it. She was Dr. Amara Johnson, forged in the crucible of adversity and cooled by the love and support of those who believed in her. She was ready to greet the world with or without her wheelchair one day at a time.

Epilogue

The Igbuzor Town Community Centre's ballroom was a sea of shimmering dresses and tuxedos, the air vibrating with the eager conversations of the gathered guests. Amara stood at the brink of the throng, her pulse racing with a combination of exhilaration, anxiety, and expectations.

One year had passed since her release from the rehabilitation hospital, during which she struggled to adjust to her new normal and rebuild her life following her diagnose. Now, six months into that year, Amara stands on the cusp of another milestone, reflecting on the incredible journey that led her to become Mrs. Jiu Adekunle, following Jiu's engagement and marriage to her. She has had an incredible year, who could have predicted that she would be leaving the hospital to attend her own wedding in the same year?

Amara remembered those early days after her diagnosis, when her uncertainty and anxiety had threatened to overwhelm her. She thought back to the times of hopelessness when the suffering and tiredness had felt intolerable and when she had questioned if she would ever feel like herself once again.

Amara had never lost sight of who she was at her heart, though—a healer, a warrior, a woman with an unbroken spirit—even in her worst times. With the steadfast belief of her medical team, the spark of resilience that had always burned bright inside her, and the love and support of her family and friends, she had drawn strength.

And now Amara was feeling pride and direction as she stood on the stage of the first annual gala of the Hope for Tomorrow Foundation. Using her personal experiences to lobby for improved assistance and resources for those children in the system that deserve better than they are receiving, she has put her heart and energy into the work of the foundation over the last year.

The audience became hushed as she rose to the stage, every eye fixated on her. Amara inhaled deeply, the weight of the moment resting over her like a shroud.

"Good evening, everyone," she said with a loud, forceful voice. "I am privileged to be here tonight—to tell my story and to honour the great work of the Hope for Tomorrow Foundation."

She stopped and let her eyes float over the sea of faces in front of her. As many of you know, I received a rare autoimmune disease diagnosis of myositis just over a year ago. It was a devastating blow that profoundly affected me and forced me to confront my own mortality in a way I had never experienced before. The audience erupted in laughter, and Amara also joined in.

Emotion drove Amara's throat to constrict, yet she persisted in trying to give voice to the trip that had shaped her. "But I never lost sight of the idea that I was not alone, even in my worst of times. When I couldn't do it on my own, my family, friends, and medical team rallied me and carried me through. They were an amazing support system.''

She inhaled deeply and felt her words weighting down the space. Our Hope for Tomorrow Foundation's work is centred on that, friends. It's about giving folks confronting the unthinkable that same level of support and attention. It's about reminding them that, even in the worst of circumstances, there is always hope, and they are not alone."

Rising in her chest, Amara had a flood of feeling, accompanied by a strong and unquestionable certainty that this was the task she was supposed to accomplish. "I am here tonight not only as a survivor but also as a thriver. I have learned to lean into the love and support of those around me, to find delight and purpose in the middle of adversity, and to never, ever give up on myself or my aspirations." She stopped and let her words linger in the air momentarily. "And I want to say to those of you who are confronting your own problems, whether they be spiritual, mental, or physical—you are not alone. You have an army of love and support to lift you. And together, we shall create a society in which nobody has to deal with these difficulties by themselves."

Amara felt love and thanks flooding over her as the crowd burst in applause. She came out of the fire stronger, smarter, and more determined than she had ever been. She firmly believed that she would dedicate her life to guiding others through her personal struggles.

She was Dr. Amara Johnson, a woman who was shaped by the furnace of hardship and cooled by the love and encouragement of those who believed in her. And one heart at a time, she was prepared to transform the world.

As the event concluded and the visitors began to disappear into the night, a sea of well-wishers and supporters surrounded Amara. Feeling a great sense of connection and direction coursed through her veins, she shook hands and gave embraces.

Among the crowd, she saw Liam, the young guy she had met during her stay at the rehabilitation centre. He was catching her eye while seated in his wheelchair, a broad smile splitting his face.

He called out, "Dr. Johnson!" and turned to face her. "That was a very amazing speech. You brought the entire room to tears."
Amara felt a knot form in her throat, a surge of emotions almost certain to overflow. Reaching out and squeezing Liam's hand, she had a surge of pride and respect for the amazing young man he had

grown to be.

"Thanks, Liam," she responded quietly. "But the true credit belongs to folks like you—the ones whose daily inspiration comes from their resiliency, and I keep fighting because of them."

Liam lowered his head, a hint of shyness creeping into his smile. "I couldn't have done it without you," he whispered softly. "You taught me that I have so much to give the world and that my condition does not define who I am. You inspired optimism when I felt like everything had vanished."

Overwhelmed by the depth of Liam's thanks, Amara felt tears pricking at the corners of her eye. She was aware that her own path had been challenging, dotted with obstacles and times of hopelessness. She also understood, however, that it had all been worth it—just for the opportunity to improve the life of someone like Liam.

Amara found herself alone with her thoughts and the weight of her calling resting over her like a cloak as the last of the visitors left and the ballroom became quiet. She understood that there would be many more fights to fight and challenges to surmount and that the path ahead would be long and meandering.

However, she firmly believed that she was exactly where she should be. Every difficulty and suffering, every setback and grief, had been guiding her to this moment, to this goal.

She considered her parents; their legacy of love and dedication is still fresh. She thought of her friends and relatives and the unflinching belief and support they had given her through even the worst of circumstances. She also considered her patients for their amazing daily fortitude and determination in the face of unthinkable adversity.

And at that instant, Amara experienced calmness and direction, like a cozy blanket. She recognized the gift she had received—the chance to use her personal struggles as a guide for others. She also resolved to use every opportunity and give her heart and soul to the healing and hope-oriented activity.

Amara felt a fresh will filling her chest as she headed out into the waiting darkness. She was going to travel a long road, a career of service and advocacy laying out before her like a straight road. She was ready to welcome it, however, and to meet whatever obstacles lie ahead with the same bravery and grace that had seen her through the worst of circumstances.

She was Dr. Amara Johnson, a lady created in the furnace of hardship by love. Every challenge she went through was another furnace, honing her will and soul. One thing Amara knew for sure as she entered the unknown, prepared to face the next challenge life would present: she was just starting.

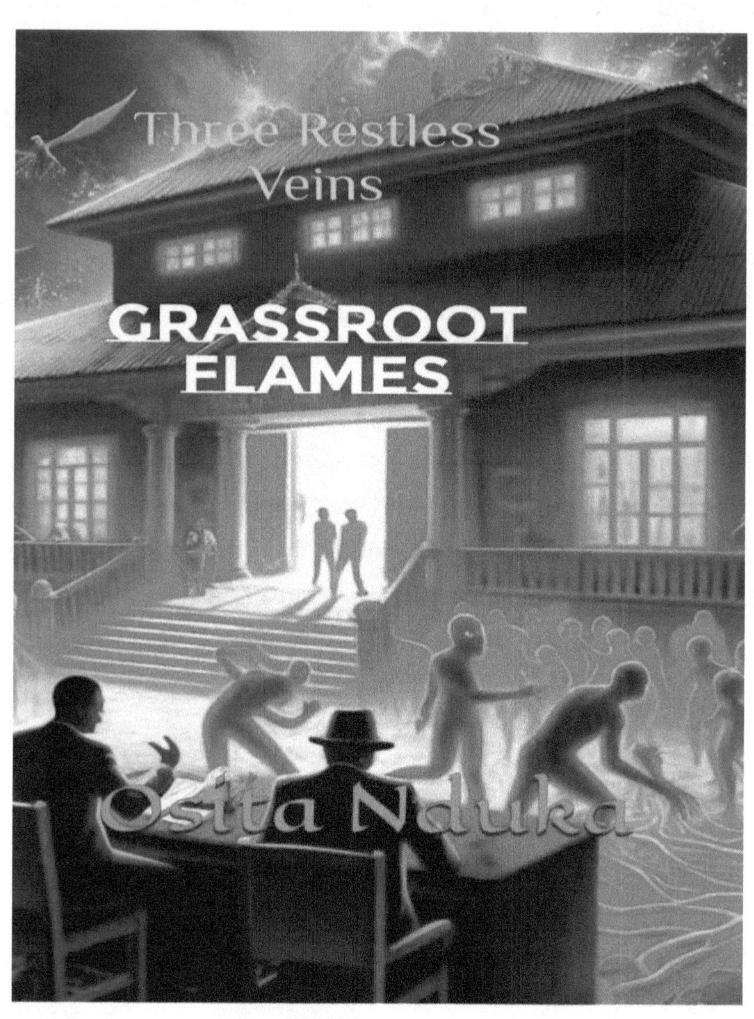

BOOK III

Main Characters

Dr. Amara Johnson: A dedicated doctor and community leader who becomes embroiled in uncovering the conspiracy threatening Igbuzor.

Nuss Johnson: Amara's brother, an adventurous rock climber who assists her in deciphering the mysterious map and confronting the town's hidden enemies.

Mayor Sholina Okoye Singh: The determined leader of Igbuzor, working with Amara to protect the town from the shadowy forces threatening it.

Jiu Adekunle: Amara's husband, providing emotional support and stability.

Emily Carter: Amara's close friend who stands by her side during the tumultuous events.

Reverend Solomon Okafor: Initially presented as a spiritual leader, later revealed to be a key figure in the conspiracy against Igbuzor.

Mrs. Okereke Miriam: The Mayor's secretary, a minor character who assists in administrative matters.

John Amiri Anderson: Amara's protégé at the hospital, who supports her in her medical work.

The Archivist (Ikenga Luti): A shadowy figure behind the conspiracy, seeking to control Igbuzor.

Clara Mohammed: A nurse at Igbuzor General Hospital.

Mr. Okerie Talel: A politician mentioned as part of the conspiracy alongside Ikenga.

Key Locations

Igbuzor: The main setting of the story, a town with a rich history and hidden secrets.

Igili: A neighboring town to Igbuzor.

Wirad: Another neighboring town.

Igbuzor General Hospital: Where Amara works as a doctor.

Community Centre Block C: Where Mayor Sholina's office is located.

The Igbuzor market district: Site of an arson attack in the middle of Igbuzor.

Old town of Igbuzor: Where the lineage map leads Amara and Nuss.

Abandoned house Okafor family building: Where the final confrontation takes place.

Hope for Tomorrow Foundation: Amara's charity organization located within Block B of the community Centre.

Prologue

The final rays of sunset bathed Igbuzor in gold and red; the light danced over the undulating surface of the river winding through the centre of the town and glancing off the tin roofs of the market booths. Perched on the steps of the old community centre, Dr. Amara Johnson surveyed the crowd before her. A sensory scene as rich and vivid as Igbuzor itself, the air smelled of flowering frangipani and the spices from surrounding food sellers.

Twelve months ago, after navigating her new normal and rebuilding her life following her myositis diagnosis, Amara left the rehabilitation hospital. She had not only healed but also flourished in that period—marrying Jiu, giving her all to the Hope for Tomorrow Foundation, and shining hope for her neighbourhood.

As she watched the guests still mixing at the Foundation's annual gala after party, Amara's thoughts returned to those terrible days in the hospital bed, her body plagued with anguish, uncertain if she would ever practice medicine again. Her present success was all the sweeter, but the remembrance of that impotence also sharpened her awareness of the fleeting nature of life.

As Amara navigated through the crowd, meeting and sincerely thanking others, the sound of champagne glasses clinking, and lively discussions filled the air. Her eyes landed on familiar faces: Emily, her constant companion; Liam from the Rehabilitation Centre, now a volunteer at the Foundation; Mayor Sholina, radiant in traditional clothing. And there, in the middle of it all, was Jiu, watching her work the room with eyes glistening with love and pride.

She heard a brief exchange as she passed a gathering of town folks. "...the lineage map has reappeared." Should they find its actual significance, she does not belong here.".

"Hushed!" Not Here. One whispered, "Too many ears."

Amara wrinkled her nose, but before she could ponder, someone pushed her towards the little improvised platform. As she replaced him, the weight of expectation rested on her shoulders, and silence descended over the assembly.

"Friends, neighbours, and fellow citizens of Igbuzor," she said, her voice clear and powerful. "I stood before you unsure of my future a year and a half ago. Today, I stand not just as a survivor but also as a woman devoted to the battle for the health and future of our community.

The audience applauded, and Amara felt a surge of feelings grow in her throat.

"But our road is far from done. New difficulties wait on us even as we celebrate our successes. "The forces at work in Igbuzor want to discredit what we have created, disturb our lovely workplace in the community centre, and rip apart our community for their own benefit."

A discomfiting murmur swept through the crowd. Amara's eyes ran over their features, reflecting to her a combination of worry and will. "I now know that real power derives from standing together rather than from alone. And thus, I ask everybody tonight: Will you be here? Will you stand with me to confront whatever storms may come, to save the community we love and the future we believe in?"

The answer came right away and was overpowering. Cheers started; hands rose in sympathy. Amara was rather proud of her people for their tenacity and unflinching attitude.
But a shudder went down her spine, even as she savoured their support. For there, in the rear of the assembly, she saw someone. The

figure stood tall and commanding, enveloped in darkness under the dazzling glow of the gala lights. Amara might have thought she saw the glitter of metal—a sword, maybe—before the figure faded into the throng, leaving only a sensation of dread Amara could not shake for a moment.

Amara found a peaceful moment to retreat, resting against the cold stone of the structure, as the aftermath of the celebration continued to envelop her. Her thoughts ran with the ramifications of what she had seen and heard. The enigmatic lineage chart, the unknown dark person, and the rumours of threats to her foundation's office at the Community Centre Block all pointed to a storm building on the horizon.

She thought about her parents and the legacy they had left behind. She thought of Jiu and the life they were creating together. She had witnessed each patient and impacted every life she encountered. Amara comprehended, with profound clarity, that this was only the beginning. Igbuzor's story was about to begin a new chapter that would test them in ways unknown.
Amara was certain that they would face the darkness together, regardless of the challenges that lay ahead. For they were Igbuzor— unbreakable, relentless, created in the furnace of hardship.

She inhaled deeply, straightening her shoulders, and then turned back to rejoin the festivities. Their toughest obstacle was yet to come. And Amara Johnson would be prepared to confront it squarely, with the same tenacity and elegance that had got her through the worst of circumstances.

She was Dr. Amara Johnson, a woman forged by love and forged in the crucible of adversity. Every tribulation she went through was like another furnace honing her soul and fortifying her will. Amara was certain as she ventured into the unknown, ready to confront the next challenge life presented: she was just beginning

PART 1

THE SMOKE

Chapter 1

Lineage Chaos

Low above the busy streets of Igbuzor, the sun cast long shadows over the town square, where Mayor Sholina was speaking to a sizable gathering of people in one of her regular community outreach programs. Her voice bounced off the nearby buildings, clear and loud.

"Fellow people, I have come to share some very important news with you today. Many of you are aware that lately we have acquired an enigmatic lineage chart—a map with mysteries about the past, present, and future of our community. I think this map is essential to unite our community instead of separating us and starting a new period of prosperity for Igbuzor as one people."

Sholina stopped, peering over the sea of faces. With emotions ranging from curiosity to mistrust, the audience hung on her every word.

She said, sadly, "There are those who would use this lineage map for their own selfish benefit." Even today, hidden rivals are quietly plotting to seize control of our community and target specific individuals as part of the ancient bloodline cleansing process. Anyone who calls here home belongs here, and it is one of us; we cannot let them succeed!"

A murmur spread throughout the assembly at this point. Along with a buzz of anxiety, unease permeated the space.

"But we will not cower in the face of any adversity," Sholina said, her voice picking intensity. "We are strong, cohesive, resilient people from Igbuzor. We shall open the secrets of these lineage charts and create a road towards a better future together. We have our own destiny!"

Amara watched intently from the plaza's edge as the crowd erupted into cheers and applause. Right in time to see the finish of the mayor's address, the young doctor had returned from her foundation's clinic. Amara, still healing from her protracted sickness, felt a flash of interest in Sholina's comments. Like the mayor's vision for the town's future, the mystery of the lineage map now fascinates her.

Still, Amara also felt the threat was hiding under the surface. Igbuzor was a political powder keg ready to blow if there were really opponents plotting against Sholina. She also sensed that the impending storm would ensnare her and her loved ones, whether they desired it or not. However, it wasn't until she looked at the lineage chart that she understood the situation.

Amara turned suddenly to see a commotion close to the front of the assembly. An enraged yell erupted, followed by a brawl. She bent her neck to observe a group of tough-looking guys marching towards the platform, where her security detail swiftly encircled a startled Sholina.

Lying! "It's all lies!" yelled the mob leader, a big man with a severely scarred face. "Sholina is unfit for heading this town! We should know the contents in the open; the lineage map belongs to the public, not to a despot like her!"

The enraged crowd pushed forward to meet a wall of local police officers as they hurried Sholina off the platform. Chaos broke out. Amara felt someone grab her arm; Emily's eyes were wide with terror.

"Come on, we have to leave this place!" Emily shouted above the chaos.
With her heart pounding, Amara surrendered to the chaotic crowd. Her head whirled as they turned down a side street.

Chapter 2

Daring edges

Miles away, Nuss, trembling with effort, hung perilously over the brink of a steep rock wall. His nerves twitched with every shaky movement of his body and sweat trickled down his cheeks as he searched for another handhold.

Nuss's passion was putting himself against the environment in a primordial struggle of will and power. Clinging to the craggy rocks, he felt a type of concentration and clarity that escaped him anyplace else out here in the wild. He understood it was a risk. Still, it gave him life.

Grasping, Nuss pushed himself upward to a narrow ledge. Breathing hard, he stopped momentarily and then turned to enjoy the breathtaking scene. The rugged mountains marched out into the horizon; their jagged tops touched by late afternoon golden light. Far below, the rich carpet of the forest canopy moved in the air.

Nuss's face split in a wonderful smile. He belonged here, on the brink, constantly striving for new heights and never turning back from a challenge. His mind drifted to his sister, Amara, as he got ready for the last push toward the peak.

He thought that they had cut her from the same fabric. He felt the same warmth in his stomach from a different location. Amara was out there battling for her patients, her community, and what she believed in as he ascended mountains. They were a powerful team, the unrelenting doctor and the determined climber.

Nuss's grin faded as he thought back to the worrisome phone call Amara had given him that morning. She had said: Trouble was building in Igbuzor. Mayor Sholina had revealed an enigmatic lineage chart, and now evil forces were preparing to seize it. Amara thought the town was about to explode.

She had advised Nuss to use caution and to guard his back on his one-person climbing trips. Nobody knew exactly who may be involved or how far this conspiracy would go. Nuss was aware that Amara would not hesitate to take action when her village faced danger, despite his reluctance to witness his beloved sister in danger. Simply put, that wasn't her nature.

Neither was it in his; Nuss had to confess as he readied his next action by chalk-dusting his hands. Though he was out here in the tough terrain, his heart was with his house and sister. And should it become necessary, he would be ready to join the battle.

Nuss's jaw tightened with determination as he turned to face the granite wall. Adrenaline shot through his veins as he once again pushed himself aloft, gracefully and fluidly ascending the pure face. Through perseverance, tenacity, and an unquestionable self-belief, he would ascend this summit as he had done so many times.

And Nuss pledged that when he went back to Igbuzor, he would bring that same passion to bear for his sister, friends, and hometown. Whatever gloom hung on the horizon; they would confront it together. And they would succeed as well.

Chapter 3

Building flames

Amara dashed through the community centre's doors today; her pulse was still pounding from the brawl in the town plaza earlier. Inside she discovered a scene of precisely regulated anarchy.

Nurses and orderlies continued to tend to the mostly minor injuries, such as scrapes, bruises, and a few bloody noses, from the turmoil; fortunately, none of them were too severe. Mayor Sholina, off to one side, was deeply involved in a discussion with a small group of grim-faced officials, clearly discussing the unsettling events of the previous day.

Upon spotting Amara, Sholina broke away from the group and rushed towards her. Up close, the mayor seemed drawn and tired, the weight of leadership clearly showing on her face.

With relief, Sholina exclaimed, "Amara, thank goodness." "I really appreciate you being safe. I was particularly concerned when the audience started acting aggressively.
"I am fine, Madam Mayor," Amara said. But out there, what on earth happened? Who were those men?"

The face of Sholina became gloomy. "Troublers. Given your lack of interest in politics, you may find it difficult to understand the rabble-rousers. But ever since I revealed the lineage map, they have been causing discontent as if they were some kind of historical magic still to uncover personally. That is far from their imaginations, however; they believe I am attempting to retain its secrets for myself or use them to solidify power and stay mayor forever."

She gave a frustrated head shake. "Never mind that I'm working day and night to use the lineage map to enhance this community, or that I have been very open about the entire affair," she said. Some just cannot look above their own avarice and distrust.

Amara wrinkled her forehead, her nimble mind already considering the ramifications. Do you suppose they were acting alone? Alternatively, could someone else be orchestrating this?

"I'm beginning to question the same thing," Sholina said with bitterness. "It's all quite deliberate and too orderly. Like someone is attempting to destabilise Igbuzor town using the talk of this lineage map to create instability so they may jump into the power vacuum."

Amara's spine shivered with cold at the thought. She had seen personally how strife and instability may split societies and leave long-lasting wounds requiring centuries of healing. Whatever goal these dark individuals had; she knew it would not be beneficial for her cherished community.

"What can I do to help?" she asked, carefully squaring her shoulders. Respected physician and activist Amara had immense power in Igbuzor. She was resolved to use that power to protect the village and assist Sholina in any way possible.

The mayor cast her a probing glance, as if assessing her potential value as an ally or possibly confidante. She nodded gently at last. "Amara, I need people I can rely on. I greatly need people of integrity like you to help me uncover this plot and maintain peace in Igbuzor. I have always respected your ethics and will. Will you be by my side in this struggle?"

Amara felt a surge of emotion as the enormity of the event dawned on her. Amara thought of her deceased parents, who had sacrificed so much for her better life. She thought of her siblings, dispersed like the winds yet united by love and affection. She thought of Jiu, who was her soul companion and her rock.

She also considered Igbuzor itself the only house she had ever known—the nursery of her most treasured memories and her strongest roots. At that moment, Amara realized she could only provide one response.

"I'm with you, Madam Mayor," she said, her voice ringing with clarity. "Whatever it takes, I will help to safeguard our town and expose the truth." The future belongs to Igbuzor. And I refuse to let hatred or avarice ruin it.

With tears shining in her eyes, Sholina reached out to grasp Amara's hands in her own. "Thanks," she answered, speaking softly. Having you by my side enables me to weather any challenge. Together, we will create a better road for Igbuzor—regardless of how hard our adversaries attempt to stop us."

Heart bursting with a strong blend of pride, will, and love, Amara returned the mayor's handclasp with one of her own. Igbuzor's spirit has started its fight. She would also remain on the front lines till quite late.

Chapter 4

Hidden Gem

Deep on one of Igbuzor's lonely streets, in a damp, mildewed apartment smelling of stale cigarettes and cloying incense, a dark man sat poring over a stack of old records. To the uninitiated eye, yellowed maps, crumbled scrolls, and fragile black sheets with heavily packed lettering would have appeared like so much mouldering trash. To this man, however, they were the keys to a power beyond simple calculating.

Despite his identity being largely unknown to the new generations of Igbuzor, he was known as The Archivist. Hunching over the table like a vulture over Carrion, swathed in black garments that covered his face, applied as he was at merging into darkness, there was no disguising the atmosphere of hate hovering over him like a deadly cloud.

Under the guidance of the late Okafor Asita, the grandfather of clergyman Reverend Okafor, the Archivist had been quietly accumulating arcane knowledge, patiently waiting for his opportunity to seize authority from the Sholina's clan and ascend to his appointed position as leader of Igbuzor with a new Mayor on the throne. He nurtured the plans for decades. That time had at last come when the enigmatic lineage map surfaced in the town he thought had been taken from his collection. He understood the secrets the lineage map concealed, secrets that, if used, might overthrow him as the lord of not only Igbuzor's crystal history, but also that of the entire area of all the neighbouring towns of Igili and Wirad.

Naturally, even for one as deeply ingrained in forbidden knowledge as himself, uncovering the secret wisdom of the Igbuzor bloodline would not be simple. The writers had cleverly concealed the true meaning of the Igbuzor bloodline, using layers of riddles and diversions to deter the unfit. Breaking those old rules would need all the archivist's subtlety and ability.

However, his lack of patience was evident. And if the simmering anarchy his operatives had unleashed in the town square a few days earlier was any guide, he had chosen his time wisely. Mayor Sholina shook, her legitimacy compromised, her foes empowered. The archivist felt he could execute his designs with impunity in the turmoil to come.

As if summoned by his melancholic thoughts, the agreed-upon signal echoed from his bedroom door, three short and two long. The archivist set the door open with an annoyed sweep of his hand, exposing a cowering underling.

"My lord," the man muttered, head bobbing in anxious obeisance. "I bring updates from our field's guys. Amara, the doctor lady, had cast her lot with Mayor Sholina. They scheme together even now to foil your plans, and Reverend Okafor is becoming weak with the plots."

Under his mask, The Archivist's lips closed into a disgusted line. Of course, becoming well-known in Igbuzor did not happen without drawing attention. Amara had been known about. He had undoubtedly underestimated her, dismissing her as just another philanthropic individual. One mistake he would not repeat.

Despite her strength, she remained merely one woman. He wielded the power to render Sholina and Amara's endeavours futile. The Archivist understood that the lineage map was just one piece of a larger puzzle, one that, once completed, would grant him complete authority. Even Amara, with her strong community connections, would not be able to stop him.

With a whirl of black robes, The Archivist rose from his seat and turned to confront his cringing servant. "Let Sholina and her pet doctor indulge in their schemes," he snarled. "I pursue the essence, while they chase the shadows. Ultimately, Igbuzor and all the mysteries it carries will be mine. I am Ikenga Luti, the only surviving archivist in this town".

The Archivist stormed out of the chamber, disappearing into the darkness of the labyrinthine hallways beyond, his terrible proclamation still resounding. He had a lot to accomplish, and finally, time was on his side. Igbuzor's reckoning was imminent; from its ashes, his long-awaited rule would flourish.

Chapter 5

Emergency Rush

The rusting tin roofs of Igbuzor General Hospital bore relentless heat from the sun, transforming the little wards into hot saunas. Amara was gently sponging the fevered forehead of an elderly lady in one of the higher-level private rooms.

Amara attempted to give her patients calm certainty even in the stifling heat for their benefit. Inside, however, her mind was whirling with the disturbing events of the last few days: the almost-riot at the town square, her mounting discomfort about the enigmatic lineage map, and Mayor Sholina's frightening warning of a plot under way in Igbuzor.

Despite being a resident of the neighbourhood, Amara enjoyed a good reputation, garnered respect, and recognized the limitations of her influence. Dealing with a conspiracy this size would need a large coalition of the willing, courageous, and moral individuals ready to put Igbuzor's wellbeing above their own limited interests. But with a community becoming more split daily, who could she trust?

Amara sighed, wrung the moist cloth, then laid it gently on her patient's brow. Mumbled something incomprehensible; lost in the depths of fever nightmares, the elderly lady Looking down at that lined, worn-out face, Amara felt a flash of protection. These were her people, the ones she swore oaths to cure and guard. She would never surrender them to ambitious schemers.

Though Amara yearned to leap headfirst into the approaching struggle for Igbuzor's future, she realized that her first obligation was to her patients. More than ever, they relied on her steady hands and calming demeanour to provide stability amidst the impending storm.

Therefore, for the foreseeable future, she will focus her efforts on this hospital and the Hope for Tomorrow foundation clinic.

The creak of the door startled Amara out of her dream. She raised her head to see Dr John walking into the room carrying a stack of medical records high in his arms. Despite the signs of fatigue on his young face, Amara's protégé managed a weary smile.
John said, "Hope I'm not interrupting," gesturing to the patient who was asleep. "I simply wanted to inquire about your well-being and dispose of these documents." From what I've heard, the mayor's address became very nasty,"

Grateful for the thoughtful gesture, Amara grinned back. She had grown to respect Dr John Amiri Anderson's idealism and his will to change things since she had taken the young doctor under her wing at the Igbuzor general hospital. Maybe when the time came, he would be among the friends she could rely on to oppose the mysterious enemies of Igbuzor.

"I'm managing," she said, circling the bed to assist him with the clumsy stack of charts. "You know, we're trying to stay focused on our job here.
Still, I have this impression that something major is approaching. Something that could permanently alter Igbuzor—and not for the better."
John's brow wrinkled as he took in her sober comments. "I have been hearing hints," he said. "Whispers of outside powers aiming to destabilize the community divide people against one another. Do you believe any of these reports are accurate?"

Amara hesitated, torn between her natural prudence and her growing conviction that John was trustworthy. She nodded very slowly at last.

She spoke subdued. "I do." "Mayor Sholina thinks there's a political conspiracy under way, some kind of scheme driven by that unusual lineage map that's surfaced. And after what I saw at that rally address that day, I find myself leaning in her direction."

She corrected John, testing his response with a questioning glance. She was relieved to see only resolution and a trace of enthusiasm flickering in his eyes.

"Whatever's going on, I want to help," John said strongly. "I went into medicine to speak up for what's right and to change things. Should Igbuzor be in danger, I will do everything in my power to defend our village."

Amara felt a surge of warmth at his courageous statement. Amara reached out to grab his shoulder, expressing her gratitude and support.

"I knew I could count on you, John," she added, smiling. "In the next days, we will need every ally we can get. I feel as if this struggle is just beginning.

As if to underscore her dire predictions, the corridor outside erupted with a flurry of activity—loud voices, pounding footsteps. Amara and John hurried to the door and out into the hallway, their silent gazes filled with warning.

Their arrival was met with barely regulated anarchy. Nurses and orderlies rushed to and from the scene, their faces tense with urgency. Two gurneys clattered by, bearing the bloodied bodies of two young boys. Everywhere was the thrum of stress, the sparkle of disaster.

Amara saw a senior nurse running by among the chaos and clutched her arm. She said, "What's happening, Clara?" She struggled to break through the noise. "What is all this?"

The nurse turned to respond, her expression dark. "Multiple gunshot wounds," she said just now. The East District appears to have been the scene of a gang battle. The conflict has resulted in at least six fatalities, with more possibly on the way."

At the news, Amara's heart contracted. In Igbuzor's less developed areas, local gang violence had long been a problem, but this degree of carnage was astounding. Given the turbulence during the town square rally address, could this sudden escalation be a coincidence? Alternatively, was this an escalation, a clue that the town's secret puppeteers had a fresh act for their performance?

Later, there would be time to consider such issues. Amara understood; right now, her obligation was obvious. Amara squared her shoulders and turned with steely determination to meet Dr John.

"Looks like we're needed in surgery," she added swiftly. "Clean and let OR 3 know. This will be a long evening.

Amara struggled to suppress a twinge of terrible dread as she hurried along the busy corridor of Igbuzor General Hospital, dodging gurneys and shouting instructions. The battle for Igbuzor's spirit seemed to have begun with great intensity. She also sensed that before it was over, she would witness more bloodshed than any community should have.

PART 2

THE FIRE

Chapter 6

Daring Cliffs

Far away, in the tough terrain that followed Wirad, Nuss gripped the windswept rock face with lean muscles that were shaking with exertion. Should his grasp fail, the fall below him was vertigo, a pure plunge that would pulverise both flesh and bone equally. Nuss had, however, long since conquered his anxiety. Out here, in the untamed areas where stone and sky held dominion, he discovered clarity he missed in the din of town.

Pausing to mark his wounded fingertips, Nuss thought of the vastness of the mountain remaining above him. To some, it would have appeared a terrifying prospect—the far-off top buried in wisps of mist, the falling ravines, the spurs of crystalline black rock laying in ambush to crush an unsuspecting climber's bones. However, Nuss found these challenges irresistible, the irresistible appeal of the task unfulfilled.

Nuss found it difficult to ignore the issues in Igbuzor, despite his heart yearning for solitude. The phone call from his sister had slightly unnerved him. A scheme against Sholina, the mayor and good friend of his family? Shadowy agents are planting strife in the streets? Nuss was intensely loyal to his community and its people, even if he showed little political enthusiasm. His fury boiled at the idea of secret enemies endangering Amara's charity house and everything he loved.

With renewed energy, Nuss clenched his teeth and hurled himself towards the rock face. His fingers reached into tiny cracks, and his toes found grip on little ledges. This was the alchemy that turned Nuss's concern into resolve—the biting of the stone, the aching of his muscles, the razor-edged clarity of the moment. Come what may, he will stand by his town and sister. As they had withstood so much before, they would ride out this storm together.

Higher and higher Nuss ascended the enormous vault of the sky, spinning above. Exhilaration coursed through his body—the basic excitement of the liberated soul. His entire universe shrank to the rock under his fingertips, the sun on his back, and the unbounded might of the wind. Here he discovered the power he would soon need, clinging to the spine of the ground. Change was arriving in Igbuzor, good or bad. Nuss was prepared to face this change with courage and determination.

Nuss used his coiled muscle to pull himself over the brink of the top in a final effort. Rolling onto his back, he battled to settle his racing heart and gazed up at the heavens. The broad stretch of the veldt, strewn with glades of umbrella thorn and bulbous baobabs like something out of a fairy tale, was breathtakingly visible below him. Far off, nearly hidden in the heat shimmer, he could barely see the gathered rooftops of Igbuzor, clinging tenaciously to the banks of the life-giving river.

From this divine vantage point—how little and delicate his hometown seemed—Nuss felt a rush of love and resolve.

Mayor Sholina would not allow his beloved Igbuzor to collapse, regardless of the web of intrigue he had discovered or the evil powers attempting to turn friends against friends and neighbours against neighbours. The furnace of these wild hills shaped his soul, and the sting of the rock and the lash of the wind cooled it. And that same spirit now cried out to protect his house.

Nuss let the tranquillity of the high mountains permeate his spirit for a long while. He inhaled deeply of the cold, thin air and felt the ancient stone thrumming underfoot like the world's pulse. Allow the power-hungry grab for their fleeting crowns while the schemers weave their webs in the shade. A man may yet discover that it lasted here, in the untamed centre of the country.

Nuss pulled himself to his feet at last as the sun started to drop on the distant horizon. Fixing the picture in his mental eye like a talisman against the darkness to come, he cast one more glimpse out over the achingly beautiful stretch of stone and sky.

Then he began his journey down into the gathering darkness, his resolve as strong as the mountain behind him.

He would be ready for whatever lay ahead in the nervous streets of Igbuzor. Nuss would be the unquestionable rock that Amara, for the sake of their family and the town's survival, must rush to destroy. Standing before the undulating hills, with the ghosts of his ancestors guiding him home, he made a vow.

Chapter 7

More Flames

The darkness hung thick above Igbuzor, the declining moon creating fitful shadows over the overhead power line tangle. Surrounded by tall piles of paperwork and a half-drunk cup of long-cold coffee, Mayor Sholina sat crouched over a broken desk in the small office at the community centre, Block C. Her face showed prominent lines of tiredness from the strong brightness of the desk light, yet her eyes blazed with the furious focus of a woman on a mission.

Standing before her, occupying the damaged desktop, was the enigmatic lineage map that had sparked so much curiosity and conflict. Its surface, a chaotic scribble of symbols and enigmatic inscriptions, defied simple understanding. For hours, Sholina had worked over the mysterious text, trying to find some kernel of significance among its twisted symbols. At least in the mayor's eyes, the lineage chart held its secrets well; fatigue was becoming a formidable opponent she could no longer ignore.

Sighing, the mayor reclined on her creaky chair, using ink-stained fingers to massage her aching temples. She had always taken immense satisfaction in her pragmatism, her ability to see through bluster and dishonesty to the core of any topic. But with its riddling cyphers, this lineage map appeared to ridicule her earthly reason. What crucial information might this lineage chart conceal to spur such frantic actions among Igbuzor's key players?

Sholina's main goal for Igbuzor's future was to support the map, realizing that it was a significant risk. Her adversaries were numerous, with very sophisticated plans. She could practically feel their activities coiling around her like razor wire, preparing to cut her down at the slightest hint of weakness or error even now. However, she understood that leaders expected decisive action, not cautious hedging. Exposing the mysteries of the lineage chart could potentially bring stability and wealth to her long-suffering village, rather than causing division.

The phone's sharp electronic trill broke the sombre silence of the evening. Sholina grabbed it before the first ring had ended, a tingle of discomfort already developing between her shoulder blades. Based on her experience, no excellent news ever arrived at this exact hour.

"Madam Mayor?" The voice on the other end of the phone sounded weak and strained, almost as if it belonged to her head of security. "I fear another event has occurred," she said. In the market district, a fire. At least two structures collapsed, and numerous others sustained damage. We are currently determining the dead.

Sholina closed her eyes, her obligations weighing her like a leaden shroud. Her voice was firm and forceful as she talked. Any sign of arson?

A moment loaded with unspoken words. "Too early to declare for sure. However, given the turmoil of the past few days, it's premature to make a definitive declaration. The security chief trailed off, allowing the quiet to speak for itself.

The jaw of Sholina tightened. After a near-riot at the town hall gathering and a violent gang clash, there has been a surge in violence in just a few short days. Ignoring the pattern was difficult. Someone was purposefully fanning the pandemonium in Igbuzor, advancing their own sinister goal by means of terror and violence. And Sholina, who knew her own hold on power, became increasingly precarious with every subsequent transgression.

"Keep me informed on the enquiry," she said to her security head sharply. "And in every high-risk location, increase the patrols. We need to proactively address this issue before it escalates.

With a leaden click, Sholina returned her attention to the mysterious map. Its transparency seemed to mock her, hanging hope just out of her grasp. However, she could afford to embrace the luxury of hopelessness. Not with such great stakes. She had to be tough and keep battling, no matter how long the odds were, for the sake of her community and its people.

The pale light the declining moon created across the office window painted Sholina's careworn face in tones of silver and shadow. Benevolent town slept fitfully on the streets below, preparing for the next explosion of turmoil and conflict. Looking down at the mysterious lineage chart that had become the centre of Igbuzor's destiny, Sholina felt as if she were standing on the brink of an abyss with nothing but her own will, stifling the howling blackness at that instant.

Chapter 8

More Emergencies

Even in the bone-weary hours of the graveyard shift, Igbuzor's General Hospital's halls were never silent. There was always the dull thrum of machinery, the repetitive beep and hiss of life support, the murmur of night nurses trading gossip over Styrofoam cups of break-through coffee. But in the predawn calm, with fatigue tugging at her limbs and the memory of hours of emergency surgery still clear behind her eyelids, Amara found even these familiar noises oddly subdued, as if muffled by a layer of gauze.

She mechanically nodded to her sporadic orderly or white-coated colleague, moving the darkly illuminated hallways like a ghostly presence. Her head was far off, caught between the terrible pictures of the devastation of the day and the nagging fear of what fresh horrors the following shift could bring. The injured just kept arriving as victims of gang violence, arson, and severe beatings in back lanes. Violence engulfed the community, as if someone had activated a hidden switch.

Unbound, Amara's memories drifted back to her conversation with Mayor Sholina, recalling the ominous warnings of dark powers spreading anarchy and dread in Igbuzor as a political ploy for the next election, all under the guise of a lineage chart. Is the terrible plan, which includes this outbreak of violence, still in place? Is this terror campaign aimed at undermining Sholina's authority and inciting chaos within the community? The very concept froze Amara's blood flow. She couldn't, however, refute the terrible logic of it.

As Amara rounded a bend, she nearly collided with a towering man approaching from the opposite side. She looked up, an apology already forming on her lips, and found herself staring into the black, fathomless eyes of Reverend Solomon Okafor. Despite his intimidating appearance, the spiritual head of Igbuzor's largest congregation appeared to have his craggy face carved from the same unyielding stone as the ancient mission church he oversaw. However, his vulpine look was particularly unsettling in the sickly fluorescent light of the hospital hallway.

"Reverend Okafor," Amara muttered, attempting to straighten herself. "I'm so sorry; I didn't see you there, and I didn't know you were back to Igbuzor."

The reverend's lips twitched with a chilly smile. "I am in between all the towns in this area, Dr. Johnson; there are no apologies required as usual. I ought to have called myself. You have had a demanding day, I know."

Something about his tone and the knowing glitter in his eyes prickled Amara's skin. With his aura of devout purity, his historical narrative of his family's genealogy as caretakers of the region's past, and his tendency to always appear to know more than he let on, Amara had never completely trusted the Reverend. Using his moral authority to stir up anger against the mayor's leadership and her friends, Sholina revealed her fears that Okafor might be one of the main architects of the upheaval sweeping Igbuzor. At first Amara was dubious but standing here under the weight of his hungry look, she could almost believe it.

"I was just visiting some of my wounded flock," Okafor said, his deep voice strangely resonating in the vacant hall. "So much misery and agony. Does it not shatter the heart? "

Not trusting herself to talk, Amara nodded numbly. The eyes of the Reverend pierced dark and shallow into hers. When he spoke for the second time, his voice was a soft, captivating whisper.

"These are challenging times for Igbuzor, Dr. Johnson. times of turbulence and doubt. At times like these, people look to their leaders for guidance and strength. In hopes."

He moved closer, his huge bulk hovering above Amara like a gathering thundercloud. "However, I am concerned that our beloved mayor might not possess the necessary qualifications for the position. She appears more interested in following ghost tales and old lineage maps than in confronting the very real pain her people endure."

Amara bristled at the suggested critique of Sholina. "The mayor is doing everything in her power to keep Igbuzor safe," she said, her tiredness suddenly forgotten in a flash of devoted rage. "She is working day and night to sort out this violence and bring peace back."

Okafor's grin grew but still fell short of reaching his eyes. "Of course, of course. It would be unwise for me to question the mayor's commitment. The mayor's voice conveyed a clear assessment of the score. "However, one may question the rationality of her priorities. Almost everyone my age has a copy of old lineage maps in their homes; perhaps her obsession with this "particular lineage map" has blinded her to the needs of the community."

He leant in closer, his voice lowering to a velvety whisper. "Dr. Johnson, you are a lady of impact. People respect you and look up to you. Perhaps you can leverage your influence to persuade the mayor to prioritize more urgent matters. Don't wait until it's too late for all of us."

Amara drew back as if in pain, her heart pounding against her ribs. Does this constitute a threat? A fore warning? Was there a deliberate attempt to separate her and Sholina? She found it difficult to know.

However, she refused to participate in the Reverend's game, having been suddenly and brilliantly convinced.

She remarked coldly, "I'm sure Mayor Sholina Okoye Singh has the best interests of Igbuzor at heart." She deliberately stepped aside. And I rely on her judgement in this and other affairs. Now, if you don't mind, I have patients to attend to.

Amara pushed past the tall priest against the need to shiver at his closeness without waiting for a reply. With twin beams of evil curiosity, she strolled down the hallway, feeling his gaze on her from behind. She could not burst into a sprint; she could not put as much space between herself and that terrible, sepulchral look.

Bursting through the hospital chapel's doors, Amara fell upon the closest pew; her knees at last gave way as the adrenaline left her body. She realized faintly that her hands were quivering like leaves in a storm. She was shivering. More than she would like to admit, the meeting with Reverend Okafor had unsettled her.

Was Sholina facing any such challenges? Not only are faceless criminals and rumour mongers using their power to undermine the mayor's initiatives everywhere, but also pillars of society like Okafor. If so, the rot in Igbuzor went far deeper than Amara had ever thought possible. Uprooting it would be a challenging task, likely costing them everything before the end.

Amara bowed her head, trying to centre herself in the peaceful haven of the church by slowing her rushing thoughts. Long deceased but so very real in her heart, she considered her foster father and mother. What advice would they have given her in such circumstances? In such overwhelming circumstances, what advice would they give her?

She found the response like a bright beam of light cutting over the darkness. They would advise her to be strong and to rapidly oppose the storm. She must adhere to her principles, regardless of the intensity of the calamity. They had not reared a girl to shuck her obligation to her society or to flinch in the face of peril. They had produced a warrior, a healer, and an unquestionably committed lady.

Amara lifted her head slowly, her mouth locked with fresh will. Reverend Okafor and his ilk might scare her, but they could also harass her into renouncing Sholina and the cause of righteousness. They were about to discover how much they had undervalued the calm power of Dr. Amara Johnson.

Getting to her feet, Amara straightened her shoulders and headed deliberately out of the church. Amara had to complete her work, and she couldn't waste time questioning or doubting. Future hung on Igbuzor's shoulders. She would not relent until she ensured that future, regardless of the consequences.

Amara saw her reflection in a dim window as she came out into the crowded hall. She scarcely knew herself for a moment—the stern set of her jaw, the steel in her gaze. She nodded slowly, adjusting to the shift. The doubtful girl, the old Amara, was no longer present. A woman, shaped in the furnace of catastrophe and cooled by loss and suffering, occupied her position with a sword of terrible intent. She was a lady who refused to surrender, regardless of the challenges that lay ahead.

Amara's jaw tightened with determination as she quickly started down the hall. The day was just waiting here. She was also prepared to face it squarely.

Chapter 9

Empty lanes

The streets of Igbuzor's market district erupted into barely controllable chaos, a cacophony of yelling voices and acrid smoke that caused eye stinging and throat catching. Emergency lights painted a vivid gloss over the assembled audience as they strobed red and blue against the night sky. Grim-faced firemen rushed over the charred remains of the burned-out structures, hissing jets of water dousing the last tenacious embers.

Mayor Sholina battled to preserve her composure amid the chaos, a steadying pillar of power for her terrified people to draw on. Inside, however, her stomach turned over a terrible concoction of fear and rage. She was certain that this fire was not an accident. It has all the traits of planned sabotage, a determined act of terror meant to raise the tension in an already volatile community.

Her evil thoughts caused a rangy figure to separate from the crowd and approach her. Sholina stiffened; her hand dropped naturally to the hidden handgun at her hip. She slumped somewhat, however, as the orange fire glow lit a shaggy mane of untidy hair and a roguish smile.

"Nuss," she nodded to him, staying focused on her walk. "I should have known you would show up later or sooner. You seemed to encounter problems everywhere you went."

Nuss shrugged and started to smile broadly. "What could I say?" My nose is tuned for thrills." The grin darkened as he considered the scope of the damage and the shell-shocked expressions on the faces of the spectators. "This was arson; not sure otherwise. Is this just another move in the sinister scheme these devils are pursuing?"

Sholina's lips became a grim line. "That's my guess; indeed. It fits the trend of growing violence and the fear campaign." She gave a disgusted head shake. "Whoever is responsible for this is growing increasingly bold. I've run out of ways to stop them."

Nuss remained quiet for a long while, staring far off. His voice was oddly subdued as he spoke once more. "Amara informed me about the lineage map. Igbuzor is believed to be in danger due to the plot you believe in. At first, I didn't want to accept it because, as a rock climber, I am used to maps on my path, some of which look like antiquated versions of myself. But after viewing this..." He waved at the Smokey wreckage and the milling throngs of terrified residents. "I'm beginning to consider perhaps you are onto something."

Sholina looked at him sidelong, startled and a bit pleased by the unexpected help. She had always viewed Nuss's daring actions and irreverent attitude as a threat to public order, leading to a tense relationship with him. She was aware, too, of his profound affection for Igbuzor and his family and his intense loyalty to his sister and his family. She would be a fool to send him away if he were ready to stand alongside her against the approaching storm.

"I could use someone like you, Nuss," she replied gently, giving her words enormous weight. Nuss is a community member who won't hesitate to get his hands dirty. She looked at him with a penetrating glance. "Are you willing to offer assistance?"

Nuss's smile flashed once again, sharp and swift like a switchblade. "I'm willing to go to extraordinary lengths to protect my community and the people I love. I have been on many adventurous treasure hunts, and I am willing to work with you and your map."

Sholina felt a sudden wave of thanks and relief and started to smile back. She felt a flutter of something she had nearly forgotten how to feel in recent days: optimism. Nuss, on her side, possessed streetwise

knowledge and dogged devotion that centred his personality as a
rock climber.
"Alright, then," she responded sharply, straightening her shoulders
and turning to see the disorganized scene once again. "Let's start
right now. We have a village to save and a mystery to figure out.
And may God assist everyone who is trying to follow our path."

As if on cue, a woman's scream, loud and sharp with dread, followed
by a furious boom of voices, sprang from the far side of the throng.
Head swung around, eyes widening as Sholina witnessed a whirl of
ferocious violence as a writhing knot of people broke out from the
crowd. People were flying with their fists and feet in a frenzy.
She murmured, already headed forward, one hand lowering to the
revolver at her hip. "The hell...?" Nuss tightened at her side like a
coiled spring, his eyes flying fast-fire across the seething throng of
people.

Then Sholina saw a familiar person in the middle of the fight, long
hair flying as she struggled with a strong opponent—a painful flash
of familiarity. Amara was fighting furiously to repel her assailant,
her face a mask of blood and will.

Amara! Torn from the depths of his throat, Nuss's yell was an
animalistic, raw thing. In a flash, he raced towards the chaos,
recklessly pushing onlookers. Sholina swore under her breath and
shot her gun off after him.

Just as Amara fell to the ground, her attacker loomed over her with
death in his eyes; they were on the brink of the fight. With a silent
scream of wrath, Nuss flung himself at the guy who was carrying
him in a tangle of twisting limbs to the ground. The other fighters
dispersed around them like roaches before a bright light, remerging
into the obscurity of the crowd.

Sholina went to her knees next to Amara, her free hand sloppily searching the pulse of the younger lady. She was greatly relieved to find the younger lady's pulse firm and consistent under her fingertips. Amara strained to sit up and gently moaned, her eyelashes flickering.

Sholina said, "Easy, easy," guiding her to a seated posture. You are safe and well. Only breathe.

Shaking her head groggily, Amara winced at the movement. What...what happened? One moment, I was helping a woman who had suffered burns from the fire: the next... She trailed off, her sharpened eyes absorbing the sight around them. Not sure? Mayor Sholina? What are you doing here?

Sholina started to open her lips to respond, but before she could say anything, a loud voice sliced through the throng. Make room! Create space for Reverend Okafor!

The gathered people murmured as the Reverend's imposing form pushed his black cassock, billowing around him like a dark cloud over the press. A group of tough men, dressed in the black and crimson uniform of the church's lay security force, trailed behind him, their faces harsh and unflattering.

Nuss, who had choked Amara's attacker, watched nervously as Okafor walked up. Sholina saw his hold on the moaning guy under him tighten just fractionally.

"Reverend," she said coldly, getting to her feet. "I was not expecting to find you here."

Okafor's grin was wan, devoid of laughter. As the shepherd to Igbuzor's flock, it is my responsibility to assist those in need. His gaze drifted to Amara, who lay unconscious on the ground, as something flashed behind them too quickly for him to notice. "I arrived immediately and learned about the fire. A massive catastrophe. Thank you; it could have been worse."

Sholina battled the desire to shudder beneath that fathomless look, feeling a quick cold run down her spine even as the heat still rolled over the burning wreckage. The way Okafor was staring at Amara— a sort of predatory desire that sent every nerve in Sholina's body screaming danger—was rather disturbing.
She met the Reverend's eyes squarely, gently straying between the younger lady and him. She squared her shoulders. "Exactly. This time we were privileged. However, I am concerned that our string of fortunate events may be coming to an end."

Okafor raised an eyebrow, his face a veneer of polite worry. Ah? Why do you say that Madam Mayor?"
Sholina inhaled deeply and felt every eye on her weight. She knew of this as a turning point. Her next words could well decide Igbuzor's own destiny.

"Reverend, I think this fire was not an accident." "I think it was part of a planned, violent, and intimidating campaign meant to destabilize our community and challenge my authority." She stopped so her words might sink in. "And now, considering what someone else has done to Amara, I have reason to believe that the conspiracy behind these assaults is far more extensive than any of us realized." "Some individuals in positions of authority and influence among us are covertly attempting to plunge Igbuzor into anarchy for their own sinister motives."

A silence descended over the tiny listening audience seated next to her, clearly shocked and dismayed. Sholina saw Okafor's eyes narrow fractionally, a flutter of something like fury flickering in their depths before disappearing beneath a mask of immense worry.

"Those are serious accusations, Mayor Sholina," he remarked gently, his voice floating effortlessly in the unexpected quiet. "I trust you have data to back them up."
Sholina stopped, too conscious of the lethal currents whirling under

the surface of the moment. She contemplated the lineage map, securely stored in the safe of her office. The mysterious symbols and ciphered inscriptions suggest a reality too explosive to voice out. A revelation that could potentially demolish Igbuzor from its foundations.

She looked directly at Okafor; a quiet challenge poised between us. "I have leads," she added, picking her language carefully. "Patterns suggest a covert hand behind the scenes. I may not yet know all the answers. Nevertheless, I will locate them. That is what I assure you."

For a long, strained minute, nobody spoke. Tension permeated the air, a sensation of teetering on the knife's brink of some irreparable tipping point. Sholina gasped to be ready for Okafor's reply.

Still, the Reverend only grinned—a tiny, cold twist of the lips. "Definitely, Mayor, you will undoubtedly uncover the truth about this matter in due course. His eyes turned back to Amara, still seated on the ground, pallid and stunned. Maybe it would be better if Dr. Johnson went back to the hospital to have her injuries looked at in the meantime. Now, at such a pivotal point, would we want our most revered doctor absent from commission?"

Sholina bristled at the gently disguised menace behind his careful words. She could not, however, discount the wisdom in his recommendation. Amara appeared seriously shaken by her encounter; those scrapes and bruises required care.

"Nuss, can you see your sister safely back to the hospital?" She asked, keeping her gaze fixed on Okafor. she spoke. "I'll hang around here and work with the emergency responders."
Nuss nodded sharply, guiding Amara to her feet with a softness that contradicted his tough appearance. "On it, boss. Later, we will catch up."

Sholina turned back to face Okafor, squaring her shoulders for the conflict to come as the siblings made their methodical way across the milling throng.

"Mark my words, Reverend," she whispered gently, her voice like winter iron. "I'll look at who is behind these strikes. When I do, justice will be served. Igbuzor is going to obtain justice."

Okafor's smile only grew wider, a skull's grin amid the flickering flame.

"Oh, Mayor, I have absolute confidence in it." Not at all doubtful. His eyes shimmered with sinister delight. "Still, the question of whose justice will prevail remains unresolved. Yours...or?

With his dark-clad minions forming ranks behind him like a phalanx of shadows, he turned on his heel and marched out into the darkness, with that terrible declaration hanging between them.

Sholina watched him depart, a leaden weight sinking into her gut. He had established the battle lines clearly. Not now could one turn back. For better or worse, Igbuzor's destiny teetered on a margin. She would not stop until she had firmly swung those balances to the advantage of her people. Regardless of the expenses.

Chapter 10

Sudden guests

The sun mercilessly scorched the broken asphalt and tanned the skins of the scuttling people in Igbuzor. Amara leans over a damaged wooden bench in the disorganized workspace of her improvised workshop, adjusting the delicate guts of a tattered radio set. Amara's thin fingers, black with perspiration, moved with deliberate accuracy as she worked, her hair stranding to her forehead. Two days had elapsed since the fire in the marketplace, and another two days had passed since her encounter with the unidentified attacker, which had left her battered and disoriented. The underlying wounds, the persistent sensation of vulnerability, and the barely suppressed terror persisted even after the bruises had faded to a sickening yellow green colour. Throwing herself into her tinkering was the only thing that seemed to work; she lost herself in the complexities of circuits and cables until the outer world vanished into a faint whisper.

A tap at the door startled her out of her dream. She raised her head, staring owlishly in the workshop's gloom. Yes? Whose is it?

"It's Emily," the muted response came back. "Can I please?"

Amara had a quick wave of relief and thanks. Her beloved buddy Emily always seemed to know just when she most needed it. "Of course, come on in."
The door creaked open to reveal a thin woman in a clean blue dress. As Emily saw Amara's messy condition and the heavy bags beneath her eyes, her kind expression wrinkled with concern.
She muttered, "Oh, honey," and crossed the room to gently rest her shoulder on Amara. You seem weary. Have you remained trapped here since the fire?

Amara shrugged and tried to generate a comforting smile. "Pretty much. You know me; I always had to keep my hands occupied." Emily's scowl just became more pronounced. "Amara, feel free to not be okay either. You've endured the onslaught and the fire—enough to shake anyone." Her hold tightened just fractionally. "For me, you don't have to present a courageous front. Always with you, here is me."

Amara felt tears tumbling from the corners of her eyes, horrified. She dropped her head and blinked them fiercely back. "I know, Em. And I really am, thank you. It's just..." She trailed off, unable to translate the knotted mess of her feelings into words.

"Just what?" asks Emily, nudged softly.
Amara drew a long, shivering breath. "I feel so helpless," she said in a little voice. "Everything I've fought for, everything I believe in, is just sliding through my hands. Mayor Sholina believes there is some great conspiracy going on in the community—that the assault and the fire were part of a planned operation meant to undermine our quiet village and discredit her supporters. And I want to help her find the truth as well as believe her. But I just feel so... ineffective." The final phrase emerged as a choking sob with tears pouring over in hot, ashamed rivulets.

"Oh, Amara," Emily said, pulling her into a strong embrace. Emily said, "You are far from being useless." You are bold, tough, and quite intelligent. Igbuzor is fortunate to have you standing up for it.

She drew back slightly, aiming her gaze directly at Amara. "Pay attention to me," she said. I, Nuss, Lilly and Mayor Sholina are with you; Jiu is away on business. We live in this together. Together, we will investigate the situation and restore our community. okay?"

Shakily nodding, Amara swiped away her tears with the rear of her

palm. "Okay," she said, managing a misty grin. "Generally."
Emily grinned back, giving her shoulder one more squeeze before backing off. " Perfect. What, then, do you say we get from this stuffy workshop for a bit? I could walk; I'm sure you could too."

Amara halted and looked at her workstation's half-disassembled radio. Part of her was reluctant to abandon the brittle sensation of control her tinkering offered her. She knew, though; Emily was correct. She knew that hiding away in this room wouldn't solve anything.

She said, "Alright," pulling back her stool and rising with a stretch. "Lead the Way."

Emerging into the sweltering heat of noon, the two buddies squinted against the strong light. The typically busy town centre was eerily quiet, and the streets were oddly empty. The entire air appeared to be tense, anticipating the next attack.

Amara found herself half-expecting danger to come rushing out at them from every shadow as they went, eyeing the shuttered windows and deserted doors with a fresh wariness. The assault had severely disrupted her sense of safety in the place she had called home all her life. Now every stranger was a possible danger, every hidden alley a refuge for an anonymous threat.

Lost in her gloomy thoughts, she barely noticed Emily stopping next to her, grabbing her arm in a swift vice grip. She snarled, gesturing with her free hand across the street.

Amara's heart pounded as she followed her gaze. There, gathered near the mouth of a little side street, were a group of rough-looking foreign males wearing torn clothing. As they passed something back and forth between them, their furtive motions and darting looks set off every alarm in Amara's brain.

One of the guys looked up as they watched, his eyes connecting with Amara's for an absolutely heart-stopping second. Something flashed in that eye—a flutter of pure, evil purpose mixed with familiarity that froze Amara's blood to icy water in her veins.
Her voice shaking, "Em," she said, I believe we should leave here. right now."

Despite the silence, the guys continued to move, distancing themselves from the shadows and making their way towards her with purposeful strides as she spoke. Amara gripped Emily's hand as adrenaline surged through her body like an electric current.

She uttered the single word "run," and with that, they vanished, destroying the empty street as if the devil himself pursued them.
As they rushed, Amara's heart hammered in her ears, and the slap of their shoes resonated off the close-set structures. She could hear their attackers' yelling jeers behind them, becoming louder and more threatening with every second.

Glancing over her shoulder, she had a flash of absolute horror at their proximity. Their expressions transformed into leering masks of sadistic expectation; the guys were now barely more than half a block behind her. She realized, sickly, that she was playing with them and relishing the thrill of their pursuit.

As hopelessness threatened to overwhelm her, Amara noticed a small alleyway cutting off the main roadway ahead. She gasped, yanking Emily toward "there!" "Certainly, they are not locals; we can easily lose them in the back streets!"

They fell into the alley, the sudden darkness following the sun's briefly blinding power. Blinking fiercely, Amara guided her eyes to change as they flew headlong down the twisted path.

Their escape, however, was brief. The alley abruptly stopped, revealing a towering brick wall in front of them. With their chests heaving, they whirled to meet their assailants and skidded to a stop. Grinning like wolves who had just caught their prey, the men strolled into the alley with predatory nonchalance. With steely eyes and a shaven head, the burly commander moved forward and gave theatrical enjoyment a cracking knuckle.

"Well, well," he said low, gloating rasp. "What are we here for? Some beautiful birds seem to have lost their way." He shook his head to convey sympathy. "Tsk tk. It's risky to navigate these streets during a crisis on your own. You can never predict the type of danger you might encounter."
Amara pulled herself up to her full height and put on a display of bravery far from her own. "We're not looking for trouble, she answered, detesting the shaking in her voice. We don't need unpleasantness here, so please let us go."

At that, the leader's smile only became narrower, shark-like. "Oh, but we really excel in unpleasantness." He continued his advance, his lackeys spreading out to obstruct any potential escape routes. "And right now, Dr. Johnson, you and your friend here are looking like the most pleasant thing to happen to us all day."

The sound of Amara's name on the thug's lips chilled her blood to ice. She knew with terrible clarity that this was not a random mugging. There should have been a planned and coordinated effort. Someone had purposefully dispatched these soldiers to pursue her. But before she could express this terrifying insight, another voice emerged from the mouth of the alley—a voice that sent a rush of pure, dizzying relief coursed through her veins.

"I wouldn't do that if I were you," Nuss replied, his normally cheerful tone gone harsh and frigid as hardened steel. Nuss retorted, "That's only if you're willing to endure the next month in pains."

Whirling to meet this fresh danger, the thugs' attitudes changed from cocky to apprehensive in the space of a glance. With feet wide and hands clenched into fists at his sides, Nuss stood at the alley's entrance. A snarl of pure, protective anger replaced the relaxed smile Amara knew so well on his face.

The commander snarled, "This doesn't concern you, pretty boy," but Amara could sense the smallest trace of doubt behind the bravado. "Walk away now; we won't remember you were ever here."

Nuss let out a low, menacing laugh. "You're mistaken in that regard, pal," Nuss said. You are threatening my sister here. This raises my level of concern. He took a step forward, his muscles tightening beneath his sweat-stained shirt. So let me tell you what. Your group retreats beneath the rock from which you emerged, leaving our community, and I won't crush every bone in your bodies. Sound fair?"

Not one moved for a tense, breathless moment. Tension permeated the air, the potential for violence thick and weighty. As Amara watched the standoff develop, heart thumping against her ribs, she gasped.

Then the commander cursed silently, spit at Nuss's feet, and motioned for his soldiers to retreat. "This isn't over," he snarled, pointing a finger at Amara and Emily and backing towards the alley mouth. "You two have backs to watch. Igbuzor is no longer as safe as it used to be. Igbuzor is no longer as safe as it once was.

The men slid back into the shadows, disappearing as abruptly as they had shown with that terrible parting shot. As the adrenaline left her system, Amara let out a wobbly breath and sank against the alley wall.

"Nuss," she managed, her voice no more than a croak. "How come you are able to locate us? How did you come to know?

Her brother was by her side right away, clutching her shoulders in hands that trembled just barely. "I didn't," he said, his eyes darting over her face to make sure she was uninjured. "I heard the noise while I was enroute to your workplace." saw those jerks running after you. His mouth remained closed, a taut muscle in his cheek. "If I had been here one minute later..."

Even though Amara could detect a hint of it in his disturbed expression, he was unable to fully grasp the concept. Their awful realization of how close they had been to tragedy brought them to doom—too horrible to contemplate.
Emily gently sobbed and pressed a quivering palm to her lips. Whispering, her eyes wide and confused, she asked, "What do we do now?" "Those guys recognized the name Amara. They were focusing, especially on her. Why would they act in such a way? "What could they possibly want from her?"

Nuss's attitude became dark. "Apart from reporting to the police, some of them already knew what's happening in the community," Nuss whispered softly. "But I have a feeling it has something to do with that damned map, and whatever secrets Mayor Sholina thinks it holds, if not, then it might have to do with our next council election." He shook his head, his eyes brimming with frustration and rage. "This conspiracy she's hunting, this shadowy game of hide and dagger, is more expansive than we could have ever imagined." And now it feels like they're hunting everyone who approaches the truth too closely.

At his words, Amara felt a shudder go down her spine and a growing sensation of anxiety slithering into her stomach. If Nuss's theory about the assault's connection to the map and Sholina's research hold true, then their combined danger surpasses her wildest expectations. Whatever the case, the adversary had just revealed its true intentions. It will not rest until it brings Igbuzor—and everyone else who dared to challenge it—to order.

"We have to tell Sholina about this," she added, a fresh tone of steel joining her voice. The extent of their readiness should be known by her. The stakes are high. She looked into her brother's eyes and saw her own determination reflected at her. "And then we have to decide what to do going forward. One thing is certain—we cannot allow them to prevail. Igbuzor is relying on us."

Nuss nodded slowly, a glimmer of immense pride flickering to life in his eyes. "Damn right, it is," he said one final time, grasping her shoulders and then backing off. Come on, let us find you two someplace secure. We'll then see the mayor. It's time we battled with these jerks and showed them what results from their misbehaviour in our community."

The three of them then started down the alley, heads up and shoulders squared. Despite their brush with risk, they remained undefeated. Amara sensed a fresh fire burning in her blood—a flame of pure wrath and unquestionable goal.

The enemy had moved in. Their turn was now here. And come what may, they would not rest until the truth—and Igbuzor—were secure at last.

PART 3

THE DELIVERANCE

Chapter 11

Smokey Crystals

As Amara and Nuss walked inside the town community centre, Block C, the sun was slinking into the western hills, colouring the streets of Igbuzor orange and gold. With its towering arches and battered stone, the magnificent old edifice had always looked to Amara as a bulwark of strength and stability, a symbol of everything that was right and beneficial in their community.

But as they hurried up the sweeping staircase toward Mayor Sholina's office, she couldn't shake the discomfort that was gnawing at the back of her throat. The meeting in the alley had shattered her illusions of safety and routine, deeply upsetting her. Igbuzor's calm exterior seemed to conceal the terrible, festering reality like a curtain.

At the top of the stairs, they saw Mrs. Okereke, the mayor's secretary, seated exactly ramrod-straight behind her desk. As they came, the old lady glanced up, her aged face wrinkling into a worried scowl.

She rose from her seat and said, "Dr. Johnson, Mr. Nuss," as she welcomed them. Is everything good? Both of you seem rather troubled.

Though she knew it didn't reach her eyes, Amara managed a tight grin. "We came to see the mayor. It's critical. a problem of public safety."

The secretary's scowled more at that, but she only nodded quickly, naturally. One minute, kindly. She vanished inside the inner office, leaving Amara and Nuss in the waiting room to cool their heels.

Amara moved restlessly, her thoughts spinning with the implications of what had transpired. The assault had been focused and intentional. Someone had specifically targeted those guys. But for what? What could they possibly expect from her silence? She was simply a doctor from a small town, possessing a strong stubborn streak and a penchant for experimentation. She was not particularly unique. Could she potentially pose a threat to their sinister plan?

Before she could delve too deeply into her anxiety, the office door opened once more. Mrs. Okereke came out swinging the door wide in welcome.
"The mayor will see you now," she replied with an enigmatic look. Go straight in.
Amara and Nuss looked at each other briefly before crossing the threshold into the enormous, hallowed space of Mayor Sholina's inner office.

The space was just as Amara recalled from her most recent visit—all dark wood panelling and tall bookcases, the air fragrant with the smell of old paper and furniture polish. Heading down over a stack of papers, Sholina sat behind her large desk. As they arrived, her eyes widened fractionally at the sight of their stern faces.

She stood up and said, "Amara, Nuss." "What just happened? You both seem as if you saw a ghost."

Breathing deeply, Amara tried to settle the trembling in her voice. "We were targeted, Mayor. The attack occurred in broad daylight, precisely in the heart of the street. A group of vicious criminals. They specifically targeted me because they knew my name. She confronted Sholina directly, emphasizing the gravity of the situation. "I believe it relates to the map and the conspiracy you have been researching. I believe they were attempting to quiet me, therefore preventing my assistance in revealing the truth."

Sholina's face whitened at her words, a flash of terror awakening in her gaze. She raised one hand to rub her head, then firmly sank back into her chair.

She said, "Dear God," in a weak and strained voice. "I never would have imagined... I never could have anticipated their boldness. She turned back to them once again, her face hardening with will. "Are you confident that they were specifically targeting you?" Could you confirm that this wasn't just a random mugging?

Nuss groaned a grimy head shake. "No way. These men were not your typical street tough; they were professionals. They made it clear that they had specific criticisms of Amara. The muscles in his cheeks twitched as his jaw closed. He mentioned an incident involving inquisitive girls who lack self-control.

Sholina gasped fiercely at that and briefly closed her eyes. Amara could see a fresh steel in their depths as she reopened her eyes, a glimmer of pure will.

The mayor remarked gently, almost to herself, "These changes everything." "If they're willing to attack citizens in the street, to threaten and intimidate everyone who stands in their way..." She shook her head and drifted off. "We have to act swiftly. Before they can do more harm, we must identify and stop the conspirators."

Amara leant forward, steadying her palms on the desk's edge. "What should we be doing, Mayor? How may we be of service?"

Sholina studied her for a long time, something like reverence igniting in her eyes. "I need you, Amara, to be my ears and eyes. You and Nuss. People in this community trust you; you have ties here. Speak with them to find out if anybody else had noticed anything unusual. Are there any indications of dissatisfaction or signs of outsiders attempting to cause disruption?

She opened a small folder in a drawer and pushed it across the desk toward them. "And you will help me comprehend this terrible lineage map," she said. For days, I had been reading over it, attempting to find its secrets. Still, I find myself running into dead ends. Her gloomy attitude matched the sound of one finger tapping the folder. "I have a sense that whoever is behind this will be able to untangle this entire sordid affair using whatever this map is concealing. We must decipher its code before our opponents outwit us.

Reaching out to pick the folder, Nuss opened it to find a sheaf of glossy photos—high-resolution shots of the enigmatic lineage chart, photographed from every angle. He whistled softly, raising his eyebrows to reach his hairline.

"This is like some Da Vinci Code-level stuff," he said, running one finger over the rich scribble of symbols and cyphers covering the paper. "You weren't joking about it being a challenging task."

Sholina's smile was thin and devoid of humour. No, I was not. Still, I trust you two. The Johnson siblings can solve this mystery better than anyone else. She leant back in her chair, tucking her fingers under her chin. Amara, I am depending on you. I count on you, Nuss. These bastards cannot rule us. We cannot let them ruin what we have so laboriously created here."

Rising in her throat, Amara flooded with feelings—a complicated tangle of dread and resolve mixed with intense, protective love for her home and people. Reaching out to grab Sholina's hand, she showed unity by feeling the mayor's fingers tighten around her own.

"We won't let you down, Mayor," she said with enormous certainty. "If this conspiracy shows up on our map, we will locate and stop those behind it. Whatever it takes is irrelevant. Igbuzor is going to obtain justice. That is a pledge.

Beside her, Nuss grimly nodded, his eyes gleaming with the same resolve. Damn right, we will. These idiots chose a town to tamper with incorrectly. They have no idea what they have unleashed.

Sholina stared for a long time, something like hope sparking deep in her eyes. "I believe you," she answered quietly. And I'm thankful—more than I can express. She inhaled deeply and squared her shoulders as if preparing for combat. "Let's start working now. We have town to rescue and a mystery to unravel. Time is also not on our side.

In the secret maze, the three of them hunched over the map. The sun sank below the horizon outside, darkening Igbuzor. But in the mayor's office, a new light had started to blossom: the fiery, unquenchable light of optimism—a people unified in defence of their home and their way of life.
No matter what happened, the light would continue to shine. Amara would see to it that way. For Igbuzor and for everyone who called it home, she would fight to last.

The struggle for the soul of the town had started.

Chapter 12

The Cave

Deeper into her study of Igbuzor's historical background, Amara came across an old book that drew her eye. The fragile pages held mysterious sections that hinted at a powerful relic buried millennia ago. The book detailed a lineage map, a convoluted path that guides the chosen individual to this potent relic and ensures their arrival before they unintentionally cause the town's destruction.

Intrigued, Amara examined the fading ink attentively in search of the mysterious signals. She pondered why it was so difficult for Mayor Sholina to decipher these words; the more she read, the more convinced she became that this lineage chart was authentic and held the key to revealing a long-hidden secret. She knew she had to discover it to sort the mysteries of Igbuzor's history and maybe even influence its present.

Amara, resolved with fresh will, went out to gather additional data, knowing that the road ahead would be dangerous and difficult. Equipped with the understanding that the lineage map would be her lighthouse to her and the fate of the igbuzor, she was ready to face whatever lay ahead.

Over Igbuzor, a suffocating blanket of blackness broken only by the weak illumination of streetlamps and the sporadic flutter of lightning on the horizon, the night hung heavily. Amara bent over her damaged coffee table in the little space of her lounge room, the enigmatic lineage chart laid out before her like a challenge.

She had been gazing at the dreaded object for hours, until the symbols and cyphers started to appear before her fatigued eyes. Besides her, Nuss lay on the worn-out sofa, flipping over a dog-eared cypher manual with his long legs dangling over the armrest.

"Any luck?" Amara inquired, her voice strained with weariness and irritation.

Nuss shook his head, grunting as he threw the guidebook away. " Nothing. Though I have tried every code-breaking device available, this one is unlike Fort Knox. The creator of this map genuinely intended for its secrets to remain unbroken."

Amara moaned and caressed her sharp eyes. She had thought that the lineage chart might be somewhat advanced, given her analytical mind and Nuss's expertise in adventures, riddles, and codes. All they had so far to show for their efforts, however, were frayed tempers and weary necks.

"There must be something missing," she said, speaking more to herself than to Nuss. There must be a pattern or reasoning that guides the placement of the symbols. The cartographer who created this wouldn't have expended so much effort to create an incomprehensible mess.

Nuss sat up, swung his legs off the sofa, and slanted forward to see the map. "Maybe we're coming at this from the wrong angle," he said, his brow wrinkled in contemplation. "We've treated it like simple code, easily understood by reason and inference. But suppose it exceeds that? What if we are overlooking a layer of significance? Amara scowled, weighing his comments. "What do you mean?"

With one finger, Nuss ran over the thick scribble of symbols on the lineage map. "Observe the arrangement of these symbols. They create patterns, not simply happenings. Their recurring themes resemble a unique language. He raised his gaze to her, clearly excited. "What if the key is that? If the lineage map aims to convey a story or a message beyond its literal interpretation, then it also holds true.

At his words, Amara had an electric rush down her spine. She saw suddenly, with a flash of clarity, that he was correct. The map represented a narrative to unravel, not merely a puzzle to solve. A hidden history awaited revelation.

She gasped, grabbing the closest pen and paper, of course. "We have lost sight of the whole picture by concentrating so much on the individual symbols." We must see the map holistically and attempt to interpret the narrative it is presenting."

Once again, they bent their heads over the map, this time driven by a different goal. As they worked over the mysterious marks, picking out connections and patterns they had missed earlier, minutes turned into hours. Gradually, laboriously, a picture of old secrets and hidden powers—of a town with a destiny much greater than any of its residents had ever dreamed—started to emerge from the tumult.

"Look here," Nuss exclaimed abruptly, pointing in the centre of the lineage map at a cluster of symbols. "These symbols repeat constantly in a certain order. They seem to be creating a kind of road map. The map stretches from the centre of Igbuzor to its edges. Amara leant in closer, her heart thumping with delight. "You are correct. Consider the emblem that appears at the beginning and end of the path. It's more detailed than the others. somewhat like a keyhole."

Nuss gazed back at her, his eyes wide with insight. "What if this lineage chart also reveals a physical location?" Amara asked. What if it's guiding us toward something else, something hidden, such as a real person?

Amara shivered, a tingle of foreboding lighting every nerve on her spine. "The secrets of Igbuzor," she spoke, her voice filled with respect and wonder. "The information lost from our forebears. Nuss, you have cracked it. This map is a road map, a trail of breadcrumbs guiding us to the most secret of the town.

They just gazed at one another for a long, heated minute, the weight of their findings hanging thick between them. Then Nuss's face broke gradually into a wide, exultant smile.
"Well then," he murmured, excitedly rubbing his hands together. "I suppose we need to begin along the yellow brick road. It appears that we are on our way to meet the magician."

Laughing at that, Amara felt an unexpected wave of ecstatic happiness rising in her chest. After all the anxiety and uncertainty of the last several days—attacks and the danger of conspiracy—it felt amazing to finally have a clear lead. There was a glimmer of hope amidst the darkness.
She added, immediately grabbing for her phone: "We have to tell Mayor Sholina." "She has to know what we discovered. If this lineage chart yields any secret information, whether it be human or power-related, it could provide the means to suppress the disturbance in Igbuzor.

Nuss nodded, his countenance austere. "In agreement. But Amara, let's exercise caution. If the wrong people find out about the development of our map, it could intensify the focus on our retreat goal. We cannot afford any more ambushes or slips-through.
Amara felt a flutter of discomfort at his remarks, recalling the icy hate the attackers held in her eyes. Nuss was correct; they were walking on dangerous terrain now, and one misstep might mean catastrophe.

Then she thought about her parents, who had been dead for a long time but were still very vividly alive in her memories. She remembered their unwavering commitment to justice, regardless of the consequences. She considered her hospital patients, and the innocent lives the recent violence had destroyed. She would do everything to protect Jiu and their uncertain new love.

She also understood, with consistent, relentless clarity, that there was no going back now. This was not just for Iggy, but also for her. Regardless of the circumstances, they remained engaged in this battle until the very end.

"We'll be careful," she said, staring squarely at her brother. "We cannot allow fear to nevertheless control us. We can't let fear rule us right now when we are so close to the truth. Iggy needs us, Nuss. We must persevere through the danger.

Nuss stared for a long, searching time. Then he stretched out gently to grab her shoulder, his grasp firm and solid.

"Together," he answered simply, his voice ringing with subdued clarity. "We confront it together regardless of what transpires. As we usually have.

Emotionally, Amara felt her throat constrict with love and gratitude for this courageous, unwavering guy who had always been her rock—her constancy in a world of tumult.

"Together," she said, the weight of that promise sinking into her bones. an everlasting, unbreakable covenant.

They then went back to the lineage map, to the meandering road leading them into the core of Igbuzor's most hidden knowledge. They ventured into the future, where fate awaited them.

Chapter 13

Crystal Smoke

Dawn was nothing more than a faint hint on the eastern horizon as Amara and Nuss slid over the quiet streets of Igbuzor, the enigmatic lineage map tightly in hand. The town was still asleep in the forgotten grip of dreams. For the two siblings, however, there could be no more sleep. They couldn't rest until they witnessed the fulfillment of their mission.

Their footsteps ringing abnormally loud in the predawn silence, they walked like ghosts over the meandering alleyways and little pathways. The terrible sensation Amara felt—that malevolent eyes were following every step they took from the shadows—was intolerable. But every time she turned to check her shoulder, the streets behind her were as silent as a stopped breath.

At last they arrived at the location where the enigmatic path of the map started—an unassuming length of crumbling brick wall in an abandoned area of the ancient town. Amara held up the map, staring in the faint light at the thick scribble of symbols.

"This is it," she said, tracing her finger over the intricate symbol that marks the start of the road. "The keyhole. The start of the trip."

Nuss pushed in closer; his brow wrinkled as he examined the fading bricks. The town teems with ancient walls. Are you sure we're in the right place? I don't see anything special about this spot."

Amara nodded, a tingle of confidence galloping down her spine. She turned to face him, a sardonic smirk tugging at her lips. "I'm sure. The map is clear. This is where the trail starts." This is where the trail begins.

Nuss squatted and shook his head. He straightened himself, straightening his shoulders, "guess not. Would have been nice, though." " Alright then. Lead on, Captain Amara. Let's explore the depths of this journey.

With their eyes fixed on the lineage chart, they embarked on a journey down the narrow street lane, following its winding path deeper into the heart of the ancient Igbuzor Road.

The ancient structures here bore scarlet, pitted faces, a result of decades of exposure to wind and rain. Amara constantly felt like they were walking over a forgotten part of history where modern norms didn't apply. They were travelling outside of time.

The lineage map led them on a meandering path, where they would turn back on themselves and deviate offside streets seemingly at will. Over time, Amara began to worry that they had missed the road and that the mysterious symbols were merely a game. However, each time hopelessness threatened to overwhelm her, they would discover another of the unusual symbols etched on a lintel or a paving stone, guiding them forward.

They were standing before a generic gateway built into a crumbling stone wall as the sun started to ascend higher in the sky, casting the town in tunes of gold and rose. The building it belonged to seemed long deserted, its windows boarded up, and its roof collapsing under years' weight.
Amara said, "This is it," holding out the lineage chart with a quivering palm. "The end of the path. The keyhole reminds me of the last time I visited this part of the town when we were younger.

Nuss wrinkled his forehead, gazing sceptically at the crumbling construction. "You sure about that, sis? It appears to be more conducive to the spread of tetanus than to the use of secret ancestral knowledge to aid Igbuzor.

Amara threw him a quelling glance, but she couldn't quite quell the flutter of uncertainty his words sent off. He made a point: there was nothing overtly amazing about the decaying wreck in front of them.

Another lost husk in a community with already too many.
A taut, alert tone in the quiet that enveloped them signalled to her that they were on the verge of a revelation that would transform everything. A barrier, once impenetrable, now stands poised for breach.

Amara inhaled deeply, then stretched out to grab the corroded door handle. Upon touching it, the door handle felt rough due to its age and neglect. It was frigid. She briefly worried it might be locked and their trip wasted.

Then, with a moan of protesting hinges, the door opened to spew a blast of stale, musty air. Beyond, a little stair descended into darkness, the tread of many feet worn smooth on its steps. Amara looked long and angrily at Nuss. She saw the same mixed exhilaration and apprehension he described—the same heady combination of fear and reckless expectation.

"No turning back now," he said, the very faintest of a smile playing at the corner of his lips. "You ready for this, sister?"

Amara straightened her shoulders and experienced an instantaneous surge of strong, unquestionable will. She thought about her parents and the sacrifices they had made to give her a better life.

She thought about Jiu and their fragile newly formed marriage.
Mayor Sholina bravely fought for Igbuzor's soul.
Startled by the force in her own voice, she responded, "I'm ready."
"Let us finish this for Igbuzor."

And they passed the barrier into the dark, waiting. The steps seemed to go on endlessly, a meandering trip to the very depths of the planet. Amara saw a rising sensation of unreality with every stride, as if they were straying into a world of myth and darkness from the concrete, sunny world behind.
Just as she was beginning to worry that they might sink permanently,

the steps suddenly stopped, leading her into a small, musty-smelling room. Redolent with the aroma of old dust and long-forgotten secrets, the air was dense and tight.

"Where are we?" Nuss spoke in a startlingly loud voice amidst the surrounding silence. "What is this place?" This place suggests the Tailor's farmhouse tales in Amara's childhood memory. As an adult, Amara never anticipated being in these kinds of circumstances. Amara shook her head and gestured to the lineage map with a quivering palm. "I'm not sure. This is where the keyhole symbol was guiding us, but what is here then, and how will this help us?"

Her gaze darted forward, cutting through the darkness. She noticed the hazy shapes of shelves filled with decaying scrolls and leatherbound volumes, as they gradually adapted to the dimness. In the centre of the chamber, a stone pedestal rose from the floor, adorned with a thick scribble of the same mysterious characters found on the lineage chart.
"Nuss," she said, her heart suddenly thumping into her ribs. Amara whispered, "I think...this is it," Nuss interjected. This is the treasure trove of our ancestors' vanishing knowledge. For generations, the secrets of Igbuzor remained concealed. The Reverend Okafor family once owned it, I believe. The Reverend Okafor family must have abandoned it many generations ago, as I remember playing around that area.

She moved closer to the pedestal, her hand out to touch the chilly, coarsely hewed stone. But before her fingers could touch, a low, mocking laugh broke the quiet—a low, mocking giggle that rose the hairs on the back of her neck and sent cold water coursed through her veins.
"Oh, I'm afraid it's a bit more than that," a voice from the shadows whispered. The secrets buried here belong to more than just Igbuzor. They belong to me—my family. Now that you've found them, I'm afraid I can't let you leave this place unscathed; this is my family's

legacy, and only the archivist Ikenga is authorized to access it but now you've crossed the boundary.

Amara whirled, her heart in her throat. Rising from the shadows like a spectre of anxiety, Reverend Okafor was there. But gone was the mask of moral virtue he wore for the residents. He replaced his mask with a pure, unvarnished hate grin, exposing the rot underneath. Amara murmured, "You," as a wave of icy, creeping terror swept over her. "Behind the turmoil, the violence. The conspiracy threatening Igbuzor was you all along."

Okafor's grin only grew wider at that; his eyes sparkled with a manic, frantic brightness. He stepped forward, his hands splayed in a hideous caricature of humility. "Oh, you have no idea, my dear. You have no idea at all; this comes from inheritance.

His voice dropped to a hiss, loaded with venom. "This town is mine on behalf of our family lineage." It's always been mine. And the power buried here, the secrets locked away—they will make me a king to rule over a new Igbuzor when your so-called mayor is displaced. The great archivist Ikenga have anointed Mr Okerie as the new mayor to preserve our legacy." "And I will not allow two meddling rats to stand in my way."

Nuss moved forward, straying between Amara and the oncoming lunatic. "You're insane," he growled, his hands closing at his sides. "Igbuzor will never bow to a monster like you. We'll stop you, whatever it takes."

Okafor laughed and flung back his head—a sound of sheer, unrestrained malevolence. "Stop me? Oh, you poor, deluded climber boy. You have no idea what you are up against. The forces I have unleashed...they are beyond your wildest imagining."

He lifted one hand, his fingers contorting into a hideous claw. "But don't worry; you will learn. Oh yes, you will learn. You will beg me for the mercy of death once I have broken your minds and ground your souls to dust: "And I will savour every last scream."

Then he shot forward, his visage a mask of snarling, inhuman rage. Amara yelled and flung herself backwards as Nuss surged to squarely meet the attack. The room went crazy—a swirl of animalistic roars of wrath and wrestling bodies.

Amara, her hands trembling, fumbled at the pedestal, searching for anything that could help them. Her fingertips touched a secret catch, and a panel opened, revealing a small chamber with a grinding sound.

Nestled on a bed of disintegrating velvet, there was a fist-sized crystal shining with an inner brightness like a live heart. Amara grabbed it and felt a sharp bolt of electric heat burn through her hand before the room started to smoke.
She whirled to face the fight blazing behind her, yelling, "Nuss!"
"The crystal! It's some kind of... gun! Use it!"
Nuss, his face smeared with blood, struggled free from Okafor's grasp and reached for her outstretched hand. His fingers wrapped around the crystal, and the chamber burst in a blinding flash of light at that same moment.

Okafor staggered back, agonizingly screaming as he scratched his eyes. Amara gasped raggedly as she blinked away the dots dancing in her sight.
Nuss had his crystal gripped to his chest and stood tall. Surrounded by a nimbus of glittering energy, it cracked and surged like a live creature. His words had a force that sent goosebumps running down Amara's spine.

"It's over, Okafor," he said, the words resonating with a terrible, unearthly sound. "The power you sought to claim... belongs to the people of Igbuzor, to those who would use it for good, not for selfish gain. You are not the intended recipients of this power.

He lifted the crystal high, and the glow—the smoke—became more intense, filling the space with a terrible, burning light. "Now feel the wrath of the people—the judgement of the common people of Igbuzor." Feel their power...and despair."

The fumes shot forward, consuming Okafor in a blaze of burning, cleansing smoke. The reverend yelled a shrill, agonized screech that continued endlessly until it reached an intolerable crescendo. Then it ended abruptly, just as it had begun.

Okafor dropped to the ground; his body twitched and smoked. Amara moved gingerly forward, scarcely daring to breathe. Was it quite completed? Have they really won?
However, Okafor's eyes opened as soon as the idea crossed her mind. But instead of the angry, terrible gaze she had anticipated, Okafor's eyes were bright and coherent, bursting with tears of relief.

The reverend said, "Thank you," his voice raspy and weak. "Thank you... for releasing me from this generational devil. I was born into the darkness of the lineage—the evil that possessed me—but now I'm free. Banished by the light of this crystal, I never knew that was all I needed to be free."

His face twisted with agony and regret as he battled to sit up. "The things I did, the horrors I unleashed on Igbuzor, were not intentional, the archivist will have my head if I didn't carry out the lineage plans." I will never be able to atone for my actions; I was coerced into them; I was not alone in this; however, please, please, believe that it wasn't me. Not really. The real me...the man I used to be would never have done such things; I lost control; this is more of a spiritual warfare targeted on me due to my clergy status's."

Amara gazed at Nuss for a considerable amount of time before becoming charged. Would that be accurate? Could the power of the crystal have really banished the darkness that had settled inside Okafor's soul?

There was no certainty at all. But Amara saw a flutter of something that could have been hope as she looked into the reverend's eyes and felt the unvarnished suffering swimming in their depths. Maybe it was just the release of a struggle waged and won—the assurance that, for now at least, the gloom had been kept at a distance.

She murmured gently, "We believe you," and reached out to assist Okafor to his feet. "And we forgive you; the evil that controlled you...it's the true enemy here; not the man you used to be, and not the man you could be again."

Nuss nodded, his fingers dropped, and the glitter of the gem dimmed. "Amara's right. What really matters now is how you take advantage of this second chance. How do you use it to make amends, to heal the wounds you helped inflict on Igbuzor?"

Okafor's eyes gleamed with a sharp, driven fire. "I will spend the rest of my days doing just that. I swear to the power that freed me and the memory of the man I once was. Look around the chamber, at the ancient secrets and forgotten lore that line its walls," he said. "And I will start by sharing the knowledge hidden here with the people. I am the only surviving person in that lineage now. We all own the wisdom of our ancestors, the authentic history of Igbuzor crystals, and politics.

The archivists Ikenga and Mr. Okerie will no longer hoard it in darkness; instead, we will bring it into the light.

Amara felt a tangled mix of relief, tiredness, and dizziness, with an unbelieving pleasure swelling in her throat. They were successful in this. Despite all the challenges, they successfully unravelled the plot that threatened their house and emerged victorious.

She knew their task was far from over, even as she enjoyed the victory. The recent events have left Igbuzor town damaged, and the recent anarchy and bloodshed have traumatized its inhabitants. Months, even years, of healing those wounds and restoring the trust and togetherness that had been so severely broken would be the task.

But they would still do it. all together.   Just as they had battled against the darkness, they would now dedicate themselves to the task of mending the damage. After all, what did Igbuzor excel at? Igbuzor emerged from the wreckage, displaying greater vibrancy and strength than before.

Amara turned to face Nuss, a faltering grin on her lips. She said, "We should go." "After all they have gone through, Mayor Sholina needs to know what has happened, and the people deserve to hear the truth."
Nuss nodded, reverently sliding the stone into his pocket. "Lead the way, little sister. It's time Iggy learned just what kind of heroes it has in its midst."

And they started the protracted ascent back to the surface—back to the sunny streets and the waiting arms of the town they loved. The storm endured; the war ended. Even though the wounds it left would always be visible, Amara knew that Igbuzor would emerge from this furnace stronger than ever.

They were humans, sculpted by intense fires and tempered by adversity to become unbreakable. And they would confront whatever evil the future contained, as they always had.

In unison. They acted courageously, compassionately, and with unwavering trust in the ability of the human spirit to overcome any challenge.
Igbuzor would go through. And ultimately, it was the biggest triumph of all.

Epilogue

As Amara walked over the meandering lanes of the ancient town, the sun was falling low over the roofs of Igbuzor, casting the heavens in tones of fire and gold. A month had passed since the last confrontation under the deserted home—a month since the plot threatening to split their community had been pulled, whirling and growling, into the light.

Lots had changed throughout that period. True to his pledge, Reverend Okafor dedicated his body and soul to healing the wounds he had helped create; now, he was under the influence of his former friends, The Archivist and Okerie. Under his guidance and with Mayor Sholina's support, he shared the ancestors' hidden wisdom with every Igbuzor resident, serving as a reminder of their shared rich history and culture.

Amara had never seen the community come together like this before, united in their efforts to rebuild the damage. Previously suspicious neighbours now work side by side; their disagreements are forgotten in the face of a shared purpose. Slowly, the conspiracy's wounds began to heal, giving way to a renewed sense of community and direction.

Regarding Amara personally, the hard-earned lessons of the past had helped her define her new rhythm in life. Her job at the hospital and her NGO continued, but now she tackled it from a different angle, with a greater awareness of the part she performed in the fabric of Igbuzor. And always by her side was Jiu—her rock, her comfort, the consistent flame guiding her across even the darkest of nights.

After enduring their shared struggles, Nuss also found a new path. The power of the crystal and the knowledge it had given had aroused something in him—a longing to explore the secrets buried in the lost corners of history, to go further into the mysteries of the earth mountains. Following the paths left by old maps and decaying books, he had started a road of his own. Drawn by the strong bond of family and the assurance that he would always have a home waiting for him, he nevertheless always returned to Igbuzor.

Atop a hill, Amara looked out over the rooftops of the town that had shaped her—the community that had made her who she was. The big baobab tree, which had been a quiet guard over the town for millennia, stood in the centre of Igbuzor, its twisted limbs extending to the distant heavens.

She considered her parents, long gone but never forgotten, and of the legacy they gave her—one of strength, compassion, and an unquestionable devotion to the greater good. She considered her neighbours, friends, and the many lives she had affected personally and in turn. She believed she would never want to be anywhere else.

For Igbuzor, it was more than simply a town she grew up in—more than just a collection of streets, buildings, and people. It was a living, breathing creature—a drapery spun from the hopes, hardships, and victories of millennia. Even if the strands frayed and darkness tugged at the weave's edges, the pattern would endure, retaining its brilliance and vividness.

Amara grinned, a surge of strong, unquestionable affection building in her chest. They cherish this community, these individuals, and the resilience that united them. Regardless of the circumstances, they would approach each task with a burning passion and a confident demeanour, enduring every challenge.

And Amara turned her feet towards home, towards the cosy hug of all the people she loved as the final light of day painted the heavens in tones of splendour. The journey ahead would be lengthy and far from complete. She knew, however, now and always, that she would never walk it alone.

Igbuzor had lived through. Igbuzor would live. Ultimately, therefore, it was all that counted. The love, hope, and unbreakable spirit that bound them would always bind them.

As all living entities must, the settlement would develop and alter. Old faces would disappear into memory; new ones would arrive. However, the essence of Igbuzor—the vibrant spirit that defined its essence—would persist, serving as a constant beacon amidst the darkness.

If that light continued to burn and the residents of Igbuzor remained united, they could endure any storm, extinguish any fire, and triumph over any darkness.

Because they were one. They were Igbuzor. And at last, it was enough. That was everything.

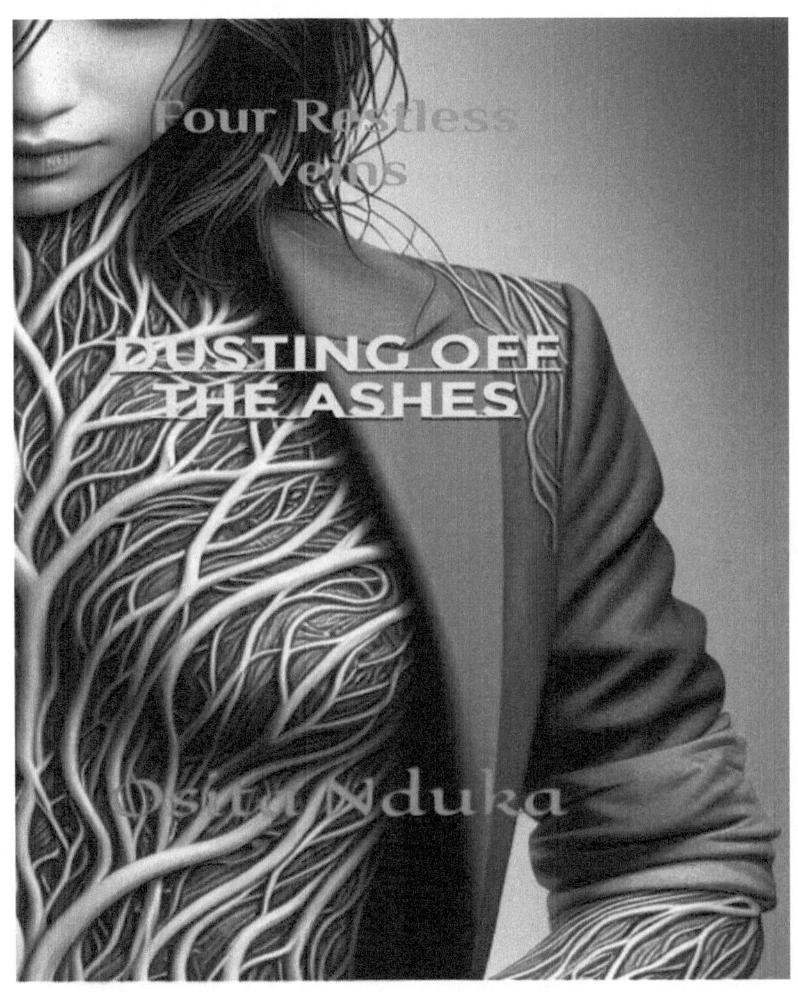

BOOK IV

Main Characters

Dr. Amara Johnson – Doctor at Igbuzor General Hospital, founder of Hope for Tomorrow Foundation

Jiu Adekunle- Amara's husband and supportive partner

Dr. Patel Sharma- Amara's mentor at the hospital

Dr. John Anderson- Amara's colleague and friend

Nuss and Zarah Johnson- Amara's foster siblings

Felicia D'Silva - Young patient with a mysterious illness

Torino Akpan - 7-year-old foster child Amara helps

Jamie Etienne - Newborn baby born with drug addiction

Mayor Sholina Okoye - Mayor of Igbuzor

Vivian Ajayi Opobo- Former foster youth who speaks at the town hall meeting

Rajendra Kumar Singh- Amara's colleague from medical school

Rev Okafor Solomon Christian – Clergyman from indigenous family who inherited secrets about Igbuzor

Key Locations

Igbuzor - The town where the story is set

Igbuzor General Hospital - Main full-time workplace of Amara

Hope for Tomorrow Foundation - Amara's NGO located at Block B in the community Centre

Igbuzor Children's Home - Local foster care center located in the heart of Igbuzor

Igbuzor Community center – Large building location for meetings and events

Igbuzor Town square - Site of the annual Community Day festival

Prologue

Rising from the streets below, the golden light of the evening sun warmed the busy metropolis of Igbuzor, creating an ensemble of sights and noises. Among these colourful depictions of life was the soaring Igbuzor Community centre housing the local general Hospital and Hope for tomorrow's foundation among other services, it a one stop junction that serves as a beacon of hope for those in need.

On the rooftop of this magnificent institution stood a woman of extraordinary fortitude and will. Her white coat blowing in the soft air, Dr. Amara Johnson looked out at the vast metropolis before her. She felt a mixture of excitement and fear as she contemplated the significance of this momentous occasion.

This was not just another hospital day for Amara; it was the start of her journey as a wife and mother. She had produced a gorgeous pair of twins. That was a turning point in her life, evidence of the relentless spirit that had seen her through the worst of circumstances.

Memories of the past year flooded her mind, each one a vivid reminder of the challenges she had faced and the path she had chosen.

She reminisced about the day her life fell apart—the political turmoil that threatened to destroy the entire town—and the day she received a crippling disease diagnosis, leaving her paralysed and questioning her future as a doctor. The next months were a haze of hospital visits, demanding physical therapy sessions, and many hours of uncertainty.

Amara had, nevertheless, not given up even in her worst hours. She had battled fiercely to recover her life with the relentless support of her husband, Jiu, her foster siblings, Nuss and Zarah, her close group of friends in Emily and Lilly among others. She had relearned how to walk, how to stand, and how to hope once again, step by agonizingly slow step.

Now, she stood tall and proud, poised to resume her career in medicine following a thorough evaluation of her abilities. She understood that the path forward would not be simple. Long hours, difficult situations, and times of self-doubt would all abound. Amara, however, was ready. She was ready to don her white coat and stethoscope once more, ready to transform the lives of her patients.

Still, her mind drifted to another calling as she stood there, one that drew at her heart with equal intensity. Given her personal experiences, her work with her NGO—which she had started to assist and empower foster children—has fresh urgency. Raised in the foster system, she was all too familiar with the sorrow and difficulty of feeling lost and alone in a society that seemed insensitive to her misery.
Amara closed her eyes, the faces of the kids she had met via her non-profit flickering before her. She had found enormous resonance in their tales of optimism and fortitude, even in the face of unthinkable hardship. She understood that her work reached right into the heart of her neighbourhood—beyond the hospital's boundaries.

Amara inhaled deeply as the sun sank below the horizon, filling her lungs with warm, energizing air. Though it was a weight she carried with pride and resolve, she could feel her obligations pressing down on her shoulders.

She realized this was her calling—her opportunity to really change the planet. She would be striving toward a better, more compassionate future with every patient she saw, every youngster she coached, and every injustice she battled.

And so, Amara went towards the door, prepared to welcome the difficulties and successes that lie ahead, with a last look at the brilliant city below. Rising from the wreckage of her own challenges, she was now prepared to support others in doing the same.

As she retreated into the hospital hallways, she turned to see the rooftop sliding away behind her. She smiled. Amara was back where she belonged, creating a path of hope and resiliency that would be evident for everyone to follow.

Sholina effectively won her election and carried on as the mayor of Igbuzor until the flames that had threatened to destroy the town were under control. Amara loved this moment of accomplishment, but she couldn't get rid of the thought of the enigmatic man who had approached her at the local festival only weeks ago with a book from Rev. Okafor, which she had not been able to access yet. Though it remained unread, the leather-bound book he had pushed into her hands now lay buried in her office drawer, its mysterious contents suggesting disclosures that may once again challenge the entire basis of her identity and her whole profession.

Amara was walking down the hospital hallway when the familiar noises and smells from the nurse's station abruptly interrupted her thoughts. With a look of concern on his face, Dr. John began to sprint towards her.
"Amara," he said, struggling to catch his breath. Thank you, God, you are here. We are currently dealing with an emergency room issue. Several of the patients arrived with symptoms they had never seen before. No medical literature had documented these symptoms.

Amara locked eyes with her colleague, a chill running down her spine. She knew then that her comeback into medicine would not be typical. As she hurriedly accompanied Dr. John to the emergency room, Amara couldn't shake the thought that this mysterious ailment had a connection to the secrets concealed in that book, given that Rev. Okafor's family has consistently been associated with secrets.

She inhaled deeply, straightening herself for whatever was ahead. Even as the echoes of prophecies and long-buried facts murmured in the back of her mind, she was Dr. Amara Johnson, ready to meet this new challenge head-on.
The ER's doors opened, and Amara moved forward into a fresh chapter of her remarkable journey—one that would challenge her abilities as a doctor, her bravery as an advocate, and her awareness of her own identity in ways she could never have predicted.

Part 1

MENTAL REFLECTIONS

Chapter 1

Practice Return

With a gentle whoosh, Igbuzor General Hospital's automated doors swung open to welcome Dr. Amara Johnson back into the field of healing and hope. She stopped for a minute, her heart bursting with both anxious expectation and nostalgia. Her grin came from the familiar smell of antiseptics and the subdued buzz of activity, reminding her of the many hours she had spent within these walls, committed to the honourable quest for medicine.

Her footsteps resounding on the polished floor as Amara made her way through the hallways, she couldn't help but consider the long and difficult road that had led her back to this moment. The preceding year had been an emotional rollercoaster, evidence of her unflinching spirit and the force of pure will.

She remembered the early days of her sickness and the conflicts the lineage map generated as the world seemed to fall apart around her. The diagnosis shattered her goals and cast a shadow over her future. Amara, paralysed from the waist down, had been facing the terrible reality that she would never walk again—let alone practice medicine. The fires in her village did not welcome her return to practice.

She had, nonetheless, resisted giving up to hopelessness even at her worst times. With the love and encouragement from her husband, Jiu, her foster siblings, Nuss and Zarah, and her closest friends, Amara found the strength to overcome the challenges. She had gradually gained control of her body through daily gruelling physical therapy sessions and many hours of rehabilitation.

Amara could feel her coworkers staring at her as she negotiated in the familiar hospital halls. Their looks combined astonishment, respect, and affection to recognize the amazing accomplishments she had made in getting back to work.

Amara turned the bend and came across two of the most powerful people in her medical profession right there. Her mentor from the beginning and lighthouse, Dr. Patel, stood next to her valued friend and confidante, Dr. John. When they saw her, their faces brightened with delight; their grins expressed the depth of their love and admiration.

Amara!" Dr. Patel spoke with pride and compassion in his voice. He moved forward, his arms out in a welcoming gesture. "It's really great to see you back where you belong."

As Amara embraced him, the familiar smell of his perfume brought back a rush of memories, and her throat tightened with emotion. Believing in her even when she had questioned herself, Dr. Patel had been a continual source of support and direction throughout her medical path.

"Thank you, Dr. Patel," she said, her voice heavy with appreciation. "Being here and having the chance to make a difference again means the world to me."

His eyes sparkling with mischief and respect, Dr. John said, "You've always made a difference, Amara. You never ceased motivating us with your courage and tenacity, even when you were battling your own challenges.
The praise made Amara flush, embarrassed by the trust her coworkers placed in her. "I couldn't have done it without all of you," she remarked gently, looking at both Dr. Patel and Dr. John. "Your encouragement and support enabled me to overcome even the most challenging days."

Dr. Patel nodded, his facial expression becoming more austere. "Amara, your accomplishments are truly remarkable." It's a testament to your remarkable character and determination to overcome a crippling disease and fight your way back to health.

Amara choked hard, his words weighing down her shoulders. She was aware that her path had been challenging, full of disappointments and depressing times. She had, nevertheless, held to the conviction that her life's goal was healing and that she could change the course of others' lives.

"I'm just grateful for the chance to be here, to continue the work that means so much to me," she added, her voice full of passion. "I'm ready to face whatever obstacles come my way; I know the road ahead won't be easy."

Dr. John reached out and placed a comforting hand on her shoulder. "And we will be by your side at every turn, Amara. You're family, not just a coworker. We are all here together.

Amara experienced a wave of warmth and thanks; the ties of friendship and a common goal enhanced her will. She knew she could conquer any hurdle and meet any challenge that lied ahead with the help of her loved ones and coworkers.

Amara felt a fresh sense of purpose and drive as the three of them stood there, bonded in their dedication to the honourable quest for medicine. She had come so far and battled so hard to take back her spot in the healing scene. She was now prepared to welcome her fate and change the lives of her patients and the neighbourhood.

Amara straightened her shoulders and moved ahead, prepared to start the next chapter of her remarkable trip, nodding one last time to Dr. Patel and Dr. John. Though she knew she had the courage, resiliency, and relentless support of those who believed in her, the path ahead would be full of challenges and victories.

And so, ready to accept her calling and leave her imprint on the world, Dr. Amara Johnson returned to the hallways of Igbuzor general Hospital, a heart full of optimism and a spirit forged in the furnace of hardship.

Chapter 2

Thermal checks

The boardroom at Igbuzor General Hospital was a spacious, well-furnished area cantered around a gleaming wooden table illuminated by the warm glow of recessed ceiling fittings. Amara sat at one end of the table, her posture straight and her expression calm, thereby releasing the tense energy coursing through her veins.

Her final reinstatement examination today would decide whether she could continue her full-time public hospital responsibilities as a doctor with the general hospital. Determined to show that she was ready to face the demands of her profession once again, Amara had spent several hours getting prepared for this meeting by reading case studies and medical publications. There has been a lot going on around Amara, and the board has seen everything and must assess her circumstances.

As the board members gathered in the room, Amara felt a flutter of anxiety. Among the most revered and powerful people in the hospital were some independent outside panel members—those with the ability to help determine her professional path. She knew several of them from her time as a medical student and resident, but there were also a few strange faces on the board since her sickness had brought fresh arrivals.

Leaning over Amara from her seat, Dr. Patel murmured, "Remember, Amara, you've earned this. To get here, you have worked more than everyone I know. Just be you and let your expertise and enthusiasm show.

Amara nodded, finding resonance in his words and the consistent presence of Dr. John on her other side. She knew that her colleagues thought of her, that they had personally seen the commitment and ability she brought to her job.
Amara inhaled deeply and concentrated on her present work as the conference chairman called it to order. She carefully noted each

board member's areas of expertise and their roles in the hospital hierarchy as they introduced themselves.
She then turned to start speaking. Getting to her feet, Amara launched her case with a strong, unambiguous voice. She explained her road, the challenges she had faced, and the ones she had overcome. She revealed her passion for medicine and her outstanding will to improve the lives of her patients.

As Amara dove into her medical knowledge and discussed the most effective patient care practices and most current treatment advancements, she could feel the board members' emotions shifting. A nod of approval and murmurs of gratitude began to replace the initial suspicion and anxiety on some of their faces.
Dr. Patel paused at one point to underline Amara's exceptional diagnostic skills and her aptitude to think imaginatively under tough conditions, pride shining in his eyes. Dr. John also left, mentioning stories of Amara's compassionate bedside manner and uncompromising patient care.

As the session progressed, Amara asked the board members questions; her responses were intentional and unambiguous. By emphasizing her recovery and the support system she had in place, she addressed their concerns about her ability to handle the rigors of her job.
The chairman finally called for a vote after what seemed like an eternity. Amara felt her heart hammering in her chest as each board member voted; the tension in the room was clear.
Amara experienced a wave of relief and happiness as the totals came together. Honouring her skills, determination, and unwavering commitment to her line of work, the board voted unanimously in favour of her reinstatement.
Amara's colleagues showered her with congratulations and delight as the conference ended. Dr. Patel exclaimed, "I knew you could do it, Amara," with his voice full of emotion and his arms around her. I genuinely appreciate you.

His wide-ranging, infectious grin grew as he continued, "Welcome back, Dr. Johnson. The hospital would be different without you.
The flood of love and encouragement from her colleagues overwhelmed Amara and caused tears to prickle at the edges of her

eyes. She knew that long hours and challenging cases would abound, that the path ahead would be arduous, and that there would be times of uncertainty and frustration.

But at that very moment, among the people who had believed in her and supported her through the darkest of times, Amara had a feeling of belonging, of purpose, and of unflinching determination.
She had battled her way to this moment, demonstrating to both the world and herself her ability to overcome even the most formidable challenges. With her white coat once again slung over her shoulders and her stethoscope around her neck, Dr. Amara Johnson was ready to embrace her career and help alter the lives of her patients and her community.

With a final thank you to the members and a touch of Dr. Patel's hand, Amara left the boardroom head held high and her heart exploding with excitement. Having the strength of her values and the support of those who believed in her, the future was clear, and she was prepared to face it straight.

Chapter 3

Days rush

The emergency room at Igbuzor General Hospital was a hive of activity, a symphony of worried voices, beeping equipment, and racing feet. Pausing at the entrance, Amara peered at the under-control chaos before her as her pulse surged with both excitement and worry.

Her new duty was the emergency room, where every second counts and every choice can perhaps save a life. Amara exhaled deeply, preparing herself for the challenges ahead, her first day back in the emergency department after licence validation as a physician with the public hospital.

Amara felt a surge of excitement pumping through her veins as she entered the confusion. Her familiar sights and sounds—the sharp scent of antiseptic mixing with the metallic taste of blood—washed over her. Her coworkers were staring at her, some inquisitive, others dubious, all observing to see how she would handle pressure.

Amara ignored the whispers of self-doubt that tried to enter her head and concentrated on the current work. She went to the nurses' station, where a charge nurse, appearing stressed, was yelling commands into a phone.
Amara responded, her voice crisp and calm, "Dr. Johnson, reporting for duty." "Where do you require me?"

Looking up from her papers, seasoned veteran Jing, the charge nurse, widened in astonishment. "Dr. Johnson, you're very pleasant. Her tone, a combination of respect and worry, "I didn't expect to see you back so soon in full time." "Are you ready for this?"
Amara locked eyes with Jing, her face set. "I'm ready," she said forcefully."

Jing nodded, a flutter of appreciation playing over her features. "All well, then. In Exam Room 3, a middle-aged man complaining of shortness of breath and chest discomfort sits patiently. Likely heart attack. Could you please take it?"

The reference to a serious case sent Amara on an adrenaline rush; her mind was already running over the diagnostic procedures and course of therapy. She said, snatching the patient's chart and walking towards the exam room, "I'm on it."

Amara saw a guy slumped on the gurney as she pulled open the door; his face was pallid and damp, and his breathing was laboured. She could see the terror in his eyes, the unsung cry for aid.
Calm and soothing, Amara responded, "Hello, sir." "Here to assist you is me, Dr. Johnson. How may I help you today?"

Amara listened closely as the patient started to explain his problems, her thoughts lightning fast as she absorbed the data. She started developing a treatment schedule after ordering an EKG, blood testing, and a chest X-ray.
Amara expertly stabilised the patient's condition alongside the nurses and technicians, amidst a whirlwind of activity. She watched vital signs, gave drugs, and made quick judgements depending on the often-shifting information before her.

Though the scenario was high stakes, Amara felt a serenity come over her—a clarity of goal refined over years of training and experience. She was aware that every act she did and every directive she issued might turn a life around.

Amara felt relief flood over her as the patient's condition started to get better. She had overcome the initial challenge of returning to work and emerged victorious. She could see the patient's eyes light up with unsaid appreciation for her talent and effort.
However, she had no time to rest on her achievements. As soon as the patient became stable, Jing was at the door with a fresh case file in hand. Dr. Johnson, a vehicle-stricken six-year-old girl, is on her way to paediatric trauma. ETA Two minutes.

Amara nodded; her thoughts had turned to be ready for the next fight. She was aware that the path ahead would be long and challenging, and pain and success would abound. Yet she found herself exactly where she should have been, pursuing her passions and enhancing the lives of her patients.

Amara felt a sense of purpose and resolve created in the furnace of her own hardships as she hurried towards the ambulance bay, ready to meet whatever obstacles were ahead. She had battled her way back to this point, showing the world and herself that she was capable of conquering even the toughest of challenges.

Now, with her obligations firmly on her shoulders, Dr. Amara Johnson was ready to welcome her destiny, to be the lighthouse of hope and healing that society so sorely needed. Though she knew she had the strength, the resiliency, and the consistent support of those who believed in her, the road ahead would be full of challenges and successes.

Chapter 4

The Charts

With her brow wrinkled in concentration, Amara pored over the medical file in her hands as the fluorescent lights buzzed quietly above. Felicia D'Silva, her newest patient, was standing outside the waiting room in the paediatrics unit. An unidentified sickness had brought Felicia to the hospital, her symptoms confusing and conflicting. She had been suffering from a high fever for days, her petite frame tormented by shivers and tiredness. The first blood tests came back negative, leaving Amara and her staff searching for explanations. Amara's stomach started to hurt as she looked over Felicia's past. She was always uneasy. This case felt as if it was a missing component from the larger picture, a piece that didn't quite fit.

Amara glanced over the chart one more time, inhaled deeply, and pushed open Felicia's chamber door. Her eyes clouded with fever; a little figure buried in a sea of white sheets stared at her with a pale, drawn face.
Felicia's mother, a young lady with worn eyes and a troubled appearance, turned up from her vigil by her daughter's bedside at the sound of Amara's footsteps. Her voice quivering with passion, she added, "Dr. Johnson." "Please, can you help my baby?"
Amara was sympathetic to the young mother when she saw her eyes ablaze with dread and hopelessness. She had seen that look many times before in the traits of parents whose dreadful hand of sickness had turned their children's world upside down.

"Mrs. Adebayo D'Silva," Amara said in a kind but authoritative voice. "I promise to help Felicia to the best of my capabilities. together, we can properly handle this."

As Felicia spoke, Amara arrived at her bedside; her hands moved with deliberate simplicity as she began her examination. She looked at the girl's vital signs, listened to her breathing, and probed her abdomen in search of any clues that might help explain her circumstances.

But as the minutes went by, Amara's irritation grew. She gave it her all but couldn't seem to get a diagnosis. Felicia's symptoms ranged widely and resisted the neat categories and practices of modern medicine.

Amara struggled to completely understand the fight the little child's body was involved in. She asked for further scans, tests, and expert visits, but every new piece of information seemed to compound the picture.

As the days passed, Amara found herself drawn into Felicia's life, spending many hours at her bedside, chatting with her mother, and attempting to unravel the complex strands of their life. She learned about the hardships and poverty that characterized the family's lives. She listened as Mrs. Adebayo opened her heart, expressing her goals and anxieties as well as her hopes for her daughter's future. And as she listened, Amara started to comprehend the wider picture—the intricate network of social and financial events that had led Felicia to this hospital bed.

It was a sobering insight, a reminder of the many difficulties her patient's encountered challenges beyond the field of medicine. She knew she had to keep battling for the life of Felicia, however, as she stared into her eyes and felt the flutter of hope and trust shining there. She could not give up.

She intensified her efforts, relentlessly striving to unravel the mystery surrounding Felicia's condition. She worked with colleagues, read over medical publications, and contacted field specialists, all in search of the secret that would open Felicia's road to recovery.

It was a demanding procedure, a trial of Amara's knowledge and will. However, she never lost sight of the broader impact her work could have on the lives of many people, including Felicia, as well as on her own.

Finally, following weeks of continuous effort, a breakthrough occurred. A fresh viewpoint, a new series of tests, and suddenly the pieces of the jigsaw started to fit together. As the diagnosis became obvious and the road ahead started to take shape, Amara experienced a surge of enthusiasm.

Felicia's situation was severe and would need long-term therapy and care; yet, for the first time since she had taken on the case, Amara felt a glimmer of optimism, a feeling that success was within grasp. Amara experienced a surge of emotions as she conveyed the news to Mrs. Adebayo, witnessing the young mother's face transform from tears of relief to gratitude. She had become a doctor for this reason, and she had battled so hard to take back her position on this planet.

Her goal is to give underprivileged people hope and healing. Amara knew she had discovered her vocation in life when she glanced down at Felicia's sleeping figure and saw the colossal swelling to her cheeks and the simple rise and fall of her chest.

For Felicia, for her family, and for the many others like her who battled against all the odds, the road ahead would be long and challenging. But anything was possible with physicians like Amara on their side, armed with compassion, commitment, and relentless persistence.

With a last squeeze of Mrs. Adebayo's hand and a quiet prayer for Felicia's ongoing recovery, Dr. Amara Johnson then emerged from the busy paediatric ward prepared to meet the next challenge and leave her imprint on the world one patient at a time.

Chapter 5

Distractive supports

As Amara entered her warm house, the smell of savory spices and boiling stew permeated the air; the stress of the day melted away in the welcoming environment. She allowed the familiar smells to envelop her, like a salve to her worn soul. She breathed deeply.

As Amara entered the kitchen, she saw her boyfriend, Jiu, rushing around the stove, his face a picture of concentration as he stirred a pot of aromatic jollof rice. He gazed up at the sound of her feet, his eyes ablaze with love and delight.

"Welcome home, my love," Jiu murmured, his voice kind and sweet. "I wanted to honour your successful official first day back at work by surprising you with a little celebration dinner."

Upon hearing his remarks, Amara felt a surge of emotions and a knot in her throat. She had nearly forgotten the importance of this occasion because she had been so preoccupied with her patients and the daily difficulties and successes.

But everything came flooding back here, in the haven of their house, with the man she loved by her side. She endured a lengthy and excruciating journey towards recovery, enduring numerous hours of treatment and rehabilitation and experiencing moments of doubt and despair when she doubted her ability to pursue her passion.

And now here she was, back where she belonged, doing what her nature demanded. It was a success, a vindication, and Amara felt a wave of thanks for the guy who had been by her side through it all.

"Jiu," she said, her voice laden with feeling. "You had no need to do all this. All the celebration I need is just having you here, helping me, and believing in me.

Strong and consoling, Jiu laid down his spoon and crossed the kitchen to carry her in his arms. "Amara, my love," he said, his breath warm against her ear. "You have done very remarkable. From the verge, you have battled your way back; you have recaptured your life and your goals. You should celebrate it every single day.

Leaching into his hug, Amara felt his body's sturdiness and weight against hers. All the hardships of the preceding year appeared to vanish in one instant, replaced by a head-to-toe sensation of calm and satisfaction.

Stuck in one another's arms and enjoying the peaceful closeness of the moment, they remained like that for a long time. Then, as if by unspoken accord, Jiu went back to cook, and Amara moved to arrange the table.

Amara sensed rightness and belonging as they worked side by side, their motions exactly timed. She should have been living in this house with this guy, embarking on a life together.

Even as she savoured the pleasure of the moment, Amara could not help but feel a flutter of anxiety—a sensation that there were still difficulties ahead and barriers to surmount.

She contemplated her patients and the numerous lives relying on her skills and dedication. She considered her neighbourhood, the social and economic injustices afflicting Igbuzor, and the many children who were suffering and striving every day.

She also considered her own route, the lengthy one she had followed to reach this place. She knew the fight would continue and obstacles and uncertainty would materialize.

But Amara knew she was not alone—that she had the will and the support to face whatever lay ahead—when she looked across the table at Jiu and saw the love and pride flashing in his eyes.

And so Amara lifted her glass in a toast as they sat down to their festive feast, her voice ringing out loud and powerful. "To new beginnings," she remarked, fixated on Jiu's. "To second chances, and to the power of love and determination to see us through."

Jiu clinked his glass to hers, flashing a broad grin. "To my beautiful, brave, brilliant partner," he murmured, sounding full of admiration. "To the woman that never gives up, who always finds a way to make the world a better place."

Amara felt calm and satisfied flood over her as she drank her wine and appreciated the tastes of the dinner. Indeed, the route forward would be challenging. Indeed, there would be obstacles to overcome.

But now, surrounded by her husband's affection and the comfort of her home, Dr. Amara Johnson felt she was right where she should be. She realized that, by focusing on each day, each patient, and each small victory, she could confront any challenges that lay ahead, armed with this knowledge and unwavering faith.

For that is the power of love, of commitment, of relentless resolve—the power to heal, to change, to make the world a better place, one priceless life at a time.

Part 2

ADVOCATING CHANGES

Chapter 6

Collaborative agencies

Amara strolled across the crowded hall of the community centre blocks; her eyes swept over the sea of people around her. She still wore her white coat, and her shoulders showed the weight of her daily tasks. She had come straight from the main hospital.

But when Amara looked around the gathered assembly of local politicians, anxious parents, and community organizers, she sensed direction and connection. These were her people—the ones she had sworn to rescue, heal, defend, and guard.

She headed toward the front of the room, where a small gathering of panellists had already settled in to decide the destiny of the many varied businesses in the town ahead of their annual one-week festival. Their looks were serious and intentional. Amara nestled among them and had a flash of anticipation and worry. She knew that the planned talks for today will determine Igbuzor's destiny and really enhance the quality of life for its most impoverished residents.

The austere-looking moderator kept the gathering under control with sharp eyes and greying hair; her voice cut through the din of argument. "Thank you all for coming," she said in a sombre tone. "We are here today to handle a topic of great relevance to our community—the welfare of our children."
Heads bent together as a collective murmur of acceptance swept across the assembly. The words set Amara ablaze with feeling; her mind turned to the many children she had met in her work—the ones suffering from poverty, from neglect, from abuse.
She thought of Felicia, the little child she had just come across, whose mysterious illness exposed a much more urgent problem: a family trying to survive, a mother struggling with money.
She also considered her own early years, the difficulties and uncertainties of growing up in the foster care system, and the numerous challenges she had surmounted along the route.

Amara listened completely as the presentation started; her head spun

with thoughts and opportunities. She heard tales of parents trying to support their family, of kids tumbling through the gaps of an overburdened system, and of a society under threat.
Amara too sensed increasing intensity and drive as she listened. She realized that she needed to act—not just observe the changes.

When it was her turn, Amara took a deep breath and spoke clearly and steadily. Her eyes flicked around the room as she added, "I have seen personally the challenges our children face working in my foundation clinic." As a public hospital doctor, I have looked after many young patients whose illnesses and injuries directly result from the social and economic inequalities afflicting our society.

She paused so her words might sink in. "But we also have the capacity to change this and truly raise the quality of life for our most vulnerable members."
Amara then discussed her own experiences, the changing power of love and support, and the significant part the community might play in supporting and empowering its children.
She talked about her work with a nonprofit organization and the initiatives she took to provide at-risk youth and foster parents with resources and support.

Amara could see the faces around her alive with promise and hope as she talked, and the atmosphere in the room transformed.
The crowd erupted in applause as she returned, the sound encircling her like a wave. Amara experienced an unexpected surge of humility and gratitude. She understood that this was only the beginning and that much more work remained.
Still, she knew she was not alone; behind her she had the support and enthusiasm of her community.

Well-wishers, parents, and community leaders surrounded Amara as the conference ended, eager to learn more about her work, get involved, and change things.

Making her way out into the chilly evening air, Dr. Amara Johnson felt she had found her calling—her purpose in life—her heart full and her mind running with possibilities. Standing up for the weak, comforting the sick, and tending to the injured is what she loves to do.

One child at a time, she improves the world with her voice, skills, and energy. Equipped with that knowledge and relentless confidence, she realised that everything was possible, that together they could build a brighter future for Igbuzor, and that no agency should be left out as the children of any agency would define next generations.

Chapter 7

Echoing voice

Amara was walking over the peaceful streets of Igbuzor, the morning mist still hanging on the ground, while the sun was just starting to show above the horizon. Shivering slightly in the cool air, she drew her coat closer to her.

Despite the early hour and the cold, Amara was filled with excitement and drive. She was on her way to the Igbuzor Children's Home, the venerable local foster care facility she had just come to call home. The facility, along with others, existed before the founding of the Hope for Tomorrow foundation. Amara had successfully tackled the challenge of sustaining some aspects of this agency services earlier in the week.

As Amara approached the building, she could already hear children laughing and chatting, the sound of small feet tapping against the worn-out linoleum flooring. Feeling a surge of love and admiration for these priceless lives, little souls who had already suffered so much in their brief time on Earth, she grinned to herself.

She opened the door and entered the familiar noises and sights in the centre. Vibrant paintings and sketches covered the walls, while toys and well-worn picture books piled high on the bookcases.

And everywhere were youngsters running, playing, laughing, their cheeks ablaze with the little pleasures of infancy.
Amara moved around the hallways, pausing to personally welcome every kid by name, give a high-five or hug, and pay attention to their hopes and stories.

She was in awe of their resilience and their ability to find hope and delight in even the worst of conditions. She also harboured an intense protectiveness, striving to do everything within her power to provide them with the much-needed love and encouragement.

The centre's dedicated carers, men and women who worked tirelessly to provide a secure and loving environment for these fragile youngsters, greeted Amara with happy smiles as she headed to the staff room.

Over the last six months, she had grown to know them well and had experienced personally the difficulties and successes of their job. She had also learned to really appreciate them as the unsung heroes of Igbuzor.

They looked grave and deliberate as they gathered around the table to begin discussing the day's agenda. There were new kids to house, medical appointments to schedule, and paperwork to submit.

But Amara sensed an undertone of irritation and fatigue as they spoke and organized. She understood that the centre was stretched thinly and that these kids' demands exceeded its means.
She also realised they had to change and find ways to do and be more.

As the meeting ended, Amara expressed herself clearly. With her gaze straying across the room, she remarked, "I know that we are all doing the best we can with what we have." "But I also know that these kids deserve much more; it's not enough."

She inhaled deeply, sharpening herself for what she was about to say. "That's why I want to propose a new initiative, a way to expand our reach, our interactions, and our influence."

Amara then went on to describe her vision: a network of support services and resources for foster families, various agency partnerships, a mentoring program for at-risk kids, and a community outreach campaign to increase awareness and support for the work of the centre.

Her remarks depicted a better future for Igbuzor's children, one in which every kid received the love and support they needed to flourish. She spoke with passion and conviction.

As she spoke, Amara could see the faces around her awaken with potential and hope. She sensed a shift in the atmosphere in the room, a spark of enthusiasm and determination beginning to take hold.

There was silence, a pause that seemed to last indefinitely, until her departure. One by one, the employees began nodding and murmuring their agreement, thereby pledging their support.

Amara experienced a surge of gratitude and humility. She realized that this was only the beginning; there was still much more to accomplish.

She was aware, however, that she had sown a seed—that she had started something that may turn around lives and alter destinies.

Her heart full and her mind racing with possibilities, Dr. Amara Johnson believed she had discovered her calling—her path in life— as she made her way back into the sunny streets of Igbuzor.

I aim to stand up for the marginalized and overlooked, providing a voice for those who lack a voice.

One little triumph at a time, her talents, passion, and relentless will to create a better future for Igbuzor's children will help her use them.

Knowing that all was possible and that together they could move mountains and create a better future for next generations, she too had an unquestionable conviction.

One little one at a time, one family at a time—one priceless life at a time.

Chapter 8

Changing policies

As Amara sat at her desk reading over the facts of her most recent patient today, the case papers felt heavy in her hands. A support group took seven-year-old Torino Akpan to the hospital; his little body showed traces of a lifetime of neglect and abuse.

Amara's heart closed with a combination of grief and rage as she went over the notes. From his early years, Torino had been in and out of foster families, bouncing from one placement to another like a human pinball.

His medical records revealed a narrative of untreated diseases and chronic starvation, as well as a range of mental and behavioural problems that had only grown worse over time.

As Amara closed the file, her jaw set with will, and she experienced a burst of determination. She understood that Torino's situation was just one of many; numerous other children were also falling through the gaps of a dysfunctional system.

Additionally, she was confident in her ability to transform this child's life.

She grabbed the phone and dialled the number for Kanneh Ibol, Torino's current foster home. She had seen the love and worry in their eyes as she held Torino's hand and murmured words of comfort, having briefly met them at the hospital and at one of her charity public screening events.

She was also aware of their suffering and the lack of tools they needed to manage the challenging responsibilities of parenting a child with Torino's background and demands.

Amara inhaled deeply as the phone rang, getting ready for the next talk. She was certain that this was just the beginning; many more would come.

She knew she was ready and had the knowledge and will to finish this and fight for Torino's future with everything she had.

The sound of a family at the end of their rope permeated the tired and strained voice on the other side of the line. But Amara could hear the optimism and thanks starting to seep into their tone as she described her strategy for Torino's treatment and care.

She pledged to be there for them at every stage and to offer the tools and support required to give Torino the greatest possible opportunity for a better future.

And Amara sensed rightness and purpose as she hung the phone. It was her duty to fulfill her call.

I aspire to serve as a healer, advocate, and champion for the marginalized and overlooked.

One little triumph at a time, her voice, abilities, and relentless will to create a better future for children like Torino reflect who she is.

Amara poured herself into Torino's case with a passion and intensity that startled even herself during the following few weeks. She put forth an enormous effort to schedule his medical appointments and link him with the therapists and experts he needs to start the protracted recovery process.

For hours she sat with him, listening to his dreams, worries, and tales. She held his hand throughout the agonizing treatments and helped him wipe his tears when dreams struck.

She also started to perceive a difference in him: a flimsy grin on his face and a spark of optimism in his eyes.

However, Amara realized that this was only the beginning, and further action was necessary. She started looking into Torino's past to see the trends of mistreatment and neglect leading him to this state.

She also uncovered startling evidence of a dysfunctional and overburdened system; government policies that prioritize operations and reward high salaries; a network of failing foster homes; and agencies that fail to protect and nurture the children under their care.

Amara's urgency to make a change was growing. She started contacting organizations, other activists, and advocates in the community, including coworkers.

She scheduled forums and gatherings and spoke at town halls and public hearings. She battled nonstop to draw attention to Igbuzor's most vulnerable children and mobilize support for new policies and programs.

She also started to notice a wave of support and enthusiasm, as well as an increasing awareness of the problems confronting the foster care system.

It was a long and challenging path with hurdles around every bend. Amara, nevertheless, never wavered or lost sight of her objective.

She understood that this was more than simply employment—more than just a cause.

It was a promise to the children of Igbuzor—a calling, a holy trust.

We aim to serve as their representative, champion, and unwavering ally in the fight for a brighter tomorrow.

Armed with that knowledge and unwavering belief, Dr. Amara Johnson understood that anything was possible and that together they could create a better world for next generations. She could move mountains. One kid at a time; one family at a time; one agency at a time; one priceless life spared at a time.

Chapter 9

Revamping decisions

The crammed town hall filled every seat and every inch of standing area to the rafters. Expectancy charged the air as something historic was about to unfold.

A panel of advocates and professionals gathered around a large table on stage, their expressions solemn and severe. Dr. Amara Johnson, glaring furiously with passion and determination, was at the core of it all.

She had called this conference and worked nonstop on assembling this group of dedicated individuals all motivated by the same goal: to expose the challenges and problems confronting Igbuzor's foster care system and to map a future together.

Every eye turned to Amara as she climbed the platform, the room motionless. She drew in deeply, feeling the weight of the event and her own responsibilities.

She then began to talk.
She spoke of the children she had known ones who had touched her heart and changed her life. She spoke about their tenacity, resilience, and unwavering attitude against seeming insurmountable challenges.

She spoke of the foster families she had worked with—those who had opened their hearts and homes to these precious children and who had done everything they could to provide love, constancy, and support.
She also mentioned the system that was systematically failing them all—the one that overworked and underpaid, the one that too often allowed youngsters to fend for themselves and slide through the gaps and plunge into darkness.

Amara could feel the atmosphere change in the room as she talked, and she could sense the spark of identification and empathy starting to take root. Driven by a shared objective, she could see the faces of the audience members come alive with understanding.

Then one by one, everybody on the platform shared their own stories and experiences, as well as their own perspectives and opinions. Among them were politicians, therapists, lawyers, and social workers. Former foster parents and children joined together, driven by a common goal to change things.

As they spoke and shared their expertise and passion, Amara could also sense the momentum building and the tide beginning to flip.

She understood that there was still a significant amount of work ahead and that this was merely the beginning. However, she also realized that launching a movement—a coalition of change—was a crucial first step.
She also came to see that she had an army of supporters and friends willing to battle alongside her to advocate for the underprivileged and speak up for the disregarded.

As the conference ended, Amara experienced a surge of gratitude and humility. She understood that this was more than simply employment—more than just a cause.
It was a promise to the Igbuzor children—a calling, a holy trust. One tiny victory at a time, she also knew she would never stop fighting or trying to make the world better for children.

Well-wishers and fans crowded Amara as she stepped from the podium, everyone eager to offer their own stories and ideas, thereby affirming their support and allegiance to the cause.

Dr. Amara Johnson believed she had found her real calling—her purpose for existing—her heart full and her mind racing with possibilities as she headed out into the cool night air.

I want to speak for those without a voice and stand up for the underprivileged and disregarded. She creates a better world for Igbuzor's children through her abilities, devotion, and unwavering resolve.

Chapter 10

Expanding Reach

The light was just beginning to appear through the windows of Amara's office as she sat at her desk, pouring over the most current figures from the child safeguarding agency reports. Driven by a strong resolve to uncover the truth behind the challenges and suffering Igbuzor's most fragile youngsters were going through, she had remained up all night.

Her brain kept going back to the town hall assembly—to the faces of the people she had met and the stories they had shared while she was working. She could still feel the energy of that room—the sense of shared commitment and ambition that had gripped hold.

She could still recall the comments of one specific young lady, Vivian, a former foster child who had spoken up close to the conclusion of the evening.

"I left the system at eighteen," Vivian remarked, her voice quivering with feeling. "And I felt I was on my own. But I was wrong. I had people who supported me, believed in me, and corrected me back on course. And that really changed everything.

Amara felt a lump in her throat as she recalled those words and thought of all the other young people who were still waiting for someone to believe in and fight for.

She knew she had to be that person—that she had to push on ahead even if the road proved challenging.

Amara was working when she heard a knock at the door. Looking up, she saw Rajendra Kumar, a fellow from her medical school years, staring into the room.

"Hey, Amara," he said, a big smile showing gladness to see you once again. "I just landed a new job in your town. Last night I heard about the meeting. The meeting sounds like it was fantastic.

Overcome with thankfulness for Rajendra's support and assistance, Amara nodded. "Yes, it was," she said with fervent intensity. But that's just the beginning. You would love visiting here; we have so much more work to do.
Rajendra nodded, his eyes reflected wisdom. He said softly, "I know." "But Amara, your community actions reflect more than just yourself." Each stride we take together is our own.

At his words, Amara experienced oneness, a spark of emotion, and friendship that filled her heart. She knew Rajendra was right—that she had a vast network of supporters and friends at her ready to fight with her for the children of Igbuzor.

Over the next four days, Amara threw herself into her job with new clarity and focus. She met authorities and politicians to advocate for more foster care system funding and resources.
Working with her hospital colleagues, she developed new initiatives to find ways to better assist and care for the children under their duty.

She also kept visiting the other Igbuzor Children's Homes to establish relationships, spend time with the kids there, and learn from the committed staff and carers who worked nonstop to create secure and loving surroundings.

Amara sensed that the momentum and shift were intensifying. She saw it in the gleam of hope and opportunity that the children she encountered reflected.

She saw it in the passion and loyalty of her friends and coworkers— in the way they joined together to encourage and uplift one another, thereby acting as a force for positive change in the world.
She also saw it in the little victories and triumphs that began to come up—the little moments of progress and transformation that added up to something more powerful than she could have ever expected.

Obstacles and difficulties still awaited her to overcome.
However, Amara knew she was heading exactly where she should be. She was on the correct road.

She also understood that she would never stop battling or striving to create a better environment for one priceless life at a time—that of the children of Igbuzor.

Sitting in her office late one evening, surrounded by evidence of her unwavering efforts and unshakable dedication, Dr. Amara Johnson felt peaceful certainty overwhelm her heart and soul.

She knew that obstacles and barriers would abound on her long and taxing trip ahead.
She knew, but she was not alone; she had a huge community of supporters and friends at her ready to fight with her, to be the voice for the voiceless and the champion for the forgotten.

She insisted that anything was possible and that together they could overcome challenges to create a better future for next generations.

One child at a time, one family at a time, one priceless life at a time—the road is still ongoing.

Part 3

OPERATIONAL STARVATION

Chapter 11

Wake up knock

The news left Amara gasping and reeling like a strike to the stomach. She attempted to make sense of what she was seeing as she glanced at the email on her computer screen—the words blurring before her eyes.

The message read, "We regret to notify you that we cannot financially support your projects and activities."

Amara wondered if Mayor Sholina knew of this choice, as she felt a surge of terror and a terrible sensation of anxiety threatening to overtake her. This cannot be happening, not now, not when they were so near to actual success in altering the whole system, changing lives, and rewriting destinies.

She considered all the young people dependent on her company—the ones who had discovered healing and hope via the offerings of programs and services. She considered the committed employees and volunteers who had given everything they had to change the world—their hearts and souls poured into their job.

She also considered her own path—that long and challenging route that had taken her to this point. Along the road, she had surmounted many difficulties and battled so fiercely to get here.

She couldn't let it all go to waste or allow this setback to ruin everything they had painstakingly created.

Amara took a long breath, then felt steely resolve, picked up the phone, and started to call. She called her board members, her contributors, and her community friends. Seeking their assistance and direction throughout this crisis, she gathered her team and supporters.

And gradually, a strategy began to take shape. Where they could, they would reduce costs; they would also simplify their processes and concentrate on their most important programs and offerings. They would network with new partners and contributors and foster fresh community connections and ties.

They would fight for every dollar and resource, taking all necessary steps to maintain their operations and their mission.

Amara could feel the weight of duty falling on her shoulders through it all—the weight of stewardship and leadership accompanying her position. She understood that her life—as well as the future of her neighbourhood and company—lay on the line for many children.

She was aware, however, that she was not alone; she had a team of committed and driven people at her side, ready to battle with her at every turn.

And so, Dr. Amara Johnson started to work, devoting herself to the job of salvaging her company and safeguarding its critical purpose with a feeling of grim determination and unwavering resolve.

She late-night pored over budgets and grant applications, spending long hours in meetings and on conference calls. Reaching out to everyone and anything that may be able to assist, she gathered her friends and supporters.

She also began to see glimpses of hope on the horizon. A local company volunteered to support one of their main initiatives; a new contributor came forward with a sizable gift.

The bits started to fit little by little, and the future started to seem somewhat safer and more brilliant.

Amara was aware, however, that the path ahead would be long and demanding and that additional difficulties and disappointments would arise. She understood that the struggle to salvage her company and assist the Igbuzor children was far from over.

She was aware, too, that she would never cease battling or trying to create a better world for those most in need.

And armed with that knowledge and unwavering belief, she persisted, one tiny triumph at a time, one day at a time.

She understood that this went beyond just employment—more than merely a cause. She worked full-time for the state hospital already.

To Amara, her foundation was a calling, a holy trust, a promise to the Igbuzor children.

She would also honour her commitment, regardless of her means or the difficulty of the path ahead.

Dr. Amara Johnson would find a way ahead with the love and encouragement of her family, friends, and community; therefore, she would keep the candle of hope ablaze.

Our actions benefit the children and their future. One priceless life at a moment.

Chapter 12

Slap in the face

Amara stood beside the incubator, staring at the little, delicate body of the infant inside while the fluorescent lights flashed above. Just a few days old, Little Jamie Etienne had been born a drug addict; his little body shook with tremors, and his screams were painful.

Watching him struggle, Amara felt a tsunami of anger and sadness as she thought about the challenges his brief existence would provide. Alone in the world, Jamie survived by depending on the kindness and generosity of total strangers. His mother neglected him, and a system designed to look after him abandoned him. Amara then thought about the government's decision to discontinue funding initiatives like hers, which would have offered Jamie tailored treatment. An outsider to this child, Amara sought to be more than just another face in apathy. She had entered his case determined to fight for his future with everything she had.

She stayed with him for extended periods of time, monitoring his vital signs and giving drugs meant to reduce his withdrawal symptoms. She embraced him tightly and spoke words of love into his little ears as he started to cry.

She also put in endless behind-the-scenes effort navigating the complex bureaucracy and red tape separating Jamie from the required therapy.

At times throughout the horrible and upsetting procedure, Amara felt fatigued and discouraged. She saw firsthand how the system failed to protect and help the most vulnerable.

She also witnessed resilience and hope, but her daily interactions with children and families revealed incredible grit and tenacity.

She found strength in their example and the knowledge that, even in the most challenging circumstances, there was always hope—always a reason to keep moving forward.

With the days running into weeks, Amara delightedly and
wonderingly observed as Jamie started to thrive under her care. His
shaking ceased; his cries became less frequent and less strong.
She also noticed the first signs of a brilliant and inquisitive
personality beginning to emerge—traces of the extraordinary
youngster he would one day become.

Even as she acknowledged these small victories, Amara understood
that Jamie's journey was far from over. He would need continuous
medical treatment and assistance as well as a loving, stable home of
his own.
She also understood that the path ahead would be long and
demanding, full of hurdles at every step.
She also knew she would fight for his future at every turn while
supporting him.

This was not merely a case or a job.
It was a calling, a holy trust, a promise to every Igbuzor child. And
Dr. Amara Johnson would uphold that commitment, regardless of the
means or the difficulty of the path ahead.

With the love and support of her coworkers, her community, and all
those who believed in the power of compassion and hope, she would
find a way ahead and keep the spark of potential ablaze.
This is for the benefit of little Jamie and all the other children who
rely on her.

Chapter 13

Our dangers

Word of the scandal struck Amara like a blow to the stomach, leaving her gasping and reeling. She fixated on the newspaper headline, the words seeming to leap out at her from the page: "Local Foster Care Agency Implicated in Embezzlement, Child Endangerment."
She stopped momentarily—not moving, not thinking, not breathing. The agency in question was one she had trusted for years to care for and safeguard the children under her supervision; she had worked closely with them, attempting to cooperate.

The thought of having been involved in something so horrific and unfathomable was nearly unbearable.
But Amara felt a strong desire to do something right, building within her even as shock and terror rushed over her.

She answered the phone, scheduling an emergency meeting of the board of directors of the Hope for Tomorrow Foundation, then visited several other agencies and stakeholders. Soon, they gathered around the conference table, their expressions sombre and serious as they scrutinized the details of the scandal.

The stories revealed a depth of sadness and frustration. Children suffered from neglect and malnutrition, while funds meant for their care and assistance ended up in personal bank accounts. Entrusted with the most precious and fragile of life, the system was abusing trust in the most unthinkable manner.
As Amara listened, a white-hot anger rising within her threatened to overwhelm her totally. She understood that they had to move fast, and that rage alone would not change things.

She started a thorough, independent investigation into the very agency and its policies together with her staff. They examined case files and financial data, spoke with foster homes and employees, and investigated every clue and trail of evidence they could come across. Because of their demanding job, they were exhausted and heartsick every day. Still, they persisted, driven by the same goal and will.

And the bits started to fit together gradually. The degree of the corruption and the mistreatment became evident; the scope of the treachery was almost too enormous to fathom.
However, Amara and her colleagues refused to give up or let the overwhelming workload overwhelm them. They gathered their evidence, built their case, and presented it to the authorities, media, and anyone else who would help them get justice.

Every move in this protracted and challenging conflict taxed their will and bravery. Still, they were unflinchingly dedicated to the children they cared for, the families they helped, and the neighbourhood they called home.
Eventually, their diligence will pay off as well. They closed the agency, arrested its officials, and charged them with crimes. They implemented fresh security measures and accountable mechanisms of control to ensure that nothing like this could ever resurface.

Amara and her team acknowledged, however, that their job was far from done, even as they celebrated their victory. They comprehended that there was still a significant amount of work to accomplish to improve the world for everyone, and that numerous children still required their care and assistance.
And so, they continued, driven on with a fresh feeling of purpose—one day at a time, one little triumph at a time.

They realized that this was not just a job but also a cause.

It was a summons, a holy trust, and a promise to the Igbuzor children.
And regardless of how challenging the road ahead may be, Dr. Amara Johnson and associates would keep their promise.

Their community, their partners, and all those who saw the power of hope and healing would assist them in determining their road forward and maintaining the blazing compassion torch.

I am doing this for the young people and the future. One precious life at a time.

Chapter 14

Blowing wind

Amara battled to make sense of the disorder that had engulfed her life in recent weeks, her head resting on her hands as she sat at her desk. The debate at the foster care agency had affected both her personal and professional life; she felt anxious and tired. She had devoted her entire being to the fight for duty and justice, putting everything she had into the investigation.

But the emotional toll and long hours had caught up with her; she was thin and tired. Her relationships had also suffered; she was separating herself from the people she most loved throughout the globe. She had skipped meals with her partner Jiu, cancelled playdates with her little children, and let her friendships slip away as she focused all her efforts on the current problem.

As she sat in silence in her office now, she felt sorrow and remorse, a nagging sensation that she had let the people most important to her down.

She glanced up to find Jiu standing in the doorway, a worried expression on his face, shocked out of her thoughts by a tap at the door.

"Amara," he said softly, then went to sit beside her. "Amara, what's happening? You left before I woke up, did you? You've been somewhat disconnected and distracted recently. tell me, am here if anything". Glancing at her husband, Amara detected love and worry in his eyes and felt her throat knotting.

She saw she had been separating herself from him, from their family, in her sole pursuit of justice. She reached out to clasp his hand in hers and apologised. "I have been so absorbed in all this, so preoccupied with trying to right things," she remarked. II have allowed it to overwhelm me, ignoring the most important things. Jiu held her hand; his touch made sense. "I understand," he said softly. ""Amara, you're involved in a significant task." t's important. But you also matter. Not less essential are your health, happiness, family, relationships, and general well-being. Tears began to fill Amara's eyes as she heard her husband speak about the depth of his love and

support. She saw he was right—that she had been neglecting the people she loved and herself in her pursuit of a bigger good. "I know," she said softly, her voice loaded with emotion. ""I feel like I must persevere and fight constantly," she said. here are high risks here, as many people depend on us.
Jiu nodded; his face marked with comprehension. I know, darling. But one cannot pour from an empty cup. You must take care of yourself, maintain equilibrium, and resist succumbing to life's events.

Amara inhaled deeply, then let his words sink in. She realized he was correct—that she had to figure out how to control the strain and stress of her job and how to carve out time for herself and her family amid the tumult. he deliberately tried to accomplish precisely that during the next few days. She assigned additional work to her staff and relied on friends and colleagues for direction and encouragement. She scheduled time for consistent meals and exercise, as well as for leisure and rest.

She also made sure she gave her connections top priority and interacted with the individuals most important to her right now. She smiled and played with her little children, had lengthy, emotional talks with Jiu, and contacted friends and loved ones she had been ignoring.
It wasn't always easy, and there were still moments of overload and tension. However, gradually, Amara began to experience a sense of serenity and perspective that had been absent during the crisis and returned to her life. he also came to see that this was a component of her calling and of her profession. She couldn't be there for the children and families she helped if she wasn't first there for herself, if she wasn't tending to her own needs and nurturing her own soul.
She felt a great thankfulness for the love and support that surrounded her as she sat with Jiu one evening, curled up on the sofa after bed-setting for the children.
She said, "Thank you for always resetting my head," softly kissing his cheek. She expressed her gratitude for his belief in me, his reminder of what truly matters, and his presence in her life. For the time being, I will focus on my responsibilities at the main hospital and let my team handle the foundation for a while.

Jiu pulled her near and grinned. "Always," he said gently. "We go through this together, Amara. Whatever happens or how difficult it becomes, nothing changes. We will address it collectively; indeed, I will consistently strive to refocus your mind like a remote control when you're losing focus.

And Amara realized he was correct at that instant. Together, they possessed the resilience to surmount any challenge and endure any adversity. heir unwavering love and commitment to each other, their family, and their community would enable them to overcome any challenges that lay ahead.

Driven by a fresh sense of power and direction, Dr. Amara Johnson went back to her work on the battle for justice and healing that had evolved into her mission.

But this time she did it with a fresh sense of balance and perspective—a realization of the need for self-care, family harmony, and self-compassion among the pressures of a life devoted to helping others. he also knew that, with the love and support of those most important to her, she would face whatever the future held with the fortitude and resiliency that had carried her thus far. She was determined to live each precious life to the fullest, one day at a time.

Chapter 15

Harden Knocks

The emergency department was a swirl of activity, a symphony of critical voices and beeping monitors filling the air with a controlled anarchy. Amara, at the centre of it all, laboured to steady a newly admitted patient with a life-threatening illness; her brow wrinkled with concentration.

She had trained for this kind of high-stakes situation, one in which every decision and action may decide whether life carried on. And yet Amara worked with precision and focused concentration, unable to rid herself of the unease that had crept over her in recent days.

She had been pushing herself harder than ever, pouring herself into her job with a single-minded dedication, ever since she delegated certain tasks to other staff members following the scandals at the foster care organizations. She had volunteered for every crisis and emergency that presented itself and took on additional hours at Igbuzor General Hospital.

However, as she stood amid the chaos and urgency of the ER, she couldn't help but question herself, a nagging sensation suggesting that perhaps she had pushed herself too far.

Her hands trembled slightly as she reached for a bottle of medicine; she felt lightheaded as she attempted to concentrate on the current work. She briefly closed her eyes to regain her composure by taking deep breaths.

She felt something was amiss, however, even as she attempted to press on—to keep going despite the stress and fatigue. She was nearing both emotional and physical boundaries.

Then, with startling clarity, she made a mistake. She made a small mistake, perhaps a hand slip that could have gone unnoticed. But in the high-stakes environment of emergency care, even the tiniest mistake might have terrible results.

When Amara realized what had occurred and saw the worried expressions on her colleagues' faces, she experienced a surge of anxiety. With her heart thumping in her chest, she quickly corrected the error and left the bedside after treating the patient.

But she had damaged her own confidence and others' faith. She could see their uncertainty and unspoken questions and concerns in their eye. She is acutely aware of the significance of these issues, which prompted her to reassess her approach following her prolonged stay on the hospital floor. r.
At that point, Amara realized she could no longer challenge herself beyond her comfort zone and endanger the lives of those she had promised to guard.

Heartbroken, humiliated, and remorseful, she left the ER and staggered along the hallway, gathering her thoughts and breathing.

Tears flooding her eyes, she leant against the wall and tried to make sense of what had happened—of how she had let herself reach this point.
She felt a small touch on her shoulder then, as if on cue, and she heard a familiar voice softly in her ear.

"Amara," Dr. John said, his voice empathetic and concerned. "What is happening?" Are you good?
Shaking her head, Amara found she could not pass the lump in her throat. Dr. John nodded, his expression compassionate.
"Come on," he exhorted her down the hall into a quiet room. "Let's talk."

And there, in the stillness and the aloneness of that room, Amara at last allowed herself to fall apart, at last letting herself face the truth of what she had been going through.

She discussed all her emotions with Dr. John, including the guilt and shame she felt for her mistakes on the job, her limitations, and the stress and pressure of her agency position, which had experienced a funding cutoff. She shared with him the toll it had taken on her health and relationships, as well as the uncertainty and doubt that had begun to creep into her consciousness.

And Dr. John listened, his steady lighthouse amid her turmoil. He gave her words of wisdom and encouragement, reminding her of her own strength and perseverance, the incredible work she had done, and the people she had touched. Realising she was not alone and that everyone around her loved and supported her to help her through whatever challenges were ahead, Amara began to slowly but progressively see hope and clarity returning.

She knew that the route of healing and self-forgiveness would not be a straight-line road; there would be difficulties and mistakes along it. She was also conscious, however, that she had the will and guts to face them and keep on speaking up for herself and for the people she supported.

And so, Dr. Amara Johnson went back to her profession, to the calling that had become her life's goal, breathing deeply and feeling reoriented.
This time, however, she did it with more self-knowledge and self-compassion, an understanding of her own limitations, and the need for family life balance and self-care.
She also knew that she would face the future with the love and support of those who believed in her, with the perseverance and will that had taken her this far. Whatever it contained.

Part 4

COMMUNITY ANNUAL WEEK FESTIVAL

Chapter 16

Festive Preparation

Over the crowded streets of Igbuzor, the light shone gloriously, bathing the vivid decorations and festive banners that covered every inch with cozy warmth. A real energy, a sense of excitement and expectancy, seemed to ignite through the masses of people approaching the town square.

This was not a typical day in Igbuzor. Today marked the start of the annual Community Five Days event, an occasion for the town's residents to gather and pay tribute to the diligence and efforts of those who had changed their life or their community.

And at the core of it all, her heart thumping with a combination of nervousness and pride, stood Dr. Amara Johnson, one of the main honourees for this year's festival.

Under the direction of Mayor Sholina, a committee of community leaders and activists picked her for her relentless efforts to better the lot of Igbuzor's most disadvantaged members.

Those who knew and loved her brought attention to her work with the Hope for Tomorrow Foundation, her advocacy of children in the foster care system, and her dedication to her patients and community. And yet Amara couldn't shake the feeling of imposter syndrome— the nagging sense that maybe she didn't deserve this honour, this recognition—even as she stood there on the podium.

She reflected on all the challenges and obstacles she had faced in the past year, such as the loss of her agency's budget, errors, uncertainty, and moments of vulnerability. She considered the many others who had contributed just as much personally to the cause and worked just as hard.

She also briefly experienced a surge of anxiety about being exposed as a phony in front of all these people who were celebrating her. This was dreadful.

Then, as if on cue, she felt a light touch on her shoulder and heard a familiar voice murmuring in her ear.

"You got this, Amara," Jiu stated in a loving and motivating tone. "You deserve this, more than anybody I know."
Amara inhaled deeply, let his words flow over her, and felt the confidence and power they carried. She gazed out at the sea of faces before her, seeing the nods and grins as well as the admiring glances.

She instantly realized that Jiu was right. She had earned this and exerted immense effort to achieve it. She encountered challenges, setbacks, and times of doubt along her journey—all of which moulded her into the person she is today.
Amara stepped up to the stage, eager to embrace the honour that had been given her. She smiled and felt reoriented.

She expressed her gratitude with a clear and powerful voice. "Thank you all for coming today and spending time honouring our work and the communities we love."
She then spoke on her own path—about the events and people who had moulded her and motivated her along the way. She discussed the kids she had seen, the families she had dealt with, and the colleagues and partners who had always supported her.

She also discussed the power of community and the remarkable outcomes that can occur when individuals unite around love, compassion, and a common goal.
"We are all in this together," she said, eyes flaming with emotion. "We all have to help to build a better world, create a future whereby every child receives love and support, and every family has the means and chances they need to thrive."
As Amara spoke, she could feel the energy in the room shifting and the spark of possibility beginning to take hold. On the faces of everyone around her, she could see it in the nods, smiles, and focused looks.

She also knew that regardless of the challenges ahead—however tough they may be—they would traverse the road together as a family.

Amara left the stage with a final word of gratitude, and a rush of emotions swept over her, setting off an emotional tsunami.

She would have done it. She had faced her uncertainties and fears, gone public, and asserted her leadership and transformative power in her community.
She also realized that this was only the beginning: there was still much more to do, countless lives to impact, and futures to shape.

Driven by the love and support of those who believed in her, Dr. Amara Johnson let herself be here to savour the happiness and celebration of what they had accomplished together in this moment. She savoured every valuable existence as it presented itself and each day as it came.

Chapter 17

Festive sunset

As the annual Community Day festival festivities began to wind down, a sea of familiar faces, each shining with pride and respect, surrounded Amara. Nuss and Zarah, her foster siblings, stood by her side with kind and encouraging looks.

"We're so proud of everything you are doing, Amara," Nuss added, gently hugging her. You have gone so far and done so much. Mum and Dad would also be very proud."

At the mention of their parents, at the thought of the love and direction they had given over their years together, Amara felt a knot developing in her throat. She considered all the difficulties they had gone through as a family and the ways in which they had encouraged and cheered one another constantly.

"I couldn't have done it without you, but this case now..." she replied gently, staring from Nuss to Zarah and back again. Without all of you. You have been my foundation and rock. Without your love and encouragement, I do not know where I would be."

Zarah grinned; her eyes misted with feeling. "We're family," she stated somewhat succinctly. That is our line of work. We are always there for each other, no matter what.

As they stood there together, caught in a moment of shared memory and thanksgiving, Amara couldn't help but marvel at the road that had brought them to this place. She considered all the challenges they had surmounted and all the happy and sad times they had experienced to Mold them into the people they are now.
She also understood that they would travel the road ahead together, as a family, as a community, regardless of what the future contained or how difficult it may be.

Amara found herself lured into discussion after conversation, each one a reminder of the amazing network of love and support she was surrounded by as the festival celebration days stretched around her into day five. She chatted with partners and colleagues, activists, and community leaders, sharing their own tales and experiences, as well as their own aspirations and plans.

Amara also felt a great deal of humility and gratitude throughout it all, realizing the great privileges and responsibilities that accompanied her profession. She understood that she had been given a gift—a chance to really change the world—to touch lives and shape destinies in ways that counted.

Amara was standing on the platform once again as the day concluded, this time surrounded by her family and friends and all those who had been a part of her trip and her achievement.

She said, "Thank you," her voice full of feeling. "Thanks everybody for coming here, for believing in me, for helping me at every stage. Your affection and your trust really humble me and make me very happy."

Looking out at the sea of faces before her, she saw hope, will, and the ferocious, unquestionable spirit burning in every single one of them.

She said, "Together," her voice ringing out sharp and loud. "We are capable of amazing things taken together. We can create a better planet as well as a brighter future for next generations and for ourselves. All it takes is love, compassion, and a readiness to show up daily and do the necessary job."

As the audience erupted in shouts and clapping, Amara felt a surge of emotions, a sense of potential and goal competing. She understood that there would be obstacles and times of uncertainty, as well as a long and demanding path ahead.

She was aware, too, that she was not alone; she had an army of fans and allies at her side, ready to fight with her to be the change people wanted to see in the world.

With a heart full of hope and a soul full of will, Dr. Amara Johnson then moved forth into the future, prepared to welcome whatever was ahead, one precious life at a time.

Chapter 18

Festive tensions

Amara's pulse thumped in her chest as she made her way to the platform on the last day of the yearly celebration, confronting the sea of faces before her for the final day before the next one in the next twelve months. The air was heavy with anxiety. She could feel the weight of their expectations, their ambitions, and their hopes firmly on her shoulders.

She knew, however, that this was the moment she had been waiting for her whole life, even as she stood there, and her hands shook gently as she held the podium's edges. She had the opportunity to share her vision of a better world, a brighter future for everyone, and her truth.

She inhaled deeply to help her relax before starting her speech. "My friends," she added, her voice loud and clear among the subdued audience. "We come here today under considerable uncertainty and substantial risk. The forces of evil and division threaten to rip apart our community and ruin what we have so laboriously created." They first stopped our money, but the community wants us to keep going; hence, we are still here."

Heads nodded with serious respect for the validity of her remarks, a murmur of agreement rippling across the assembly. Amara stopped momentarily to allow the weight of the occasion to settle her.
"But even in the face of such great adversity," she said, her voice rising with every syllable, "I believe that we are empowered within us to overcome, to rise above the challenges that confront us and emerge stronger, more united than ever before."
She spoke of her own path—of the challenges and successes that had moulded her into the woman she was today. She spoke about the individuals who had motivated her along the road—the mentors and supporters who had believed in her even when she questioned herself.
She also talked of the children, the priceless life entrusted to her care, the ones who looked to her for direction, love, and support.

"These children are our future," she added with fervent conviction in her voice. "They will be the ones carrying on the task we started and inheriting the planet we leave behind. And it is our holy obligation, our serious responsibility, to make sure they have every chance to flourish, develop, and become the finest versions of themselves."

Amara could feel the vitality in the room changing as she talked, and she could sense the spark of potential and optimism starting to take hold. She could see it in the expressions of those seated around her, leaning forward to hang on every word.
"But we cannot do this alone," she said, her voice rescinding.
"Without the support, the love, and the dedication of our whole community, we cannot create a better future. If we are to conquer the darkness threatening to surround us, we must stand together, unified in our goal and will.
She stopped momentarily to let her words linger in the air, observing as those who listened delved deep into the hearts and thoughts of each other.
"Therefore, dear friends and fellow residents of Igbuzor, please join me in this battle." You can stand side by side with me in this battle.

The audience burst in yells and ovations, the sound filling Amara like a tsunami of love and encouragement. She felt a knot in her throat, and tears sprung at the corners of her eyes as she relished the warmth and brightness of their embrace.

Her voice full of enthusiasm, she said, "Together, we can achieve great things." We can reduce the gaps separating us, heal the past, and create a future appropriate for our best wishes and goals. Bravery, empathy, and a willingness to love and serve with all we have—and all we are—are all it takes.
As the final words left her lips, Amara had deep and persistent knowledge that she was exactly where she was supposed to be, doing exactly what she was supposed to be doing. She felt serenity and direction sweep over her.
She realized that the road ahead would be long and arduous, full of obstacles at every turn. She retreated off the platform, and the clamour of the crowd still resonated in her ears.

She knew, too, that she was not alone; she had an army of supporters and friends at her side, prepared to fight alongside her to be the change people yearned for in the world.

Then Dr. Amara Johnson entered the future ready to greet whatever lay ahead, one valuable life at a time, a heart full of hope and a soul full of dedication.

Chapter 19

Festive Dawn

Amara felt a little touch on her shoulder as the celebration was coming to an end and the throngs were gently spreading into the darkness. She turned, her eyes widening in shock as she came upon a stranger—a guy with sharp eyes and an aged, wise-lined face.

"Dr. Johnson," he continued, his voice low and urgent. I must speak with you. It's a critical issue.

Amara stopped momentarily, her head whirling with questions and uncertainty. Who was this guy, and what could he possibly want with her? However, the intensity of his gaze and his look conveyed to her that she should not dismiss this moment.

She looked around to see no one observing, then nodded and followed the stranger to a quiet area of the plaza. Her voice was tight with expectation as she asked, "What is it?" "What must you tell me?"

As she leant closer, she felt the warmth of the man's breath against her ear. His murmur, "There is something from Rev. Okafor as a thank you for helping him regain himself from all the village mysterious evils that had tormented his whole life," sent a shiver down Amara's back. "It is about the forces poised to bring down everything, everything, not about the lineage chart or a secret about your history here or about who you really are. This encompasses everything; he gestured towards his pocket and expressed his gratitude.

Amara's heart raced as the implications of his words swirled in her mind. She had always known that there were riddles about Rev. Okafor's family, queries left unmet for as long as she could recall. She only heard rumours, but the stranger confirmed her deepest fears; the Rev. Okafor family remains mysterious, despite his pledge to freely share the region's crystal legends.

"What would you mean?" With a somewhat shaky voice, Amara questioned the man claiming to be a disciple of Rev. Okafor. "Amara is staring at the man's pocket; what secret is in there?"

The guy shook his head, a depressed grin flickering at the margins of his lips. "I cannot tell you everything even if I know them," he said regretfully. "Not yet. Nevertheless, know this: the truth is out there, just waiting for you. And once you discover it, everything will transform.

He took out a small, leather-bound book from his pocket. He pressed it into Amara's hands and said, "Take this; it's the last gift from our dying clergyman." "They will both mentor you on your whole trip." Amara gazed down at the book, her fingertips following the aged and battered cover. Even with the weight of the book in her palms and the sense of destiny and purpose radiating from its pages, she is not ready to read another Okafor family mystery.

Then the stranger disappeared, melting back into the shadows as if he had never been there at all, just as quickly as he had shown. Amara stayed there for a long time, her mind racing with thoughts and doubts. She knew she should be afraid; the sight of this mysterious guy and the secrets he claimed to hold should make her terrified and anxious.

Instead, she experienced a unique tranquillity, a reassuring certainty that this path was her destiny. She always knew that the Okafor family narrative had more to offer than the pieces she had managed to piece together over the years—more to her own identity.

With this book in her hands and the promise of answers just beyond the horizon, she realized that the time had come to confront her history and confront the reality that had long eluded her.
She inhaled deeply, straightening her shoulders, slid the book into her pocket, then proceeded inside her office drawers. She is not ready for the long, difficult road ahead, even though she knew there would be obstacles at every turn.

Nonetheless, once she was ready, she knew she had the will and bravery to see this through to the very finish.

Driven forward, ready to accept whatever was ahead, one valuable truth at a time, Dr. Amara Johnson had a heart full of hope and a spirit full of determination.

Epilogue

As the sun sank, Amara was ascending the meandering route to the
hill with a view of Igbuzor. Underfoot, the dew was still clinging to
the grass; the air was cool and clean.
Stopped temporarily at the hilltop, she gazed down at the large town.
The streets were calm and quiet; the houses and buildings remained
buried in the fog of morning.

Still in early morning calm, Amara could feel the liveliness of the
area—the sense of promise and possibility that seemed to pulsate
through the air itself. She had grown up and raised her family; the
neighbourhood had shaped her into the lady she was today.

Even as she stood there, savouring its beauty and majesty, she
couldn't get rid of the sensation that there was still so much she didn't
know—that many mysteries and riddles were just beyond her grasp.
She carried the leather-bound book the stranger had given her, a
constant reminder of the journey ahead. She had poured many hours
over its pages, attempting to interpret the cryptic hints and latent
meanings found therein.
Though she struggled to make sense of it all, Amara knew she was
on the right track and would find the answers she sought.

She considered the events of the last year, the successes, and the
obstacles that had taken her to this point. She considered the subtle
and significant changes she had impacted in the lives of the children
she had assisted as well as the families she had supported.
She also thought about the group of friends and supporters who had
remained by her side, believing in her even when she doubted
herself.

She realized she couldn't have done it alone; her success and
resilience were proof of love, compassion, and shared goals.

She also realized that, irrespective of the mysteries and riddles the
future may bring, she would address the challenges ahead with the
same courage and persistence that had led her there.
Her vocation and purpose were to defend life. She battled for justice,
equality, and a brighter future for everyone seeking to soothe the

grieving and heal the ill.

She would not waver until she achieved her goal of loving every child, supporting every family, and honouring every life with all its beauty, complexity, and wonder.

As the sun rose higher in the sky and spread its warm, golden glow over the settlement below, Amara breathed deeply and filled her lungs with the pure, clean air.
Then, ready to greet whatever lay ahead, one beautiful moment at a time, she turned and proceeded down the hill with a heart full of hope and a spirit full of determination.
She knew the journey would be long and difficult, but she also knew that she had the love and support of all those who believed in her—in her work and the planet she helped fight so hard to create.

Armed with that knowledge and unwavering belief, Dr. Amara Johnson moved forth into the future prepared to meet whatever obstacles were ahead, one priceless life at a time.

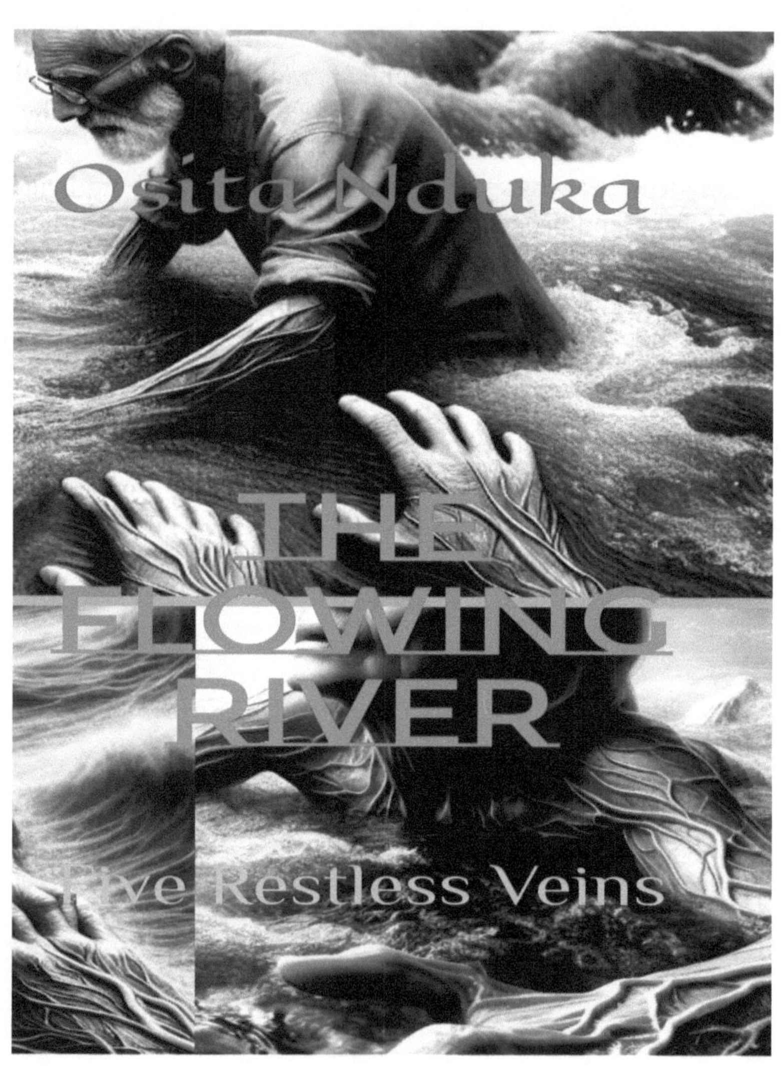

BOOK V

Author's Note

Closing the last part of the Restless Veins series, I would like to sincerely thank you for accompanying Amara on her incredible trip through childhood to adulthood. The lifeblood of this story has been your consistent support and energy.

Though Amara's narrative is fictitious, I hope the ideas of resiliency, family community, and the need to appreciate one's history speak to you personally. To create a realistic and relevant environment in building this planet, I have looked to actual locations and vocations. Aimed at captivating viewers from various walks of life, the varied spectrum of dramatic themes spun throughout the series was a conscious decision.

Saying goodbye to Igili, Wirad, and Igbuzor, along with their vibrant ensemble of personalities, excites me to welcome you on a fresh journey.

Look forward to my next work, "The Unbreakable Egg.".
An adventure, mystery, and sci-fi trilogy meant to keep you on the edge of your seat.

Thank you once again for joining the Restless Veins family. I hope Amara's narrative resonates with you and perhaps inspires you to embrace all the aspects that define you.

Until our next literal trip...Ciao! Ciao!!

Main Characters

Dr. Amara Johnson – Local Doctor, community leader, NGO founder

Jiu Adekunle - Local Plumber, Amara's husband and partner

Jenny Alonso- Amara's birth mother

Nathan Okechukwu - Amara's birth father

Nuss Johnson - Amara's foster brother, adventurer

Zarah Johnson - Amara's foster sister

Emily Carter- Amara's childhood friend and a local lawyer

Mayor Sholina Okoye - Leader of Igbuzor, Amara's mentor and ally

Councilman Okorie Talel - Corrupt official fighting to take over from Mayor Sholina

Rachel Mendoza - Journalist, undercover investigator working with Gayan

Mr. and Mrs. Johnson - Amara's deceased foster parents

Amara's children (unnamed)

Dr. Patel Sharma - Amara's mentor

Lilly Adebayo - Amara's close friend

Rev Okafor Solomon Christian - Giver of mysterious book

Council of Elders - Shadowy group of corrupt Indigenous officials

Mr. Gayan Okorie Ngannou- Known local Media team leader

The archivist Ikenga Luti – Leader of the shadowy Indigenous elder's council

Key Locations

Igbuzor - The town where the story is set

Igbuzor General Hospital - Amara's workplace

Hope for Tomorrow Foundation - Amara's NGO located at Block B of the community centre

The newly built Isiolu educational wing and community health clinic at Igbuzor

The Johnson family home

Amara and Jiu's Family home

Wirad - A coastal neighboring town where Amara and Jiu have a getaway

Prologue

Dr. Amara Johnson was standing on the balcony of her house, staring toward the horizon as the sun sank over Igbuzor, casting orange and pink colours across the heavens. A reminder of the active community she had devoted her life to serving, the warm air brought the smells of cooking fires and blossoming flowers.

She carried the leather-bound book the enigmatic stranger had given her during the final day of the yearly celebration of the town. She had lost it for months in the whirlwind of her hectic office job, but recent circumstances had brought it back into her consciousness.

The pages of the book teemed with mysterious symbols and cryptic notes, suggesting mysteries long buried in Igbuzor's past. Amara had discovered disturbing links between the present and past Igbuzor political environments, as well as the forces attempting to destroy her NGO, when she began to decode its contents.
More than that, however, the book appeared to speak of a higher destiny, a role Amara was intended to play in determining the course of not only Igbuzor but maybe something much more.

Amara sensed someone behind her as she stood there, lost in contemplation. She turned to see Jiu, his face marked with love and worry.

Quietly approaching her, he said, "You're thinking about the book again, aren't you?"
Amara nodded, bending into his hug. "I can't shake the feeling that we are about to encounter something profound, Jiu." Something is going to transform everything.

Jiu planted a kiss right at her temple. "We will face whatever happens together." We, including you, me, our children, and our entire family, both biological and adopted, will confront any situation together.

Amara's heart began to tremble as she mentioned her blood kin. After years of estrangement, Jenny and Nathan, her biological parents, had just reached out, expressing a desire to re-connect. It was a difficulty she hadn't anticipated, yet another layer woven into the already complicated fabric of her existence.

"Do you think I'm doing the right thing?" she whispered, her voice barely audible. "Meeting with Jenny and Nathan is mean."

Jiu stopped momentarily to give his comments great thought. "I believe," he finally said, "that you must listen to your heart." You have always been one to believe in second chances and the healing power of love for past hurts. Perhaps this is your chance to heal a part of yourself that you were unaware was still wounded.

Amara nodded, buoyed by his constant support. She became excited as she gazed out over the place she loved so very much. Whatever obstacles lied ahead—reconnecting with her biological parents, learning the book's secrets, confronting the dishonest forces endangering her work—she knew she wouldn't tackle them alone.

Amara inhaled deeply, then turned back towards her home, the coziness of her family, and the promise of a fresh day. She murmured, "Come on," to Jiu, a grin flickering at the margins of her lips. "Let's go inside. Tomorrow will be very significant.

Closing the balcony doors behind them, neither Amara nor Jiu noticed the faint glow emerging from the leather-bound book, a subtle pulse of light that seemed to beat in tune with the rhythm of Igbuzor itself. Amara had prepared the stage and positioned the players accordingly. Amara's amazing trip was about to start its last chapter.

PART 1

THE RIVER TRIP

Chapter 1

Sitting on the Riverbank

The sunset sunbathed the vibrant gathering in Amara's yard in warm light. Friends and relatives were celebrating Amara's recent achievements from the community annual award—her excellent recovery, the founding of her NGO, and the general delight of being together again. Laughter and conversation filled the air. Everyone seemed to have forgotten the financial burden Amara's NGO had to bear due to the generosity of a few contributors.

Amara went through the throng in her lovely house, her heart full and her smile brilliant. She stopped to give Emily, her childhood best friend and now a rising legal star, a hug. Emily said, "I'm so proud of you," in her ear. "You have gone so far."

Tears stuck in Amara's eyes. She had come far, quite definitely. From her difficult beginning as a preterm baby born to parents battling addiction, to her stint in the foster system, to today, it was a journey she could scarcely believe.

Her eye strayed to Jiu, her boyfriend and rock, working the grill with a ridiculous apron and a smile. He drew her attention and winked, his pride and affection clear. Amara's heart surged. Building a future with him excites her.

The celebration abruptly came to a halt. Amara looked to see what had caused the abrupt change in the mood as two strangers were walking into the home but remained at the door; none of the neighbours knew these two old people. Two people she had never quite recognized and never expected to see again were standing timidly at the yard's edge.

As her long-lost parents arrived, Amara felt Jiu's calm hand on her shoulder. Their faces mixed trepidation with hesitant delight. Jenny said, "Amara," with tears shining in her eyes. "We have sorely missed you."

Amara stood still, her head whirling. What is this about?
Blood is usually thicker than water, so naturally, Amara pointed at them with a perplexed look. Father?" Amara murmured the words in a skeptical tone. Even after all these years, they remained clear and unambiguous. The birth parents are Jenny and Nathan. Jenny and Nathan slowly nodded in agreement with Amara.

Amara experienced a surge of emotions that included shock, wrath, uncertainty, and a startling undertone of optimism. Here, what were they doing? Why now, after so much time? How could they have known anything about our home? Right now, what do they want?

As a little girl, she had dreamt about this moment so often, picturing warm hugs and emotional reunions. But the truth was considerably more nuanced. These individuals not only brought Amara into the world, but also allowed addiction to take control of their lives, leading to her removal from their care.

Looking at them now, Amara could see her own traits reflected in their lined features. The resolute chin of her mother and the kind brown eyes of her father stood out. She could also see, however, the traces of challenging lives and difficult decisions.

Between them, the stillness weighed heavily with unsaid words and ancient hurts. At last Nathan cleared his voice. "We know we have no right to just show up like this," he added, his voice sharp with feeling. "But we have been labouring to correct problems. Above all, we wanted to visit you to share with you our pride in the lady you have grown to be."

Tears blazing in the back of her throat burned Amara. She wanted to be angry with them, demanding explanations for their lack of presence when it was most needed. But another side—the one that had laboured so hard to mend and pardon—murmured that everyone deserved a second chance.

She moved forward, bridging their gap. "I think we have a lot to talk about," she said quietly. "Why won't you come inside?"

Amara could feel the weight of her loved ones staring back at her as she guided her parents inside the home. She understood that this unexpected meeting would raise many questions and bring back memories of past suffering for all of them. She was strong enough, however, to confront it—to hear her parents out and choose if, going ahead, they would play any part at all.

Amara inhaled deeply to be ready for the challenging but necessary talks ahead. It was time to confront her past and perhaps weave its ghosts into the fabric of her present.

Chapter 2

Flashing river waves

Memories of her early life washed back to Jenny and Nathan as Amara relaxed into the living room with her biological parents. She could almost smell the stale cigarette smoke filling their little flat, and she could almost hear loud shouts and slamming doors waking her from her little mattress at night.

Even though she was too young to fully understand what was happening, she could sense the strain and desperation in the air. Barely more than children themselves, her parents had been utterly unprepared for the responsibilities of motherhood.

The first memories Amara had been a flurry of movements and change. They bounced between relatives' sofas and dark hotel rooms, never seeming to settle in one spot for very long. Her parents would often disappear for days at a time, leaving her in the care of whoever was available to pick her up.

However, there were also fleeting moments of affection and brightness. Amara remembered curling up for nighttime reading with her mother, her gentle voice soothing her to sleep. She recalled her father tossing her high in his arms, his laughter loud and mixing with her joyful screams.

There was an undertone of affection even amid the turmoil, a feeling that her parents were doing their best. But the seductive lure of their addictions usually undercuts their best.

Amara could clearly remember the day everything turned around. Quietly seated on her little cot, she was attempting to ignore the progressively loud and hostile words emanating from the kitchen. Suddenly, her parents became quiet, followed by a loud bang and the sound of broken glass.

The kitchen scene was filled with chaos. Broken dishes scattered the floor, and among all of this was her parents, falling asleep under the effects of yelling at each other with a viciousness Amara had never seen before. Amara was looking at all that was happening at the time with tears running silently down her face. They were so lost in their own suffering and passed out they didn't even notice when the social worker, Mrs. Thompson, Sgt. Kazley, and ambulance crew came onto their property to take Amara as a baby.

The cops arrived that night, hauling Amara away from the only family she had ever known. She remembered clinging to her social worker's hand as she watched her home vanish into the distance and followed her to a waiting automobile.

Amara wandered between foster homes throughout the next few years. Some were kind and helpful, doing their best to provide her stability and affection. Others, on the other hand, were less kind and helpful, making Amara feel more like a burden than a child, until she encountered the Johnson family.

She held onto her parents' love as an innocent child even as she realized they were losing their battle with addiction. Every time they relocated her to a new house, she hoped for the moment they would return, clean and sober, ready to reunite as a family. Though they never did.

Under the soft encouragement of her instructors, the unwavering support of her social workers, and finally the pure love of the Johnsons, the foster family that would permanently alter her life, Amara gradually learned to find her strength and her family elsewhere.

Years later, Amara sat opposite Jenny and Nathan, marvelling at the journey that led her to this point. She had battled so hard to create a life of meaning and direction and had endured so much.

Amara saw the weight of her birth parents' regrets—the years of suffering and self-loathing—and stared back from their eyes. She could, however, also see a flimsy but driven will to right things.

She replied gently, "Tell me everything," reaching out to hold their hands in hers. "I am listening."

And Amara felt calm come over her as Jenny and Nathan started to talk; their voices shook with feeling. Long overdue, this was a reckoning that may mend past hurts and create fresh starts.

She was ready to hear their narrative—ready to confront her history and figure out how to spin it into the woman she had evolved into. Amara understood that every step she took, every struggle she faced, and every victory made her who she was. She also took enormous pride in that person, scars and all.

Chapter 3

Calling for the river baits

Amara felt a rush of emotions churning in her chest as Jenny and Nathan's comments swept over her. Knowing their struggles and how far their addictions drove them was enlightening and devastating.

They discussed their encounters with young individuals in high school, describing their journey as two lost yet drawn-together souls, guided by their shared demons. Amara's unplanned pregnancy occurred during a period of youthful recklessness, amidst a backdrop of drugs and hopelessness. However, Jenny's discovery of Amara's pregnancy provided a glimmer of hope—a chance to transform their lives.

It seemed to work for a while. Driven to provide a better life for their child, Jenny and Nathan kept clean all during the pregnancy. But the demands of new fatherhood and the always-hovering threat of addiction were too much to handle.

Jenny, tears streaming down her cheeks, said, "We loved you so much, Amara." But we were young and unprepared. Though every day was a hardship, we felt we could manage it.

Nathan nodded with a gloomy look. "The drugs had a powerful pull on us." Each time, we reassured ourselves that we would truly achieve sobriety. That is the last time. Then the appetites would strike, and it seemed as if nothing else mattered."

Amara listened as her heart ached. She could see the unvarnished suffering on her parents' cheeks, the weight of years of sorrow and remorse. She wanted to be furious with them, demanding to know how they could have prioritized their addictions over their children's. However, her dedication to knowledge and treatment revealed the subtle nature of the illness that was engulfing them.

Nathan's voice broke as he spoke. The most agonizing experience was losing you, Amara; we endured job losses, evictions, and overdoses, but none of these were as painful as losing you. When we woke up and discovered they had taken you away, it felt as if all the light had disappeared from our planet.

Tears were pricking at Amara's own eyes. She felt abandoned and spent many years wondering how her parents could have left her behind. Hearing about their pain and seeing their profound and lasting love for her despite their flaws gave her a different viewpoint.

Jenny added, gently, "We made many attempts to become clean." "We wanted to be the parents you so well deserved. However, the addiction intensified with each passing moment. We felt trapped in a dream that we couldn't escape.

Amara reached out to clasp her own mother's shaking hand. She answered, "I understand," softly and gently. "Addiction is a dreadful illness. Addiction neither identifies you as a wicked person nor implies that you love me less. You were unwell, and you needed aid.

Jenny began to weep, her shoulders shaking. "We so sorely needed assistance. However, we were too embarrassed and terrified to ask for help. We claimed we could manage it on our own. We also lost the most valuable item we have ever owned.
Nathan leant forward with a fierce gaze. "Losing you woke us up Amara, It made us realize that we needed to change, both for you and for ourselves. Our aim was to become individuals you would be proud of even if we never crossed paths again. again."

Amara felt a knot in her throat. She had retained for all these years a picture of her parents as self-serving, irresponsible individuals who had thrown her aside. Indeed, the people in front of her were shattered, but they also were profoundly human, battling a struggle she could not conceive.

She added gently, "I'm proud of you for getting help." "I understand that it couldn't have been easy." And I appreciate you coming back into my life and being honest about your path.

Jenny and Nathan looked at one another, a flutter of optimism visible in their eyes. "We know we can't change the past," Nathan remarked. "But, if you're game, we may be part of your future. We aim to enhance the wonderful family you've established, not to displace it, but to acquaint ourselves with the remarkable woman you've transformed into.

Amara reclined, her thoughts spinning. It was a lot to absorb—a significant change in her perspective of her past and her role in the world. She understood that including her biological parents in her life would be a journey with plenty of emotional work, limits, and patience needed.

Gazing at their optimistic, haunted expressions, she knew it was a journey she was ready to embark on. She saw in their narrative parallels of her own: a story of resiliency, of conquering the challenges, of choosing to love and light in the face of darkness.

"I would like that," she murmured gently, a grin flowering on her face. "I too would want to get to know you. To choose a path forward, collectively."

And Amara felt a piece of her heart that had long been absent slip in place as Jenny and Nathan's faces lit up with delight and relief. She had dedicated her life to building a family of choice, but now she was receiving a precious gift: the chance to reclaim a portion of her blood, her legacy.

Amara knew it would not be simple. She had to navigate through years of suffering and separation, mend old injuries, and cultivate new trust. She was prepared for the challenge yet eager to embrace the possibility of a future filled with all the shattered pieces of her past.

Since Amara fought and survived. She also understood that the best victories often sprung from the most severe scars. She would weave this fresh thread into the fabric of her life with love and will, producing a design more exquisite and complicated than she had ever dreamed.

Chapter 4

Incoming river current

Amara was struggling with a rainbow of contradictory feelings in the days after her birth when her parents suddenly reappeared. Reuniting with her birth family and filling in her personal history was also exciting. But another aspect, the one that had learned to be cautious of loss and disappointment, murmured warnings in her ear.

She comprehended that cultivating a bond with Jenny and Nathan would require a nuanced dance, requiring transparent communication and clearly defined boundaries. She wanted her vision of an instantaneous family to fall apart under the weight of unrealized aspirations—not to rush headlong into it.

Amara was also keenly aware of how this abrupt shift would affect the other significant individuals in her life—those who had supported her consistently. She understood that her loved ones would respond differently—complicatedly—to this fresh news.

She started looking first to Jiu, her rock and boyfriend. As always, his constant presence and unwavering support soothed her tormented spirit. However, Amara also observed a cautious wariness due to his deep affection for her, as well as an undercurrent of protection in his demeanour.

Pulling her near, he said, "I'm here for you, no matter what." "But you also have to be cautious, guarding your heart. Amara, you have worked rather hard to create a decent life. I want you never to suffer once again."

Amara nodded and leant her head on his robust shoulder. "I know," she mumbled. "And I promise, I'm into this with an open mind." I don't see a fairy tale reunion. However, I do believe that I should give them an opportunity to explore whether we could be in each other's lives in a constructive manner.

Jiu planted a kiss on her forehead, his touch a mute pledge of encouragement. "Then that's what we'll do," he stated with firmness. "Together."

Amara then contacted the Johnsons, the foster family adopting her and loving her as their own. She understood that the notion of her birth parents coming back may be disturbing for them, a reminder of the impermanence that always lurked under the surface of foster family life.

First to express her worries was Zarah, her confidante and foster sister. Her brow wrinkled with anxiety; she questioned, "Are you sure about this, Amara?" "I know how much you yearn for a relationship with your birth family, but I don't want you to be setting yourself up for more heartache."

Nuss, her foster brother, interjected with a sober focus, replacing his typically light-hearted manner. "We're your family, Amara," he added with outstanding conviction. "We will always be your family, wherever. You have nothing to owe these folks."

Overwhelmed by the great love and commitment emanating from her foster brothers, Amara felt tears welling up in her eyes. She answered quietly, "I know." "I could never forget it; I could never replace you in my heart." To determine whether Jenny and Nathan fit into my life, however, I do believe I need to at least attempt to know where I come from. My affection for each of you remains unaffected.

As Amara considered the Johnsons, the foster parents who had showered her with so much affection and encouragement, she experienced a wave of sadness. Her life had been profoundly empty after their terrible death in an automobile accident; she was still learning to negotiate.

As she faced this new challenge, she longed deeply for their presence to offer their gentle guidance and unwavering support. Despite her absence, Amara could sense their love surrounding her, guiding her.

She contacted Zarah and Nuss, the Johnson siblings she now considered her own. Together, they had all suffered the death of their parents; their common pain had strengthened their relationship.

"I wish Mum and Dad were here to help me out," Amara said, her voice quivering just slightly. "They seemed to always know the right thing to say—the right road forward."

Zarah drew Amara closer, placing an arm around her shoulders. "They are here, in a way," she said softly. They are present in the teachings they imparted and the love they offered us. I know Amara would be proud of your kindness and bravery in facing this.

Nuss nodded, tears gleaming in his eyes. Unshed tears. Indeed, he said. "Your dad's smart mind and Mum's great heart speak to me. You, sister, reside in you. And in each of us."

Leaning into the hug of her siblings, Amara found strength in their unbroken link and shared past. They still had each other even though they had lost so much. And it was rather strong.

Amara found comfort in the support of her chosen family and friends as she negotiated the complicated feelings around the homecoming of her biological parents. One of her childhood closest friends, Emily, was always kind and encouraging.

"I can't even imagine how overwhelming this must be," Emily

replied with sympathetic eyes. But from what I know, Amara. You possess an abundance of love and forgiveness. Though you should trust your emotions, do not be hesitant to establish limits. You deserve pleasure and tranquility.

Another buddy, Lilly, offered a shoulder to weep on and a listening ear. "I'm here for you, no matter what," she said. "Amara, you have seen so much. But you've always emerged stronger. This is yet another chapter in your amazing narrative.

Not even Amara's mentor and advisor, Dr. Patel, had wise advice to offer. "You have a rare opportunity, Amara," he added, kindly glistening eyes. "You have a rare opportunity to build fresh relationships and mend past hurts." Even though it won't be easy, I have faith in you. You have the grace and will to manage whatever comes your way."

Amara had peace come over her as she listened to the words of encouragement and support from her loved ones. Indeed, this was an emotionally demanding period. Indeed, she had to confront both new anxieties and old traumas. Still, she was not alone. She had an army of love and encouragement behind her, ready to catch her should she trip.

Amara then decided to let her biological parents know about a relationship, with deep breathing and a resolute heart guiding her choice. She understood it would be a route with many curves, a path full of both delight and suffering. However, she knew this was the path she had to take—part of her story.

Amara entered this new phase of her life knowing the love of her chosen family and the bravery of her own beliefs. She was prepared to welcome all the bits of her past and thread them into the fabric of her future. Whatever was ahead was just waiting for her.

The furnace of hardship forged Amara into a lady, tempered by the love and encouragement of those who believed in her. Deep in her spirit, she also knew she had the will to withstand any storm and come out on the other side stronger and more compassionate than before.

Chapter 5

Waves ignited

As Amara battled whether to allow her biological parents, Jenny and Nathan, into her life, her thoughts kept wandering toward the journey that had brought her to this place. Though the journey had been full of incredible challenges and unimaginable pain, it also had accomplishments that enabled her to become the woman she is today.

Amara recalled her early years in the foster care system, when the wounds from the abandonment of her original parents were still raw and bleeding. She remembered the uncertainty and fear that had filled her young heart—the sense of aimlessness in a world that seemed so frigid and random.
Still, there had been flashes of hope—spikes of light guiding her ahead—even in those darkest years. She thought about the kind social workers who had stood up for her, the professors who had nurtured her skills, and the friends who had stood by her side no matter what.

The Johnsons, the foster family, arrived and brought about a profound transformation. Amara had never felt like she did when she entered their cozy, friendly house. She felt like she belonged. The Johnsons had given her the valuable gift of family, relentless support, and pure love, in addition to a roof over her head and food on the table.
Amara's heart ached as she thought about Mr. and Mrs. Johnson, the parents she had chosen, who adored her and guided her with such elegance and knowledge. Her terrible loss had left a void in her life that would never fill, and it still left her breathless when she allowed herself to fully experience it.

Amara could still feel the intensity of their love encircling her; however, even in her loss, they were still supporting her. She had learned so much from the Johnsons about resiliency, about finding delight and meaning even in the face of unthinkable hardship. Family was about far more than just blood; they had told her; it was about the people who showed up daily to love and encourage you over the ups and downs of life.

Amara came to see from thinking back on her path that each step and difficulty had helped to define her into the person she was now. Her early abandonment had caused her immense empathy for the suffering of others and a strong drive to assist and heal wherever she could. Her foster family's affection and direction had instilled in her a strong desire to achieve—to change the world.

And now Amara knew she was using all the power and knowledge she had acquired over the years as she stood on the brink of a fresh connection with her biological parents. She was aware that the path ahead would not be simple, that obstacles would arise, and that uncertainty would strike at times.

However, Amara realized she was no longer a lost, damaged girl. She was a survivor, a fighter, and a woman who had come to see beauty and purpose in even the most terrible of environments. She had the skills and the help she needed to gracefully and boldly negotiate this new phase of her life.

And so, Amara decided to give her biological parents an opportunity, breathing deeply and hoping broadly. She didn't owe them anything, but instead, she owed it to herself to explore every facet of her story, thereby asserting every aspect of her identity.

She came to see that the road toward forgiveness and reconciliation would be long and meandering, with both happy and sad incidents. Amara knew, too, that she was ready for the work—ready to squarely confront her past and find out how to thread it into the fabric of her future.

Rising from the flames, Amara was a woman who had become even more sensitive, even more resilient, and even more driven to follow a life of meaning and purpose. Knowing the love of her chosen family and the power of her own beliefs, she also believed she could overcome anything.

She was ready to welcome every aspect of her existence—the darkness and the brightness, the agony and the delight, the past and the future.
She was poised to be the hero of her own story, to create the next chapter with love, bravery, and an open heart. And whatever lay ahead, Amara knew she would confront it head-on, with the elegance and strength defining her path so far.

PART 2

THORNS ON THE RIVER TRIP PATHS

Chapter 6

Listening to the water splash

As Amara sat across from her biological parents in the comfortable living room of her house, a surrealistic feeling washed over her. These two people had lived only in her mind for so many years, in the foggy, half-remembered visions of her early life. Now here they were, real and bloody, bursting with anxious energy, eager to fill the gaps in her past.t.

Jenny spoke first; her voice shook with emotion. We want to tell you and explain so much, Amara," she said. We should first, however, apologise. We are aware that our decisions and behaviour caused you much suffering. No day goes by without thinking of you or regretting events, even though we cannot change anything."

Nathan nodded, tears flashing in his eyes unshed. "Amara, you were born at a time when we were very young and inexperienced. We believed that having a kid would somehow make everything right, provide the means to conquer our addictions, and create a true life together. The reality, however, was much more difficult than we had ever dreamed.

Amara listened carefully; her heart ached with a combination of old grief and fresh insight. She could see the suffering carved on her parents' faces from years of grief and remorse.

"We tried, Amara," Jenny said with a broken voice. "We really worked hard to be excellent parents to you. However, the drugs and our lifestyle had a strong hold on us. Every time we thought we were making progress; something would set us back. And you were the innocent one, the one most affected by our shortcomings."

Nathan reached out to gently grasp Jenny's hand in support. "We experienced numerous moments of despair," he said softly. The most challenging aspect was losing you, Amara; we faced job loss, eviction, overdosing, but losing you was the most difficult. Our entire world seemed to have collapsed when CPS hauled you away. We realized we had let you down in the worst possible way.

Tears were pricking at the margins of Amara's eyes. She had spent so many years feeling abandoned and unloved, but when she heard the genuine anguish in their voices, she began to see that the enormous force of addiction had driven her parents' behaviour rather than a lack of love.

"We went to rehab so many times," Jenny remarked, wiping away her tears. "Every time we promised it would be the last, we would get clean for real and figure out a means of getting you back. Despite our best efforts, we consistently failed and reverted to our previous behaviours. We felt trapped in a dream, unable to break free.

Nathan nodded; his face tormented. "The years went by, and from a distance we saw you flourish despite all the difficulties you encountered. Amara, you really were very pleased with yourself and in wonder at your fortitude and will. However, we understood that we had no right to intervene in your life or to return after enduring such immense pain.

Amara slanted forward, her brow wrinkled. She inquired, gently, "What changed?" "Why stretch out now, after all this time?"

Jenny and Nathan glanced at one another, a flutter of hope flickering between them. "We have been clean for six years now," Nathan replied with a firm voice. Despite its importance, maintaining our sobriety has been the most challenging thing we have ever done. We have been attending meetings, working with sponsors, and actually doing the necessary research to grasp our addiction and create a fresh life."

Jenny nodded, a faint smile adorning her face. "And part of that effort has included addressing our history and owning up to the damage we've inflicted. Amara, we want to try, despite the knowledge that we can never undo our past actions. We wish to be in your life in any manner that is comfortable for you. We aim to enrich the family you've established, not to take its place, but to discover the remarkable woman you've transformed into."

Amara sat back, her head whirling. It was a lot to absorb—a whole rereading of the story she had been living for so long. Looking at her biological parents, however, she had a flutter of something fresh in her heart—the sincerity and optimism in their eyes.

Reconfiguration. comprehending. The prospect for a fresh start. She understood it would be difficult and uncertain. Amara, nevertheless, also knew she could muster the will to rise from the past and create something fresh.

She murmured gently, "Thank you for telling me all of this," reaching out to grab her parents' hands. "I understand it cannot have been simple. And I value your candour and readiness to admit your faults. I will lie; it's a lot to digest. However, I am prepared to embark on this journey and explore its potential outcomes.

Tears streamed down Jenny and Nathan's cheeks as their faces sparkled with hesitant delight. "Thank you, Amara," Jenny murmured. "We appreciate you considering us. We swear to do everything in our ability to be worthy of your confidence and pardon.

Looking at her biological parents, Amara sensed something changing deep within her—a piece of her heart long hidden away beginning to break free. This was a different chapter, a fresh chance for her to heal, mature, and redefine what family meant to her. Having children of her own now, Amara understood what it meant to be a parent.

Amara knew this would be a fantastic tale. Ups and downs, times of connection, and hardships would abound. She was nonetheless prepared to welcome the intricacy and depth of her narrative.

Amara was a lady who had discovered beauty from shattered bits and strength amid difficulty. She knew she could weather any storm and could emerge even stronger and more compassionate on the other side, with the love of her chosen family and the cautious promise of this new relationship.

Chapter 7

Clapping waves

As the initial shock and emotional turmoil of her birth parents' return began to subside, Amara found herself increasingly captivated by the details of their story, the hidden aspects of her own past. She saw that her own healing process depended critically on her knowing about their path, challenges, and successes.

And so, Amara asked Jenny and Nathan to tell her their whole tale, a combination of fear and will. Once again, they gathered in Amara's cozy living room, sharing a dish of homemade cookies and steaming tea on the coffee table as a small gesture of comfort before the challenging conversation that lay ahead.

Jenny inhaled deeply, her hands securely gathered on her lap. "I guess the best place to start is at the beginning," she remarked quietly. "Nathan and I met when we were barely adolescents; both of us were already rather deep with drugs and booze. Our common suffering and our need to flee the tragedies of our own childhoods united us.

Nathan nodded; his tone serious. We thought we were unbeatable and could do anything with each other back then. However, we were just two lost children navigating life through self-medication.

Amara listened carefully; her heart hurt for the young, fragile forms of her parents. Their narrative had echoes of her own hardships, the way unhealed scars may spread and affect generations.

"When I became pregnant with you, Amara," Jenny said, "it was a wake-up call, a moment of clarity among the tumult. We felt compelled to cultivate better lives for our child and embrace change as well. For a while, it seemed like we were on the verge of success.

Nathan's expression relaxed, and he cast a far-off glance. "Those early days with you were some of the happiest of my life," he remarked gently. "Holding you in my arms, seeing you develop and evolve... it felt like a miracle, a chance at atonement. I felt that my love for you would be sufficient to keep me pure, to give me the will to conquer anything."

As Amara well knew, however, the hold of addiction was not readily reversible. Jenny and Nathan related the gradual, agonizing breakdown of their sobriety—the way previous traumas and habits had seeped back in and undermined the brittle foundation they had sought to create.

"We would have periods of clarity, moments when we would get clean and try to put our lives back together," Jenny recounted, tears welling in her eyes. "But something would always happen—a job loss, a fight, a trigger we couldn't resist—and we would fall back down the rabbit hole."

In the crosshairs of their vicious cycle, Amara could feel her own tears ready to flow, her heart bleeding for her parents and for her younger self.

"Losing custody of you to the system was the darkest moment of our lives," Nathan continued, his voice full of feeling. "It felt as though all the brightness had disappeared from the earth, as though we had failed in the one area that truly mattered." After that, both of us Amara began to spiral out of control, and Nathan stopped.

Nathan exhaled shakily, his eyes fogged with terrible recollections. "We spun hard after your loss, Amara. Deeper into our addictions, both of us sought to dull the pain of our failed parenting. There were moments when I felt I would not survive and when the thought of just not waking seemed like a comfort."

Jenny stretched over to clasp Nathan's hand, a sign of unity and common loss. "We lost our house, our employment, and our sense of ourselves. We lived in and out of rehab centres and the streets. Despite our dreadful circumstances, we couldn't seem to break free.

Amara's heart tightened upon witnessing her parents at their lowest point, engulfed by an illness that had stripped them of everything that held significance. She could clearly understand how addiction would undermine even the strongest of ties and transform love into a twisted, desperate tool.

"It went on like that for years," Jenny said, remorse weighing her voice. "We could never make it stay, although we would have fleeting spells of sobriety. The remorse and the shame—the weight of what we had lost—always followed us and pulled us down.

Nathan nodded; he looked far away. Only after we had reached our lowest point did things start to change. I suffered from a terrible overdose. Before they could bring me back, I was clinically dead for many minutes. And as I woke up in that hospital bed, something within me simply changed.

Amara slanted forward, her heart in her throat. She had come so close to never having the opportunity to know her father outside the shadow of his addiction, to permanently losing him.

Nathan described it as if someone had turned off a switch. Suddenly, it felt impossible to live another day under the hold of addiction. I knew I had to change and find a way out, not only for Jenny and you, Amara, but also for myself.

Tears glistened in Jenny's eyes; her grin was shaky but pleased. "My own overdose served as a wake-up call as well. Seeing him like that—so near death—made me realize how much I still had to lose and how much I wanted to live. Right there in that hospital room, we signed a contract pledging to do whatever it takes to get clean and create a life worth living.

Rising in her chest, Amara experienced a flood of feelings combining pride with loss and cautious optimism. Her parents' expressions revealed strength and resolve, and she could see the hard-earned knowledge that only comes from reaching the bottom and pulling oneself back up.

"It wasn't easy," Nathan said. "Recovery never is. We often felt tempted to give up and revert to our previous behaviours. But we had each other, and Amara, we carried memories of you. The idea of one day deserving of your pardon and of your affection kept us going even on the worst of days."

Jenny nodded, blotting at her tears. "We worked the stages, acquired sponsors, and developed a support system. We learned to face our demons rather than run from them and be honest with each other and ourselves. And we began to recover gradually, daily.

Amara sat back, her head whirling with what she had heard. This was a tale of enormous suffering and loss as well as of resiliency and the relentless character of the human spirit. Now looking at her parents, she could see the marks they bore as well as the hard-earned peace and strong love that had taken them to this point.

"Thank you for sharing all of this with me," Amara replied gently, her voice laden with feeling. "I know it couldn't have been simple to revisit those experiences. But I am so proud of you both and in wonder at your bravery."

Tears spilt freely down Jenny and Nathan's cheeks as their smiles brightened. "We are the ones who really admire you, Amara," Jenny replied. The grace and compassion you've shown us after all we've done is beyond our wildest dreams."

Looking at her biological parents, Amara saw something sliding in place—a missing piece of her own tale at last finding its home. Her legacy, her history, is a narrative of love lost and discovered as well as of struggle and atonement.

Though the path ahead was yet unknown, Amara knew she was prepared to travel it with an open heart, to welcome all the happiness, suffering, and complexity that accompanied joining this flawed, wonderful family.

Chapter 8

Widening surface currents

After the emotional disclosures from her biological parents transformed the days into weeks, Amara found herself negotiating a difficult terrain of emotions and responses from both within herself and from those closest to her. While part of her heart wanted to forgive and reconnect with Jenny and Nathan, another part feared more pain.

Her loved ones' responses, each of which handled the news of her birth parents' return in their own unique manner, reflected this inner struggle. Amara could see the worry written on Jiu's face, as his protective instincts appeared to be fighting with his desire to back her decisions. She was aware of his intense and relentless love for her, but she also knew of his anxiety and urge to protect her from any further suffering.

One evening, as they sat on the sofa, Jiu said, "I just don't want to see you get hurt again," Amara's head resting on his shoulder. "Your journey has been rather remarkable, my darling. Reopening these old wounds and allowing your biological parents to come back is a danger.

Amara moaned and curled up nearer Jiu's coziness. "I know it is," she responded gently. "Believe me, I often question and worry about myself." I feel compelled to act for their and my benefit. She's trying, Jiu. They truly are striving to be better and atone. And I want to give them that opportunity."

Jiu planted a kiss at the top of her head, his arm encircling her. "I understand," he said in a whisper. "And I will be here for you regardless of everything. I only urge you to be cautious with your heart and remember to prioritize your own well-being."

Grateful for Jiu's love and encouragement, Amara nodded. Amara knew he would support her through whatever lay ahead, as he had been through every previous difficulty they shared.

Not everyone in Amara's life at the time was nearly as sympathetic. Nuss was having trouble seeing Jenny and Nathan back in the picture. Amara could feel the resentment boiling behind his typically laid-back attitude—the way his jaw tightened at reference to her biological parents.

One day, Nuss finally expressed his frustration, saying, "I just don't get it." "After everything they did, how could you welcome them back? Amara, they don't deserve your pardon. They are not worthy of you."

Amara felt her own rage rising; a protective impulse triggered. Fighting to keep her voice calm, she replied, "It's not about what people deserve, Nuss." It's about what I believe to be correct for me and what I need. I'm not justifying what they did; rather, I'm choosing to live in the present and pay attention to the work they are currently doing."

Nuss shook his head and laughed scornfully. "People who like that don't change, Amara. They will just do you more damage; then where will you be? You will discover yourself precisely where you began gathering the fragments of your heart.

Nuss's sharp comments wounded Amara, causing tears to sting at the corners of her eyes. "I know you're just trying to defend me," she whispered softly. But Nuss, this is my choice. My path forward. You must value it even if you disagree with it.

Nuss's visage softened, a flutter of guilt over his cheeks. Reaching out to clasp Amara's hand, he apologized. "I didn't want to irritate you. Amara, I just love you so very much. I detest the idea of you suffering any longer."

Amara hugged back and grinned waterlily. "I know you do," she replied. "And I adore you for it. But Nuss, I am not the same terrified little daughter I used to be. I have all of you to depend on, and I am stronger now. I can manage whatever comes, of course.

The anxiety and uncertainty were wearing on Amara as the days went by and she negotiated the challenging dynamics of her newly enlarged family. She had always yearned for her biological parents; there were times when she could see the bond and moments of intimacy. There were miscommunications, old wounds, and new worries that could have weakened their tentative trust.

Amara leant on the love and encouragement of her selected family through it all, finding strength in their consistent presence in her life. She realized that no matter what happened to Jenny and Nathan, she would always have a house and a family with the people who had supported her through every challenge.

But Amara also knew she couldn't allow her dread of possible suffering to keep her from the chance of healing—of creating something new and beautiful from the ruins of her past. She then kept on the road to reconciliation one step at a time, deep breathing and a heart full of cautious optimism guiding her.

The compassion and wisdom of those who believed in her shaped Amara into a lady of resilience. She possessed a deep-seated determination to confront the challenges ahead and emerge from them with even greater strength and compassion.

Chapter 9

Witnessing the earth rotation

As the emotional rollercoaster of reuniting with her biological parents continued, Amara found herself more depleted—the constant tug of optimism and dread, progress, and failure wearing on her normally strong spirit. She could see herself beginning to unravel at the margins, the weight of the circumstances dragging down her heart and head.

Amara found herself in a vulnerable state when she discovered a medical emergency at her workplace with a young patient's life hanging precariously. As Amara rushed into the operating room, adrenaline flowed through her veins, and she felt a surprising clarity—a crystallization of what really mattered in the long run.

Working relentlessly to save the baby, Amara threw the last ounce of her expertise into the delicate surgery with laser clarity and calm hands. Minutes felt like hours as she traversed the difficult terrain of the surgery, each decision holding the weight of a life in balance.

It stopped as suddenly as it had started. The child stayed calm, avoiding the situation. Amara felt a surge of emotions sweep over her as she stepped away from the operating table; her heart hammered with relief and exhaustion, and tears started to tingle at the edges of her eyes.

The sheer enormity of what she had just gone through appeared to eclipse the worries and tensions of her personal life at that very moment. Saving a life and participating in something so great and important helped me put everything else in context.

Amara considered her own early years and the many medical experts she had seen throughout her foster system. Indeed, the physicians and nurses who attended to her bodily needs were important, but so were the ones who reminded her she mattered and was deserving of love and care.

Those moments of empathy and human connection, amidst turmoil and uncertainty, had stayed with Amara and influenced her decision to pursue a career in medicine. Now, after enduring her own challenges, she experienced a renewed sense of purpose and direction that cut through the chaos of her personal issues.

Amara slanted her face to the heavens and let the cold wind sweep over her as she left the hospital that evening. She considered her biological parents, the suffering, and the hope their homecoming brought into her life. She considered her chosen family and the unwavering love and encouragement that had gotten her through every obstacle.

And in that instant, Amara knew she could manage whatever lay ahead, gracefully and resiliently negotiating the complexity of her growing family. Ultimately, love was what counted most—the ability of human connection to heal and change even the worst of wounds. Amara inhaled deeply and gratefully, then headed into the evening prepared to meet the next phase of her trip with a fresh feeling of serenity and perspective. She was aware that ups and downs, joyful times, and stressful events would still occur. Furthermore, she was confident in her abilities and support to navigate through any challenge and discover beauty and purpose even in the most challenging circumstances.

Amara kept this fresh clarity with her in the next days, allowing it to direct her contacts with her biological parents as well as with her loved ones. She approached every discussion and shared moments with an open heart, eager to listen, understand, and find the common ground that would serve as the foundation for something new and lovely.

Amara could sense the old wounds healing and the stresses gradually but beginning to relax. Of course, there were still times of doubt and uncertainty, as well as natural worries and questions around the margins. However, there were also moments filled with laughter, shared memories, and cautious aspirations for the future.

Amara clung to the love and the courage that had gotten her this far—the unquestionable sense of self created in the furnace of her events, through everything. With the knowledge she gained from living a complete and bold life, she knew she would face the obstacles ahead with bravery and compassion.

Amara was a warrior, a healer, and a woman who had mastered the ability to find hope in the most challenging circumstances. Using that light as her guide, she grasped the possibility of transforming even the most shattered pieces into something complete and beautiful.

Chapter 10

Shaking off the water gravity

After the emotional turmoil of her birth parents' return, Amara found herself drawn to the job that had guided her through many life's challenges: her relentless efforts with her NGO, Hope for Tomorrow. Surrounded by the laughter and conversations of the children they served, Amara felt a sense of purpose and clarity that had been difficult to come by in recent weeks in the bright, bustling halls of the community centre housing the organization.

Amara chose to further her road of reconciliation with Jenny and Nathan here, in the middle of this active, loving group. She had been considering the possibility for some time, rolling it over in her thoughts like a smooth river stone, calculating the possible hazards and benefits. But after witnessing the transformative power of love and support in action and witnessing children who had endured so much pain and suffering blossom under the caring hands of the NGO staff and volunteers, Amara realised it was time to give her birth parents the same chance for healing. It's time to direct some of her recently acquired vitality into her philanthropy.

Amara asked Jenny and Nathan to join her for a day of work at the community centre so they could experience what it's like to grow up in a government-constructed family structure. She inhaled deeply and felt a sense of apprehension and expectation. She didn't know how they would react or if they would understand this invitation to a world that had become so important to her.

To Amara's surprise and delight, Jenny and Nathan enthusiastically accepted the offer, their eyes shining with a blend of gratitude and apprehension. And so, Amara was strolling through the vibrant, art-filled corridors of the community centre on a beautiful Saturday morning, her birth parents by her side, eager to start a new chapter in their shared journey.

There was initially a clear feeling of uneasiness, a rigidity in their exchanges as they negotiated this foreign ground together. But as the day wore on and they threw themselves into the work at hand—reading stories to wide-eyed toddlers, helping older kids with homework and art projects, serving warm meals and warmer smiles—Amara could feel something starting to shift, a tentative bridge of understanding and empathy beginning to form.

She watched Jenny read from a well-worn picture book while seated cross-legged on the floor, surrounded by a gathering of laughing toddlers hanging on her every word. Her mother's face was soft, her words gentle—a taste of the loving spirit buried for so long under the weight of pain and addiction that Amara had never seen before.

Nathan, too, appeared to come alive in this setting, his often-austere manner giving way to a fun, captivating vitality as he assisted a group of middle schoolers create a sophisticated Lego structure. Amara could see glimpses of the father he might have—the patient, attentive presence lost to her in those vital early years.

Tired but content, Amara found herself seated next to Jenny on a bench in the beautiful courtyard as the day came to an end and the kids started to return home. Though laughter and conversation filled the air, they sat quietly, lost in thought.

Jenny tentatively reached out and gently grasped Amara's hand. At the touch of her mother's warmth and love, Amara experienced a shock. She raised her head to see Jenny's wet grin and tears glittering in her eyes.

"Thank you for this, Amara," Jenny said, her voice rich with feeling.

"Thank you for allowing us to participate in this in your life." Seeing you here and the outstanding job you are doing makes me very proud. And it helps me realize even more how much I still must learn about being a good mother and how much I miss it.

Amara felt her own eyes filling up, a knot building in her throat. She murmured gently, "You're here now," gripping her mother's hand. "That's the important thing." Every one of us is developing and learning. This is a crucial aspect of our journey, both personally and collectively.

Jenny nodded, one tear running down her face. "Amara, I want to go with you. I want to be in your life, in any manner you will allow. Instead of replacing you, I want to learn from you. Even though it's taken me an excessive amount of time to arrive, I'm here to be the mother you truly deserve."

Amara felt a surge of emotions rising in her chest—a mixture of love, loss, and cautious hope. Her voice almost above a whisper, she continued, "I want that too." "Together, I want to figure out a future path. It will not be simple, and it will not happen overnight. But being here, seeing you with these children, inspires me. It gives me hope that we may mend, that from the shattered bits of our history we may create something fresh and lovely.

Jenny nodded in agreement and grinned over her tears. "One step at a time," she murmured quietly. "One day at a time. We'll sort things out together.

Amara and Jenny were sitting hand in hand; a delicate yet valuable moment of connection and understanding blossomed between them as the sun began to set above the community centre, casting a warm, golden light over the courtyard. Even though it was small, it was a significant step toward the healing and development that can occur when hearts are open and love has time to blossom.

For Amara, it also served as a reminder of the power of her job and the magic that may result from individuals gathered in a compassionate and serving attitude. Her NGO was not just a job or a passion project; it was a tool for transformation—a place where broken hearts could find solace and hope could emerge from the crucible of adversity.

Amara had serenity and direction come over her as she said goodbye to her biological parents that evening, seeing them stroll hand in hand, quietly speaking and hesitantly smiling. Her calling was to be a lighthouse in the darkness, a hand extended to those who lost their way.

With the love of her chosen family, the support of her community, and the growing awareness of her biological parents, Amara knew she was exactly where she was supposed to be—doing exactly what she was supposed to be doing. The path ahead would be long and meandering, filled with obstacles and failures. Amara was ready for the road, ready for all the pleasures and losses, successes and hardships.

The compassion and wisdom of those who believed in her shaped her into a lady of resilience. She understood then that everything was possible, that even the most shattered souls could find their way home, and that strength was her basis for knowing that anything could be mended.

PART 3

ARRIVING AT THE EDGE OF THE RIVER

Chapter 11

Looking deep

Over the course of the weeks while Amara continued to negotiate the delicate dance of developing a connection with her biological parents, she became more appreciative of the strong basis of love and support she had in her life. Her job at the NGO, her close-knit group of friends, and naturally her rock and companion Jiu kept her grounded and reminded her of her own strength and resiliency in the face of even the most difficult obstacles.

In this atmosphere of thanksgiving and introspection, Amara found herself sitting down for a heart-to-heart with Mayor Sholina, the lady who had grown over the years to be both a mentor and a close friend. They gathered at their regular location—a little corner table in the neighbourhood coffee shop—where the rich scent of freshly brewed coffee mixed with the soft buzz of conversation around them.

"Amara, my dear," Sholina started, her eyes shining with love and tenderness. "It's wonderful to see you. Given everything that has been happening, how have you been managing?"

Amara sighed, a little grin flickering at the margins of her mouth. She cradled her hot cup in her hands and remarked, "It's been a journey, that's for sure." "Some days I find more simplicity than others. Still, I consider myself to be in a decent state generally. One day at a time, I'm learning to be patient with myself and the process."

Sholina nodded, her face one of empathy and comprehension. "That's really vital, Amara. Healing is slow and seldom a straight road. Still, I must admit—your handling of things has really been outstanding. Your kindness and elegance are very inspirational."

The compliments caused Amara to flush with warmth, and she felt pride and direction flowering in her breast. "Thanks, Sholina," she murmured gently. "That's a lot, from you. For both personally and professionally, you have been absolutely a lighthouse. Without your guidance and encouragement, I'm not sure where I would be."

Reaching across the table, Sholina lightly squeezed Amara's hand. "You credit me too much, darling. Your resilience and strength originate from within. I am delighted to be on your journey, witnessing your triumph over even the most formidable challenges.

They sat in easy quiet for a bit, drinking their coffee and appreciating the little pleasure of one another's presence. Sholina's face then became reflective, a glimmer of delight flickering in her eyes.

"Speaking of your path, Amara, I really have some updates for you. We have been making significant progress in Igbuzor thanks to your unwavering efforts and the support of this amazing community.

Amara slanted forward; her interest sparked. "Really? Of what kind of news?"

Sholina's grin became broader, her pleasure and gratification clear in every syllable. "Well, as you know, we have been working hard to revitalize the town—to create a stronger, more resourceful community for every one of our neighbours. And we have been able to achieve some very remarkable progress owing to the kindness of several important contributors and the commitment of our local officials.

She then went into great detail on the several projects and initiatives under way: the new educator centre and job training programs, helping residents develop useful skills and find meaningful employment; the affordable housing developments, guaranteeing everyone a decent place to call home; and the new community centre, providing a safe, nurturing environment for children and families.

"And at the heart of it all, Amara, is the work that you and your NGO have been doing," Sholina added, her voice bursting with respect. "Your ability to unite people, inspire hope, and heal... has been the impetus for a great deal of good change. You should feel truly satisfied with the lives you have touched and the impact you have made.

Overwhelmed by the scope of what Sholina was sharing, Amara felt tears prickling at the margins of her eyes. Her efforts, in the hope of creating a brighter future for the children and families of Igbuzor, had poured her heart and soul. Hearing this, however, and seeing the tangible proof of the impact she was making was nearly overwhelming.

"I... I don't know what to say," Amara began, her voice full of feeling. "I just am very appreciative and humble to be involved in this. It's everything I've ever wanted to know—that we are really changing things and providing individuals an opportunity for a better life.

Sholina nodded; tears of pride and delight glistened in her own eyes. "You are a gift to this town, Amara. You serve as a remarkable example of what we can accomplish when we guide with affection and persistently support each other. I also realize that this is a starting point. We can accomplish anything under your leadership and with the amazing people who support our cause."

Amara felt serenity and direction settle over her as the talk veered to other subjects: the pleasures and tribulations of parenthood, the newest novels they were reading, the little pleasures of a good cup of coffee, and a meaningful chat. Indeed, there were still difficulties ahead, as well as healing scars and building bridges. But at this moment, surrounded by love and encouragement, propelled by the thought that she was really changing the world, Amara felt she was precisely where she was supposed to be.

And Amara felt a fresh will and hope as she hugged Sholina farewell and vowed to see her once again very soon. She was prepared to meet whatever lay ahead—to keep battling for the family she had created, for the town she loved, and for the brilliant, beautiful future she knew was achievable.

Amara was a lady of unlimited compassion, of strength, of resilience. She knows that anything is possible and that even the worst circumstances can lead to a brighter day with love and encouragement from those who believe in her.

Chapter 12

Building thunderstorm

Nuss broke into Amara's comfortable house, his face ablaze with enthusiasm and expectation, as the sun was just starting to sink below the horizon and the sky was a stunning mix of oranges and pinks. Curling up on the sofa with a book and a warm cup of tea, Amara glanced up in surprise and began to grin at her adored brother's infectious vitality.

"Amara!" "Amara!" Nuss erupted, nearly leaping to his feet. "You never would have guessed what just transpired. I have the most amazing news!

Amara lay down her book, intrigued. "Well, don't keep me in suspense," she said, patting the couch's adjacent seat. "Come on, leak. What's got you so agitated about?"

Nuss collapsed down next to her, his eyes shining and his smile broad. "Okay, so you know how I have recently been very into rock climbing. I've practically made rock climbing my sole focus outside of my job and family responsibilities".

Amara nodded with a gentle chuckle. "Yes, I am very aware of your fixation with climbing large structures. I'm not sure how you manage to avoid vertigo."

Nuss waved a hand of contempt. "Psh, when you have the correct tools and mentality, heights are nothing. However, that's not the focus of this discussion. I received an invitation to participate in this highly exclusive climbing trip. Like Amara, we are talking world-class athletes. The finest of the best."

Amara's eyes widened, a mixture of pride and worry rising in her chest. "Wow, Nuss, that's really amazing. Really, I am very proud of you. But isn't it also, I wonder, very risky? Though you're a fantastic climber, these are professional athletes you're referring to."

Nuss's face softened, his hand stretching out to gently squeeze Amara. "I know it seems strong, and trust me, I'm not treating the chances lightly. But, sis, this is a unique opportunity. This is an opportunity for me to push myself to the limit and uncover my true potential. And I will be accompanying some of the most seasoned mountaineers worldwide. They'll have my back, as I will have theirs.

Amara sighed, caught between her innate urge to shield her brother from injury and her want to help his aspirations. "I simply worry about you, Nuss. You are brilliant, powerful, and fearless. However, the thought of you standing on a distant mountain facing unknown dangers worries me.

With his chin on the top of her head, Nuss gently hugged her. "I can see that it works, Amara." And I could see. However, I feel compelled to act. I want to demonstrate to myself that I can surmount any obstacle and confronting my concerns. You've consistently demonstrated this throughout time.

Amara turned back, staring at her brother with a misty grin. "I learned from the best," she remarked gently. "Watching you grow up—the way you always managed to find the fun and the adventure in even the worst circumstances—it gave me strength, Nuss. It still performs."

Nuss smiled, his eyes flickering curiously. Well, you know, I also learned from the finest. My amazing, tough, relentless sister. She has overcome numerous challenges and emerged more resilient than anyone I've ever encountered. Amara, if I could be half as courageous as you are, I believe I could handle whatever this trip presents."

They simply sat there for a long time, hugging each other and savouring the coziness of their unwavering relationship. Amara then gently withdrew, her expression solemn but full of affection.

"Okay," she said, inhaling deeply. "Sure. If this is what you need to do, I fully support you. I need you to promise me that you will be careful, listen to professionals, and avoid unnecessary danger. You must also ensure the safe and sound return of the item to me. Because, brother, I cannot lose you. Simply cannot."

Nuss smiled gently, his eyes full of comprehension. "Amara, I swear. I promise I'll be cautious, and I'll come back to you. Ever. You will always be with me, sis, whether you like it or not.

Laughing, Amara swiped at the tears starting to run down her cheeks. "I think I can live with that," she added, her voice soft with love. "As long as you promise to bring me back a souvenir from the top of whatever shockingly high peak you end up conquering."

Pulling her in for another brief embrace, Nuss laughed. "Deal." We are approaching the summit with unwavering determination.

As the evening progressed and the conversation shifted to other topics, such as the latest antics of their NGO kids, the progress Amara was making with her birth parents, and the delicious new recipe Jiu had prepared for dinner the night before, the initial shock and anxiety of Nuss's announcement began to fade, replaced by a sense of pride and excitement for the adventure that lay ahead.

Amara knew how difficult the next few weeks and months would be for everyone, not just Nuss. It was never simple to see someone you love to take on a project so large and possibly perilous. She also understood, however, that this was a vital component of Nuss's path—an opportunity for him to soar and find his own strength—just as she had many times in her own life.

And so, Amara felt serenity come over her as the night got late and Nuss eventually walked home, her foot light and her heart full of expectation for the climb to come. Indeed, there would be uncertainties and doubts, anxieties, and fears. But there would also be delight and triumph—the unearthed excitement of seeing someone you love passionately and boldly pursue their aspirations.

Amara deeply understood the essence of life: the ups and downs, the struggles and successes, and the enduring bonds of love and family. With Nuss by her side and the love and encouragement of all the amazing people in her life, she understood that everything was possible and that she could climb even the tallest mountains, one resolute step at a time.

Chapter 13

Fresh sea air breath

Nestled away from the bustle of the city and a haven of tranquility and old-world appeal, the little, lovely beach town of Wirad is today a hidden gem. As Amara and Jiu walked hand in hand around the streets, the salty sea wind tousling their hair and the warmth of the sun on their faces helped them to feel serenity and contentment flood over them—much-needed relief after the emotional roller coaster of the last few weeks.

Jiu had conceptualized this last-minute weekend trip. He had seen the toll the recent changes in Amara's life had been having on her, the way her normally vivid spirit had started to fade beneath the weight of so many contradictory feelings and obligations. Driven to give her an opportunity to relax, rejuvenate, and reconnect with the happiness and calm that had always been such a natural part of her existence, he had whisked her away to this magical small village with a little bit of careful preparation and a lot of love.

Amara could feel the knots of tension in her shoulders starting to relax as they meandered around the little stores and galleries along the main street, marvelling at the exquisite, handcrafted goods and the friendly faces of the residents. The tightness in her chest would be easing with every breath of salty sea air. She leant into Jiu's firm warmth, thanks beyond words for his consistent presence and his unflinching love and support.

She said, "Thank you for this," softly squeezing his hand. Even in my ignorance, I understood exactly what I needed. Jiu, you're my rock. My refuge from the tempest.

Jiu grinned down at her, his eyes full of devotion. "You're my everything, Amara," he added understatedly. "My heart, my house, and my cause for living. "I would go anywhere and do anything to see you grin like that."

Overwhelmed by the depth of feeling in Jiu's remarks, Amara felt tears spring at the margins of her eyes. How had she been so fortunate to find love of this kind? They built their relationship on mutual respect and trust, with the certainty that they would support each other no matter what life threw at them.

Amara felt lightness and delight bubbling up inside her as the day wore on, and they explored the many pleasures of the town: the little bookshops and cozy cafes, the breathtaking views of the ocean from the cliffside walking paths—Amara was exactly where she was meant to be, with exactly whom she was meant to be.

Then Jiu led her to a secluded, small cove, where the sand was smooth and warm beneath their feet. As the sun began to dip below the horizon, it painted the sky with a magnificent array of pinks and golds. He laid a blanket and made a picnic basket loaded with all of Amara's favourite foods: crusty bread and creamy cheese, juicy figs and honey, green olives, and a bottle of crisp red wine.

The only music they could hear as they settled down to savour their feast was the sound of the waves slamming against the coast and the distant scream of seagulls. Jiu looked to Amara, his face suddenly solemn and full of feeling.

"Amara," he said, his voice gentle yet firm. "Although I had long wanted to accomplish this, the time never felt quite perfect. But being here with you, in this magnificent area, surrounded by so much love and beauty, I cannot imagine a more ideal time.

Amara's heart started to speed, a flutter of excitement and expectation rising inside her. Can this be...?

Then Jiu was reaching into his pocket to retrieve a small velvet box. Opening it with shaky fingers, he unveiled the most beautiful ring Amara had ever seen: a thin band of gold capped with a glittering diamond that seems to catch all the hues of the sunset.

"Amara Johnson," Jiu remarked, his voice laden with feeling. "I knew you were the only one from the time I first met you. You are the other half of my soul, the missing piece of my heart. You have been our two children's mother, closest friend, partner, and lighthouse during the worst of times. And I want nothing more than to be by your side, creating a lifetime full of love and joy and many experiences."

He inhaled deeply, staring right at her. "Amara, will you repeatedly marry me? For now, and always, will you be my wife and my friend in everything?"

Amara paused, unable to talk or breathe, then guessed it was so nice; yet, we are already married, so he is proposing once again. Since they started dating and getting married, Amara had completely forgotten it was their anniversary. The love, delight, and strong feelings that surged within her were too profound for mere words to express. Amara suddenly recognizes the day and goes through an emotional rollercoaster, tears streaming down her face. She wonders how she missed the day and how her spouse startled her.

Then, however, she found her voice among the tears running down her cheeks. With her heart filled to the brim, she repeated, "Yes," recalling the day. "Yes, Jiu, a thousand times indeed. I love you more than I could have imagined. And I am eager to show you exactly how much I have to offer for the remainder of my life.

When Jiu slid a beautiful ring upon her finger, drew her into his arms, and kissed her with a passion and compassion that took her breath away, Amara felt a sense of rightness settle over her, a bone-deep confidence that this was precisely where she was supposed to be.

Indeed, there would present difficulties. Indeed, there would be periods of confusion and doubt as well as terror. But with Jiu by her side, with the love and support of her amazing family and friends, Amara felt she could face anything, that she could create a life of purpose and meaning and eternal love.

As the sun sank below the horizon and the stars began to glitter in the velvet sky, Amara and Jiu hugged each other tightly, their hearts filled with gratitude, delight, and the promise of a lovely future together.

Chapter 14

Riverbank feast

The Johnson family house was humming with activity; the warm conversation of loved ones gathered was filling the air with the smell of home cooking. This family reunion, the first since the untimely death of Mr. and Mrs. Johnson, the adored parents and grandparents who had been the centre of the clan for so many years, was a diverse event.

Despite the undertones of loss and nostalgia, there was still a sense of delight and celebration, acknowledging the enduring ties of love and family that had always been the Johnsons' strongest point. And for Amara, who had grown up in this house surrounded by the joy and love of her foster siblings and parents, it was a homecoming in the most literal sense.

Her heart filling with love and thanks, she greeted aunts and uncles, cousins, and family friends, moving among the throng with Jiu by her side. She glanced around and saw happy smiles and extended arms, reminders of the amazing support system she had been blessed with, the family she had chosen, and who had selected her in return.

Two people, however, among the sea of familiar faces, caught my attention; they hung hesitantly around the margins of the assembly, their looks a combination of apprehension and cautious optimism. Amara insisted on inviting her biological parents, Jenny and Nathan, to the reunion, a gesture of inclusivity and healing not readily available to certain Johnson clan members.

As Amara observed Jenny and Nathan from across the room, she could see the tightness in Zarah's shoulders. She could also sense the anxiety emanating from Nuss as he engaged in a polite yet detached small conversation with Jenny and Nathan. She understood that for her foster siblings, who had been by her side through all the suffering and uncertainty of her early life, the concept of inviting her biological parents into the fold was a challenging one, full of complicated feelings and unresolved traumas.

But Amara also realized that if there was any chance of moving forward and building a future with all the pieces of her past, she needed to have this conversation and build a bridge. Her heart pounding with a mixture of fear and resolve, she took a deep breath, squeezed Jiu's hand for courage, and then moved towards where Jenny and Nathan stood.

She whispered gently, "Jenny, Nathan," and gave a little grin. "I'm delighted you could make it. Being here with everyone must be a bit overwhelming, right? But I want you to know how much it means to me that you're here and that you're ready to participate in this family gathering."
Jenny's hands reached out to grab Amara's, tears filling her eyes. She said, "Oh, Amara." "We are the ones who appreciate it here. We appreciate you giving us this opportunity and extending your family and heart to us. We haven't yet earned it; we know we haven't. But here we are, trying. And we will do everything necessary to show ourselves worthy of your confidence."

Nathan nodded; his face austere. "Amara, we understand that we cannot undo the past due to the suffering we caused. But we want you to know that we are dedicated to being a part of your life in any way you find suitable. That means getting to know those who loved and helped you when we couldn't.

With tears stinging at the edges of her eyelids, Amara felt a knot form in her throat. She understood that this moment, this hesitant olive branch, was a turning point, an opportunity to start the protracted and challenging process of forgiveness and healing. Before she could reply, however, a voice emerged from across the room like a dagger piercing through the buzz of activity.

"Well, isn't this cozy?" Zarah spoke in a high-pitched and brittle voice. "Going back to take what is theirs—the prodigal parents. Not considering the years of neglect, abandonment, and trauma. We simply welcome you with open arms, correct?

The room grew silent, all eyes shifting to the conflict that was developing. Amara felt the tension pulsing in the air like lightning, and she could see the hurt and rage carved on Zarah's face.
She started "Zarah," her voice gentle yet consistent. "I understand that this is challenging," she said. I am aware of the ongoing pain and anger. To continue and achieve peace, we must be ready to have tough talks and face the past."
Nuss ahead, his expression mixed. "Amara, we merely want you to avoid suffering another wound. We have witnessed the toll their decisions have placed on you here. How can we believe that this will be different?"

Amara inhaled deeply, looking from her foster brothers to her biological parents and back once again. "I know you have questions, Nuss. You're correct; assurances are not given. What I do know, however, is that clinging to hatred and bitterness and neglecting to even consider forgiveness does not mend anything. It just leaves us mired in the past and caught in a misery cycle.

With her posture open and vulnerable, she turned to face Jenny and Nathan. "I'm not suggesting it will be simple. It's possible that there will be challenges and uncertainty. I am, however, indicating that I am ready to attempt to engage in the necessary rebuilding and reconnection activity. Whether by blood or choice, we are all family. Family is about showing up, even when things are difficult. Especially under difficult circumstances.

Silence descended for a long while as the weight of Amara's words

hung in the air. Then, Zarah's shoulders began to soften gradually, with the harsh lines of her face only slightly relaxing.
"You're right, Amara," she murmured gently. "You're right; as much as it hurts, as much as I want to shield you from any further agony. We must try to heal the past and move forward.

She turned to Jenny and Nathan; her look was cautious but not aggressive. "I'm not going to pretend that any of us—including myself—find this simple. You have much to prove and plenty of trust to build. But I'm ready to give you a chance for Amara's sake— for the benefit of this family. This is your chance to demonstrate your growth and commitment to becoming a part of our wild, amazing, and chaotic family.

Jenny and Nathan collapsed with gratitude and relief, tears streaming down their cheeks. "Thank you," Nathan said in a whisper. "We value your presenting us with a chance and openness to attempt. We are ready to move systematically even if our route forward is lengthy."

As the tension in the room began to relax, Amara experienced a range of emotions before timid optimism and possibility grabbed centre stage. Family was all about, she understood: the readiness to love and forgive, to confront difficult circumstances together, to develop even in the face of uncertainty, adversity, and doubt.

Knowing that whatever obstacles were ahead, she gazed around at the faces of her loved ones and at the intricate pattern of her life spun from so many strands, knowing that she would face them with the courage and endurance always her best gift.
She was Amara, the woman emerging from her past to create a purposeful, focused life. Love of her family—both old and new— made her feel that everything could heal; she felt even the most damaged hearts could find their way home.

Chapter 15

Incoming storms

The sound of the phone ringing interrupted Amara's office, where she had been reading over the most recent data from her NGO's many projects and initiatives. She had been in peace here. She scowled slightly and looked at the wall clock; it was rare for someone to be phoning at this hour, particularly on her personal line.

She sighed and grabbed the receiver, preparing herself for perhaps yet another crisis or pressing need. "Hey, this is Amara speaking."

She had been anticipating the voice on the other end of the call. It was the voice of the director of the local child welfare agency, a lady she had closely collaborated with over years to help foster children in the system have better lives.

"Amara, I'm so sorry to bother you at this busy hour," the stressed-out lady remarked in a hurried voice. "But we have a matter that calls for your immediate attention. We've received some extremely serious allegations about your NGO.

Amara felt her heart drop, a chilly knot of anxiety building in her gut. "Allegations?" What type of accusations? Has our money already been discontinued?

The lady stopped momentarily, as if searching for the appropriate words. "Amara, I worry that your company has seen some more instances of mismanagement and fraud. There are concerns regarding the theft of funds intended for children's programs and the involvement of some of your employees in illicit activities.

Amara felt as if the earth had collapsed beneath her, as though she were descending into a deep hole of astonishment and incredulity. Her voice quivering, she muttered, "That's... that's not possible." "I trust every single person of my staff fully; I know exactly each other. There has to be some error, some misinterpretation."

Amara had a terrible feeling of doubt creeping in; a little voice in the back of her mind was suggesting maybe—just maybe—there was more going on than she had ever realized, even as the words left her lips.

The lady on the phone sighed loudly, her tone compassionate yet strong. "I know how hard this must be to listen to, Amara. However, the allegations are extremely serious and stem from various sources. Even though it pains me to say it, we must begin a thorough investigation of the operations and finances of your non-profit organization.

Closing her eyes, Amara battled the tears that threatened to run down her cheeks. This could not be happening now, not when they had come so far and accomplished so much. Scandal and mistrust have tarnished their reputation, making the thought of their labour, the lives they've impacted, and the future they've contributed to almost unbearable.

Even in the midst of her shock and misery, Amara felt a flutter of resolve, a defiant rejection to let this failure define her or the job she had dedicated her life to.

"I understand," she responded, her voice calm and steady in spite of the turbulence within her. "And I assure you, I will do all in my power to help the enquiry and find the truth about this." If my company has experienced any misconduct, I am eager to learn about it and assist in rectifying the situation.

The lady on the phone appeared to pause momentarily, as if considering Amara's statements. "I believe you, Amara," she murmured at last, her tone softening just slightly. "And I know that at heart you have always acted in the children's best interests. You should know that this investigation will be thorough and objective, and if we find misconduct, the consequences could be severe.

Amara nodded even though the lady was blind. "I understand," she said, her heart filled with sorrow but her determination unwavering. "For the sake of the children and the integrity of our work, I'm ready to face whatever comes next to keep our agency accreditation, even without your department funding," she said.

Amara felt a rush of tiredness sweep over her as she hung up the phone, the weight of the news and the problems ahead squarely on her shoulders. Even though she was exhausted, she knew she would not give up. When so much was at stake, the futures and lives of numerous vulnerable children were in danger.

Amara grabbed up the phone once again, prepared to begin calling and gathering the soldiers, inhaling deeply and silently praying for strength. She would need every ounce of love and encouragement from her amazing network of family and friends, who had always been her rock and haven, as well as every ounce of support and knowledge she could summon in the days and weeks to come.

But Amara felt a flutter of hope, which will ignite in her heart even as the path ahead seems dark and unknown. She had overcome hardship before; she had seen storms and come out stronger and more resilient on the other side. She confidently headed to her beloved workplace, resolute in her determination to persevere through any challenge.

The air hummed with the sound of conversation and children laughing at play while the busy streets of Igbuzor were alive with the dynamic energy of a town in action. But among the daily grind, anxiety had started to sink in, a shadow of doubt hovering over the town like a gathering storm.

Since the leaked news of the funding cut-off, whispers of corruption and scandal have been circulating, with tales of backroom deals and dubious connections threatening to erode the fundamental basis of society. At the heart of it all was Amara's cherished, reputable NGO, which she had devoted her heart and soul to create, now facing accusations of mismanagement and fraud.

Head in her hands, Amara sat in her office, surrounded by a mound of menacing-looking papers on her desk. The news had blinded her, and the abrupt probe of the NGO's funds and operations had totally startled her. It seemed like a betrayal—a terrible turn of events threatening to ruin all the wonderful work she and her team had done and all the lives they had touched and changed.

Despite her amazement and incredulity, Amara understood one thing: these claims were untrue, part of a smear campaign by her political rivals, who were attempting to undermine her authority and silence her voice. She had always understood that her work, along with her support for the underprivileged and vulnerable, would stir up controversy and create strong rivals. She never imagined, however, that they would target the very company that had been a lifeline for so many and go to such extreme lengths.

Startled from her thoughts by a pounding at the door, Amara turned to find Jiu's troubled face staring in. "Hey," he replied gently, entering the office and shutting the door behind him. "I saw your comment regarding the regulatory commission's call; how are you managing?"

Amara groaned and ran her fingers over her hair. " Frankly? I am enraged, afraid and just overburdened. Jiu, it seems unbelievable that this is occurring. After everything we have done—all we have created—to have it all jeopardized like this, it is simple.

Jiu gathered Amara into his arms with two swift steps across the room. "I understand, darling. I realise. But we will resist this, right? We will demonstrate that the NGO is acting above and beyond all standards and that these accusations are unfounded. Amara, you have a vast array of supporters in your corner. There are numerous people who back you and your work.

Amara nodded, finding power in Jiu's relentless encouragement. "You are correct. We cannot let them ruin what we have created or let them triumph. But Jiu, I find myself concerned. I'm worried about the potential impact this situation may have on the children and families we support. They depend on us; they are relying on us. What if..."?

Jiu gently pressed Amara's lips to quiet her worries. "Remember, no what ifs." We will proceed day by day, one step at a time. Rallying the troops and straightening our ducks will then help us begin erecting our defenses.
Amara drew a long breath and squared her shoulders. "You're right." We must retaliate and demonstrate our capabilities. First, we need to ensure that everyone in the team agrees and willing to do whatever it takes to restore the NGO's reputation.

Amara's office turned into a war room of sorts during the next several hours, a hive of activity as her supporters and coworkers convened to plot and strategize. Emily, Amara's lifelong friend and now a bright legal thinker, was carefully reading contracts and financial figures. Ever the explorer, Nuss offered to undertake some on-the-ground reconnaissance using his connections to compile information on the movements of their opponent.

Still nervously adjusting their role in Amara's life, Jenny and Nathan also insisted on providing any kind of assistance. "We may not have been there for you in the past, Amara," Nathan remarked, his voice sharp with feeling. But right now, we are here. We will also do whatever it takes to help you and safeguard the amazing job you are doing."

Amara felt overwhelmed with gratitude and love for the incredible people in her life, the family she had built, and the friends she had gathered. With their support, she believed she could face and endure any challenge.

Despite their tireless efforts to gather evidence and refute the unfounded accusations, Amara couldn't shake the feeling that there was more to this than initially appeared. The timing of the inquiry and the rapid spread of rumours appeared too systematic and deliberate to be mere coincidences.

Amara was sitting in her office late one night, trying to understand a particularly enigmatic piece of evidence when she had a startling realization.

She had placed the book from the stranger during the final day of the yearly festival celebration from Rev. Okafor someplace in her drawers and never had an opportunity to read it. She has been extremely busy, but today Amara decided to look at the book. With trembling hands, Amara rummaged through her office drawers until she found the leather-bound book intended as a thank-you gift. She examined it from fresh angles. She discovered the name of a dishonest official who had been working to undermine her NGO from the moment she expressed support for Sholina, a powerful businessman with close ties to the corrupt members of the former council, including the archivist Ikenga Lutian and Mr. Okorie. He had bought off almost all well-known members of the society, encouraging them to use their excellent reputations to help Sholina ruin the society.

As the bits started to fit, Amara's heart pounded. Amara realized that this wasn't just a smear campaign. She had long disregarded this concerted effort, a desperate attempt by the old guard to hang onto power and suppress anybody who challenged their hold on the town.

Her financing was stopped.

She saw then that the battle ahead would test her will and will unlike anything else, therefore raising more stakes than she had ever dreamed. Amara also knew, however, that she was not alone; she had an army of love and encouragement at her ready to stand with her and fight for what was right.

Amara grabbed up the phone and dialled Sholina's number, resolvedly. It was time to bring the corruption and falsehoods that had lingered in the shadows for far too long to the attention of their opponents.

"Sholina," Amara murmured, her voice firm and powerful. "I believe I understand the true nature of things here. I also have a scheme. However, I will require your help and the assistance of everyone we can trust.

Amara could almost see Sholina's smile over the phone as she spelt forth her doubts and plan. "I'm in," the mayor responded, her voice buzzing with enthusiasm. "Let's do this, Amara. Let's defeat these tyrants and demonstrate to them the true nature of Igbuzor.

Amara couldn't help but grin fiercely and determinedly, lighting her entire face. Indeed, the path ahead would be challenging, and the fights would be fierce. She knew, however, that nothing could stop her—that justice and truth would ultimately triumph—that her family was at her side, with the love of her hometown and the power of her principles.

Amara felt peace come over her as she hung the phone and gazed out over the glittering lights of Igbuzor—a strong, unquestionable trust in the power of love and resiliency to transcend even the darkest of circumstances. She murmured, "Thank you, Reverend Okafor, wherever you are."

She considered her darling children soundly asleep in their beds, blissfully ignorant of the tempest raging around them. She considered Jiu, her soul mate and friend, who had been her support through every challenge and success. She also reflected on the woman she had become—moulded by the love of those who supported her and the crucible of adversity.

Amara said to the night sky, "Bring it on," her eyes shining with will. "We are prepared for any eventuality. We are Igbuzor; therefore, we will remain unbroken."
Amara returned to her desk, ready to face whatever lay ahead with bravery, elegance, and an unwavering faith in the power of love to triumph.

PART 4

STRENGHTS OF THE WATER CURRENTS

Chapter 16

Riverside scrabbles

The early sun bathed Igbuzor in a gentle, golden glow, warming the village. Despite the serene beauty of the dawn, an undercurrent of tension ran through the streets—a feeling of expectation and anxiety that set everyone's nerves on edge.

With a hot cup of coffee in one hand and a pen in the other, Amara bent over her desk in her NGO office, busily jotting notes and thoughts as her mind raced to fit the bits together. She had perused the leather book many times.

Amara was aware that there was a limited amount of time left to restore their reputation and identify the true culprits behind the smear campaign, as the investigation into the company's finances had intensified significantly.

For the past three days, she had scarcely slept, her entire attention devoted to her current tasks. Jiu had tried to persuade her to relax and reenergize at night and take breaks, but Amara had waved aside his worries with a resolute grin. She added, "I can't stop now, love," and planted a small kiss on his cheek. We cannot stop when we are so close to the truth. I promise to take a long nap once this task is complete. perhaps even a vacation."

Knowing better than to argue with his wife when she displayed that fire in her eyes, Jiu let out a grunt. Holding her hand, he murmured, "Just remember to take care of yourself, darling, okay?" "You run yourself into the ground, and you are no good to anyone."

Amara nodded, moved by Jiu's concern. She realised he was correct and that if she was going to see this battle through to the finish, she had to pace herself. She wanted to relax now, but the stakes were too high, and the consequences of failure were too severe.

A tap on the door startled Amara from her thoughts, and she glanced up to see Emily peering in, her face etched with grim resolve. The attorney remarked, "I think I found something," waving a big folder. "Something huge."
As Amara indicated for Emily to come in and lock the door behind her, she experienced an adrenaline spike. Lean forward excitedly; she said, "What is it?"

Emily laid the contents of the folder over Amara's desk, exposing a set of email printouts and bank paperwork.
"I conducted a thorough review of the bank records and recent communication to identify any anomalies or red flags." And at first glance, everything appeared perfect.
Amara nodded; she looked over the papers, her brow wrinkled in concentration.

Emily said, gesturing to a run-through of transactions, "But then I noticed something strange." "These gifts arrived shortly before the commencement of the enquiry." These gifts originate from shell companies, which lack any commercial presence or history. As I dove deeper, I realized they all shared a trait.

She grabbed a printout—a blurry picture of a guy shaking hands among a gathering of suited candidates. "This individual, Councilman Okorie, is the centre of everyone's attention." In the past, Councilman Okorie has been one of our most vocal critics, pushing for the NGO's closure. The anointed contender to succeed in Igbuzor leadership is Okorie Talel.

As the ramifications of Emily's revelation seeped in, Amara felt a cold run down her spine. "So, you are saying...?"
"Okorie seems to have been funnelling money into the NGO via various persons, only to turn around and accuse us of fraud and corruption. This is Amara's arrangement. Amara uses this

arrangement as a tool to denigrate and silence us, all while bolstering his own financial interests.

Amara's thoughts raced as she struggled to process this new information. Now everything made sense—the timing of the inquiry, the speed with which the rumours had spread, and the viciousness of the assaults on her and the NGO. She understood this was not just a political power move. This personal.

She spoke more to herself than to Emily. "Why would Okorie go to such lengths to ruin us? What might we have done to him?

Emily shook her head, a grimace flitting across the edges of her lips. "I don't believe it speaks of us, Amara. It seems to be about power. Okorie and his allies fear our work and how we are strengthening the Igbuzor people. Their days of corruption and greed are coming to an end; they understand that if we succeed, we must demonstrate to the community a path based on justice, compassion, and equality.

Amara felt a surge of anger and determination coursing through her body. That was it, then. Once again, the old guard—the same powers that had sought to quiet her mother and wipe out her family—was at work crushing anybody who dared to question their rule.

However, they had devalued the tenacity and drive of her and the people she fought for. Amara insisted that they could not destroy the NGO's optimism and change.

"Okay," she said, her voice strong and exact. "This is our scheduled response. Emily, keep looking for any trace of evidence tying Okorie and his associates to this fraud. Nuss, please contact your contacts to learn about Okorie and his friends' actions and goals.

She looked at Sholina, who had been listening closely, and saw a sudden flare in her eye. "Sholina, in this regard we will need the town's help." Could you inspire the masses to see the real situation and the value of our revolt?

Sholina nodded and began to grimly smile. "Consider it accomplished, Amara." The Igbuzor people are always with you. We cannot allow these bastards to prevail.

Amara felt overwhelmed with gratitude and love for her team—the incredible people who had consistently supported her. She knew that with them at her side, nothing was too big to overcome and that anything was achievable.

"Okay then," she said, smacking her hands together. "Let us get right to work. We have a dishonest councilman to dismantle, and we have a neighbourhood to protect.

Amara resolved herself silently as her team scattered to concentrate on their own jigsaw pieces. The road forward would be difficult, indeed, and the conflicts would be intense. She was ready to meet any obstacle, however, with conviction and audacity.

She was Amara, the woman rising from her history to create a life of meaning and direction. She also knew that nothing could stop her, and that justice would ultimately run through with the love of her family and the power of her community.

Amara considered her children, her priceless daughters, who drove everything she did. She considered Jiu, her soul mate and friend, who had been her lighthouse over every storm.

And she considered Igbuzor, the place her heart had come to call home. The town provided her with an opportunity to adapt and transform her circumstances.

She would battle for every one of them. She would not stop until she exposed the truth and permanently banished the shadows of corruption.

Amara inhaled deeply and driven, went back to her desk, prepared to meet whatever difficulties lay ahead. Even though the battle was just beginning, Amara knew with unwavering clarity that love, and justice would ultimately prevail

Chapter 17

Diving deep under

Each member of Amara's team was prepared to participate in the intense battle that was about to begin. As they were ready to face their toughest enemy yet, there was a tangible buzz in the air, a thrumming undercurrent of tension and expectation.

Rachel, a new member of Mr. Gayan's media team hired from a nearby town, Wirad, is not known in Igbuzor; she is always the adventurous journalist assigned to go undercover, gathering intelligence and proof of Mr. Gayan's unethical behaviour from within the ranks of Councillor Okorie. Rachel Mendoza has never been one to back down from a challenge; this was a perilous job that demanded equal parts cunning and bravery.
With her cover narrative and secret recording devices in hand, Rachel left the enemy camp with a brief embrace and a murmur of "be careful" from Amara guiding her. She was determined not to disappoint her friends and the community, realizing that the success of their entire plan hinged on her ability to blend in and gain the trust of those who would dismantle the NGO.

Emily, possessing a robust legal intellect and unwavering determination, persistently examined bank records and email correspondence in search of the conclusive evidence that would connect Okorie and his associates directly to the false allegations against the NGO. Driven by a strong blend of coffee and righteous outrage, she worked nonstop, knowing that every bit of evidence she found moved one step toward justice.

True to tradition, Nuss launched himself into the chaos with his trademark mix of charm and daring. Drawing on his vast network of connections and his remarkable ability to hunt secrets, he sought to expose the covert web of relationships and backroom agreements allowing Okorie's plot to grow. From the dingy pubs to the corridors of power, Nuss tracked the money and rumours to create a terrible picture of corruption that stretched to the top tiers of Igbuzor's elite.

Rallying the people of Igbuzor to rise and fight for the spirit of their town, Sholina, the unwavering mayor and Amara's closest friend, went to the streets and the radio. Her comments, a clarion call to action that moved the hearts and brains of every person she talked to, were passionate and convincing.

"My friends," she said, her voice resonating over the town square. "We are at a crossroads, a moment of truth that will define the future of our community." On one side, there are those who would want to quiet and control us by means of falsehoods and intimidation, therefore preserving their hold on authority. On the other hand, we have the power and resiliency of a people united, a people that understands that every man, woman, and child who calls Igbuzor home shapes our future rather than the hands of a corrupt few." The assembly burst in shouts, their faces ablaze with hope and will. Watching from the sidelines, Amara felt a surge of pride and thanks for the amazing lady who had evolved from just a coworker to a real friend and mentor.

Jenny and Nathan emerged as unexpected characters in the unfolding drama. When they first contacted Amara, offering their aid and support in any capacity they could, she had been reluctant, uncertain of their intentions, and still struggling with the complicated feelings of their shared history.

Amara started to view them differently, however, as she witnessed them commit themselves to the struggle and use their own special senior talents and contacts to support the exposure and enquiry of Okorie's actions. These two individuals, who had made terrible mistakes in the past and caused much suffering, were now striving to atone by using their own hard-earned knowledge and resiliency to contribute to making the planet a better place.

It was a strong reminder of the ability for development and transformation that every human heart has, and Amara felt a twinge of something that could have started her toward forgiveness.

As the days turned into weeks and the net tightened around Councilman Okorie and his friends, Amara witnessed the tension and expectation intensifying. As her staff worked around the clock to compile the evidence required to bring the dishonest officials to justice, late-night strategy discussions and secret meetings became the norm.

Of course, there were periods of uncertainty and anxiety when the weight of the work ahead of them seemed insurmountable and the hazards too large to handle. Still, Amara clung to her confidence in the power of truth and the enduring ties of love and community that had carried them this far.

She considered her children soundly asleep in their beds, blissfully ignorant of the tempest raging around them. She considered Jiu, her rock and friend who had been by her side every step of the way, providing his unflinching support and unqualified love.

She also considered the courageous and tenacious souls of Igbuzor, who had survived so many storms and come out stronger and more bonded than ever. No matter how difficult the chances seemed, they were the reason she battled and the reason she would never give up.

Amara could feel quiet resolve settle over her as the last pieces of the jigsaw came together and the day of reckoning approached. She knew the journey ahead would be dangerous and that their opponents would do anything to maintain their privilege and power.
She also knew, however, that she was not alone; she had an army of love and justice at her back, poised to stand with her and fight for what was right. Equipped with that knowledge and unwavering trust in the kindness and resiliency of the human spirit, Amara entered the future prepared to meet any obstacle.

The players are all in position; the stage is ready. The final act, the pivotal moment that would determine the fate of Igbuzor and all those who called it home, was rapidly approaching.

Amara inhaled deeply, squared her shoulders, and raised her chin. She felt a wave of pride and thanks as she turned around at her team and at the faces of the individuals she most loved and trusted worldwide.
"Alright, everyone," she began, her voice firm and clear. Here it is. This is the moment we've all been striving for. "Though I know the journey has been long and the struggle has been difficult, every single one of you has given your all, your heart, and your soul to this cause."

She stopped, her eyes ablaze with emotion. "It makes me very glad to be standing with you—to name you my family and friend. And I know that we can do this together. We can expose the truth and create Igbuzor where everyone, from all walks of life, may grow and prosper without regard for background or situation."

Cheers and clapping erupted, giving the crowd a tangible buzz of enthusiasm and determination. Amara grinned, a flood of affection and connection coursed over her.
She answered, "Okay then," slapping her palms together. "Let us do this. Allow us to demonstrate for them the transformational power of justice and love."

The squad then dispersed, with each member contributing to the grand drama that was about to unfold. With her heart bursting with hope and will, Amara watched them depart.
She understood that the fight ahead would try them all and that ambiguity and doubt would periodically cause anxiety. She also understood, however, that they had something their opponent could never comprehend: the resiliency of love and community, the power

derived from group effort against hardship.

Equipped with that understanding and a strong and lasting trust in the power of the human spirit, Amara turned to face the future her family, community, and country all deserved, ready to fight for them.

Amara knew, with every thread of her existence, that they would triumph and that the light of truth and justice would shine against the shadow of corruption and greed in the last clash.

They, as Igbuzor people, would not succumb to silence or disintegration. United in love and goal, they would stand tall and strong, creating a world wherein every kid may grow up safe and cherished and free.

Amara entered the fight prepared to lead her squad and her community toward a better, more fair future, driven fiercely in her heart. The moment had come to record a fresh chapter in the history of Igbuzor, and Amara knew, with certain conviction, that it would be a narrative of victory, of resiliency, of the ongoing strength of the human spirit to overcome even the darkest of circumstances.

She inhaled deeply, grinning as she felt the love and power of her family and neighbourhood course through her. They were set. They grew together. They would also not stop.

They joined the fight, determined to shape and win the future. They went all out to win for their loved ones and the future.

Chapter 18

Surviving the waves

The successful sting operation was a testament to Amara's team's meticulous planning and flawless execution. As the meticulously planned trap for the dishonest officials and their allies unfolded, it was a sight to behold.

With her sharp tongue and fast wit, Rachel had crept into the inner sanctum of Councilman Okorie's operations, masquerading as a rich investor eager to lubricate the wheels of her commercial activities with a few strategically placed bribes. She had performed her job to perfection, caressing egos and dropping clues until the councilman and his allies had been all too happy to divulge their secrets, never thinking that every word they said was being recorded for future generations.
Rachel had also informed the rest of the team when the time was right, once she had gathered all the necessary data.

Emily had presented the damning financial records and email trails to the authorities, laying out the complex web of corruption and dishonesty that had let Okorie and his allies operate with impunity for so long. She had a forensic eye for detail and an unwavering commitment to justice.
Nuss's streetwise sense and network of connections throughout Igbuzor enabled him to coordinate the swift response of the local law enforcement, ensuring the capture of dishonest officials before they could escape or destroy evidence.

As the public face of the operation, Sholina hosted press conferences and town hall meetings to keep the community informed and involved, ensuring that the truth remained unburied and unforgotten. Her dominating presence and unmatched ability to inspire the people had been especially important.

Against the might of corruption and money, it was an incredible victory of justice and the pure human spirit. Seeing the once-powerful councilman Okorie and his friends being taken away in handcuffs, their faces marked with astonishment and wonder, Amara also felt pride and thankfulness for the incredible team that had made everything possible.

Even with their enthusiasm, Amara knew the conflict was far from over. As the dust settled and the full extent of the corruption revealed itself, it became evident that the rot had penetrated much deeper than they had initially thought.

Rumours circulated about massive amounts of money flowing through offshore accounts, backroom deals, and intricate relationships spanning decades. Ultimately, in the end, Amara shuddered at the mention of the Council of Elders clan, which belonged to the archivist Ikenga Luti. She previously heard rumours about this shadowy organization, whispers of a group of powerful men and women manipulating Igbuzor's events from a hidden position, shaping the town's history to suit their own agenda. She had consistently dismissed these tales as mere rumours, relegated to the realm of neurotic delusions and conspiracy theories. Amara could not ignore the reality as it looked.

As the evidence began to mount and the connections became evident, Mr. Okorie's role became increasingly significant. Driven by the Okafor family, the Council of Elders played a central role in the corruption, nearly destroying her beloved village for several decades. The book handed to Amara contained comprehensive information, Reverend Solomon Okafor did her a wonderful favour.

Having not shared the contents of the leather book gift with the entire group, Amara experienced a surge of wrath and resolve as the knowledge set in. With the whole group, Amara felt a surge of wrath and resolve as the knowledge set in. It was more of a spiritual

conflict, and she realized that accepting the Elders Council of the
Archivist would be the fight of her life, requiring every ounce of
bravery and fortitude.

She knew she was not alone; she had the love and encouragement of
her amazing family and friends, as well as the strength and
knowledge of her entire community behind her. Knowing this,
Amara believed she was prepared to meet whatever obstacles lied
ahead—that unwavering trust in the ability of the human spirit to
overcome even the worst of situations would equip her.

She considered her children—her darling infants—the brightness of
her life and the motivation behind everything she achieved. She
considered Jiu, her soul mate and friend, who had been her
lighthouse throughout every tempest.

And she considered Igbuzor, the place her heart had come to call
home. The community provided her with an additional chance, a
place where she felt a sense of belonging and had the power to
transform things.

She would battle for every one of them. She would relentlessly
pursue justice for the Archivists Council of Elders, ensuring the
permanent removal of their generational corruption and avarice from
Igbuzor.

Amara inhaled deeply, savouring the love and fortitude of her family
and neighbourhood. She grinned. Although the fight was far from
over, they had scored a fantastic victory today with council member
Okorie.

There would be more challenges to overcome. But Amara
understood, with unflinching clarity, that they would meet and that
they would come out stronger and more bonded than ever before.
They, as Igbuzor people, would not succumb to silence or
disintegration. United in love and goal, they would stand tall and
strong, creating a world wherein every kid may grow up safe,
cherished, and free.

Amara turned to her squad, her eyes glistening with thankfulness and commitment, driven fiercely from within. "Thank you," she responded, her voice rich with feeling. "I appreciate your bravery, tenacity, and unflinching devotion to justice. Today we have attacked greed and corruption and shown the world the power that love and community can produce.

She paused, gazing over the faces of her dear friends and supporters. Despite everything, our mission remains incomplete. The Council of Elders continues to lurk in the shadows, manipulating discontent and causing division. We must maintain our resilience, stay vigilant, and never surrender the struggle."

The gathering was vibrantly energetic and determined as a chorus of shouts and clapping erupted. Knowing that whatever obstacles lied ahead, Amara felt a rush of pride and love go over her; she would meet them with the strength and support of the most amazing individuals she had ever met.

She answered, "Okay then," slapping her palms together. "Let's return to our job. We have a community to protect and a future to build; we will not relent until we eradicate all corruption and enable every child in Igbuzor to grow up with hope and possibilities.

The crew then dispersed, with each member assigned to handle the next stage of the fight. Amara watched them depart, pride and resolve bursting in her heart.

She understood that the battle would be challenging, and the journey ahead would be lengthy. She also understood, however, that they had something the Council of Elders would never comprehend: the strong ties of love and community, the strength derived from gathering against hardship.

Equipped with that knowledge and strong, deep trust in the power of the human spirit, Amara turned to face the future, ready to guide her team and her community into a better, fairer one. Amara could not wait to demonstrate to the Council of Elders the actual might of Igbuzor; they had no clue what they were up against.

Chapter 19

Taking deep breath up

Today at the general hospital in Igbuzor, it appeared as though the hunter had become the prey. Amara's body had once crumbled under the strain of human tension, and after many weeks of battles, she found herself back in the hospital bed, her blood pressure high and her legs sore. The hospital room remained silent, except for the soft beeping of the vital sign monitoring monitors. The vivid, relentless energy that had always seemed to propel her every movement was a stark contrast to her closed eyes and weak breathing. She lay calm and pallid against the clean white linens.

With a drawn face and red-rimmed eyes from sleep deprivation, Jiu crouched on a chair at her bedside. Holding Amara's hand in his own, his thumb softly circles her skin as if he could restore her to health only by pure love and dedication.

Jenny and Nathan stood silently on the opposite side of the bed, remorse and concern clearly on their faces. Amara had positioned herself in front of the dishonest council officials to shield the community from the violent outburst of one of the council's henchmen, thereby absorbing most of the impact, both physically and psychologically. They had been presented to witness the daily struggles Amara endures on behalf of the community.

What a busy girl Jenny and Nathan had produced; they had felt a flood of terror and guilt beyond anything they had ever gone through. Their daughter, the child they had brought into the world and abandoned, was the woman who had every reason to hate them but felt compelled to give them another chance.

She lay wounded and bruised in a hospital bed, battling for her life; they blamed her for their own weakness and cowardice.

Jenny put out a quivering palm to sweep a hair strand off Amara's forehead. Her voice strangled with tears; she said, "I'm so sorry, baby." "I'm so sorry we missed you when you needed us; we let our own demons split our family."

Nathan nodded, unshed tears glittering in his own eyes. "We should have been better," he murmured weakly. "We should have been your parents, giving you unconditional love and protection. But Amara, we let you down. In every sense that counts, we failed you.

Jiu stared up at them, his face a combination of sympathy and grief. "You're here right now," he remarked gently. "That's all that counts. Amara is aware of your affection for her and the effort you have been making toward righting things. Even when individuals cannot see it in themselves, she has always found the good in them.
Their hearts full of the weight of their previous errors and the anxiety of losing the daughter they had just lately gotten to know, Jenny and Nathan glanced at one another. But as they gazed at Jiu, at the love and loyalty that glowed so brilliantly in his eyes, they felt a flutter of hope start to grow in their hearts.

It was possible for their family to heal and grow if Amara could forgive them and open her heart to them after all their suffering and anguish.

As Amara remained mostly unconscious, her body battled to recover from the horrific emotional and psychological damage she had suffered. Hours became days. Jiu and her parents stayed by her side too, alternately holding her hand and giving words of love and support in her ear through it all.
Friends, coworkers, and community members affected by Amara's relentless labour and unflinching dedication to justice joined them in

a steady stream. They sent cards and flowers, tales and memories, and their own prayers and best wishes for her quick recovery.

Even Emily, Sholina, and Nuss, who had been working nonstop to compile evidence against the Archivists Council of Elders, who had turned to violent politics, took time out of their hectic schedules to sit with Amara, hold her hand, and remind her of all the reasons she had to keep fighting.

Amara began to gradually show signs of recovery daily. Her vital signs steadied; her breathing became more robust, and the colour started to show up on her cheeks. The physicians hailed her improvement as a miracle of modern medicine and the relentless human spirit.

When she opened her eyes at last, blinking faintly against the brilliant fluorescent lights of the hospital room, Jiu's face first caught her attention—his eyes gleamed with tears of relief and excitement. He muttered, "Welcome back, my love," then softly kissed her forehead. "You nearly scared us there."

Amara tried a feeble grin, her hand grasping his with all the force she could muster. She croaked, her voice strained from disuse, "I'm sorry." "I meant not to worry you."

Jiu shook his head and smiled broadly. "Don't regret, Amara. You put yourself on the line to protect the ones you love, like you do constantly. You're that way, which is one of the many reasons I love you."

Amara's eyes strayed to her parents, seated at the foot of the bed, their features tinged with both relief and anxiety. She whispered gently, "Mum, Dad," tears flooding her eyes. "You are here."

Jenny came forward, her own eyes shining. "Of course, dear, we are here. We promise to never abandon you again. Not at all.

Nathan nodded; his voice charged with feeling. "We Love You,

Amara. And we really admire you—the amazing lady you have evolved. Although we know we do not deserve your pardon, we swear to dedicate our lives seeking it."

Amara felt a surge of emotions rising in her chest—a mixture of love, gratitude, and a deep sense of belonging that came from being around the people who mattered most to her. She murmured quietly, "I forgive you," her voice shaking with the weight of the words. "I want us to be a family once again, and I forgive you and love you. A true family is one that always supports each other.

Mindful of her injuries but unable to control the desire to pull Amara close, Jenny and Nathan's faces crumpled with relief and delight as they grabbed her into a strong, uncomfortable embrace. Jiu joined in, his heart brimming with love and pride as his own arms encircled his bride and her parents.

And in that instant, as the four of them held each other, their tears mingling and their hearts pounding in unison, Amara realized that everything she had endured—every battle, every suffering, and every moment of doubt—had been worth it. She wanted to experience the pure love of a family that would always support her, regardless of the circumstances.

She knew there would be more difficulties ahead. Meanwhile, the Council of Elders continued to heal their wounds and naturally strategize their retribution plans. They would need to heal both physical and mental scars, which would require time, patience, and a significant amount of bravery to overcome.

But Amara also knew that she was not alone—that she had the affection and encouragement of the most amazing individuals she had ever met. Her family, friends, whole community—they were her strength, her foundation, the rock upon which she would create a better, more equitable future for Igbuzor and those who called it home.

Amara started to feel a clarity of vision she had never known as the days stretched into weeks and she gradually rebuilt her strength. She understood that her brush with death had transformed her and had eliminated all the doubts, anxieties, and insecurities that had hitherto kept her back.

She was no more the terrified little child left behind by her parents or the enraged adolescent who had attacked the planet in agony and uncertainty. Now a woman, she was a leader, a force for justice and change in a society sorely lacking both.

Armed with that understanding, unwavering trust in herself, and the ability of love to overcome anything, Amara began the daily rebuilding of her life and her community.

She put forth an enormous effort with Jiu and her parents to mend the past and create a fresh link of trust and understanding that would get them through any obstacles. She found courage and inspiration in Emily and Nuss, as well as all her amazing friends' relentless support and cause devotion.

She continued to fight, standing up for the people of Igbuzor and those subjected to exclusion and mistreatment by the dishonest systems of authority that had held sway for an extended period. Using her position and power, she denounced injustice wherever she came across it, therefore highlighting the sinister aspects of their society and motivating others to join her in the fight for a better world.

It wasn't easy, and there were times when the weight of it all threatened to crush her, when the forces arranged against her felt too enormous and too strong to resist. Amara never gave up, however; she never lost sight of the vision that had propelled her for so long—a society in which every kid could grow up secure, loved, and free, where every individual had the chance to flourish and realize their full potential.

Gradually, that vision began to materialize and turn into a reality. Legal action was taken against the Council of Elders for all the atrocities, which led to the gradual elimination of their extensive network of corruption and avarice. Men and women of integrity and compassion committed to serving the people rather than their own self-serving needs arose as new leaders. Sholina remains the council mayor.

And through it all, Amara stayed at the centre—a lighthouse of hope and inspiration for everyone who had been affected by her relentless labour and her relentless devotion to justice. She was a hero to her hometown and a role model to a new generation of leaders who would continue her legacy long after her death.

More importantly, however, she was a daughter, a wife, a mother, and a friend. She was a lady who had risen from the flames of hardship stronger, more compassionate, and more resolved than ever to help make the world a better place.

And Amara knew she had discovered her actual calling—her purpose for being—as she gazed out over the village that had grown to be her home. She was determined to make the most of her second chance at life—to make the most of every breath and every pulse—and to leave the planet in a more beautiful state than she had found it.

Amara emerged from the shadows prepared to meet whatever obstacles lied ahead, a grin on her face and a song in her heart. She knew she would never be alone—never be without the love and support of the amazing individuals who had grown to be her family, regardless of what the future held.

And with that love, that unwavering link of compassion and togetherness, Amara felt that everything was possible—that even the worst of circumstances might allow the dawn of a new and better day. She was a lady of strength, of resiliency, of limitless optimism, and she would never stop fighting for the planet she knew was feasible.

That was her legacy, her pledge, and she meant to uphold it no matter what.

Chapter 20

Storms choreography

As Amara ascended the meandering road to the community centre, the sun was sinking over Igbuzor, painting the sky an amazing spectrum of oranges and pinks. Today, she remained resilient, rising above the grip of hospital beds, dishonest council members, and all those who had threatened to consume her pure spirit. The mayor's efforts and support resulted in two projects: the grand opening of the new Isiolu educational wing and the community health clinic, a celebration of triumph over adversity, and a fresh start for Amara and her loved ones.

Standing at the door, Amara looked at the shining new construction and felt pride surge in her heart. The tenacity and will of her people gave them hope for the future they had fought for. Following the drop of the fraud case against the NGO and the punishment of the offenders, Igbuzor flourished under the collective efforts of its people.

"Can you believe it?!" Jiu softly spoke and gently squeezed her hand. "We indeed did it."

Amara grinned and bent into his hug. She nodded. "We did." "All of us, collectively."

She saw familiar features in the swelling throng as if on demand. Nuss, his smile infectious, was proudly showcasing the state-of-the-art computer lab he had contributed to, complete with a curriculum that prepared the upcoming generation for the digital era. His face was brown and worn from his most recent trip, but his eyes gleamed with the same cheeky glimmer she had known from infancy.

"Amara! " Nuss cried out and moved through the crowd. "You will not believe what occurred on the trip! At the top, I discovered myself. I discovered the bravery and strong will I never had known I

possessed.
Her heart brimming with joy for her buddy, Amara, gave him a firm embrace. "I always knew you had it, Nuss." The bravest person I have ever known is you.

Emily stood nearby, deep in conversation with a group of surrounding attorneys about the free legal aid clinic that the centre planned to operate independently, ensuring its long-term sustainability. Mayor Sholina greeted both residents and dignitaries, her face beaming with joy as she made her way through the crowd.

But as Amara strolled with her two kids, her breath stopped in her throat when she saw Jenny and Nathan. Her biological parents stood somewhat back from the throng, their expressions a combination of wonder and doubt. As Amara recalled the long, challenging road that had taken them all to this point, she had an emotional explosion.

She inhaled deeply, then moved closer to them, her kids running ahead. Crying, they flung themselves into Jenny and Nathan's arms: "Grandma! Grandpa!"
Amara followed more slowly, her grin subdued and hesitant. "I'm so happy you could make it," she added gently.

Jenny reached out to cup Amara's face, and tears sprung to her eyes. Sweetheart, we wouldn't have missed it for the world. What you and your colleagues have done here is amazing.

Nathan nodded; his voice was sharp with feeling as he drew Amara into a hug. "Amara, we really admire you. Therefore, we are pleased with the woman you have become.

As Amara came back to their hug, she felt tears stinging at her own eyes. Despite the genuine, honest, and optimistic nature of their new connection, it was not flawless. And at that moment, surrounded by the love of her biological parents, her husband and children, and the family she had chosen, Amara felt fullness she had never experienced before.

Everyone turned to the improvised stage when someone tapped a microphone. Standing there, Mayor Sholina looked around the assembly with glitter in her eyes.

"My friends," she said, her voice ringing out sharp and loud. "Today marks the beginning of a new era for Igbuzor, not just the inauguration of a structure. This Isiolu Centre stands for the very best of who we are—a community that values its own and sees the ability of healthcare and education to change lives."

She stopped, looking across the assembly for Amara. "And one lady—a woman who has never ceased advocating for the residents of this town—owns most of this debt. Would you kindly come onstage with me, Dr. Amara Johnson?"

Amara experienced a flashback as she moved among the cheering audience. How many times had she stood before her community like this, inspiring them to act or celebrating their victories? However, this occasion seemed somehow more significant and distinct. Mayor Sholina warmly gave her the microphone as she arrived on stage. Amara inhaled deeply and peered out across a sea of recognizable faces.

"Thank you all for being here today," she said, her voice firm despite the feeling rising within her. "Looking at this centre, I see more than just concrete and building materials." I see the culmination of years of our unwavering dedication and hard work. I see the aspirations of many youngsters who will now have access to high-quality education and the opportunity to develop into the leaders and change agents of tomorrow. Families who no longer must choose between putting food on the table or obtaining the necessary medical treatment have hope.

She stopped, looking around the assembly. Above all, however, I find this group to be very resilient and strong. Together, we have surmounted poverty, corruption, division, and a terrible epidemic. Despite numerous setbacks, we have consistently risen again. We have never given up on one another or ourselves. We have never lost faith in the power of love and unity to triumph even in the most challenging situations.

Amara tried not to conceal tears that started to trickle down her cheeks. "This new Isiolu educational wing and the community health centre are evidence of everything we have in Igbuzor—our identity. We are healers, teachers, warriors, and visionaries. Our shared goals and hardships, as much as blood, bind our family together. Our common humanity defines us. Our community understands that working together is the best way ahead and that, if we do this, there is no issue too big to tackle."
She inhaled deeply and let her words linger in the air for a time. "So let us make a pledge to each other as we stand here today in the shadow of this magnificent new edifice." We promise to always remember those around us, the love we share, and the things that truly matter. We pledge to constantly strive for our best selves, help those in need, and strive for a society where every individual can live with dignity and every child can dream without limitations. We must remember that our greatest asset is not our possessions, but our essence.
Amara lifted her fist in the air and let her voice roar. "We, Igbuzor, are here, and together, there is nothing we cannot do!"

Amara felt a flood of love and thanks as the audience burst in thunderous yells and clapping. She considered all the people who had been on this road: her husband Jiu, her steadfast friend in life and love; Nuss and Emily, her dear friends who had stood by her side through every struggle; Mayor Sholina, the mentor who had believed in her vision from the very beginning; Jenny and Nathan, the parents she was gradually learning to forgive and embrace; and the innumerable others who had lent their time, money, or relentless support to help her realize this dream.

The rest of the festival unfolded in a blur of tears, laughter, and heartfelt conversations. Children running around the new school's hallways, their eyes ablaze with excitement and possibilities, delighted Amara. Listening to patients' tales of restored health and optimism, she embraced those who had already benefitted from the services of the Tomorrow Foundation clinic. Blinking back tears as they sliced the ribbon to formally open the new health centre, she joined hands with Jiu to mark this moment of success.

As the sun began to set, bathing the shining edifice in a warm glow, Amara found herself slightly off from the throng. She was absorbing everything. Jiu showed up at her side, her arm around her waist. He said gently, "What are you thinking?"
Amara leant towards him, a grin flashing at her lips. "I'm thinking about how far we have come," she remarked. "I'm thinking about all the hardships and disappointments, all the moments we felt we would never make it," she said. We did, however. We exist here. And nowadays..."

Her eyes strayed to the children playing on the grass, to the staff and volunteers still humming with enthusiasm, and to the community leaders now deep in conversation about the next project and the next challenge. She trailed off.
Jiu said, "And now, we keep moving forward," while tightly hugging her. "We use this amazing gift—this place of healing and education—that we have received to continue growing." To continue dreaming. We must continue fighting for the planet we know is within our grasp.

Amara nodded, then turned to squarely face him. "Together," she said, pressing her forehead against his. " ALWAYS together."
As the community they loved celebrated this fresh beginning all around them, Amara felt a deep sense of calm settle in her bones as

they held one another tightly. She understood that the journey ahead would be extensive, requiring her to overcome new obstacles and engage in battles.

She also knew, however, that they would face whatever came as they always had hand in hand, heart to heart, strengthened by the solidified links of love and solidarity that had taken them this far.

For these were the inhabitants of Igbuzor, in all their exquisite, untidy, magnificent humanity. They were trailblazers, survivors, warriors, and visionaries. They were family, in every way the term suggests.

All they were, were, and would become was that. Rising together to greet the brilliant dawn of each day, they were a community.

Amara looked one final time at the centre that personified so many aspirations—at the town that had permanently grabbed her heart—at the husband, children, and friends who had grown to be her home as the first stars started to shine in the purpling heavens.

Then she turned and headed on into the waiting darkness, ready to welcome whatever was ahead, a soul full of thanks, and a spirit eager for all the experiences yet to come.

This was only the beginning. They are continuously creating a legacy that will endure for millennia, akin to a never-ending river; it marks the start of a story that future generations will read. From the beginning of all that they were, to all that they would become, united amidst all the turmoil of their unique veins, they would always triumph together.

Epilogue

Igbuzor was softly golden as the sun sank low on the horizon. Perched on the balcony of the recently built Isiolu educational wing and community health centre, Amara peered over the busy town she had devoted her life to helping. A monument to healing, progress, and harmony, the centre stood as evidence of the distance they travelled.

Besides her, Jiu gripped her hand; his presence served as a continual reminder of the love that had seen her through all of life. She smiled, thinking their relationship had grown stronger with each challenge.

As Amara gazed out over the town, her thoughts drifted back to the path that had brought her to this point. Her soul breathed from Igbuzor; she was born in Igili. Her biological parents, Jenny and Nathan, had played a transformative role in her life, reviving a past filled with both suffering and healing. Through forgiveness and understanding, they created a new partnership that embraced the present while honouring their common history.

While the fight against corruption had tested the resolve of their society, it also revealed the true strength of Igbuzor's spirit. Amara considered Emily, Nuss, and Mayor Sholina—the unflinching supporters who had seen her through every conflict. Together, they had revealed the truth and set the foundation for a society more open and fairer.

The leathered book and its disclosures had forced Amara to face her own fate, to see that her own path was naturally connected to the fate of Igbuzor. It had shown her that the relationships we create and the love we share define real power rather than the old secret knowledge.

Amara heard children laughing in the courtyard of the new centre as the final rays of sunshine illuminated the sky with vivid colours. Among them were her own children, the next generation to carry forth the goals and principles she had battled so valiantly.

"What are you wondering?" Jiu inquired gently, standing alongside the railing.

Amara grinned and slanted into his hug. "I'm considering how all the components of my life—the challenges, the victories, the loves and losses—have come together to define me. to define us as unique individuals.

Her eyes blazing with passion, she turned to face him. "We are everything that we have been, right now, and all we may become. And taken all together, nothing is impossible."

Amara knew as darkness descended over Igbuzor that one chapter was closing while another was just starting. Challenges will always abound, injustices to combat, and lives to repair. She was, however, ready. They were all poised.

They were Igbuzor, a community bonded by love, reinforced by hardship, and unified in their ambition for a brighter future; they were flowing like a river. And in that oneness lay their most authentic legacy and greatest strength.

Amara looked one final time at the life she had created the place she loved, and the future just waiting for them. Then she headed towards home, towards everything they were, and all they would become among their restless veins—a heart full of thanks and a spirit blazing bright with purpose.

9 781763 782129